ALSO BY JEFF GUNHUS

ADULT FICTION

Night Chill

Night Terror

Killer Within

Killer Pursuit

The Torment of Rachel Ames: a novella

MIDDLE GRADE FICTION

Jack Templar Monster Hunter

Jack Templar and the Monster Hunter Academy

Jack Templar and the Lord of the Vampires

Jack Templar and the Lord of the Werewolves

Jack Templar and the Lord of the Demons

Jack Templar and the Last Battle

A THRILLER

RESURRECTION AMERICA

USA Today Bestselling Author

JEFF GUNHUS

SEVEN GUNS PRESS

Printed in the United States of America

Cover design by Extended Imagery
Book design by Inkstain Design Studio
Edited by Mandy Schoen

Text set in Dante.

Library of Congress Cataloging-in-Publication Data
Gunhus, Jeff
The Torment of Rachel Ames / Jeff Gunhus

FOR NICOLE

AUTHOR'S NOTE

Many early readers of *Resurrection America* commented on the science used in the story. While I've certainly taken liberties, most are surprised to learn much of the technology I describe already exists in the world. For example, amputees already have prosthetic limbs controlled by sensors embedded in their brains, the Unites States Department of Defense is developing autonomous kill drones, and experts warn that the interconnectivity of our modern world has created an Achilles' heel which, if attacked, could hobble the world for a generation.

But it is the most outlandish events in this book that have people wondering if I jumped the rails from science to pure conjecture. You know, taken my creative license out for a spin only to crash the family car into a tree. Could, they ask, this actually happen?

I don't want to give things away, but I'll share this with you. When you come to the science that seems to challenge credulity, just know that too is based on reality. I'll share more at the end of the book, but when you ask yourself whether the events here could really ever happen, the answer is yes. They already are.

I hope you enjoy *Resurrection America*.

PART ONE

CHAPTER 1

A *crackling, static-heavy transmission blasted* from the radio, filling the small-town jail with the frantic voice of Deputy Manny Garcia.

"Sheriff? You there? Come on, Rick, pick up." Then, as an afterthought a few beats later, he added, "Over." Maybe to make it sound more official.

Sheriff Rick Johnson heard the deputy's voice all the way down by the bathroom where he was about to enjoy a long sit with that week's *Sports Illustrated*. There was no one else in the jail since Manny was his only deputy and there weren't enough evildoers in the town of Resurrection to fill up either of the two cells in the back of the building. It'd been a quiet morning, just the way Rick liked it, and he groaned at the thought of his eager-beaver deputy disturbing his day. Rick was only ten years older than the new recruit, but he felt like a father with a hyperactive kid on his hands.

"Come in, Sheriff." A pause, filled with static. "Rick. Where are you? You're not going to believe what I just saw. It's gonna blow your mind," Manny said. "Shit, man. Answer the radio."

Rick frowned at the use of the swear word. He knew some of the old folks in town liked to use their own police scanners to eavesdrop on the radio chatter. At least they used to. With the Internet, they could easily tap into something with a little more action like the NYPD or Miami SWAT team, so he supposed most of them listened to those to get their fix. There probably wasn't much risk that one of the town's good citizens would have picked up the comment. Still, he liked to run a professional operation. Cussing on the official radio wasn't part of the drill. He folded his beloved *Sports Illustrated* and tossed it on the small magazine rack outside the bathroom.

"This better be good," he shouted, even though he knew Manny wouldn't be able to hear him without toggling on the radio.

"Sheriff, you're not gonna believe what's going on up here," Manny said, his voice lowered into a whisper. The interference was getting worse. The next words tumbled around inside a swirl of static. "It's ... huge ... the old mine ... c'mon man ..."

A high-pitched squawk burst from the speakers, loud enough to make Rick wince as he crossed the room to grab his handheld radio. He spun the volume knob down, the fingers in his prosthetic hand giving him a little trouble with the dial, but the ear-splitting sound just got louder. Then, suddenly, it went silent.

The mine? What the hell was the kid doing up there?

"Manny," Rick said into the radio. "Come in, over."

Nothing. Not even the usual static. He thought the battery might be out, but a quick check showed the meter on the radio's side had five green bars. Full charge.

"Pieces of shit," he mumbled to himself. He hit the button again. "Manny? Where are you?" He paused. Silence. "If you're talking I'm not reading you.

Move down the mountain to get a better signal. Do you copy?"

He felt dumb for asking. If the kid could tell him that he copied the message, then he'd be able to talk to him. He stared at the radio, waiting for something to happen. But it was dead.

There were two backup radios on the charger station. Chances were that the radio just blew out on him. Part of the Get America Working Again program, GAWA for short, meant that all of the electronics that used to be manufactured over in Asia were now made right in the good old US of A. Rick liked supporting the labor unions as well as anyone else, and GAWA seemed like a good idea on paper, but he missed having technology that actually worked. The stuff from the revitalized factories of the rust belt was good, but it wasn't China good.

Rick grabbed a spare radio off the charger. "Manny. Come in, acknowledge."

Nothing.

He tried the other one.

"Dammit, Manny. Are you there?"

Dead air.

Rick suppressed a shiver as cold sweat appeared on his hands and forehead. He braced himself against his desk and took a few deep, shuddering breaths, trying to regain his composure. He closed his eyes and focused. This was Resurrection, Colorado. It wasn't a barren desert in a foreign land. There were no Jihadis stalking his men, waiting for him to make a tactical mistake and send them to their deaths. Silence on the radio meant a malfunction, that was all.

He opened his eyes and felt back in control. Manny had probably seen a big ten-point buck or a grizzly bear. That would explain the excitement in the kid's voice. He felt himself settle down even more.

"Manny? Come in. Come in."

When he didn't get an answer, he grabbed his keys and gun holster and headed to the front door. "If you can hear me, I'm coming your way. I'm heading to the mine on the main service road."

As he left the building, he knew he wasn't being honest with himself. He really didn't believe his deputy had called about spotting some game animal. Sure, the kid had been excited, but there was something else in his voice too. He wasn't sure what his deputy, an ex-Marine and gun-wielding law officer, had seen up by the mine, but whatever it was had done more than get the kid excited.

Something had scared the shit out of him. And that wasn't good.

CHAPTER 2

The fence wasn't supposed to be there.

Rick stared out through his windshield of his Chevy Blazer, leaning forward so he could see all the way to the top of it. The damn thing was at least twenty feet tall, with razor wire coiled across the top to add another two or three feet. A heavy fabric lined the inside, blocking his view of the mine. The dark green color of the fabric made the yellow signs posted down the length of the fence stand out. Each of these was emblazoned with a lightning bolt and the promise of seven thousand volts to anyone crazy enough to get too close.

"What in the hell..." he whispered.

He'd been up to Resurrection Mine a thousand times in his life and never seen anything like this barricade. As a kid, he used to visit his dad at work back when the place was in operation. Even then, there was no more than a chain-link fence around the work yard in front of the mine's entrance. Even after the mine closed, the security had never been anything special. As a teenager, he and his buddies would break in to explore the old shafts, drink beer, and talk about conquering the world. Outside of some big warning signs and a padlocked gate on the mine itself, there had never been much effort to secure the site.

What was really strange was that he'd come up to the mine as recently as a month ago to take a look around and make sure none of today's teenagers were as dumb as he'd been when he was younger. On that trip, he hadn't seen any sign of activity in the area. And on the drive up, there'd even been a tree down across the access road that'd required him to take the old Blazer off-road just to get past it. With the main access road cut off, the place ought to be abandoned.

The fence wasn't supposed to be there.

Rick parked on the steep slope right before the spot in the access road where he knew it flattened out into the mine's parking area. The spot was so steep that his Blazer slid backward a few inches on the gravel before settling in. He turned off the engine, put on the emergency brake, placed his hand on the door handle ... and hesitated. Every alarm bell was going off inside his head. The first thing he'd taught the new guys in his unit back in the day was that if something doesn't belong on scene, then it was put there to kill you. The first time you second-guess yourself is the time you lose either your life or a limb. He flexed his prosthetic left hand, then let go of the door handle and grabbed the radio mounted on the dash.

"Manny, this is Rick. You copy?"

Nothing but static.

"I'm up at the mine. Main road. In front of this weird fence. If you can hear me, make your way over to my position. Over."

Static.

He considered the chances that Manny's radio was receiving but couldn't send. It was possible. The last few years spent using American-made electronics had proven there was no end to the ways they could malfunction. He hoped his deputy just had a flat tire or some mechanical problem and that's why he wasn't at the mine where Rick had expected to find him. But another look at the fence told him there was more than a flat tire at work. He hoped there was a simple explanation for it all. The fence. Manny's absence from the spot of his last radio transmission. But his gut told him he was hoping for too much.

Rick put the radio back and tried his cell phone. Coverage was spotty on a good day up on the mountain, and today wasn't shaping up to be good at all. Sure enough, zero bars.

He sat there, the wind whistling in the Blazer's dried and cracked window seals. The noise only added to the feeling of isolation as he stared at the fence. He considered his options, not really liking any of them. He couldn't go get backup; Manny was his only deputy. He couldn't call anyone; all of his coms were down. That left only one real option: to get out and take a look around. But he didn't like that option either.

Because the fence wasn't supposed to be there.

He looked around the Blazer. Nothing moved outside except the pines slowly bending in the breeze. There were no squirrels on the ground. No birds flying between the trees. He stretched to look out of the passenger window, and then twisted to look out the back. Looking for anything alive. Anything at all.

Nothing moved.

It was dead outside.

At the thought, he felt his throat tighten and his heart thump in his chest. He closed his eyes and, just that fast, he was standing in a farmer's field in Afghanistan, the faceplate of his bio-chem suit fogging up as he spun in a circle, surrounded by dead livestock in every direction. Cows. Pigs. Horses. Birds that had dropped right from the sky.

He jerked his eyes open, gasping for breath. It'd been a while since he'd had that particular flashback, but he didn't need a reminder of what came next. The Pashtun village, mostly women and children, dead just like their animals.

Rick shoved open the door and climbed out, gasping for air. He stumbled a bit and settled himself, his hands on his knees, getting his balance, getting right with himself. As he stood there, a bird called from the trees to his left. A second bird answered. And the simple sound made him grin and shake his head.

"Get your shit together, Marine," he said. As the words came out, he spotted a set of tire tracks on the gravel road. It'd rained the night before, enough to smooth out the surface of the road, but it'd been sunny all day. Even in the cool, fall temperatures, the road was dry, which was why he hadn't spotted the tire tracks earlier. They were Manny's, had to be. He'd said he was at the mine, freaking out about something he'd seen. A massive fortified security fence, erected without anyone in town knowing about it, fit that bill. Rick's own little trip down Jihadi memory lane was testament to the power of the fence to cause fear. He followed the tracks up the hill toward the gate and then stood there, staring at the ground.

The tire tracks continued right up to the gate and disappeared inside.

He didn't like that at all.

To the left, next to an old tree stump so that it wasn't immediately visible when approaching from the road, was a sturdy metal post topped with a video camera and a speaker. Rick fought a sudden wave of anger at being watched, hating the thought that someone might have seen the way he'd stumbled out of the Blazer. But he pushed the anger back easily enough. It was his fault for being sloppy and not noticing the post earlier.

He waved at the camera. "Hello? Anyone in there?"

No answer. He bent down to see if there was some kind of call button next to the speaker. There wasn't.

"Hello?" he said, louder. "I'm Sheriff Rick Johnson. I need to speak to whoever's in charge in there. Hello?"

Still nothing.

Rick crouched down to see if there was any space under the gate so he could get a look inside. The fabric and the fencing went all the way to the ground. He wasn't sure if that part of the fence was electrified too, but he wasn't about to take a chance.

He stepped back and looked for a way to get a glimpse over the fence. The mine entrance was at the back of a little draw in the mountain face, at the end of the V in the rock. The fence stretched across the entire length of the mining operation, nearly four hundred yards from end-to-end, connecting the two sides of the draw.

He knew, from lazy summer afternoons, that trying to climb the sheer rock face at either end of the fence line was impossible. And that had been with two good arms. Although there was an argument that his prosthetic was more powerful than his original equipment, he still didn't think climbing the face was an option. There was a second entrance to the mine, an old emergency shaft, but that was over in the next valley. Judging by the amount of security in front of him, he didn't think an unplanned appearance at the back door was the way to go.

The fence poles were positioned on a steep incline so that any trees growing downhill from the fence weren't tall enough to give a vantage point into the area in front of the mine. He looked around for any nearby ridgelines he might be able to hike to, but the draw was positioned in a way that made getting a look in nearly impossible.

He'd been in enough forward operating bases during his military career to recognize how well the place was sealed off. Whoever had set up camp inside had either gotten really lucky or they knew what the hell they were doing. And Rick didn't believe much in luck.

He went back to the Blazer, tried his radio again, and listened to the static for a few seconds before switching it off. Staring at the gate, he rifled through his options again, reluctantly realizing he didn't have many. He got back out then went around and opened the rear door. He rummaged through the stockpile of traffic cones, flares and first-aid kits until he found the crowbar that went with his wheel jack. As he walked toward the gate, he was a little more observant than he'd been before. This time he noticed several cameras around him attached to different parts of the fence. Some wireless units were positioned up in the trees. He pictured somewhere there was a bank of TV monitors and a security guard watching his every move from a dozen angles. The least he could do was make it exciting.

With a grunt, Rick heaved the crowbar at the fence. On impact, it exploded into a fountain of sparks. He ducked as the metal bar came flying back at him like a missile and passed over his head, right through the Blazer's windshield.

"Shit," Rick said, standing up. He stared dumbly at the shattered glass, feeling like an idiot. A few inches lower and the crowbar would have taken his head off. He looked back at the video cameras, imagining someone on the other side having a good laugh at his expense. That put him in an even worse mood.

The air reeked of burnt ozone. Rick was no expert on electrified fences, but he would have bet good money that the voltage was a lot more than advertised, not to mention the amps. Whoever erected the fence meant it to be a lethal deterrent.

He took off his hat and wiped the sweat from his brow even though the temperature hadn't cleared sixty. A hawk cried overhead, and he found himself wishing he had a hand drone to activate and send over the fence to reconnoiter the area for him. Even one of the civilian jobbers would have done the trick. Although he was starting to suspect that whoever was on the other side of the fence would have countermeasures for anything sent over to get a better look.

He decided to walk the length of the fence to look for a gap in the fabric mesh. He didn't hold out much hope that he'd find one, but he felt like he at least needed to try. A path about four feet wide made walking it easy. He looked up and down each section, feeling like a kid trying to find a hole in the fence at a ballgame when he couldn't afford a ticket. Section after section showed that the fabric was a professional job. There were no corners turned down or short edges to give him a peek inside. Just green fabric and steel mesh with thousands of volts coursing through it. The whole thing had the smell of someone with military expertise.

The end of the fence terminated into the mountain but also curved out and up along the rock wall. Even though the face was as climbable as Rick remembered, there were also long strands of razor wire bolted into the rock to block access. And he found one more thing that added to his anxiety level. A double set of boot prints in the soft dirt. One walking down and another walking back. It was impossible to know for sure, but his gut told him that he was tracing Manny's footsteps. But where in the hell had he gone?

An overwhelming sense of dread washed over him, just as it had in the Blazer. The looming fence seemed to stretch higher, and the ground felt tilted beneath his feet, giving him a feeling of vertigo. His heart jackhammered and his breathing sped up. A ringing filled his ears. Part of his brain recognized the signs of a panic attack, the kind that used to grip him and twist him sideways back when he first came home from the war.

Naming something wasn't the same thing as controlling it, but it was a start. He closed his eyes, trying to focus his breathing, grasping his left bicep right above the joint of his prosthetic hand. Holding on to what was real. What was actually part of him.

Slowly, the panic ebbed. His heart rate returned to normal and he was able to take a deep breath, even though when he exhaled it came out ragged and slow. He took another breath, eyes still closed, and this one was smooth and clean. He was centered. Back in control.

But when he opened his eyes and looked down the fence line, it took everything he had to keep that control in place.

The gate was open. And he was no longer alone on the mountain.

CHAPTER 3

R*ick's hand moved toward the* gun on his belt but he immediately felt ridiculous for the gesture. The man standing outside the gate was almost two hundred yards away. His Glock was basically useless at that distance. Still, despite feeling idiotic, he took comfort in the feel of the gun's cool steel under his fingers, and his nerves steadied.

It wasn't Manny waiting for him as he'd hoped. It was a man in a suit, dark and formal, waving Rick toward him. Rick pulled his hand away from his gun and started the long slog back, squinting as he approached to get a better look at the stranger waiting for him.

The man watched him walk the entire distance, standing with his feet shoulder width apart, chest squared to him. The suit was buttoned up, but the jacket tails still whipped around in the mountain breeze. As Rick got closer, he noticed the man's only concession to being in the mountains were the rugged boots he wore instead of fancy dress shoes. He also realized the man was older than his upright posture indicated from a distance.

The man appeared to be in his early or mid-sixties, with silver hair carefully combed back and parted perfectly to one side. His face was etched with deep grooves that spoke of experience and a life lived the hard way. There was a self-confidence in the way the man stood with his squared jaw thrust forward, his cold blue eyes taking in every detail. A confidence that could have been arrogance, except that the man's bearing and the expression on his face conveyed the sense that the confidence had been well earned. When Rick finally reached him, the man gave a thin, pained smile.

"How can I help you?" the man said.

Rick stifled a laugh. "Where do I start?"

The man smiled, a little more genuinely now. A little pride sneaking into the expression. "You're wondering how all this happened without you knowing about it?" the man said, indicating the fence.

Rick nodded. "The thought had crossed my mind. That and a dozen other questions. Like whom I'm talking to."

"Of course," the man said, "introductions first. My name's Hank Keefer. And you are Sheriff Rick Johnson, correct?"

Rick glanced at the gate and noticed two small holes had appeared in the fabric covering the fence. Through each of these poked the barrel of a gun pointed at him. Whoever this Hank Keefer was, he was well briefed and traveled with a security team. Rick worried what Manny might have gotten himself into. The sheriff decided to hold off on asking if the man had seen his deputy.

He nodded to the guns. "I do have questions for you, Mr. Keefer, but first you better tell whoever's behind those weapons over there to put them down. Guns make me nervous."

Keefer didn't look towards the fence; his eyes stayed locked on Rick. "Sorry, of course." He waved his hand and the gun barrels pulled back inside the fence and circles of fabric were reaffixed into position. "A lot of our mining operations are in third-world countries so our habits reflect that. We have to remind ourselves that we're in the good old USA."

"So, that's what you're doing here? Mining?"

Keefer laughed. "What else would we be doing?"

Rick shrugged. "Been a mine up here for over a hundred years. Hell, there's probably been a half-dozen different owners since I've been born. No one's ever put security like this up here before."

The man looked at the fence as if he were contemplating the size of it for the first time. "Like I said, we're used to operating in some very bad places. Sudan. Bolivia. New China. Congo. We have a protocol we follow."

"The folks down in Resurrection probably don't consider their town part of that list you just gave."

Keefer's face showed a flash of annoyance for the first time. It was there and then gone just as quickly. He nodded to the fence. "You think it's too much?"

"Depends on what you guys are really doing in there."

Keefer laughed, but it was cold. "You're a suspicious one, aren't you?"

"Just trying to figure out—"

"No, I understand," Keefer interrupted. "A major mining company moved into town, created a high-tech secure perimeter fence, started operations, and not a single person in town knew anything about it. Not even the sheriff who's supposed to be looking out for things."

Rick ground his teeth, feeling the truth behind the man's words. Undoubtedly, he felt like a fool that something like this could happen right under his nose without him noticing. He felt no reason to lie about it. "It's a little embarrassing,

I'll admit it. But why bother? Why all the secrecy?"

"I could tell you, but then I'd have to kill you," Keefer said, delivering the joke in a flat, lifeless voice that made Rick's skin crawl. The man stared him down for a few seconds before giving him a wink. "You need to relax, Rick. I'm kidding. It's from an old movie."

"Yeah, *Top Gun*. I know it." He pointed down the mountain. "There are hundreds of people in Resurrection who know how to work this mine. But you haven't hired one of them. Why?"

Keefer blew out an exasperated breath. "For the same reason as the secrecy. The reality of what we're doing here is only going to upset people in town. Perhaps to a point where there might be some trouble. We wanted the site to be online first if possible before announcing."

Rick took a step back, feeling like he was finally about to hear something approximating the truth. "Announcing what?"

"The reason we haven't hired anyone."

"And that is …"

Keefer pointed to the fence behind him. "This mine is going full auto," he said. "It's our competitive advantage. A small handful of men operating machines that can do the work of hundreds."

"You mean robots," Rick said.

"See, that's a word we just don't like to use. It's too loaded with sci-fi expectations. People think of androids walking around with pickaxes, wrapped in synthetic skin like those Asian sex worker bots they see on the news. These are just smart machines, safely operated from a control room on the surface by a human. Once we're fully up and running, the trucks taking the ore out of here will be driverless, but still supervised by a person."

Rick took it all in. He'd seen the backlash against automated factories in industrial cities. Whole factories burned to the ground by angry mobs. And it wasn't only factories. Everything from cab companies to fast food restaurants that had tried to go full auto had first been picketed, and then vandalized and become a hot-button political issue. Presidential candidate Mayfield had made it a central campaign promise, and after taking the oath of office had hammered the nail in the full auto coffin with his Get America Working Again (GAWA) legislation. But some things never change, and GAWA had carved out exceptions for those with the most powerful lobbies in Washington. Problem was that Rick knew mining wasn't one of them.

"You open this mine and it's full auto, you're going to need a taller fence," Rick said. "Once word gets out, the feds will be here to close you down. If the men in town don't arrive here first. All this twenty-foot-tall fence will do is cause a run on twenty-four-foot ladders at the hardware store."

Keefer glanced at the destroyed windshield of Rick's Blazer but didn't comment. They both knew the fence wouldn't be breached by an angry mob. The man pulled out a neatly folded piece of paper from his inside jacket pocket. He handed it to Rick. "Times change, Sheriff. Don't you watch the news? The world's on fire. Countries putting walls up. Trade's nonexistent. And on how many fronts is America waging the war on the Jihadis? Turns out America needs raw materials more than she needs a couple hundred jobs in Resurrection, Colorado. The feds were the ones who invited us in."

Rick unfolded the piece of paper. It was an official-looking document from the Department of Labor, but the heading on the page told the whole story.

GAWA Exemption Awarded to CZ Corporation: Resurrection Mine, Colorado.

Rick flipped to the second page and saw the signature line.

Terrance Ruiz, Secretary of the Interior.

"You can keep that if you want," Keefer said. "It's just a copy."

Rick folded it and put it into his pocket. "You think this is going to make things any easier with the town? Or the fact that your robots are *supervised*? This mine is the only hope they have. Once they see it's back in operation but that none of them are needed to—"

"I thought ten million dollars of town infrastructure and job training would help ease the pain," Keefer said. "I was going to contact Mayor Wilkins. She goes by Bertie, right? Anyway, I'm going to ask her to facilitate the money. Or do you think I should ask Jack Lougner, the town treasurer? But I heard he spends a little too much time at Roscoe's Bar and Grill. What do you think? Who do you think I should give the money to? I mean, it is your town and all."

Keefer grinned, and Rick sensed the man knew exactly what he was doing, signaling that he'd done his homework and knew the town well. If it was meant to rattle Rick a little, it hit the mark.

"The mayor will tell you the same thing I did. These people don't want a handout, they want a job. They don't want your money."

Keefer shrugged. "Funny, your deputy didn't feel that way."

CHAPTER 4

R*ick felt a wash of* cold over his body. "What do you know about my deputy? I got a radio call from him that he was up here."

"You just missed Deputy Garcia. We invited him in and had a nice chat. I asked him to do the same thing I'm going to ask you to do."

"Oh yeah? What's that?"

"Keep what he saw up here to himself. You know, give us a few days to make last minute preparations before we announce our presence to the town."

"I'm sure Manny told you the same thing I'm going to," Rick said. "You can go to hell."

The man's eye twitched and the muscles in his neck bulged. Rick took note of the signs of a raw temper just under the surface of the cool exterior, and filed it away for later use.

Keefer pulled a stack of money from his jacket pocket. Nice, crisp, hundred-dollar bills. Based on the thickness, Rick guessed it was nine to ten grand.

"He did say that, but with a little convincing, he decided to take a few days of vacation time."

"Bullshit," Rick said.

"Check your voice mail. He said he was going to leave a message for you."

Rick grabbed his phone. "I don't get any reception …" His voice faded as he saw four bars on his phone. And a flashing icon of a telephone indicating he had a message. He looked quickly back at Keefer and hated the smug bastard even more.

"Go ahead," the man said. "I can wait."

Rick pressed his screen and turned away from Keefer. His shoulders slumped when Manny started to speak.

"Hey, Rick, it's me. I just wanted to let you know that I … uh … needed to take a little time off. Nothing big … a few days, k? I had … you know … I thought I saw something up at the mine. That's why I called you. It wasn't anything. Just Iraq again. Shit's in your head, you know? Look, I'll explain when I get back. Sorry, man. I'm really sorry."

Then the phone clicked off.

"Did you want to play it again?" Keefer said.

Rick clutched the phone to his chest and shook his head.

"It's not a bad deal," Keefer said, waving the money like he was gently fanning himself. "No one gets hurt. If anything, it makes things smoother for everyone. The federal government wants this place operational, so you can't stop it. All we're talking about is *when* people in town find out we're up here. If it's today, there'll be confusion and panic because we're not quite ready to announce the benefits package for the town. You said yourself that when people find out the mine is going full auto, there'll be hell to pay."

"Option two?"

"You say nothing. The town finds out in a few days when we have the community money figured out. We'll have a meeting in the town hall and tell everyone the good news."

Rick snorted a short laugh. "Good news?"

"What's better? The mine is closed forever, everyone clear out? Or here's ten million dollars, let's find a way for everyone to stay?"

Rick nodded. Mining was a thing of the past, he knew that. But it was the only thing about half of the working age men in town had ever known. Maybe a job training program was exactly what the town needed. It was better than anything else they had going on to save the town. "A few days?" Rick asked.

"I can do it in two," Keefer said.

"How much are those days worth to you?"

Keefer's eyes narrowed. He held out the money. "About this much."

"I want five million dollars."

Keefer burst out laughing. There was movement behind the fence and Rick saw the holes in the fabric open, followed by gun barrels. Keefer saw the same thing and waved them away. The barrels withdrew but the holes remained open.

"Son, you're not worth five million dollars. No one is."

"It's not for me," Rick said. "I want it for the town. Up from your ten million."

"I don't think—"

"That's nothing to you guys. You and I both know it," Rick said. "And I figure it's worth twice as much not to have the entire town up here a couple of hours from now picketing this place." Rick indicated down the hill. "Tomorrow's the Fall Festival. People from all over are coming into town. Most of them from other mining communities. Bet we could get a thousand people up here. The press would eat that."

Keefer narrowed his eyes, looking Rick up and down as if just seeing him for the first time. "Marines always were a pain in my ass."

Rick ignored Keefer's show of knowledge about his background. He almost let a *Oorah* slip, but instead just stared the man down.

"Fifteen million and I get three days," Keefer said. "Anything sooner and it goes back to ten. The town gets out of control once it finds out and it's on you. The money goes away. All of it."

Rick assumed the money was off the table if the town blew up either way, so he didn't feel like he was giving anything up. He knew he couldn't tell anyone, not even Bertie. If she knew then she'd call off the festival and march right up the hill herself. No, he'd have to keep this secret. What difference would two days make? "Agreed," he said, holding out his hand.

Keefer shook it, and when he did, he pressed the stack of cash into Rick's hand. When Rick pulled his hand away, there was ten thousand dollars in it.

"Down payment," Keefer said. "Do with it what you want."

Rick weighed the money in his hand. "Really?"

"Sure," Keefer said, his tone saying he'd known all along Rick could be paid off. "It's all yours."

Rick bent the paperclip back slightly on both the front and the back of the wad of bills. Then, with a quick movement that made Keefer flinch, he chucked the money at the fence. When the paper clip hit, the money exploded into a ball of spark and flame, sending tiny fragments of paper money into the air like confetti.

"Oorah, asshole," Rick said. He turned and walked back to his Blazer, a smile spreading across his face. He might have to do business with the man, but that didn't mean he had to like it.

He climbed into the Blazer, brushed the glass from his seat and cranked the engine. When he looked up, he saw Keefer standing right where he'd left him, feet firmly planted, arms at his sides, hands slowly flexing open and closed. It looked as if he was thinking about running after the Blazer and ramming it like a bull. Even from twenty feet away, Rick could clearly see the man's face and the unbridled anger burning there. Rick had seen that expression more than a few times, usually in combat right before someone did something stupid that got them killed.

As Rick threw the Blazer in reverse, the rush he'd felt at his little ethical stand with the money faded away. Keefer's eyes bore into him and left him wondering if he'd made a huge mistake. Whoever Keefer really was—Rick didn't believe for a second he was some corporate operations manager—one thing seemed certain. He wasn't a man you wanted to piss off.

As Rick drove away, he figured his last stunt had blown that in a big way. In one morning, he'd discovered a high-security outpost thirty minutes from his office that had been erected without his knowledge, discovered the mine jobs were going to be forever carried out with robots, lost his only deputy to a bribe and then agreed to lie to everyone in town about everything he'd seen. On top of that, he'd made an enemy of the man who seemed to hold the future of Resurrection in his hands.

And it was only eleven o'clock. It was gearing up to be a shitty day.

CHAPTER 5

H*ank Keefer watched the Blazer* drive down the mountain, small dust devils kicking up from the rear wheels. He slid his jaw back and forth, grinding his teeth. God, he would have liked to have stepped out from the part he was playing and just beat the young sheriff to a pulp right then and there. He'd come close, mentally justifying that it would have been good for his men to see that their leader hadn't lost his step. But that was reaching, and he knew it. A missing sheriff would mean search parties and calls down the mountain. No, this was better. The situation was contained and they were still on schedule.

The sheriff was no more than an ant under his boot. If he had the time later on, he'd enjoy paying the man back for the disrespect he'd shown. Meanwhile, he had important work to do.

Hank took a deep breath and let out some of the tension in his neck and shoulders. When he turned around, the men in protection detail already had the gate open and were in positions on either side of him, facing out to the surrounding forest as if they expected to be attacked at any minute. These were good men, hand-picked by Keefer himself for both their loyalty and their dedication to the cause. He knew being out in an exposed position with an armed man had made them nervous, but they were professionals. If the sheriff had tried to lay a hand on Keefer, he would have been put down.

Keefer walked through the gate and the men followed. A hum filled the air as the electricity was pumped back into the fence once the gate was closed. He turned and looked at the wall stretching in either direction, pleased with the progress of the operation.

The plan had always factored in discovery by the locals during the construction phase. In fact, they'd gotten away with it longer than expected. Using only back access roads that hadn't been driven on in years, and keeping everything in stealth mode, had cost more and stretched the process out, but the anonymity had been worth it.

They were so close to being operational that he'd started to think they'd be able to get through construction completely without being discovered. The arrival of the young deputy that morning had been an unwelcome turn of events, but nothing he couldn't handle.

Keefer turned and looked over the rows of trucks lined up in the yard, all scrubbed and looking good. Mechanics worked on a few of them, but he knew from the reports that these were routine maintenance checks. Beyond that were the old mine buildings, mostly empty shells with broken windows, and half-covered with bushes and creeper vines. They'd set up shop in the most intact building for office space, and rolled a few trailers onto the site too. But that was just for show in case there were aerial photos from a private airplane or a drone.

The real headquarters of the operation was a few thousand feet below ground, safe and sound.

The only disappointment from the morning was that the radio jamming had failed, allowing the deputy's call to get through to the sheriff. Communication control was an essential part of the operation and their first test had been a failure. The man responsible was an expert in the field, the best available, but he'd gotten sloppy. Three weeks of working without discovery at the mine had made the team complacent. Now with the Boy Scout sheriff out there as a wild card, Keefer knew he had to tighten up his ship. It was almost game time, and they couldn't afford any more mistakes.

Carlos Estevez, his number two at the mine, walked out of the office building and met him in the middle of the yard.

"You let him go," Estevez said. It came out as a statement, but there was a question buried inside it. Keefer raised an eyebrow.

"And?"

"The guy didn't want the money," Estevez said. "Goddamn Boy Scout. You trust a guy like that?"

Keefer didn't like the tone in the man's voice. "We had options with him. He didn't see what that deputy did. It was your men he saw outside the fence, let's not forget that. This is your mess I'm cleaning up."

Estevez didn't flinch at the reprimand. He looked at the road where the Blazer had disappeared. "Lot's riding on what we're doing up here. Makes me nervous having someone like that running around, especially when we're this close to being operational. Would have been better not to have any loose ends."

Keefer looked the man over. Estevez was thirty years younger and better looking than he'd ever been despite the ridiculous tribal tattoo swirling up from his neck to his jawline. A weight room junkie, Estevez was a beast, walking with his arms out from his sides because of his bulging muscles. Still, Keefer had seen him on the sparring mat doing martial arts, and his thick arms did nothing to reduce his agility and speed. He wondered how the fight would go down if the younger man ever challenged him physically.

"He won't tell anyone," Keefer said. "I know men like that."

"Seems risky."

Keefer clenched his jaw. He wasn't used to explaining himself to anyone, and it was hard for him to allow it. The only reason he did was because he had an unsettling feeling that Estevez had a point. Removing the sheriff wouldn't have been hard. With a single hand motion, it would have been done. The deputy's fate had been an easier decision to make because after what he'd seen, there was no letting him go. But once they'd explained what they were doing, once they gave him a little tour inside the fence line, he'd been an easy convert. The voice mail he'd left the sheriff had even been the kid's idea. Easy.

But the sheriff was different. And now Keefer was thinking that maybe he'd made a mistake letting him leave.

But what was more unpredictable: The fallout of a sheriff gone missing, or a man with a five-million-dollar incentive to keep quiet for three days? Not that Resurrection would ever see any of that money, but the sheriff didn't know that.

"This was always built into the contingency planning," Keefer said. "We're lucky we went this long without being discovered. Let me worry about it. You have your own timeline to meet. And your own men to control." He turned and walked toward the mineshaft entrance, a half-circle hole in the rock face that looked like something out of an old Western movie. Rusted railroad tracks led from the yard and disappeared deep into the opening. Work crews were affixing a massive metal door into the side of the tunnel, sparks flying from several welders operating at once.

"We'll be ready," Estevez said, a half-step behind him.

"Hmm ..." he said, letting the younger man feel his doubt. "It's times like this that I miss your dad. He was the best operations man I ever worked with."

Keefer suppressed a grin as Estevez's muscles clenched under the man's thin sweater. He expected the reaction since the young man was forever trying to escape his father's shadow, but he also meant what he said.

Alejandro Estevez had been his right-hand man through a career that could have filled multiple books of memoirs. It was on his deathbed that he'd convinced Keefer to take his son into his confidence on the plans the two of them had developed after so many years of watching America rot from the inside. The younger Estevez hadn't hesitated when given the opportunity to join the cause and had proven himself capable over the last two years, even if he did forget his place from time to time. While he'd meant to put his second in command on his heels a little with the comment, Keefer had found himself missing his old friend as he neared the finish line of the project that the two of them had dreamed up together. The project that would make right all that was wrong with the world.

"We'll be ready," Estevez said. "You can count on it."

Keefer nodded. He looked to his right where a line of trucks shielded another car from view. He walked in that direction and felt Estevez follow, now a full step behind him. It was a simple act of submission, but Keefer took note of it. They reached the driver's side of the vehicle, a police car, and stood in front of the blown-out window.

"We're doing important work here," Keefer said. "The most important work imaginable. To save the world, sometimes you have to be willing to do the unthinkable." He pointed inside the police car where Deputy Manny Garcia's bloody body slumped over the wheel, the back of his head splattered against the passenger seat. "Take the good deputy here. He would have helped, said he was willing. But we can't risk newcomers. Why can't we risk newcomers?"

"Can't be trusted."

"Right, can't be trusted. And when you don't trust someone, sometimes you have to make the hard decisions about them."

"I'm on board," Estevez said. "Anything you say. You know that."

"Yes," Keefer said, crouching down so that he was staring into the open eyes of the dead deputy. "But next time you question one of my decisions, even in private—"

"I didn't mean to—"

Keefer held up his hand, his eyes never leaving the deputy's face. Estevez fell silent.

"Just never make it so I have to make a hard decision about you," Keefer said. "Are we clear?"

"Crystal," Estevez said.

Keefer reached out and pushed the dead man's eyelids closed. "Then go get my mountain ready. I want to be operational by this time tomorrow."

Estevez turned on his heel and hurried toward the mine. Keefer smiled and patted the deputy on the shoulder. The body slumped to one side, the movement exposing the dead man's forearm and his US Marine Corps tattoo.

Keefer's smile disappeared. He stood up and walked back to the mine, picking two men for burial duty. Whether he knew it or not, the soldier in the police car had been sacrificed so that his country might live. The Marine deserved a decent burial and Keefer would make sure he got one.

CHAPTER 6

R*ick drove down the mountain* in silence. His phone had again lost service and the radio gave nothing but static, so he really didn't have a choice in the matter. Even so, he wanted the silence. He needed to think.

The shock of hearing Manny stuttering and stammering as he explained he was taking a few days off work had turned to anger. He'd given the guy a chance when no one else would. Put his own neck on the line with the town to give a fellow Marine a place for a soft landing. And how had Manny repaid him for the effort? He'd taken a ten-thousand-dollar bribe and probably headed out to Vegas.

Rick had a mind to call in the squad car as stolen and put out an APB on the son of a bitch. Halfway down the mountain, he'd convinced himself that tough love was exactly what his deputy needed. A Chevy Impala with a law enforcement shield and the words RESURRECTION SHERIFF painted on both sides would be spotted within an hour of him putting the word out. Maybe less if Manny was on the freeway. He'd be pulled over, cuffed, read his rights and tossed into holding until Rick went down to get him out. Lesson learned.

But by the time Rick was on the outskirts of town, he'd settled down a little. He knew that Manny, like all recent vets who'd spent time eye to eye with the Jihadis, was always a few clicks of the dial away from losing it. Some junior highway patrol officer trying to put the Marine in handcuffs could easily spin out of control and the result would be an altercation Rick wouldn't be able to clean up with a few phone calls.

Besides, he was going to have enough on his plate when CZ Corp finally made their announcement in town. The money would help, but it wasn't going to placate some of the die-hards in town. The fifteen million at stake gave him some leverage though. If enough people knew the money was tied to how calm things stayed, then the town leaders, especially Bertie, could use that fact to pressure the troublemakers to control themselves. The money would go a long way to helping the town get on its feet again. That was thirty grand for every man, woman and child in town. Not life-changing money on its own, but Rick had listened to Bertie's wish list enough times to know that the money would make a big impact on the town in her capable hands. He imagined the job training program she could put together. Maybe even lure a company or two from Denver to set up telecommuting centers. Without the money, his brain knew what his heart refused to admit. Resurrection wasn't going to make it.

As he pulled into his small town, he felt like he was looking at a terminal patient doing the best it could not to give up hope in the face of an incurable disease. It was a pity because the bones were there for a great city. The founding fathers had been nothing if not confident when it came time to lay out the town's common spaces. Unlike other small mining towns in the surrounding area, which had packed downtowns with clapboard houses crammed together as close as possible, Resurrection was designed to live up to its name and be the center of rebirth for the entire area. The original owners of the Resurrection Mine directly above town saw this spot as a future county seat, maybe one of the leading cities in the state eventually. As such, they parceled out an oversized square park bounded on three sides by streets and a ring of storefronts. On the fourth side was city hall, an impressive granite building with columns and a dome. Putting on airs, as Rick's mom used to say. More like dressed for a party that never happened.

One look at the shuttered businesses and vacant buildings with broken-out windows and peeling paint told the real story. The mine had petered out in the 1950s and so had the prospects for the town. Rising gold prices, and advances in mining techniques that made it more cost-effective to extract the mine's low-grade ore, reopened the doors every now and then, but this was always short-lived. Then a real boom came when Genysis, America's leading tech company, paired up with the University of Colorado that was running experiments in a deep lab, using the natural shielding properties of a half mile of solid rock.

But that run only lasted four years. Once they developed shielding technology that replicated the effect of the mine, they moved out and closed up shop like the corporate a-holes they were. Rick had seen it coming a mile away, but that hadn't made him any less mad about it. Everyone in town got hurt when Genysis left, a fact he had to remind himself of when he felt like complaining about his own personal loss in the deal.

After Genysis, the town and its people slowly slipped into disrepair. The buildings were in need of a paint job and the citizens in need of more than a monthly check from the government. Rick admired President Mayfield and his Get America Working Again program, but his GAWA initiatives sure weren't reaching up to their little hamlet nestled in the Rocky Mountains. In the end, Resurrection was no match for the hopefulness of its name. The running joke was that a resurrection always needed a death to get the process started, and the town was certainly fulfilling that half of the equation.

The overworked shrink who ran group counseling for vets at the VA had argued that Rick had created an unhealthy link between the town's survival and his own. Maybe, but he didn't care. Thoughts of home had pulled him through hell and back. He wasn't about to let it slip away.

Which is why, even though he was shaken up by what had happened up at the mine, he couldn't help but stop the Blazer and take some pride in all the activity in Town Square. Normally deserted on a Thursday morning, the streets were filled with pickup trucks and delivery vans. Volunteers raked leaves and put up vendor tents. There was a huge stage being erected in front of the town hall and a dozen men and women, most of them people Rick had known since grade school, were all smiles as they worked.

"Trying to get out of work, Sheriff?" came a woman's voice from behind him. He startled and twisted to his left. Mayor Bertie Wilkens, an elegant woman in her sixties, (no one knew for sure if it was early or late sixties and she wasn't telling), walked up next to the Blazer with a cup of coffee in her hand. She wore work clothes, jeans and a flannel shirt, that both had a little paint on them. A tall woman, she reminded Rick of a deer when she moved, graceful but always on guard.

She shook her head as she looked over the bruised and battered vehicle. It wasn't lost on her that the town's vehicle was missing a windshield.

"What happened here?"

"Had to go off-road to get around a fallen tree," he said with a shrug, as if that explained everything.

"Probably cost more to replace the windshield than the hunk of junk is worth." Every year, she offered to buy a new rig for him, but he didn't see the need. It was a 2015 model, but it'd been a workhorse for nearly a decade and it was the only rig he'd ever used as sheriff. The suspension was a little stiff and it jostled him pretty good on the rougher roads, but it wasn't like he was conducting high-speed chases down the freeway. The closest he ever came was when some of the Harley guys decided to get off the beaten track on their way up to the massive bike rally in Sturgis. If any of them wanted to outrun him, they could do so easily. But a new Blazer wouldn't have made any difference. Harley Davidson, now that was one piece of American manufacturing that still got it right.

Normally, he'd be happy to see her, but after his interaction with Keefer, he'd planned to avoid her as best as possible. The fewer questions she asked, the less likely he'd be in a position to have to lie to her. And, like most politicians, Bertie was a talker.

"No, ma'am, I'm ready to work," he replied. "I'm heading over to help old man Roberts get his grills out." He rolled the Blazer forward a few inches, hoping Bertie would take the hint. Instead, she put a hand on the truck, causing him to put on the brakes.

"Heard he's starting his world-famous pork tonight so it'll be done and perfect by lunch tomorrow."

Rick took a breath. He knew Bertie well enough that he wasn't going to get out of there without a little jawboning. He played along.

"I'm helping him with it," he said, trying to sound more relaxed than he felt. "Promised he'd share his secret recipe with me."

"Gonna be the best Fall Festival yet," Bertie said. "Bet we get over two thousand here by lunch."

"Not if people find out I helped with the cooking. I'd suggest you keep that under wraps."

As impatient as he was to get going, he always enjoyed an easy banter with her. He liked seeing her face glow as she watched her town come together to throw a party. It made him feel normal, just two public servants doing their jobs. And normal was all he wanted.

Things could have gone in a different direction for him, and Rick knew that. Bertie had taken a chance on him when he'd come back from the war a broken man, and not just because of the arm he was missing. Rumors followed him back into town, hushed conversations of a mission gone wrong in Istanbul. No one knew the details for sure, and no one was about to ask. Word got around quickly about the nightmares he suffered, and most people wondered how smart it was to give a man like him a gun and a badge. But she'd told people that Rick Johnson was Resurrection's finest before he went off to war and he was even more qualified than ever now that he was back after traveling the world. She'd stuck her neck out for him, and he'd never forget it. Bertie could have told him to jump off a canyon wall and his only question would have been what she wanted him to yell as he did it.

"Where are you coming back from?" she asked.

He shifted uncomfortably in his seat, cursing himself for lingering too long. "Took a drive up the mountain. Clear my head a little."

Bertie arched an eyebrow, exactly the way she used to when she was his school principal instead of his mayor and his employer. "Manny go with you? I haven't seen him around."

"Went out alone. Not sure where Manny is." That part was true.

Her eyes narrowed and she pursed her lips together. "You've always had the worst poker face, Rick Johnson," she said. "What aren't you telling me?"

Rick looked out the windshield, trying to escape her eyes looking right through him. He couldn't lie to her, not Bertie, so he chose to keep quiet. He thought she might draw her own conclusions, and he was thankful when she did.

"Look, I'm glad you took a chance on Manny," she said. "You know that." She paused, searching his face for a reaction. Getting none, she probed, "Is he doing the work?"

They both knew she wasn't talking about his job as deputy. Manny was a vet, and nowadays every vet had work to do when they got home. The Jihadis might not have been able to sail across the ocean, but they did a pretty good job of transforming each Marine into a ticking time bomb during their tour of duty.

Rick nodded. It'd occurred to him that the kid getting the hell out of Dodge might not have been because of the money, but part of a PTSD episode. Hell, that whole crazy thing on the mountain had nearly triggered one in himself. Manny had sounded nervous on the voice mail, but that also could have been because he knew he was letting Rick down. "He's a good man. Let me track him down and talk to him first. I'll shoot you straight with how he's doing once I know. I promise."

She reached into the Blazer and put a hand on his arm. "Can you stay objective with him?"

"Were you objective with me when I came back?" he asked. "Because if you were trying to be, then you were pretty terrible at it. I was more off my game than Manny, and you know it."

Bertie reached in and squeezed his cheek, playing up the gesture like she was a long-lost aunt. "But look at this face," she said. "I never could resist this face."

He rolled the Blazer forward and Bertie stepped back, smiling.

"And that's right where we end the conversation," he said. "Bye, Mayor."

"See ya, Sheriff," Bertie called out, tipping her coffee cup toward him. "Don't forget about old man Roberts. We need those grills set up. Gonna be the best festival yet. It's going to put us back on the map."

And she walked away, not knowing how that the next day her Fall Festival and her beloved town would take its place in the history books, but for all the most terrible reasons.

CHAPTER 7

R*ick rolled down Main Street,* parallel to the stage being set up in front of the town hall. Bertie's enthusiasm was infectious. Maybe it was going to be an amazing event. If they really were going to have a couple thousand people in the Town Square tomorrow, he was going to miss having Manny to help him out. But he'd figure it out. He always had. He considered that Keefer and CZ Mining Corp might end up being the town's opportunity for a new start.

And that's all he wanted, just to give Resurrection a shot to live up to its name and be the place he knew it could be. The money would give them all that chance.

But he had to keep it a secret. He knew he couldn't tell Bertie, least of all. She wouldn't agree to keep something like this from the town. And if by some miracle she did agree, she'd tender her resignation as mayor afterward out of guilt for keeping it from people.

No, it had to stay a secret like he'd agreed with Keefer. He just hoped he could avoid direct questions about where he'd been that morning. There were a lot of things small-town people could forgive. Looking someone in the eye and lying to them wasn't on that list.

He turned into Town Square and parked in his spot in front of the jail. The work done over the last couple of hours was impressive. The stage at the city hall step was complete and decorated with red, white and blue bunting, reusing the same weatherproof plastic material the town used for Memorial Day and the Fourth of July, saving a buck in hard times.

Most of the vendor stands were either fully built or as least had their metal frames put together. He spotted Big Mac Davis mowing the grass at the far end, and his son, Lil' Mac, walking behind him with a leaf blower, scattering the dried leaves and grass trimmings in a whirlwind that appeared to be making more of a mess than anything else.

The ladies from Old Pines Retirement home were manning a refreshment stand for the workers, all wearing floral dresses and wide-brimmed hats as if they were going to the Kentucky Derby instead of a mountain town fall festival. If past behavior was any indication, he was sure there was a flask or two of bourbon hidden in the folds of those dresses.

Dahlia Stevens, an attractive redhead dressed in jeans, flannel and a quilted vest, with hair pulled back into a ponytail, spotted him from a distance and walked toward him. Rick felt a twinge of excitement and awkwardness. She intercepted him as he climbed out of the Blazer.

"People have been asking where you were," Dahlia said. "I told them you had a habit of disappearing unexpectedly."

"Good morning to you too," he said. He wasn't surprised at the comment. One thing that attracted him to her was that she spoke her mind. He enjoyed it when she called out people on their issues, saying aloud what most people would just think or mutter under their breath. But it wasn't as enjoyable when he was the one under fire. "Town's looking good," he said, walking away from the jail and into the square.

Dahlia gave her head a shake, not quite believing he was going to try to blow off her comment. "You said you were spending the night," she said. "That usually implies you're going to show up at some point. Usually dinner."

"Sorry, something came up."

She grabbed his arm and pulled him to a stop. She was five inches shorter than him but somehow still managed to seem like she was towering over him. "Charlie spent the whole night looking out the window for you."

Rick looked away. The image of her five-year-old waiting up for him was brutal. "I should have called."

"Yeah, you should have," she said. "Whatever this thing is that we're doing, don't think it's not scary and confusing for me too. It's been two years, but it doesn't feel like it. Not at all."

Rick's memory flashed him an image of Jerry Stevens's funeral up at the Resurrection cemetery. Rick and a handful of others from town in their dress uniforms. Dahlia all in black, accepting the folded flag and the wooden box with the Purple Heart.

"I get that," he said, feeling lame as the words came out. By the fire in Dahlia's eyes, he knew they'd fallen flat with her too.

"You get that? Maybe what you don't get is none of that matters to me. Only Charlie does. Don't show up on me because you're freaked out or having a tough night for some reason? Fine. I told you early on that we'll take it slow. But don't tell Charlie you're going to do something and then not do it. You don't get unlimited chances with my son. You get one, maybe two. You blew the first one, and now you're on maybe."

Rick nodded, accepting the beat down because he knew he'd earned it. Like in most small towns, the relationships at work were complicated. Rick had known both Dahlia and Jerry since they were all kids together, riding bikes all over town, fishing out of Bateman Creek, sneaking beers when they were teenagers. Jerry's death had been another blow to a town that, like so many towns across America, had gotten used to bad news arriving by way of soldiers in uniform knocking on a front door. But it'd struck Rick particularly hard. Jerry had reenlisted for a fourth tour, but he hadn't. Jerry was six feet underground, his little boy fatherless, and his wife looking for comfort with another man. The fact that the man was Rick filled him with such conflicted emotions that he found it hard to think straight about it. Fortunately, Dahlia was willing to do the thinking for both of them.

"This is when you say something," she said. "Make it good."

"I don't have an excuse. I'm sorry," Rick said. "I got … I got … I don't know. Just let me make it up to you."

Dahlia stared him down, the hardness in her eyes slowly disappearing until it was replaced with the soft sympathy that ate him up every time it was directed at him. Embedded in that look was the understanding that he was damaged goods, a work in progress. But the message was clear. She had the patience for it, but not if her son was affected by it. She spoke softly, the same way she did the few times she'd lain on the pillow next to him in his bed. "You already have me, you big idiot. I want you to make things right with Charlie."

He smiled and nodded. *Big idiot* meant they were OK. He wanted to hug her, feel the comfort of her body against his own. He told himself he didn't care what people thought, but he did. And so did she. They'd decided three months ago, when things started to happen between them, to keep their relationship under wraps. The only person who knew about it was Manny, and apparently he was long gone.

Dahlia pointed to the park. "Well? What're you waiting for?"

Rick saw Charlie running through the gaggle of old ladies at the refreshment stand, a helicopter in his hand banking turns through the obstacle course. The sight caught him off-guard. Jerry had been a Marine helicopter pilot, shot down by a Chinese-made rocket used by the Jihadis. His ghost was everywhere.

But Dahlia's hand gripped his, down low and behind his back where no one would see. "He'll be happy to see you." He squeezed her hand and started to walk toward Charlie, but she held on tight to stop him. "Just tell him you couldn't make it last night. Don't make something up, all right? Don't lie to him."

He nodded. "I get that," he said, giving her a wink. This time it came out confident and assured because he did get it. He understood the power of the truth and having someone to rely on. So as he left her and walked toward Charlie, he was determined always to be those two things for the boy, regardless of what happened between himself and Dahlia. He would tell the boy the truth, always. The irony of the thought wasn't lost on him as he walked through Town Square, knowing that the people surrounding him, the people he'd known since childhood, would get nothing but lies from him for the next two days.

CHAPTER 8

R*ick could tell Roberts was* happy to see him and Charlie arrive in the staging area for the cookout. There were a dozen large grills and smokers spread out on the grass along with three big drop sheets covered with miscellaneous parts.

"'Bout time you got here," Roberts said. "I could use some smarts to get all of this together."

"Sorry, got here as soon as I could," Rick said.

"I said smarts," the old man said, "so I obviously wasn't talking to you, Sheriff." He pointed a finger blackened with grease at Charlie. "I'm talkin' to you, little man. You come to show me how this is done, ain't ya?"

Charlie looked at the pile of spare parts and then back at the grills. "It's like Legos. But we're not following directions. Just building stuff any old way we want to."

Rick laughed, a little too loudly based on the scowl from Roberts. Charlie was smart as a whip. When Rick had walked over to talk to him, he'd gotten the cold shoulder at first, but after a short apology they were fast friends again. When he invited the kid to come and help put the grills together, he'd whooped like he'd been given free-range of a toy store. What Rick hadn't counted on was the way Charlie slid a hand into his own as they walked the length of Town Square. Or the way it felt perfectly natural walking that way with him.

"Not quite, Charlie," Roberts said. "We're putting them together exactly how they're supposed to be. It's just that we don't need directions. Directions are for pansies."

"I use directions all the time," Rick said.

"See my point?" Roberts gave the boy a wink.

Charlie giggled and picked up a rotisserie motor with two hands and inspected it. "Which one does this go on?"

Roberts looked from grill to grill, pointing to one and then the other. Finally, he pointed at Charlie. "Do you know how to do eeny, meeny, miny, moe?"

Rick put a hand on Charlie's shoulder and pointed to a Weber grill. "It goes to that one. C'mon, I'll show you how it works."

Roberts smiled. "Watch the sheriff close, son. If he messes anything up, you let me know."

"Yes, sir," Charlie said, giving the old man a smart salute.

Rick noticed that the simple act took Roberts off guard and his smile disappeared for a second before coming back more as a wince. The wars had impacted everyone at some point, and it was the damnedest things that could bring back a tough memory. A kid playing soldier was just about the last thing the people in Resurrection wanted to see.

"Let's get to work, Charlie," Rick said. "We're going to have two thousand hungry people here tomorrow. If we don't have barbeque ready for them, there'll be a stampede."

Rick grabbed a small toolbox from the ground by Roberts's feet and patted the old man on the back. "Don't worry, it'll all work out. Always does."

The two men shared a look, knowing full well they weren't talking about barbeque and grills anymore. They also knew that things didn't always work out, not really. Still, Roberts nodded. "Damn right," he grumbled. "'Cause we're not pansies, right, boy?"

Charlie grinned and giggled again, then fell into step behind Rick to work on grills and smokers and get the town ready for its big day.

It wasn't until after lunch that Rick had to tell his first lie about the mine. He didn't like to lie as a general rule, but he really hated doing it to Bertie.

As mayor, she was going full speed all day. The Fall Festival was her baby, an event she brought back from the ash heap only four years earlier. Most of the old-timers remembered the town's heyday when the Resurrection Fall Festival was the event of the year. People came in from as far away as Boulder and even Denver to get a taste of small-town mountain culture, enjoy a parade, eat pit beef and funnel cakes, drink hot apple cider and marvel at the aspen trees blazing orange, red and yellow.

But as the town suffered through the dark period of the last couple of decades, the challenges of the mine closure, the tragedy of the Jihadi wars, the rise of Imperial China through the Pacific Rim, and the overall sense that the world was sliding inexorably into an abyss, no one felt like throwing a party. It'd taken every bit of Bertie's skill and infectious enthusiasm to get the first one off the ground. Even then, it had been a disaster.

The morning of the first festival, a thunderstorm had ripped through town, laying waste to the minimal decorations and the few vendor tents set up in Town

Square. But as is common with mountain storms, it lasted less than an hour, giving way to the sun soon after. The people of Resurrection came out like city dwellers leaving shelters after a bomb raid, took one look at the damage, and declared the festival over and the entire thing a fool's errand. The good old days were over, they said, and it was a ridiculous notion to chase what was gone forever.

Bertie hadn't said a word. She just rolled up her sleeves, walked out into Town Square, and got to work repairing the soggy, torn decorations. Rick was one of the first people to join her, grabbing a huge downed branch and dragging it out of the way. Pretty soon, the rest of the town joined in. There was no discussion or debate, just one person after another leaving the sidelines and getting back into the game of remaking their town. Someone figured out how to pipe music through the loudspeaker system in the square and soon they were all cleaning up and dancing to the Rolling Stones. Mick Jagger was a prophet that day. It wasn't the festival the town wanted, but it was exactly what it needed. After the clean-up was done, the party went well into the night, and the Resurrection Fall Festival was reborn.

Since then Bertie was on a mission each year to make the event bigger and better, using it as a tool to bring the town together in a way it hadn't been in years. Rick had hoped that she'd be so busy that their paths wouldn't cross and she wouldn't have a chance to ask him about Manny. He should have known better.

"How's the fried chicken?" Bertie asked, directing the question at Charlie munching on a leg like he was a caveman. Dahlia had brought it from home and she, Rick and Charlie had made a little picnic out of it.

"Good," Charlie said, licking the grease off his fingers. He held it out to her. "Wanna bite?"

"No, you go ahead," she said. "Get big muscles."

"Like Sheriff Rick," he said, flexing his bicep. "Look at that."

"Whoa," Rick said. "Careful, you're gonna poke someone's eye out with that thing."

Charlie laughed and went back to chewing his chicken leg.

"Town's looking good," Dahlia said.

Bertie looked across Town Square, the pride obvious in her eyes. "We're getting there." She turned back to Dahlia. "Mind if I borrow Rick for a minute?"

"Take him," she said. "He's eating all the biscuits."

Rick stood up and grabbed a biscuit from the straw basket on the blanket. "Just for that, I'm taking this one for the road."

He and Bertie walked down the sidewalk that went through the center of the park. Once they were out of earshot, Bertie glanced back at Dahlia and Charlie. "That's real nice."

Rick looked back. "Yeah, Charlie helped me all morning. He's a good kid."

"That's not what I was talking about."

Rick looked away, hoping she caught the signal that Dahlia was a topic he didn't want to discuss. "So, what's up?" he asked, knowing full well why she'd pulled him aside.

"Uh oh," she said. "Is it that bad?"

"What are you …" His voice trailed off as she gave him one of her patented arched eyebrow looks. "OK, I talked to Manny. He's having a tough time."

"How tough?"

"Tough enough. He's going to take a few days off. Get his head back on straight. When he returns, I'll make sure he goes to his support meetings with the group down in Elk's Ridge."

Bertie walked in silence for a while. Rick felt pleased with himself. Technically, everything he'd said was accurate.

"What did he see up at the mine?" Bertie asked.

That was the question he'd been dreading. Rick knew the woman next to him had liar-radar like no one else he'd ever met, but he didn't have much of a choice. If he confided in her, then she'd feel it would be her moral duty to either tell the town right away, or keep the secret and then resign as mayor for lying to people. He didn't want to put her in that position if he could help it.

"Nothing from what I could get out of him," he said. Technically, another true statement. "I know he served time in Tora Bora in Afghanistan. Maybe being in the mountains triggered him. Maybe seeing the mineshaft. Hard to say."

She searched his face, but didn't linger too long.

"Hmm ... hard to say," she said. "So there was nothing unusual going on up at the mine? No activity of any kind?"

Rick felt himself tense up. She was getting too specific. Then it suddenly occurred to him that maybe she already knew what was going on up there. Maybe they'd already reached out to her in advance to smooth the gears in case they were discovered early in the process. His stomach turned over at the idea that maybe there was a stack of hundred-dollar bills somewhere in Bertie's house, a gift from the CZ Corp for her silence and her assistance when they needed it.

"Nothing worth talking about," he said. Again, almost true.

Bertie put her arms across her chest and looked back over at Dahlia and Charlie, now folding the blanket thirty yards behind them. "You've got a good thing there," she said. "The three of you."

"We're just—"

"You live in a small town, Rick. The only people who think the two of you are keeping some kind of secret are you and Dahlia." She reached out and grabbed his arm. "You have your own reasons for keeping it quiet, but just know everyone thinks it's a good thing. Even Jerry's folks."

"Jesus," Rick muttered, taking his hat off and wringing it with his hands. The idea of Jerry's parents knowing he was with Dahlia made him nauseous.

"I'm only bringing this up because ... because ... it's a good thing you have going," she said.

Rick pushed back his embarrassment and took another look at Bertie. She was biting her lower lip, a little habit that only showed up when she was nervous. He'd missed it before because he'd been so caught up trying not to tell her about the mine, but Bertie was rattled about something.

"What's all this about? What's going on here?"

Bertie hugged her arms tighter to her chest. "Someone contacted me a couple of weeks ago. Said they weren't sure, but they thought they'd seen some kind of activity in the data lines running from that research lab they used to have in the mine."

She didn't explain further; he knew the lab she was talking about, and he had a sinking feeling that he knew where the conversation was going.

"This person wanted to know if I knew of a new buyer or any activity up there. I told them no and that we'd know about it if there was anything going on. We hung up and I didn't hear from them again. I thought that'd be the end of it."

Rick felt a pain in his side. All the pieces were fitting together for him now. Bertie's nervousness. Her insistence that he had a good thing going with Dahlia. All of it.

"But I'm guessing that wasn't the end of it," he said.

Bertie pointed toward the stage in front of city hall. Standing in front of it was a woman he thought he'd never have to see again.

"I tried to handle it without getting you involved. But she wanted to talk to you," Bertie said. "I'm sorry."

"Yeah," Rick said. "So am I."

CHAPTER 9

"Surprised to see you here," Rick said as he walked up to Cassie Baker, trying to keep the emotion out of his voice but sensing he wasn't doing a very good job of it.

"Hi to you too," she said. "Bertie thought I shouldn't bother you. I said you wouldn't mind. Hope that was all right."

"Depends on why you're here." He came to a stop in front of her and stuck his hands in his pockets.

She was still undeniably good looking, still with the intense, questioning brown eyes and perfect olive skin, a gift from her mother. But that smooth complexion came as a package deal with a fiery Italian temper. The last time he'd seen her, she'd worn her hair down well past her shoulders, but it was shorter now and pulled back into a ponytail. A nod to efficiency, he guessed. No time for long hair when you worked in a lab seven days a week trying to change the world. She was dressed in jeans and a sleek, high-performance jacket zipped up to the collar. He noticed her hiking boots looked brand new, the outline of the price tag sticker still visible on one of them.

"New girlfriend?" she asked, nodding over to Dahlia. "Cute little boy."

At least she looked nervous, Rick thought. It made him feel a little better. "What brings you up here? I'm guessing it's not the Fall Festival."

"I didn't even know it was going on. Town's looking great. Bertie was telling me it'll be the biggest one yet. A couple thousand people maybe?"

"Should be a good time," he said plainly, clearly closing down that line of conversation. He waited for the real reason she was there.

An awkward silence followed. Rick glanced back through the park and saw Dahlia and Charlie walking across the north side. He watched her for a few seconds and then caught her quick glance his direction. From the distance, he couldn't make out the expression on her face, but he was sure she wasn't smiling at him.

Cassie cleared her throat. "OK, so this couldn't be more awkward, so I'm just going to get to the point."

"That would be great," he said.

"I'll make this quick," she said, matching his tone. "I'm still working with Genysis—"

"I wouldn't say that name too loud around here," Rick said. "Some people are still pretty angry about how that whole thing went down. Some people hold a grudge. Some people find it hard to forgive."

Cassie pursed her lips. "Some people? Well, that's their prerogative. Maybe it wasn't handled well, but what happened, happened. And it was three years ago. Grudge or not, there's no changing it now."

"That's for damn sure."

Cassie blew out an exasperated breath. "Maybe this was a bad idea."

"What makes you think that?" he snapped.

Rick took a breath and reined himself back in. Seeing Cassie had stirred up emotions he hadn't felt in a long time, feelings he thought he'd faced and dealt with. But seeing her so unexpectedly had brought the heartbreak and the bitter anger roaring back. Still, he liked to think he was a better man now. And she was right, it was a long time ago. He held his hands up.

"I'm sorry, it's just ... you just caught me by surprise is all."

"You're right. It's my fault. I tried to send someone else up here," she said. "But most of the old team that worked in the mine are gone. Off working in start-ups or cashing in by freelancing."

Rick tensed at the mention of the mine. "Mine's been closed for years. Genysis was the last one to turn the lights off up there. You all locked the door and got the hell out of here."

The last words held their edge. When he said *You all*, he actually meant Cassie, and they both knew it. She didn't take the bait. "Genysis only leased space. When the mine sold, we were the first to get booted."

"Genysis could have bought a thousand mines the size of Resurrection if it wanted. Leaving was a choice, so don't suggest it wasn't."

Cassie balked at his tone. She tried to steer the conversation in a different direction. "Anything going on up there? At the mine, I mean."

"I haven't been up there in a while."

"Funny, Bertie told me you were up there just this morning."

He cleared his throat, feeling like one of the teenagers he busted smoking weed down by the river. *What do you have there? Uh ... cough, cough ... nothing, Sheriff.*

"I was up that direction today, but didn't go all the way to the mine itself. There was a downed tree in the road so it would have been at least another mile hike up the mountain." Hiking had never been Cassie's thing, so he threw that part in as a deterrent. Unfortunately, he could tell she wasn't buying it.

"Here's the thing," she said. "When we moved, most of the lab was left intact. Just the infrastructure, I mean. Anything that could be removed, Genysis took with them. There was some hope that a research group from a university might take it over. Maybe a collider to study subatomic particles, or even radiation trials for the space program. The mine was perfect for that, the depth naturally blocking all external radiation. All particles, really. Except for neutrinos, of course."

"Of course, not the neutrinos," Rick said, already lost. The common ground in their relationship had never been understanding the science that Cassie had been involved with. During their almost two years together, he never got past a grade school understanding of subatomic particles. To be fair, she never learned police procedures either.

She made a face, letting him know she was aware he was making fun of her, but it didn't slow her down. "All the tech gear was stripped out except for the data trunk lines, the fiber optic cables that connected the lab to the outside world so we could send evals to super cs around the world, whenever we could get time."

He remembered super cs were supercomputers, the massive systems Cassie would obsess about, complaining about her lack of access the way he supposed astronomers complained about fighting to access the best telescopes in the world. He was amazed at how standing there talking to Cassie about neutrinos and super cs made the last three years drop away and feel like only a couple of weeks. It was like they were just restarting a conversation they'd put on hold when something interrupted them for a short time. Only that interruption had left him devastated.

"I've got a lot going on today," he said. "Can you get to the point here?"

Cassie appeared taken aback, but then settled into a cool reserve. "Sure, I know you're busy. Bottom line is that we left some sensors on those data lines, just in case someone else restarted the lab."

"Genysis wanted to spy on them? Nice."

"It wasn't like that. The sensors can't read the data, only measure the flow. Technically, those lines are still Genysis property. If someone else is going to try to use them, especially if it's a competitor in our space, then we'll get an injunction and pay the thirty-million-dollar price tag to remove the data lines."

"And you're here because the data lines are being used again?" Rick asked. He pictured Keefer and his high-security fence. He said it was to protect the mine from the inevitable backlash over going full auto, but Rick wondered now if that was just a cover. Maybe they were doing something instead of mining behind those walls.

"If that were the case, that would be easy," Cassie said. "And Genysis lawyers would be up here, not me. No, it's more complicated than that. We recorded three bursts of data over the lines, sent out over regular intervals, and each with identical sizes."

"There's your proof then. Time to call the lawyers, I guess." All Rick wanted was to buy enough time to get through the two days he'd promised Keefer. He hated the idea of robot workers running the mine, but it wasn't like there was a line of companies fighting to buy the place. He figured it would take until Monday for the Genysis lawyers to do anything. By then Keefer would have made his announcement to the town and the promised money would be safe. The more Rick had thought about it, the more he'd convinced himself that the money was the key to saving the town. He wasn't about to let Cassie wreck it over some data lines Genysis wanted to protect.

"Again, not that easy," she said. "We're thinking there might just be a malfunction in one of the sensors."

"Why's that?"

"Because once we started to analyze the data packets, we discovered they were unlike anything we'd seen before. To say they were gigantic is to miss the idea completely. Like trying to really understand the scale of a single person standing next to the solar system."

He'd forgotten how animated she got when talking science. She was still the same science geek he'd fallen for years ago. Still the same woman who'd broken his heart when she'd chosen to move back to Denver, leaving behind Resurrection and the wedding ring he'd offered her on a bended knee. He was thinking about that moment, when she said the words that caused a chill to run down his spine.

"Either the sensor up there is busted and sending phantom readings," Cassie said, "or someone is doing some seriously big science in my old lab, using data compression techniques unlike anything I've ever seen. Either way, like it or not, I'm going up there today to find out which it is."

CHAPTER 10

K*eefer cradled the phone and* leaned back in his chair. He rubbed his eyes, trying to push back the headache that always seemed to accompany a conversation with Brandon Morris, the CEO of Genysis. The call was going as it usually did, with the younger man talking and Keefer biting his tongue so he didn't say anything stupid that would turn off the spigot of endless funds. Morris was a bona-fide genius when it came to technology—a couple billion dollars of net worth attested to that fact—but he was also one of the most annoying people Keefer had worked with.

He often thought dealing with Morris was half the reason the Pentagon had cancelled his program. The top brass cited ethical concerns as their reason for shutting him down, but a decade of fighting the Jihadis hadn't left many scruples in the military. If he'd delivered a weapon that worked, the chiefs would have worked out any moral issues that got in the way.

But the program had racked up only failures while devouring resources from America's much-diminished military budget. Dislike of the Genysis founder only made it easier to scrap the program and shutter the whole project. The fools had missed one of the great discoveries of the twenty-first century by only a couple of years. Lucky for the country, Keefer had never given up, selling Morris on the idea of continuing in secret.

Relying on Brandon Morris had been a flaw in the project from day one, but access to the tech, let alone Morris's cash, had made it a necessary evil.

"You're her boss," he said. "Just tell her to come back to your offices for an important meeting."

"You don't know this woman," Morris said. "She thinks she's on to something. If I call her off, she'll just push harder." The man groaned and Keefer hated him for his weakness. "I told you we should just do this overseas. It would have been so much easier."

"We're past that now."

"I could have built everything you have up there. I still don't understand why we couldn't have just done this in Asia. No laws. None that the authorities would have used, anyway."

Keefer clenched his jaw until his teeth hurt. They'd had this conversation a hundred times, but the man would never really understand why the project had to be conducted on US soil. Why it had to be Americans that saved America, not some backward culture that ate rice and fish and prayed to Buddha. Or worse, bent down to Mecca five times a day. No damn way that was going to be how America took back its rightful place in the world. But it didn't matter that Morris didn't get it. Not anymore. There was no turning back.

"We've been through all this. It had to be here. Nowhere else," Keefer said as calmly as possible. "But we're wasting time. What's done is done. Our first round of diagnostics checked out. We're online and on schedule to start tomorrow."

"But she's going to trace this back to me before that," he said. "After we're operational, it won't matter. But if it doesn't work, if something goes wrong before ... this wasn't part of the plan."

That's what it always came down to for Morris. Getting caught. Tarnishing his reputation as the wunderkind destined to save civilization from itself through technology. He didn't care about the mission, only himself.

"Nothing's going to go wrong. And if it does, it's not going to trace back to you. I promise," Keefer said. He took pleasure in knowing that, if the mission went south somehow, all arrows actually would point to Morris as the crazed mastermind behind everything he was doing. When you needed a patsy, why not use one of the most well-known men in the world?

"I'm nervous," Morris said. "I think we should postpone. M ... maybe we should ... you know ... rethink this."

A ringing filled Keefer's head and he felt his heart rate ratchet up. The headache that'd been waiting in the wings erupted with full force, stabbing behind his right eye. The idea that they could be so close to changing the world, only to have this ass even utter the word *postpone,* filled him with a blinding rage. If he'd been in the same room with the young man he might have choked him with his bare hands. He stood from his chair and slammed his hand on his desk so hard that pain shot up his arm.

"Don't you dare turn weak on me, Brandon," he said. "This program is days from being operational. Don't you ever suggest we do anything except push forward, do you understand?"

"Y ... you ... you can't talk to me like that," Morris stumbled. "I ... I pay for—"

"You knew the stakes going into this. You knew what we intended to do. But maybe you didn't fully appreciate who you were going into business with.

I want you to listen close, because this might be the most important thing you ever hear. Are you listening?"

"You can't talk to me like—"

"I asked you, are you listening?" Keefer shouted into the phone, channeling every drill instructor he'd ever had into his tone.

A long silence followed. Keefer thought for a second that Morris might have hung up, but then a small voice came over the line. "I'm listening."

"If you do anything, and I mean anything, from this point forward to jeopardize this project," Keefer said, his voice so calm that it was almost a whisper, "I'll kill you. If I die, one of my men will kill you. And before you wonder if I can make good on that threat, I want you to look around the next time you take a walk on the grounds of your fancy estate, or work late in that beautiful corporate headquarters of yours, or slide into the back of a chauffeured car. When you see people near you, people who look like they're just doing menial tasks, they're likely men I put there. Men loyal to me. Men who will do anything I tell them."

"Keefer ... I didn't—"

"And when I do it, when I kill you, I'll take my time. I'll get creative. As much of a genius as you are, you can't even fathom the things I've seen done to the human body. After it's over, after you beg for death as a mercy, other people will hear about what you had to endure, and their balls will crawl into their stomachs just from the description of it."

There was a chugging cough on the phone. It sounded like a gag reflex, and it made Keefer smile.

"Playtime's over, Brandon," Keefer said. "Shit just got real. Do you understand?"

Silence.

"I said, do you understand?"

Morris's voice came back soft and frightened, like a child. "Yes, I understand."

"I'll deal with Cassie Baker," Keefer said. "If you think that would be best."

"Yes ... whatever you think," Morris said. "Thank you."

Keefer smiled. It felt great to finally speak his mind and to reassert himself at the top of the food chain. "Don't worry, Brandon. Tomorrow you'll have everything you want. Together, you and I are going to change the world. Great progress can only be derived from great sacrifice."

"I haven't heard that quote before. Who said that?" Morris asked.

"I did," Keefer replied as he hung up the phone.

CHAPTER 11

R*ick figured he'd bought himself* some time, but only one day. He intended to come up with some other reason to delay when it came down to it. With the festival going on, and him being the only law enforcement in town, it wouldn't be too hard to concoct a minor emergency he needed to deal with. His head was still spinning from Cassie's sudden appearance. He'd thought he was over her. Over the side-splitting ache he got from missing her. Over the embarrassment of having the only marriage proposal he'd ever given be rebuffed by a woman unwilling to leave her career behind.

To be fair, she'd begged him to move to Denver and marry her there, but he couldn't pull that trigger. The two of them, as stubborn as they came, took what could have been one of the best nights of their lives and turned it into a fight for the ages. Hopeful discussion about options for working things out turned into finger-pointing and judgment. Once it got down to an argument of who was being more selfish, the knife was lodged squarely in the back of their relationship. Three days later, Cassie was gone, back to Denver and a high-flying career saving the world from itself, and Rick was left with an empty house, memories of their time together, and the dream of what might have been if she'd stayed.

He'd considered playing the part of peace-broker. Even tried to bring himself around to the idea of leaving Resurrection for the city life, making a trip down the mountain to wander the streets and try it on for size. But it didn't fit him. Resurrection was more than just a town to him; it was a way of life. It was what he'd held onto through all the shit he'd faced with the Jihadis. Somehow, if Resurrection died, then he felt like he might not be able to make it either. Leaving it behind wasn't an option for him. Besides, in Denver there were too many people, too many sudden noises, too many things to trigger memories he didn't want to have.

The guy who led his support group–none of them liked to call him a therapist, just *their guy*–told him it showed that he hadn't really dealt with all the stuff in his head yet, only buried it under a thin layer of dirt. He suggested moving might be a good step for Rick, force him to confront some of the demons that had followed him back home. It all sounded well and good, except for the part about dredging up the past and dealing with it. As far as he was concerned, that part of his life was just some bad dream that enough time and distance could wear down, like rain hitting a sand castle on a beach. Even the artificial limb attached at his left elbow felt real enough that he could almost forget the real flesh and blood arm he'd left out in a Middle Eastern desert. Almost.

But, in his heart, he knew the past always had a sneaky way of catching back up. Cassie was proof of that.

"You taking her up to the mine?" Bertie asked, falling into step next to him as he walked through Town Square away from the stage.

"Tomorrow," he said. "She needs to get into the old lab to check on something. I'll need to rig some safety gear, just in case."

Bertie walked in silence for a few steps. He looked over and saw the pinched look on her face.

"What?" he asked.

She stopped. Part of him wanted to keep walking, but he couldn't bring himself to be rude to her, so he pulled up and waited.

"I like Cassie," Bertie said. "She's smart, nice, and about as pretty as they come."

"And?"

"And I think you have time to take her up to the mine today, let her see what she needs to see, and then have her get the hell back down to Denver where she belongs."

Rick tried to suppress a grin and failed. They lived in a small town so everyone knew everyone else's business. When Bertie had found out what happened between him and Cassie, the full extent of her maternal protectiveness had been on full display. Rick had half thought Bertie might make the trek down to Denver to give Cassie a piece of her mind. Hell, she may have actually done it without him knowing. He saw that same look now, only she likely thought she was protecting Dahlia and Charlie this time too.

The problem was that he did have time to take Cassie up to the mine. The story about getting the gear ready was the only thing he'd been able to come up with on the spot. Fortunately, Cassie seemed to have accepted the explanation. Bertie wasn't going to be as easy. She knew it would take all of ten minutes to grab what he needed to make a trek into the mine. What he really wanted to tell her was that if he took Cassie up to the mine, and she saw the militarized fencing around the property, she and Genysis were going to go ape-shit. Good-bye secrecy. Good-bye fifteen million. But that was exactly what he couldn't say.

"I think it's better to go up tomorrow," he said. "After the festival."

Bertie looked skeptical, but didn't say anything. That just made it worse.

"With Manny on his leave of absence, I need to be here."

"You understand that it might seem to some people like you're looking for a way to keep her around for an extra day?"

Rick didn't need to ask who *some people* were. He was already on his way to find Dahlia. "That's not it. The machine she needs to check out is on the lab level. That's a few thousand feet underground. I'm not going down there with just a flashlight and a granola bar."

Deidre Jacobs, the self-appointed festival decorations committee chair, walked up. "Sorry, Bertie, but we need you over at the stage," she said. "Millie wants to put balloons across the front, but it looks just horrible. Horrible. Like a little kid's birthday party. We need you to settle it."

Bertie didn't take her eyes off Rick. "I'll be right there," she said.

He gave her a wink. "Duty calls."

She stepped forward and punched him in the chest. Hard.

"You've got a good thing going. Don't mess it up."

He watched her walk away, Deirdre waving her hands frantically toward the stage. Not for the first time, he considered that Bertie must have the patience of a saint to do her job. He'd certainly benefitted from her gentler qualities over the years, but the sore spot on his chest where she'd punched him was a good reminder that even she had her limits. He liked the idea of Keefer negotiating with her. Knowing Bertie, the town would end up with twenty million dollars for its trouble.

That was if he could just keep Cassie off the mountain for a couple of days and not destroy his relationship with Dahlia in the process.

Bertie had that part right, he did have a good thing going, and that was usually the time when he messed it up. He realized he didn't want that to happen this time. He had to make sure his beautiful, rich, brilliant ex-girlfriend arriving unannounced in town didn't send things spiraling in the wrong direction.

He found Dahlia in the building that used to house Miller's Hardware Store. As it had been abandoned for the past five or six years, the festival committee had commandeered the storefront as its headquarters. It looked like a politician's campaign office the night before an election. Signs piled in a corner. Flyers being copied on an ancient, wheezing Xerox machine. A group was putting together welcome packages for the vendors ready to ply their wares to the large crowd expected in the morning. Dahlia stood behind a table to the side, folding brochures, and barely looked up when he came in.

Conversation in the room fell a few octaves when he stepped through the door, staying just loud enough not to make it completely obvious that everyone in the room knew that Cassie Baker was back in town. He ignored the sidelong looks and went over to the table where Dahlia studiously had her head down, doing her work. He walked behind the table and picked up some brochures to fold.

"I forgot to thank you for lunch," he said quietly, aware the people in the room were doing their best to listen while trying to look like they weren't.

She nodded. "No problem."

He leaned over, wrapped an arm around her waist and gave her a short kiss on the lips. "I appreciate it. I really do."

She tensed up at first; months of keeping their relationship secret made such a public display of affection a shock. But when he pulled back, she was both blushing and smiling.

"You're welcome," she said. "Now start folding."

He did as he was told, taking note of the other grins around the room, coupled with knowing, satisfied looks. Dahlia nudged him playfully with her shoulder and he knew they were all right.

Now, all he needed to do was keep Cassie off the mountain for a couple of days and everything would be fine.

CHAPTER 12

C*assie made the turn onto* the mountain and headed up toward the mine.

She felt a small pang of guilt after promising Rick that she'd wait until after the Fall Festival to go up the mountain with him. He'd been so adamant that she figured it would just be easier to agree than to argue. She intended to at least see if there were any obvious signs of activity up there. Besides, she technically wasn't breaking her promise. The mineshaft itself would be locked up so she couldn't get in even if she wanted. She was going *up to* the mine by herself. Her promise was that she wouldn't go *into* the mine. Big difference.

But she knew Rick wouldn't think so.

Seeing him had been unexpectedly emotional for her. Of course, she'd known that she'd see him on her trip, and that it had the potential to be awkward. But the whole thing was more intense than she'd imagined. That he was the last real relationship she'd had didn't help either. For the last three years, she'd been married to her career and it hadn't left time for much else. There'd been the periodic fling to blow off some steam and get her head on straight, but nothing that even came close to resembling an actual adult relationship.

Seeing the town had also filled her with mixed emotions. She saw how her life could have been. Wife of the town sheriff, mom to a kid or two, maybe running a small consulting business from the back room of a house out in the woods. There was an appeal to it, especially on the days when catering to the massive ego of Brandon Morris, CEO of Genysis Corp, felt like babying the most truculent child on the planet.

But her life in Denver put her on the cutting edge of science. Seeing Rick's prosthetic arm, a Genysis product, brought that home more than the accolades from her scientific peers or the awards that crammed her office. At the crossroads between the machinery and Rick's nervous system were algorithms that she'd created. Each movement was in response to neural firing, but it was her work that translated that not only into fine motor skills, but also into a passable reproduction of a nervous system. The result was a new life not only for Rick but for hundreds of thousands of amputees from the war. The brain-machine interface Genysis had developed with her work at its core was light years beyond any BMI tech anyone else was able to pull off. When she wondered if it was worth the sacrifices she made, she only had to meet a single soldier using Genysis tech for her to stop feeling sorry for herself.

Besides being a royal pain in the ass, she had to admit that Brandon Morris was an unmitigated genius.

The shielding he'd developed to replicate the conditions in the mountain labs was so out of the box that even peer-reviewed articles on the technology still led to calls of false data. But it worked and, instead of conducting experiments in the depths of the world's mines to shield from radiation, Genysis could now operate anywhere in the world. While it hadn't been good news for towns like Resurrection that enjoyed the income from their operations, it'd led to exponential growth of their work. In fact, they'd accomplished their original ten-year goal of a fully functional artificial limb in only two years. But they were on the edge of doing so much more. Actually unlocking the power of the human brain to connect to wearable tech was within reach.

Morris had also made good on his promise to her that her work would remain non-weaponized. Genysis as a company refused all military contracts as part of their mission statement, part of the attraction for young idealistic geniuses coming to work there. Her suspicion that Morris had fallen off that path was what prompted her to secretly place the sensors in the mine on the way out. She'd used the word *we* when she described to Rick the placement of the sensors on the data line. In reality, there was no *we*. She'd done it in secret herself, not even telling her closest assistants about it. If the lab and her work were being used for military purposes, she wanted to know.

She took the switchback on the road carefully, glancing down the steep drop on the side and wishing she'd rented an SUV instead of driving her electric-powered Ford Mustang. It was pretty and fast, a throwback to the glory years of American prowess, but it had no business being on a dirt road. Although the same could be said of herself. If anything, she should have delegated the task to some low-level employee to check out the data fluctuations from the mine and get back to her.

But there were three complications to that. First, the sensors she'd left behind weren't supposed to be there to begin with. She'd taken great pains to hide them from the techies that scanned the area once the lab shut down. While it would be easy for her to find them again, trying to explain their location to someone else would have been nearly impossible and made her look like she'd lost her mind. Second, if the sensors, which were her own creation, were malfunctioning somehow, she wanted to know why out of professional pride. And third ... well, that was the toughest one. She hated to admit it, but the first two reasons were BS and she knew it. Once the sensor had gone off, she'd jumped at the opportunity to come up to Resurrection to see Rick. But the way he'd acted so strangely had piqued her interest in what might actually be going on at the old mine.

"Shit," she said, hitting the brakes and sliding the Mustang to a stop on the gravel.

In front of her, stretched across the road, was a thick fallen pine tree blocking her way. She sat with the engine idling, looking back and forth across the length of the tree. The needles were still all green so it was a recent fall. There didn't seem to be any way around it that didn't include going off-road, something she wasn't about to try with her Mustang. She calculated where she was on the winding road in relation to the mine, and estimated how long a hike up the mountain would take. The distance wasn't the problem, but she knew the elevation gain would destroy her. Twenty minutes a day on a treadmill followed by twelve hours at a desk in a computer lab wasn't exactly great training for an alpine climb.

She got out of the car and walked over to the end of the fallen tree. She hadn't seen any other debris on the way up that she would have expected if there'd been a storm in the area over the last few days. It was curious that this particular tree, perfectly placed to block the road, had fallen here. Part of her expected to see a saw cut and a pile of wood chips at the stump, proof that someone had closed down the road on purpose.

But when she got to the base she saw the entire root system still hung from the end, covered with fresh dirt. The hole in the ground was on the edge of a steep slope, right on a drainage ditch for the road. It wasn't hard to imagine the tree growing for years with its base slowly being eroded away with every rain. Her conspiracy theory of someone trying to stop her from going up the mountain lost its steam. The only conspirator seemed to be Mother Nature, and she didn't usually pick sides in disputes.

Cassie walked the length of the tree, the curious part of her scientific mind looking for anything of interest. She saw a large bird's nest but no eggs on the ground. Spring was for babies, not the fall right before the mountains descended into the ravages of winter. She stared at the empty nest, feeling a swell of emotion at the sight, surprised to find that she was blinking back tears.

Logically, she knew her response was disproportionate, that she was assigning more meaning to the broken nest than was healthy. The scientist in her knew that she was experiencing a hormonal surge as her body communicated to her that her last few years to bear children were upon her. But knowing that, even being at peace with her decision not to have kids, did nothing to protect her. The body didn't fight fairly. Its programming told it that the continuation of the species was a prime directive and it could use any means necessary to get more humans into the world. It was the reason she found herself staring at new mothers with their children. And why she had to fake her smiles at baby showers thrown for her friends. Intellectually, she was at peace with her decision. Emotionally, she was a wreck. She knew over time her intellect would win the fight. It always did.

And it looked like Rick had won his fight too. The trek up the mountain was doable but it was more than she was willing to bite off. She didn't have any water, and a quick check of her phone showed that there was no cell service. All she needed was to twist her ankle on the top of the mountain and have to hobble all the way back down. No, she would wait it out and go up with Rick as planned. With his Blazer, he could cut a trail around the tree or just tie on to it and winch it to the side. It was only twenty-four hours, and there was the Fall Festival between now and then. She took a deep breath and decided to try to relax for a day, something she hadn't done in the last three years. It would be good for her.

CHAPTER 13

K*eefer watched the woman on* the surveillance camera's feed as she turned and climbed back into her car. She mangled the three-point turn on the road but eventually got the Mustang around and headed back down the mountain toward Resurrection. He was surprised she hadn't noticed the marks on the tree trunk where the chains had been attached by his men when they pulled the large pine down across the road. For all Morris's talk of her genius, she'd missed big clues, but it was a miss that had saved her life.

He didn't like to kill people and avoided it unless it was completely necessary. He doubted the history books would reflect that fact about him. In fact, he knew they wouldn't. He would be labeled a monster, he would be vilified and hated, but it didn't matter. He would know the truth and someday the world would come to thank him. At least the part of the world he cared about would. Hell, they might even erect statues in his honor. Keefer grinned at the thought.

He would like that.

Keefer pulled out his cell. No signal. He signaled the young soldier manning the communications station. After flicking a few switches, the soldier nodded for Keefer to go ahead. He looked back down and saw there were five bars. He pressed a number and waited for the person on the other end to pick up. He didn't mind letting Cassie Baker off his mountain, but he wanted to make sure she didn't come back.

"Sheriff," he said into his phone, "this is Keefer. You've got a problem."

CHAPTER 14

R*ick hung up the phone.* He didn't know how Keefer had gotten his cell number, but he did know he hated feeling like he was on call to do the man's bidding. It'd been a long time since he'd taken orders from anyone, let alone from a smug bastard like Keefer. He swallowed hard, trying his best to hide his frustration with the position he found himself in.

"Who was that?" Dahlia asked. They'd finished folding the pile of brochures and were now helping with the vendor welcome packs.

"You know how it is," he said. "Someone's always getting into trouble somewhere in this town."

"If only we had better policing."

"Hey now," he said, giving her a pinch and then a kiss. He enjoyed how natural it already felt to be affectionate with her in public. "I've got to go check on things."

"Check on things, huh? Sounds like someone's trying to get out of work," Dahlia said.

Rick pointed to the spools of ribbon she and three other ladies were using to add flourishes to the vendor care packages. "Folding paper I can do. This stuff you're doing now is way above my pay grade." He leaned in a little closer, but kept his voice loud enough for the other ladies to hear. "Dinner tonight at my place? You and Charlie?"

Dahlia blushed, but she smiled. He could tell she liked being out in the open about their relationship too, even if it was going to take some time to get used to. "You bet."

"Great, I've got some great frozen pizzas."

"Make it my place," she said. "Seven o'clock."

Rick pretended to be offended. "You don't like my pizza?"

She shooed him out the door and he took the chance to duck out. He looked back through a side window and saw the other ladies peppering Dahlia with questions now that he was finally out of earshot. He worried that it might be overwhelming for her, but she seemed happy. And, to his own surprise, he felt pretty damn good himself.

His mood soured when he looked across the square to the Franklin Hotel. Most of the rooms in the old place were occupied as rental units, but there were still a few traditional hotel rooms available. It was where Cassie was supposed to be staying, but a quick scan of the parking spots showed that her fancy electric Ford Mustang was nowhere to be seen, further confirming what Keefer had told him on the phone.

He reached for his radio, thinking he would call Manny to tell him to be on the lookout for the car, but stopped himself. In the middle of the discovery on the mountain, Cassie's arrival and the complications with Dahlia, he'd nearly forgotten about his missing deputy.

Well, not really missing. The voice mail had been purposefully vague, but the message had been loud and clear. Manny had taken the money Keefer offered and gotten the hell out of town in a hurry. Rick pulled out his phone and called him, undecided if he was going to lay into the kid or guilt-trip him. Probably a little of both. But he didn't get the chance. Voice mail.

"Manny, it's Rick." He paused. A voice mail was a terrible way to communicate to start with, but he also knew that once he got going, he might say something he regretted. He'd given Manny a shot, gone out on a limb as Bertie had reminded him that morning. Taking a bribe and leaving the day before the town's biggest day of the year was a funny way to repay the kindness. With the anger building, he knew leaving a long message wasn't going to go well. Instead, he just said, "Got your message. Just call me to discuss."

He hung up and strode across the square to the hotel, noticing the automatic lights already clicking on. The days were getting shorter and a chill came down from the mountain on the evening breeze. Usually he preferred the longer summer days, but darkness falling meant he'd gotten through the first day of keeping the new mining operation a secret. Tomorrow the town would be busy with the Fall Festival so there was no reason for anyone to go exploring up the mountain. Then, if the Festival went well, the town would be fat and content after a day of eating, drinking and recalling better days. There would be cleanup to do and a Denver Broncos game on TV to keep everyone occupied. No one in town had been up to the mine in months and he didn't see any reason why anyone would go up there during the most exciting day of the year.

Anyone except Cassie.

The Mustang turned the corner and drove down Elm Street to the hotel. Rick had a hint of nostalgia seeing the car's clean, classic lines, but found himself missing the throaty sound of an internal combustion engine. He just couldn't get used to the quiet *hum* of electric cars even though they far outnumbered gas cars on the road now. Even the military had transformed their fleet of vehicles once the battery technology enabled days of mission time on one charge. Still, in a fight, he preferred the older equipment. There was something undeniable about the roar of massive diesel engines when the cavalry rode in with their heavy armor to extract them from a tough position. He'd seen Jihadis scramble back into their tunnels just from the sounds of the engines, not something the hum of the electros would ever do.

He watched the Mustang silently pull into a parking spot, subconsciously adding the soundtrack of a muscle car motor in his head. He remembered that Cassie used to tease him about being born ten or twenty years too late. When it came to music, movies, clothes and cars, she was right. But as he flexed his robotic left hand, articulating each finger individually, feeling the cold air on his hand as he did so, he knew he owed his quality of life to being born in today's age. Twenty years ago he would have had a stiff, lifeless prosthetic with a metal claw at the end for picking at things. Then again, if he'd been born twenty years earlier, he might never have lost his arm fighting against the Jihadis to begin with.

"If I didn't know better, I'd think you had me under surveillance, Sheriff," Cassie said, climbing out of the car.

"I'd only have to do that if I thought I couldn't trust you to keep your word not to go up to the mine without me." He nodded toward the Mustang's tires and the dirt covering them. "Cruising the back roads for fun?"

"Still have the passive-aggressive thing going on I see," Cassie said. "If you want to accuse me of breaking our agreement, just say it."

"You broke our agreement."

"See? Didn't that feel better?" She turned and walked up the steps in front of the Franklin Hotel.

Rick bit the inside of his lip and shook his head, whole arguments from years earlier flooding back to him.

"You promised," he called out.

"I promised not to go into the mine," she said, barely slowing down. "I didn't say anything about going up to the mine."

"That wasn't what I meant and you—"

Cassie stopped. "Doesn't matter anyway. There's a tree down near the bottom of the road. Blocks the whole thing. We'll need to off-road to get around it or move it somehow."

He followed her up the steps until he was even with her. He had her by six inches and he noticed she took one extra step up so that she was taller than him. "If you'd listened earlier, I told you there was a tree in the road."

"See? You were right about something."

Rick shook his head. "Can we just agree that—"

"I'm not going up there. The road's blocked."

"Sorry if I'm not convinced, but letting obstacles stop you isn't really your thing," he said. "A tree in the road hardly seems like something that could stop you."

She smiled, obviously taking it as a compliment even though he didn't mean it as one. More like a diagnosis of an illness.

"Once you decide to do something," he continued, "it doesn't matter what it takes, right? As long as you accomplish your goals, everything else be damned."

He knew the comment would bite and he didn't much care. The smile disappeared from her face.

"So that's how we're going to do this?" she asked.

"What do you mean?"

"You said everything else be damned. But what you wanted to say was every*one* else be damned," she said. "We're talking about you. About us. OK then, let's talk about it."

Rick felt a surge of heat on his neck and face as he prepared to engage. It was the conversation he'd played out a thousand times in his head since she'd left him. All the biting one-liners were ready. All the things to say that would hurt her the worst. He opened his mouth, but then stopped himself. He took a step back and slowly drew in a deep breath. A feeling of calm came over him as he realized he not only didn't want to have the conversation, but that he didn't need to have it either. Instead, he just shook his head and smiled. "What's past is past. I'm fine leaving it there if you are. In fact, I'm going to leave it there even if you aren't."

Cassie crossed her arms. She looked flustered for a second, geared up for a battle of words that apparently wasn't coming. But she forced a smile. "That's good with me. I just need your help getting into the mine tomorrow and then I'll be out of your hair."

"After the festival."

"After the festival," she agreed.

"And you swear not to go up the mountain alone until then?"

"I told you—"

"Jesus, can you just swear it, Cassie?"

"Okay, I promise not to go up there."

Rick turned his back and walked down the hotel steps. "Sleep good. Big day for Resurrection tomorrow." As he walked away, he listened for the stairs creaking behind him, but there was nothing. He knew that if he turned around she'd be there, watching him walk away. It took a lot of willpower not to turn around.

But dinner was waiting for him at Dahlia's house. Bertie was right. He had a good thing going there.

CHAPTER 15

D*inner was a hit. Rick* ate two massive helpings of pot roast with carrots, onions and cabbage all over a bed of mashed potatoes and brown gravy. It was perfect comfort food. He'd treated Dahlia and Charlie to dinner at Roscoe's before, but they'd never eaten at one of their own houses as a group. They'd convinced themselves that it was so they wouldn't confuse Charlie, but the truth was they were both scared of it.

Eating at home together felt like another step forward in whatever it was they were doing. But the night felt like the most natural thing in the world. They sat around the table, laughing, telling stories, listening to Charlie's excitement over the festival the next day. Dahlia had changed from her work jeans and sweater into a dress, nothing fancy, but she looked beautiful as she beamed with pride at her boy. She had her hair brushed out and there was the soft scent of perfume in the air. Rick found himself unable to take his eyes off her.

After dinner, they did the dishes together while Charlie got his pajamas on for bed. The small TV was on with the sound turned down. Rick glanced over long enough to see a snippet of President Mayfield at a press conference. The ticker on the bottom of the screen indicated the president was announcing a new monument to be erected in memory of America's civilian casualties, but the screen flashed to an aerial view of the devastated landscape of Washington, DC. Rick's stomach clenched even though he'd seen the footage a thousand times before. The flyby started right over the spot where the twenty-kiloton bomb had gone off near the White House, leaving just a smudge on the ground where President Harrison and most of his Cabinet had died five years earlier. The shot soared over the wreckage in the familiar smooth glide of a flying drone, moving to the ruins of the US Capitol building, only scorched by the edge of the fireball, but shattered by the air blast. The loss of life that day had been devastating. Years of war and terrorism on America's soil had hardened the public to body counts. But there was something about seeing America's monuments decimated and left in charred ruins that still caused Rick to well up.

Dahlia reached across him and turned the TV off.

"Room for dessert?" she asked.

"I want some," came Charlie's cry from the back room. The single-story rambler meant that no one was ever too far from anyone else.

"We'll see how fast you can get your jammies on," she called back.

Rick tried to shake the image of DC from his head. He took the roasting pan from her hands and dunked it into the dishwater.

"You OK?" she asked.

He nodded. She knew better than anyone that the darkness of the world outside Resurrection was still fighting for position inside his head. He thought of telling her about the flashback episode he'd experienced up at the mine. Hell, he thought about telling her everything about Keefer, the mine, all of it. He didn't want there to be secrets between them. Not ever. But he couldn't bring himself to do it. He wanted to be her support, not a source of even more burden.

"I'm fine," he said, forcing a smile.

Dahlia wasn't leaving it there. "Any word from Manny?"

Rick glanced to the hallway, wishing Charlie would hurry up and save him. He shook his head. "No, not a word."

"That's not like him, is it?"

Rick scrubbed the bottom of the pan, his agitation with Manny helping to cut through the grease and bits of stuck food. It was a fair question, but he didn't know how to answer it. Twelve hours earlier, he would never have believed his deputy and friend would take money from a stranger and toss aside all loyalty to him so easily.

"I don't know if it's like him or not, to be honest," he said. "I thought I knew him. I thought he was a friend ..."

Dahlia took the pan from him to dry it. "He is a friend. And even friends make mistakes. You always say yourself that recovering from the things you guys saw, the things you had to do over there, was two steps forward, one step back."

"On a good day."

"Exactly," she said. "This isn't about you, it's about him. Getting better. Anchoring back in the real world."

Rick grinned. "I should stop telling you what we talk about in group."

"No, it helps me too," she said. "Isn't that what tonight was? Anchoring?"

He wiped his hands dry and then pulled her to him, their bodies pressed against each other. "Thank you for a great night," he said before kissing her.

"Ewwww," came Charlie's voice from the doorway.

Rick pulled back, knocking a plate off the counter with his hip. He reached for it with his left hand and snatched it out of the air with his artificial hand, catching it easily.

"Cool," Charlie said. "How'd you do that with your fake arm?"

"Charlie," Dahlia said.

"No, it's fine," he said. "Me and Charlie have talked about my arm before. Want to check it out up close?"

Charlie shook his head. "Mom says it's rude."

Rick laughed. "No, it's fine. Want to know how it works?"

Charlie glanced at his mom, uncertain.

"Go ahead," she said.

"Awesome," Charlie said, touching Rick's arm. His eyes were wide. "It feels like a regular arm."

"That's the point." Rick pulled up his shirt sleeve so that his elbow was exposed. The joint was enlarged and boxy, the only part of the limb that appeared unnatural. "This is where the brains of the arm stay."

"You have brains in your elbow?" he said, pulling his hand away. "Gross."

Rick laughed. "Not real brains. A microcomputer that processes everything that millions of sensors all over the artificial skin feels."

"Just like nerves," Dahlia said.

Rick saw she was as interested as Charlie. He realized she'd never asked details about his arm either. "Exactly like nerves. Charlie, let me see your arm."

"Why?" he asked suspiciously.

"Don't worry, I won't hurt you." Charlie extended his arm. "Now close your eyes." Charlie fidgeted but closed them. Rick gave him a small pinch. "Feel that?"

"Yeah, you pinched me."

"How do you know?"

"Because I felt it."

"Did your skin feel it or did your brain?" Dahlia asked, picking up on his line of questioning.

"My skin," Charlie said, opening his eyes. "That's where I felt it."

"Yes, but when I pinch you here, the nerves in your skin send a signal to your brain that says *hey, something's pinching us over here*." Charlie giggled at the silly voice Rick used. "And your brain does one of three things. It freaks out and tells your body to move away from what's pinching you."

"Like when something burns you," Dahlia added.

"Exactly," he said. "That's an involuntary reaction. Or the brain thinks about the information and decides to either do something about it or not. You opened your eyes and decided to leave your arm here because you know I'd never, ever hurt you."

"That's a voluntary reaction," Dahlia said. "But what's the third thing?"

"The brain sometimes just ignores what the nerves are telling it. Charlie, have you ever been playing in the woods with your buddies and, when you got done, realized that you had some cuts or scrapes on your elbows or knees?"

"Yeah, one time I was just gushing blood and I didn't even know it until I got home. It was so cool."

"I wouldn't say it was gushing," Dahlia said. "But you did need a Band-Aid."

"There you go. If our brains processed every single thing our bodies felt, it would overload us. Figuring out what's important, what's not important, how to react to it or not react, has to be done almost instantly, millions of times a second."

Charlie pointed to Rick's elbow. "All that happens in that little computer in your elbow?"

Rick shook his head. "It'd take a supercomputer the size of this room to pull it off, so I use the most powerful computer in the world instead." He tapped his head. "Wires go from the processor here and up directly to my brain. It may not look like much, but the human brain is capable of an unbelievable amount of computing power. Better than a lot of even the fancy ones the military uses."

"Then why are people so stupid sometimes?"

Rick and Dahlia both laughed. "You figure that out, you let me know." Charlie's brow crinkled, showing that he didn't understand. "People only use a portion of their brains. Maybe as little as ten percent. If we could tap into our brains completely, we'd have the most powerful computer in the world."

Charlie poked Rick's arm with his finger. "But does it do any superpower stuff? Can you crunch rocks or anything?"

"Nope, but it can scoop ice cream," he said. "As long as it's all right with your mom."

"Two scoops," she said. "Normal sized though. I know all the tricks."

Charlie ran to the freezer to get the ice cream. Dahlia crossed the room to get him a bowl, sliding her hand across Rick's shoulder as she did. He shivered at her touch, wishing the house was bigger or Charlie was a heavier sleeper. But neither of those were the case, so it wouldn't be until Charlie was back in school Monday when he and Dahlia could be alone together. He knew it was for the best; he wanted to be careful with Charlie. Still, he couldn't make the weekend pass fast enough.

Dahlia put three bowls on the table and handed him a scooper. "We don't want the kid eating ice cream alone, do we?" she said.

Charlie whooped and Dahlia went to the fridge to get Hershey's chocolate sauce. As Rick scooped the ice cream, he happened to look up and see his friend's photo on the wall staring back at him. The picture showed Jerry smiling, looking right at the camera. In Rick's mind, the look was one of approval. And it was the first time he'd ever felt that his buddy would have wanted him to be in his house, taking care of his family for him.

At that moment, Rick realized that was exactly what he had decided to do. No matter what, he would protect Dahlia and Charlie. It was a heavy thought, but it felt right and natural. He gave a slight nod to the photo on the wall and scooped out ice cream for the three of them, content for once that he was doing the right thing.

But the second they sat down to eat, his phone rang. He pulled it out of his pocket, half-expecting to see it was a call from Manny, but it wasn't. He answered it.

"Hi, Bertie, kind of late, isn't it?" he said.

"Sorry," she said, sounding shaken up, "but I need you to come down to the square."

"Can't this wait until the morning?"

"No, Rick. Now," she said. "Right by the stage. It's about the mine."

His mind raced as to what she could have found out. "Bertie, what do you—"

But the phone was dead. Dinner was over.

CHAPTER 16

T*he glow of lights illuminating* the facade of city hall extended over the stage set up at the base of the stairs, where Bertie was standing with three men. A utility truck was parked next to the group, the kind with an extendable bucket for accessing telephone and power lines. The men were dressed in work overalls with a logo patch on the chest with the letters CZ. Still, the uniforms didn't mask the fact that all the men were broad shouldered and fit.

"Thanks for coming," Bertie said, not bothering with any formalities. "These men say you know about the instruments they're installing around town. Is that true?"

The men stared Rick down as if daring him to contradict them.

"You guys are a little early, aren't you?" he said.

"So you did know about this?" Bertie said, incredulous.

One of the men stepped forward. Rick noticed a tattoo under the collar of the man's overalls and that extended to his jawline. He'd seen that same kind of tattoo on some of the younger guys in his group session at the VA, never above the jawline unless they'd had the work added onto after getting out of the service. Regulations had been relaxed with the need for more bodies in the fight, but Uncle Sam still drew the line on face tats. When Rick asked why they'd gotten it, the answer was right out of high school. *All the cool guys were doing it*. In the military, the cool guys were the bad asses. Rick couldn't tell for sure whether the man in front of him was one of the bad asses or just another wanna-be, but judging from the man's steely glare, he had a pretty good idea.

"I told the mayor that CZ Corp inherited Resurrection Mine in bankruptcy proceedings," the man said. "We've inherited the liability for the air and water quality around here so we're just putting monitors up. That's it."

Rick nodded. "Yeah, but I thought you guys were coming next week." He turned to Bertie, his stomach clenched from having to lie right to her face. "They called yesterday, but I thought with the festival and everything, it could wait."

Bertie tilted her head as he talked, sizing him up. He hoped that in the low light, her innate talent as a human lie detector would be off.

"Why are you guys out here in the middle of the night?"

"That's what I want to know," one of the other men grumbled.

The spokesperson for the three shot him a look. "Our last job went long, then Martell over there got us lost."

"All the mountains look the same," the man who must have been Martell complained. "And the phone reception for navigation is shit… sorry, ma'am," he quickly added.

If these guys were playing the part of the blue-collar technicians, they were doing a good job. Still, Rick knew Bertie was a tough customer.

"This still doesn't make any sense to me," she said. "The mine's been closed for years and you guys show up in the middle of the night? What's the rush?"

"Ma'am, you and me both wouldn't mind getting the answer to that question. I offered to come up Monday to install, and my boss ripped me a new one. I don't make the rules, I just follow them."

"Can you guys give us a minute?" Rick said.

"We only have two more to install and we're done," the man with the tattoo said. "And we're going all the way back to Boulder tonight, so …"

"Just two minutes."

The man nodded and waved the others back toward the truck. They groaned, hamming it up a little too much, Rick thought. Once they were out of earshot, he turned to Bertie, his hands in the air.

"My bad. I should have told you right away."

"Hell yes, you should have. I walked out here and saw them installing things on my lampposts in the square. I thought they were Jihadis."

Rick tried not to laugh at the idea of Resurrection being a target for Jihadi mercenaries. Not exactly a high-value asset. "You were so busy with the festival. I didn't think you needed this on your radar right now. If I'd known they were coming tonight, I obviously would have told them to call you first. I'm sorry."

Bertie seemed to relax, taking comfort from his explanation. A reaction that made him feel even more terrible because he knew it was based on the trust she had in him.

"No, you were probably right. I don't think I'll be able to sleep tonight, that's why I was out here walking around in the first place. On a normal night, no one would have noticed." She glanced over to the truck. "CZ Corp. Ever heard of it?"

"No, you?"

"No." She pulled out her phone and typed in a search, poking her phone with her fingers. She didn't like what she saw. "Dang, reception's out. Zero bars. Been like that all day."

Rick pulled his own phone out and saw the same thing. "I noticed that too. Maybe they're doing something with the cell tower."

Bertie eyed the truck. "Do you believe them, or do you think this CZ Corp is thinking about reopening the mine? God, wouldn't that be great? Exactly what this town needs to get back on its feet again." She must have noticed something change in his expression because she took a step closer to look him in the eye.

"Do you know anything else about this?" she asked. "Anything else you thought could wait until after the festival? If so, I want you to tell me now." When he didn't respond immediately, she took him by the forearm. "Are they reopening the mine?"

Rick shook his head. "I don't know," was all he could manage. "I'm sorry," he added kind of pathetically. He was sorry, but not for the reasons Bertie guessed.

She pulled away from him, her jaw set and her eyes hard. A look of betrayal. She didn't believe him, and he felt terrible for it.

"If you want, I'll stay with them until they're done," Rick said. "Make sure they're above board."

Bertie nodded. "Do that. Something feels off about this whole thing. First Cassie shows up asking about activity at the mine and now this. I don't believe in coincidences."

"Let's get through the festival and then we'll worry about it after," Rick said. "Try to get some sleep. I'll watch things out here."

They said good-bye and Bertie slowly walked the width of the park back to Elm Street and then disappeared down a side street where she owned one of the nicer houses in town. Rick waited until she was gone before heading over to the utility truck. The men stood ready; the pretense of sloping their shoulders and feigning disinterest was gone.

"Is it handled?" the leader said.

"Why didn't Keefer tell me you guys were coming tonight?"

"Ask him yourself."

Rick's phone rang. He raised it and checked the screen. Five bars and Caller ID showed it was Keefer calling. He answered it.

"I thought we had an agreement," Rick said into the phone.

"Calm down," Keefer said. "Those air sniffers are for your own protection."

"Why's that? What are you guys really doing up there?"

A long pause.

"You were sloppy today. The scientist coming up the mountain. The mayor questioning my men. I hope I can expect better from you tomorrow. There's a lot riding on this. The man in front of you is Estevez, my second in command. What he says goes, understand?"

"I don't like this," Rick said. "There's more here going on than ... hello ... Keefer?"

The line was dead. No bars.

"We're getting back to work," Estevez said. The other members of his team immediately went into action.

"Let me see what you're installing," Rick said.

Estevez hesitated, and Rick thought he might just ignore him. Instead, he said, "Martell, bring over one of the sniffers."

Martell jogged over, carrying a device not much larger than a cell phone. He gave it to Rick who turned it over in his hand, inspecting the flared end that was an open intake area. The bottom was a speaker. He'd seen this kind of device before.

"This is a bio/chem early-warning system," he said. "Why do you need sirens here in town?"

"I told you that already," Estevez said. "It's a sniffer, measuring air quality, particulates, humidity, everything. Keefer told me you know about the mine. That it's going full auto."

"Yeah, so?"

The man grabbed the device back from Rick and tossed it to Martell. "The autodrive vehicles need environmental data points to adjust their ..." Estevez stopped and sneered. He turned to Martell. "Would you listen to me? Trying to explain science to a Marine grunt." He looked back at Rick. "Just keep doing what we tell you, when we tell you, and you'll get paid. Got it, grunt?"

Rick fought down the impulse to scrape the shit-eating grin off the man's face with a right hook. Even against the three of them, he figured he could hold his own in a fight, but he wouldn't get away unscathed. The thought of having to explain a black eye and a busted lip tomorrow didn't sound appealing. Especially when he pictured having to explain it to Bertie who was already suspicious.

Martell spoke up and broke the silence. "Sir, where do you want the last two devices installed?"

Estevez smiled at Rick. "See you around, Sheriff. Thank you for your help."

Rick watched the man walk back to the truck. He stood there, taking slow breaths to calm himself as the team drove the utility truck to first one light pole and then another, affixing the sniffers with metallic tape. They worked fast and quietly, and it was clear why no one else had noticed them in town.

Less than five minutes later, the truck drove out of the square, coming right past him as it left. Estevez was in the front passenger seat and as he passed, he held a finger to his lips as if hushing a child.

Rick didn't know how everything was going to play out over the next few days, but he had a distinct feeling that he and the man who'd called him a grunt were going to meet again. And the next time wouldn't be as pleasant.

Rick headed home, his heart filled with his feelings for Dahlia and Charlie but heavy with the burden of the secret he was keeping from everyone that mattered to him. In the middle of it was Cassie, a confusing wrinkle thrown into the mix that he wasn't sure how to respond to.

The world might have been crumbling to its knees, the US might be facing threats from every angle, but somehow Charlie made him think there was still hope for the world. He just hoped the next few days didn't mess it up. At least he had the festival to look forward to. It was Resurrection's crowning moment. What could possibly go wrong?

CHAPTER 17

T*he crowd was larger than* anyone expected. Rick stood on the stage next to Bertie and looked out over a sea of people filling Town Square. The main parking lots had been filled by ten o'clock and the overflows were reaching their limits. Every side street was lined with cars, and more than a few driveways were blocked by out-of-towners eager to park close to the action. The wide path that ran down the center of the square was lined with awnings and tents, most of them flying brightly colored flags that flapped in the breeze. All the storefronts that faced the square had their doors wide open, and sidewalk sales extended out into the streets that were now blocked to traffic, turning it into a huge pedestrian area. Music pumped through the sound system on the stage, an eclectic mix of oldies from the 50s and 60s. Bertie nearly vibrated with excitement at the sight of it all.

"How many do you think are here?" Bertie asked.

Rick scratched his head. "I was never good at guessing crowds. Has to be well over a thousand."

"Over two thousand, I'd say," Bertie said.

"Could be."

Bertie pointed to the grilling area. "Look at the line up for the food and it's not even lunchtime yet. I don't think old man Roberts has ever had so many people willing to try his cooking."

"Is there a first-aid tent for food poisoning?"

Bertie jabbed him in the ribs with her elbow. If there were any hard feelings about the night before, they'd long since faded as the lines of cars entered town. Most of the few hundred permanent residents of Resurrection all had jobs to do, and Bertie acted as their commanding officer. He'd enjoyed seeing her assigning tasks and adjusting to small issues as they came up. It'd been a long time since he'd seen the town look so alive.

"You did it, Mayor," he said, holding out a hand to shake hers.

"We did it, Sheriff," she replied, pushing the hand away and giving him a hug. "Now, go enjoy yourself. Dahlia and Charlie are over running the pumpkin bowling game."

"I'm working. I'll see them later."

"Don't be ridiculous. These are all people from a few towns over. I don't think we've attracted any roving bands of anarchists to our little festival."

He was going to remind her that last night she'd thought Jihadis were planting bombs in their little town, but he decided to leave it alone. He checked his watch. Almost eleven thirty. "You have half an hour before you talk to the crowd, so I'll make you a deal. I'll go have some fun if you agree to do the same thing."

"Deal," she said. "I might try some of old man Roberts's pulled pork."

"Maybe wait until after your speech," Rick said. "Just sayin'."

"You're terrible. Get out of here."

Rick climbed down the stage and worked his way through the crowd. His uniform helped as people moved aside when they saw it, often giving him a deferential nod as he passed. Even so, it was crowded enough that it took him a while to make his way across the square to where the games were set up. As he approached the area, he saw Cassie right in front of him. Her back was turned and he hesitated, his first instinct to work his way around her without being seen. He'd woken up that morning wanting to see and talk to her. Given that, he thought it was better if he just avoided her completely. He was about to dodge to his right when she turned. His intention must have been obvious because her face fell when she saw him.

"Hey, Rick," she said, walking up to him. "Big crowd."

"Biggest ever. It's nice to see."

The crowd thinned a bit and Rick looked up just in time to see Dahlia staring in his direction from the games area. He expected a look of jealousy or anger from her because he was standing there with Cassie, but he got neither. Just a confident smile and a wave. He returned her wave just as the crowd closed back in and blocked his view. Cassie caught the exchange.

"That's Leila, isn't it?" she asked.

"Dahlia. She was married to Jerry."

"Your friend who died in Syria. I remember the funeral."

Rick just nodded and looked past Cassie into the crowd, pretending to scan for suspicious faces. Really he was just searching for a distraction from the memory of Dahlia as the grieving widow, sobbing at her husband's grave, clutching her infant son's hand.

"What time do you want to head up to the mine?" Cassie asked.

Rick pointed to the crowd around them. "Depends on all these people. Once the crowd clears, I'll have a better idea."

Cassie frowned, not liking the answer. "But we're going today. No matter what."

Rick nodded. "We're going underground so it's not like we have to go during the day, right? Once we're in the mine, it's dark no matter what time we go." It looked like she was going to press him on it, so he held up a hand. "I promise, we'll go up there before the end of the day. All right?"

That seemed to placate her. "OK," she said. "In the meantime, I'm going to buy some arts and crafts shit that I don't need and will never use."

"The town of Resurrection thanks you," he said, happy to shift away from the topic of the mine. He knew that she was going to be livid when he came up with some reason to delay for another day. This impression she was doing of an easygoing person would be gone and she'd be looking for things to chuck at his head. He had no clue how he was going to pull off the extra delay, but he didn't have time to worry about it now. He checked his watch. Only fifteen minutes until twelve. He'd missed the chance to do anything more than just say hi to Dahlia and Charlie and still make it back in time to introduce Bertie on the stage. But he had an idea. "Catch you later," he said to Cassie, pushing past her before she had a chance to say anything else.

He worked his way over to the games area. Dahlia saw him coming and waited for him next to the row of hay bales that formed the pumpkin bowling lane she manned. A little girl rolled an enormous pumpkin at a set of bowling pins, knocking them all down but one. Dahlia edged her foot over and tipped the final pin, sending the girl into screams of delight. Charlie went about setting the pins back up for the next bowler.

"Hey you," he said.

"Hey yourself," she replied, leaning over the hay bales and kissing him.

"Ran into Cassie."

"I saw you. She's still pretty," she said. Just an observation, not even a hint of jealousy.

"Not as pretty as you."

She laughed. "Is that your attempt at sweet-talking me?"

"Maybe. How am I doing?"

She nodded. "Not too bad, actually."

The PA system squealed with feedback from a microphone. Rick turned and saw one of the teenage kids, who was helping with the technology, tap the mic. "You think Charlie would want to come on stage with me when I introduce Bertie?"

"Yes, please, can I, Mom?" Charlie burst in, knocking over the bowling pins he'd just set up.

"Sure, but behave yourself and do whatever Rick tells you to do, all right?"

Rick reached over, took hold of the boy's arms and pulled him over the top of the hay bales to his side. "We'll come find you after Bertie's speech."

They waded into the crowd. This time Rick reached his hand out and Charlie grabbed onto it. They made short work of the distance and climbed onto the stage right at noon. Bertie gave Charlie a high five and handed Rick the microphone.

"Let's get this party started," she said.

Rick turned the mic on. "Hello and welcome to the Fall Festival in Resurrection, Colorado," he said. Heads turned toward the stage and the crowd redirected itself slowly so that it was oriented toward him. "If we could have your attention for just a few minutes, that would be great." As planned, he saw the vendors stop selling their goods and pointing to the stage, everyone helping herd the cats. Surprisingly, the big crowd arranged itself naturally in front of the stage, filling Town Square. It was a sight to see.

"Thank you. My name is Rick Johnson. I'm the sheriff of this town."

"Yeah Rick!" someone called out from the crowd and there was a roll of applause.

"I just want to welcome you all and tell you how much we appreciate you coming into town to help us celebrate." For a crowd that size, it was remarkably quiet. "These are tough times, we all know that. Not only here, but in this whole country. All around the world, really. Sometimes it can feel like we've lost something. Like we've left the best part of ourselves behind. Like maybe the world is in a downward spiral and there's no way to fix it." The square was dead silent. This wasn't the feel-good chat anyone there had expected. Rick reached a hand out to Charlie and waved him forward. Charlie ran to him, showing no sign of being shy in front of so many people. "This is Charlie. And he doesn't feel that way, do you, Charlie?"

Rick put the mic in front of him. "Nope," he said. "Look at this festival. It's sweet."

The crowd laughed and Charlie flashed them a thumbs-up sign. Rick put a hand on his shoulder. "As long as there are Charlies in the world, then we can have hope. And when we have hope, we can put our heads together and get to work on solving the problems that face us. What this festival shows us, is that our best days are behind us only if we let them be. It just takes effort, and a leader to put that effort to good use. Here in Resurrection, that leadership comes from our mayor, Bertie Wilkens. Give it up for her."

The crowd burst into enthusiastic applause. Bertie took the mic and waved to the crowd. Once the crowd calmed down, she said, "Wow, what great words from our sheriff, Rick Johnson. Are you gunning for my job, Rick?" The crowd gave her a polite laugh. "But seriously, Sheriff Johnson has been one of the best things that has—"

The slow *whirr* of multiple sirens winding up came from different parts of the square. They slowly cranked up into high-pitched wails, the ubiquitous air raid sirens that had been used for decades. One by one, the sirens reset back into the lower registers only to build again.

The crowd shifted uneasily, many looking to the sky for threats. It was a perfect, blue sky, so it couldn't be a tornado. The military vets in the crowd scanned the sky out of a different instinct, but there were no warplanes doing a strafing run.

Bertie looked at Rick. They both knew it was the sniffer alarms installed the night before. But why?

Rick took the mic from Bertie.

"Folks, this is just a malfunction of some new equipment that got installed. There's nothing to worry about," he said, speaking loudly to be heard over the sirens. "Just stay where you are until we can get these sirens turned off."

The sirens grew louder. It seemed impossible that such a noise could come from the small devices on the light poles. Some of the people in the middle of the square were getting restless, a few pushing their way out of the mass of people. Rick didn't like the look of that.

"Please stay put where you are," he called, his voice echoing through the town. "This is not an emergency. There's nothing wrong. All we have is a false alarm. Just hold tight where you are. Please."

His voice took on more urgency as more people pushed and shoved to get out of the middle of the square. He knew that with a crowd that size, there was a tipping point where the whole place could descend into chaos.

"How do we turn the sirens off?" Bertie yelled at him.

Rick shook his head. He had no clue.

Charlie wrapped himself around his leg, terrified.

"Everyone stay calm," Rick said into the PA system. "Everything will be—"

The sirens stopped. Abruptly, like the throw of a switch.

Rick's ears were still ringing as he reached down to Charlie and hoisted him onto his hip. He put on a smile that matched the sense of relief he felt.

"Well, folks, our little town wanted to make an impact on you today, but that wasn't exactly what we had in mind."

Nervous laughter rolled through the crowd. There was even a smattering of applause. Rick felt the rush of working a crowd and decided to push it a little more. He turned to Bertie.

"Mayor, I told the kids who set up the PA system to have some kind of sound if your speech went a little long. I guess we have some overachievers on our hands."

More laughter; even Bertie gave him a chuckle, even though he knew she was seething behind the smile plastered on her face.

"Here's the mic back, Mayor. But I'd keep your remarks short, because I don't … I don't know if …"

The crowd murmured and turned restless as the unmistakable sound of helicopter blades echoed off the mountain walls. It grew louder and louder until the aircraft burst out from behind the canyon wall and soared over the town. Some in the crowd screamed as the downdraft pelted Town Square, whipping the flags in the air.

There were speakers attached to the helo's landing skids. A man's voice, calm but authoritative, belted out a message.

"By order of the federal government, this area is under quarantine. Assistance is on the way. Individuals attempting to leave the area will be subject to the use of force. This quarantine is effective immediately."

The message repeated, and all hell broke loose.

PART TWO

CHAPTER 18

"E*veryone calm down," Rick said* into the mic. "We'll find out what's going on. Just stay calm."

But calm wasn't on anyone's mind. The outer edges of the crowd took advantage of not being locked into the mass of people and scattered toward the side streets. Rick was grateful all the cars were parked away from the square, many of them in the auxiliary lots outside of town. All he needed was someone panicking and plowing their car through a sidewalk full of people.

Bertie took the microphone from him. "Please, remain calm. We don't want anyone getting hurt."

The helo banked hard and made another pass over town.

"… this area is under quarantine …"

Parents picked up their kids, most of whom were crying now from all the noise and picking up on the fear in the crowd.

"... Individuals attempting to leave the area ..."

The crowd in the center of the square pushed in all directions, everyone with a different idea of the fastest way out of town. Vendor tents collapsed as people pushed through them.

"... subject to the use of force ..."

Earsplitting screams came from the right side of the stage. Rick saw people stampeding through the open space of old man Roberts's barbeque area, knocking over smokers filled with hot coals, upturning entire propane grills. The screaming came from a man holding up his arms, blackened and burned.

"Please. Everyone. Stop!" Bertie cried out.

Charlie nearly had Rick in a stranglehold, his face burrowed into his shoulder.

"I'm scared," Charlie whimpered.

"You're going to be all right. I got you."

Charlie leaned back and Rick saw the tears streaming down the kid's cheeks.

"What about Mom?"

Rick spun around and searched the crowd for Dahlia. From his position on the stage, he had a good view of the games area. He looked frantically at the people running back and forth. Finally, he spotted her, crouched behind the wall of hay bales, the pumpkin bowling alley effectively making a safe zone from the crush of bodies. Her eyes were wide with fear, but they were fixed on him and Charlie.

Rick grabbed the microphone from Bertie. "Dahlia. Stay there," he shouted. "Can you hear me?"

Dahlia waved her hand in the air, acknowledging that she had.

Screams erupted around the square. Something new was happening. Each of the four streets that exited the square had a stream of people pushing and shoving to leave. But now, the tide turned and people were running back into the square.

"What the hell?"

He saw it at the street at the north end first. From his angle on the stage, he could see up most of the road.

A massive machine rolled down the street toward the square. Rick knew the equipment and knew people were making the right decision to get out of the way.

The armored assault vehicle looked like something out of a science fiction movie. Heavy armor-plating was set at odd angles to distort radar imagery. Short antennas stuck out all over the body. These were the sensors for the AAV's camo capabilities. By evaluating the scene behind it, the machine could change the thin outer layer to mimic it perfectly, effectively hiding the AAV from sight, even when it was on the move.

But whoever was driving it now didn't want the stealth. They wanted the full, awesome impact the machine delivered as it rumbled down the street.

As if seeing an AAV in his hometown wasn't enough, the sight of the support walking next to and around the machine sent chills down Rick's spine.

They were dressed in bright yellow hazmat suits, not the light-weight stuff the military gave the Marines when there was a bio/chem threat, but the heavy-duty gear the military gave out when the personnel entered an area where bio/chem was confirmed present.

AAVs and men in hazmat suits appeared at each of the four roads entering the square. Rick spotted movement on the rooflines to his left and right and saw flashes of yellow at regular intervals taking position.

Both the men on the roof and the support teams around the AAVs all had one thing in common.

They were heavily armed and their guns were pointed at the crowd.

CHAPTER 19

T*he AAVs rolled to a* stop at the mouth of each of the streets, and men in hazmat suits formed a human chain on each side, cutting the roads off completely. The helo made another pass overhead.

"Move to the center of the square and remain calm. The containment teams are here for your protection only. Please move to the center of the square and remain calm."

The arrival of so much firepower did have a calming effect on the crowds. One or two armed men constituted a terrorist attack. A hundred men with armed transports and a helicopter was the government. Their government. And while there were certainly people in the crowd who didn't trust the government, they preferred it over a nest of Jihadis any day of the week.

The pushing slowed and then stopped, the mood in the square shifting from panic to fear and apprehension. The helo angled forward and sped out of town, at least taking the constant *thump* of the rotors and the wind from the downdraft out of the equation.

The square was remarkably quiet with the helo gone. People milled around, almost as if a collective shame was setting in for the initial response. People that had been knocked down during the melee were helped up and dusted off. A few of the locals took positions in front of the tipped over barbeques and directed traffic around the area.

Rick noticed more and more people holding their cell phones up, trying to get a signal. He pulled out his own phone, on impulse really, hoping like everyone else that he could use it to get some answers.

No service.

"You heard them, folks. Move slowly back into the square." It was Bertie, using her best calming voice. Rick recalled the same tone when he was a little kid and Bertie walked through the gymnasium during a tornado warning. At that moment, she hadn't been their principal, but their mom, soothing, calming. And she was doing it again now.

"It's going to be all right," she said. "Excitement's over. Just come back into the square and we'll get things sorted out, all right?"

To Rick's amazement, the crowd moved to the sound of her voice, the stampede reduced to a shuffling walk back to the square where people filled in shoulder to shoulder, facing the woman on the stage with the calm voice.

Bertie turned the mic off and leaned over to Rick. "What in the sweet hell is going on?"

Before Rick could answer, an engine roared from the street to the left of the stage. The AAV moved to one side and a smaller command Humvee drove past. It hopped the curb and drove onto the grass, slowly enough to give people a chance to move out of the way. A group of six armed men in hazmat suits followed close behind it in what Rick recognized as a classic protection stance. He noticed the faceplates were not uniform but a combination of mirrored reflective glass and clear. By the time the vehicle came to a stop in front of the stage, all eyes in the square were on it.

Both doors swung open. The driver was in the same bright yellow suit as the rest of the soldiers, but the figure that stepped out from the passenger side had a dark blue hazmat suit on. The protective detail fell in around the figure in blue, guns at the ready. The entire group went to the stairs, but only the person in blue climbed onto the stage, his head down as he walked in the heavy gear.

As he got closer, Rick saw that the suit had external air tanks. The most advanced suit he'd ever worn as a Marine going into a hot zone had been equipped only with air scrubbers, not independent air systems like the ones deployed here. The helmets had bubbled faceplates like astronauts wore, wrapping around for a two-hundred-seventy-degree view. This man walking up the stairs had a clear glass version instead of the mirrored reflective type, so when he reached the stage and looked up, Rick had a perfect view of the man's face.

Keefer.

"Sheriff," he said, his voice coming out of the speakers on the suit.

"What's going on here?" Rick asked.

"I'm sorry," Keefer said, the strain in his voice evident. "There's been an accident." Keefer raised a gloved hand toward Bertie, indicating that he wanted the microphone. "I think it best if I explain to everyone at once."

The quiver in the man's voice could be heard even through the speaker. Gone was the cockiness Rick had seen up at the mine. That wasn't good.

Bertie handed him the microphone and he held it clumsily in the gloved hand. He turned and looked Rick right in the eye. "I'm going to need your support and help over the next few hours. Can I count on it?"

Rick nodded. He didn't know what was going on, but whatever it was, this was no drill. And it sure as hell wasn't about an automatic mining operation coming into town.

"What's going on?" called out someone from the crowd.

"Yeah, what's with all the guns?" came another cry.

In seconds, the voices swelled, demanding answers. The protection detail on the base of the stage raised their guns.

"My name is—"

The PA system squelched with powerful, screeching feedback and Keefer held it away from his mask. The feedback went on for another second or two, causing a couple of thousand people to cover their ears. As soon as is dissipated, Keefer slowly raised the microphone to his suit until the barest trace of feedback started again.

"Sorry," he said. "My name is Colonel Henry R. Keefer, United States Army, Special Weapons Division."

A murmur passed through the crowd.

"Obviously, based on the assets you can see on display in this square and the announcement from the helo, we're here today under very serious circumstances." He paused, stretching out the tension. The square was dead silent. "What I'm about to tell you will cause many of you great concern. It could lead to panic like what we just saw when we arrived, but I need you all to remain calm so that no one else gets injured. Let me be clear. I'm here to tell you about a terrible problem, but I come with a solution."

"Just tell us what happened," a man in the crowd yelled, but this time dozens of people hushed him quiet. Keefer held them in his sway.

"The solution I bring is a complete one. With it, comes the guarantee that every single man, woman and child in this square goes home tomorrow, safe and sound."

The murmurs started again. Rick heard the word *tomorrow* over and over. Finally, a young woman in the first few rows from the stage spoke up. "The helicopter said quarantine. Why would they say that?"

Voices slowly rose in agreement, the agitation increasing. Keefer held up his hand and the crowd silenced again.

"I'm going to be completely honest with you," he said. "As Americans, you deserve it. The first piece of honesty is to admit to you that I have orders not to tell you the entire truth. My orders are only to tell you the bare minimum. I've followed orders all my life, but today I'm choosing to break them and tell you everything." He pointed up the mountain. "The federal government recently took over Resurrection Mine to conduct a secret weapons testing program and create a new generation of biological agents."

Rick clenched his hands at his side. The high-security perimeter made sense now, but he felt the fool for being so easily played by Keefer earlier. But the worst of it was that he, like every adult in the audience, felt a shuddering terror at the mention of biological warfare. The most basic public fear since the Jihadi attacks started was another nuclear device in a major metro area like the one in DC. But the people who really followed the news analysis, and who paid attention to the expert talking heads, knew the real risk to the human race was a weaponized biological agent that got out of control. Rick had never imagined there would be one cooking in his backyard.

"I must remind you of what I said at the start," Keefer said. "I come with a hundred percent solution. I want you to remember my promise as I tell you what's happened here. If you cooperate, everyone's going home tomorrow safe and sound."

"Stop treating us like children and tell us what happened," an old woman in the crowd yelled.

Keefer acknowledged the woman with a raised hand. "You're right, ma'am. I just don't want there to be any panic." He turned back to the crowd. "A little under an hour ago, the lab went live. One of our systems, several of our systems actually, failed simultaneously. An extremely dangerous biological agent was released in the air. Our sensors indicate this entire area was impacted."

The fear in the crowd was palatable. People pulled their loved ones closer. Parents clutched their children.

"What does that mean?" Rick said. "Is there a chance we've been infected?"

Keefer didn't turn toward Rick, but his helmet nodded to show that he'd heard the question. "I promised you the truth, so here it is." He paused, his voice cracking under the strain of the moment. "Based on our models, there is an infection rate for this town of one hundred percent."

CHAPTER 20

R*ick watched carefully for any* signs of panic in the crowd. His own heart pounded in his chest and it was everything he could do to keep from running off the stage to seek safety. It was a natural human response to the threat; fight or flight. But how did a person fight something unseen?

"What's a virus?" Charlie whispered in his ear.

Rick clutched the boy tightly. He realized he was holding his breath, as if that would somehow thwart the invisible virus in the air. He saw dozens of people lift their shirts and sweaters to their mouths as makeshift masks, pathetic attempts but something he understood. Doing anything was better than nothing. Better than thinking of the virus in his body.

"It's like the cold," Rick said, pulling it together. "Or the flu."

"If it's just the cold, why's everyone acting so weird?" Charlie said. "It's scary."

Rick nodded. "I know, but everything's going to be okay." He raised his voice so

Keefer could hear. "That's what you said, right? Everyone gets to go home?"

Keefer glanced back at him. Rick thought he caught a glimpse of the same contempt Keefer had shown him up on the mountain, but the expression was gone a second later. "That's right. If there is full cooperation, everyone is going to be all right."

The crowd was getting restless. Whispered conversations gradually turned into discussions. Some of those turned into shouting.

"You did this."

"We can't trust them."

"He's full of shit. We're all going to die."

The armed men around the square raised their guns at the crowd, but Keefer didn't look worried.

"We have a vaccine," he said into the microphone. Just in case people didn't hear it, he said it again, louder this time. "We have a vaccine and it is completely effective if taken within three hours of infection."

This had the crowd's attention. It fell mostly silent, except for the sound of crying here and there.

"The United States government is fully aware of the situation. Today our facility went operational and, as a precaution, military units were on standby. As we speak, there are units mobilizing to create perimeters five and ten miles out." Keefer looked over the crowd. "I see many of you trying to use your phones. We're actively jamming all communication to the outside world."

A protest rose from the crowd. Rick didn't even bother to check his phone again. Even the radio attached to his belt gave off a low, gurgling static when he turned up the volume. All of his communication issues with Manny that morning suddenly made sense.

"This is only a temporary measure," Keefer continued. "Necessary to keep panic from spreading outside of this town. We will allow communication again once this situation is resolved and President Mayfield can address the nation with the facts of what happened here."

The mention of the president quieted the crowd. Keefer seemed to pick up on this so he pressed in on it. "I've spoken to President Mayfield personally. He asked me to convey his best wishes, his promise to use all resources at his disposal to resolve this and, above all, his anger over what's happened. He promised a full accounting for those responsible once the crisis is over."

The speech had a sobering effect on the crowd. Still, there were some who weren't so easily convinced.

"Why should we believe you?" someone asked. "What if you're just making that up so we don't panic?"

Worried faces turned to Keefer. Rick saw the same faces from his vantage point and saw the need in their eyes. They wanted to believe Keefer so badly, for themselves, for their family and friends around them. They wanted to believe that they would live, go home safe and sound tomorrow like the nice man promised. But there was doubt on the faces too. Something about getting the news of salvation from the same man who just delivered a death sentence on the town.

"The virus is resilient. It's been created to be. So it's still in the air, still active, still lethal without the vaccine." Keefer raised his hands to his helmet, hesitated, then unsnapped the latches around the metal neck collar. There was a hiss as the pressure from the suit released into the air. With great ceremony, he closed his eyes and lifted the helmet off his head. Then he took a deep breath and opened his eyes.

"Now we're in this together."

CHAPTER 21

T*he medical tents were set* up, one in each of the four corners of the square. They were massive white structures that arrived on flatbed trucks as tightly packed cubes of support trusses and fabric. Once offloaded into position, and the area was cleared, the cube was activated with a remote control device and it slowly opened as soldiers in hazmat suits, none of them following Keefer's lead in removing their helmets, pulled and adjusted the fabric to make sure it fell into place.

In only a few minutes, the eight foot by eight foot cubes had transformed into sixteen hundred square foot tents, forty feet to a side, with taut fabric ceilings and walls. Rolls of carpet were spread to cover the grass. Metal poles with chains between them organized the spaces into long waiting lines that looked like those at an amusement park. Only there was nothing amusing about getting an inoculation against a weaponized virus.

While they were setting up, Rick took Charlie to find his mom. She ran up and grabbed him, the emotion getting the best of her. Rick wrapped his arms around them both, whispering assurances that they would be all right. As he held them, he felt the guilt clawing at him from the inside. As the hazmat troops marched through town, he couldn't help but wonder if he could have stopped all this if he'd blown the whistle on Keefer right from the beginning. But there would be time for guilt later. Rick knew he had to focus on making sure everyone in town got through this alive.

Rick checked the rooflines around the square. He didn't like the way the snipers still had their guns trained on the crowd, eyeing them through their scopes. Seemed like overkill for a crowd of scared civilians who were cooperating.

"Look," Dahlia said.

He followed her eye line to the stage and they watched together as a massive digital clock was erected on it. There were just over two hours on it. And it was counting down.

Keefer was on the stage, huddling with Bertie. His blue hazmat suit was in a pile on the planks and he now stood dressed in his field fatigues emblazoned with the American flag patch, and the eagles on his shoulders showing him to be a full-bird colonel. Once the clock was in place, he tapped the microphone to get the crowd's attention.

"Ladies and gentlemen, this clock to my right is our new personal Lord and Savior," Keefer said. "We have exactly this amount of time to get everyone vaccinated. Like I said, the vaccine is one hundred percent effective if administered within three hours of infection. This is because it has been genetically engineered as a time-release device. No one will display symptoms before this clock reaches zero. So that headache you have? Or that cough the person next to you has? That is not the virus. I want to make that clear so no one gets unduly concerned.

"The time-release has practical uses as a weapon, but it's also a built-in failsafe if there was ever an accidental release like we had today. This next part's important so I want you to hear this clearly," he said, pausing for effect. "The virus is one hundred percent fatal for anyone not given the shot before this clock reaches zero. One hundred percent. But with your help, we'll get through everyone with plenty of time to spare. Mayor Bertie has a few words for you."

Keefer handed the microphone to Bertie.

"The colonel has assured me that there is more than enough time and plenty of vaccine for everyone who has been infected. To make this point, both the colonel and myself will be the last ones to receive the vaccine."

This announcement made heads nod. There was even some clapping that spread throughout the square.

"If there are any anti-vaccine folks out there, this isn't your day. Everyone gets a shot. Everyone. If it helps, this is technically not a vaccine but an antidote, so they'll still let you in the anti-vaccine meetings or conventions or whatever it is you people do." This got a slow trickle of laughter from the crowd. "There is only one risk and that is that we miss vaccinating everyone," Bertie continued. "And that can only happen if we don't follow the plan. If we keep our heads and just follow instructions, everyone will be vaccinated in plenty of time."

Hazmat troops moved through the crowd, distributing wristbands. It was Keefer who spoke next.

"The wristbands you are being given tell you which tent to go to. Numbers one through four. It will be scanned when you are vaccinated so we can track it. Because your mayor is only half-right. The risk of not following the plan and missing someone is not just that someone here would get sick. It's that once sick, that person would become highly contagious. They could infect everyone around them, even if they've gotten the shot."

"How is that possible?" a man near the front shouted.

"Because when the virus turns active in the host, it mutates. The vaccine you're getting doesn't protect against that."

A rumble rolled through the crowd.

"Why don't you give us a vaccine for the mutated virus too? Why chance it?" a woman shouted. A chorus of voices rose, supporting the idea.

Keefer held up his hands for quiet. "We don't have the vaccine for the mutated version."

The crowd noise increased. It started as small, concerned conversations, but it quickly turned more aggressive. Shouting came from the area near the stage. Rick couldn't make out the words, but he didn't need to. People were angry. Voices rose all across the square, piling on and turning mean.

"He's losing them," Rick said to Dahlia. He eyed the snipers again. They looked ready for action. He pushed Dahlia and Charlie toward one of the large trees and had them crouch down next to it. If the crowd panicked and stampeded, the tree would at least give them some protection.

On stage, Keefer waved his arms for quiet. He spoke into the microphone but his voice was drowned out by the crowd. The soldiers standing guard in front of the stage raised their guns. Even so, the more agitated people in the crowd started to push forward.

Keefer pulled a gun from his side, raised it into the air and fired three quick shots.

The crowd froze. The angry cries stopped and the square fell silent.

Slowly, Keefer lowered the gun, scowling at the people in front of him.

"I'll tell you one thing we're not going to do," he said, his measured cadence adding a level of menace to his words. "We're not going to panic. We're not going to lose our focus on the job we have to do. Because, losing our focus means we all die. Every last one of us. And I will not let that happen, understand?"

He had their attention. Everyone stood silent, collectively looking guilty.

"We can blame people later. We can get mad later. Right now we're just going to get everyone taken care of so we can all go home tomorrow."

He paused again, and then pointed to the soldiers around him and the snipers on the rooftops.

"Take a look around you. This is serious business, people. Deadly serious. No one can leave the area until the inoculations are complete. If someone were to leave the area and become contagious, we wouldn't be able to stop it from spreading across the entire country. Any attempts to leave will be dealt with by lethal force. Hear me when I say this. There won't be any questions asked. If one of these soldiers even thinks you're trying to leave, God as my witness, they will stop you. These men didn't sign up to hurt Americans, but do not doubt for a second that they won't pull the trigger if it means saving the country."

Keefer looked across the crowd, letting that last sentence sink in. Slowly, he held the mic out to Bertie. As the mayor took the mic, Dahlia leaned in to Rick and he pulled her and Charlie in tight to him.

Bertie adjusted the microphone, giving herself time to collect her thoughts. Finally, she cleared her throat. "I know everyone's scared. Heck, I am too. But that's okay. It's okay. It's ... it's ..." She paused and looked down at the ground in front of her. Rick thought she wasn't going to be able to continue.

"C'mon, Bertie," he whispered.

Then she looked up and, even from a distance, Rick could see her square her shoulders to the crowd as she leaned into the microphone.

"Raise your hand if you want to go home safely tomorrow." She raised her own hand in the air. Only a few in the crowd followed her lead. "Go on, raise your hand if you want to get out of here safely."

Rick smiled. He'd seen her do this same thing dozens of times at school assemblies when he was a kid. Only then it was, *Raise your hand if you want to make a difference in the world* or *raise your hand if you want to be proud of what you do with your life*. All around him, the crowd of two thousand people raised their hands. He saw Dahlia and Charlie had already raised theirs and were looking at him. He put his own hand up and gave Charlie a wink.

"OK," Bertie said. "Everyone with their hand up is getting out of here safe and sound." Her voice rang with such authority that even Rick felt a surge of relief from the words. That was Bertie's gift; she could make people believe.

"Here's how we're going to do it. Once you get your wristband the soldiers are passing out, put it on and go to the tent as indicated by the number one through four. You can see there are big numbers on the tents to direct you. Once you get there, you'll be in a holding area until the troops here get a final head count."

She looked to Keefer for affirmation and he nodded. It was brilliant, Rick thought, to have her give the instructions. A kind old woman, beloved by the locals, made it feel like they were getting directions to where the apple dunking and three-legged races were being held.

"Once you get your vaccine, you'll get a green wristband to show you're done. Again, there is plenty of the vaccine to go around and more than enough time for everyone to get one. You'll be released into the general area by the stage once you have a green wristband. We're working on food and drinks for everyone."

"When do we get to go home?"

Keefer took the mic back. "Once we finish the inoculations, we'll then need to stay here under observation for twenty-four hours as a precaution."

A collective groan passed through the crowd. Rick couldn't help but find it funny. Two thousand people had an untreated lethal virus in their body, and they were upset at the inconvenience of staying in the square overnight. He wasn't looking forward to it either, two thousand stressed out people in a small area didn't sound like a fun Saturday night, but if it meant that they all survived, it was a small price to pay.

"If I could have Sheriff Johnson and Cassie Baker meet me at the stage please?" Keefer said. "The rest of you, please begin moving to your appropriate area. Thank you."

Dahlia looked at him oddly.

"What's Cassie got to do with all this?" Dahlia said.

"I have no idea." He waved over a hazmat soldier. "Can I get three of those, soldier?"

The yellow-suited trooper came over and gave him a nod. "The colonel just called your name, Sheriff."

"I know. I just want to be sure I'm in the same holding area as these two."

The soldier dug through the bag of wristbands he carried and handed him three. All of them had the number one next to a bar code. "I suggest you get up there, sir. The colonel doesn't like to wait."

Rick thanked the soldier and helped Dahlia attach her wristband. It was thick plastic with one end sliding into a hole like a zip tie. Once it was on, it wasn't going anywhere.

"We're going to need gardening shears to get this off later." Dahlia laughed nervously.

Rick heard the stress in her voice but saw that she was being brave for Charlie. He attached Charlie's wristband and then his own. He put his wrist next to Charlie's, pointing to the two number ones. Dahlia lowered her wrist next to theirs.

"See? We all match," Rick said. "So, we're going to be together."

"Can we come with you now?" Charlie asked.

Rick crouched down so he was eye level with Charlie. "I need to go help make sure everyone's okay. You stay here and watch your mom for me." He unsnapped his sheriff's badge from his chest and put it on Charlie's shirt.

"Don't you kind of need that?" Dahlia asked.

"People saw me up on stage." Rick shrugged. "And if they didn't, I think the rest of the uniform will tip them off. Besides, my deputy needs a badge, right?"

"Deputy?" Charlie said, turning the badge so he could see its face. "So cool. Does that mean I get to boss people around?"

"Just your mom."

Dahlia playfully tugged on one of Charlie's ears. "Just you try it."

Rick stood and gave Dahlia a wink. "I'll be back soon. If you need something, you send one of these soldiers to get me."

She hugged him and the strength in her arms surprised him. She was terrified, they all were on some level, but the composure she had in place for Charlie had been nearly perfect. Now, in his embrace for only a few seconds, he felt her body heave with two quick, ragged sobs. Then, just as fast, she reached up with her hand to wipe her eyes. When she stepped away from him, her smile was back in place.

"Go get 'em, cowboy," she said. "Go save the world."

"Yes, ma'am."

As he walked away he pointed to Charlie, then to his own eyes, then to Dahlia. He mouthed the words, "Watch her."

Charlie gave him a thumbs-up.

The crowd moving toward the nearest tent crossed in front of him and his view of Dahlia and Charlie was cut off. He turned and made his way to the stage, fighting down the premonition that leaving them alone was a terrible mistake.

CHAPTER 22

"Why *did he call you up* here?" Rick asked, walking up to Cassie who stood waiting twenty yards in front of the stage. "How does he even know who you are?"

"You knew about this, didn't you?" she said, ignoring his question. "That's why you didn't want me going up to the mine."

Rick pushed past her and she fell into step next to him. "I knew there was a mining operation up there. Nothing like this. Now why are you here?"

"I don't know," she said, nodding toward Keefer walking toward them. "But I don't trust this guy one bit."

Keefer walked down the stairs. Gone was the uncertainty Rick had seen in the man's movements when he first addressed the crowd. The assertive alpha man asshole he'd met on the mountain was back.

"Dr. Baker," he said, holding out his hand. "I was both happy and disappointed to hear you were here."

Cassie looked confused. She didn't reach out to shake his hand. "Have we met before?"

"We have mutual friends," he said, pulling his hand back awkwardly. "And I'm a fan of your work. What you've created is truly transformative. Your technology will change the world in more ways than you can imagine."

"And what exactly is it that you do, Colonel?" she said. "When you're not poisoning entire towns with lethal viruses, that is?"

Keefer grimaced. It took Rick a second to realize it was the man's attempt at a smile.

"I'm from the Special Weapons Division, so I've worked with your boss, Brandon Morris."

"Genysis doesn't do any weapons contracting," she said, looking uncertain at the mention of Morris's name. "The only defense contracts we have are the integrated prosthetics." She looked at Rick's arm on reflex.

Keefer's grin was genuine this time. "You get my soldiers put back together so they can return to the fight. That means weapon to me."

"The intention of the program isn't—"

"Sorry to interrupt," Rick said. "But there are a couple of thousand people who don't give a shit whether you two have met or not. Or what Brandon Morris is doing to make his next billion dollars. All they want to do is get home safe."

"I still want to know how you knew I was here," Cassie said, undeterred by Rick's outburst and unwavering under the colonel's stare.

"You're smart, you put it together," Keefer said.

Cassie looked around the square and then up toward the mine. Rick could physically see the moment when she reached her conclusion. "Son of a bitch. This whole thing is Genysis," she said, her voice taking on a distant quality.

"You are working with Brandon. He told you I was coming up here. What is he spying on me?"

"See, you are smart," Keefer said. "That might come in useful." He paused as a group of people passed by, attaching their wristbands. "Let's talk somewhere private."

Rick felt his stomach turn over. A private talk connoted bad news. Given the situation they were in, any bad news had the potential of being catastrophic. The options marched through his head.

There really isn't a vaccine.

There isn't actually enough of the vaccine to go around.

There isn't enough time to logistically make it all work.

Rick pointed behind tent number two. "My office is right over there."

"I know where it's at. Unfortunately, we've already needed to use it today." Keefer turned to a member of his personal detail. "Have the mayor brought over to the sheriff's station." He waved to the other hazmat troops next to him. "Let's go."

The soldiers formed a protective bubble around Keefer, two in front, two on either side and one to the rear, and marched through the crowd. Rick and Cassie had to hustle to keep up, falling in behind the rear soldier.

"Nice that Genysis could make an impact on the town again," Rick said.

"I didn't know anything about this. Genysis doesn't do defense contacts. You've seen the public stance. You have to believe me."

Rick shrugged. "Doesn't matter. In some ways it's better."

"How so?"

"Because as long as what Keefer promised actually happens, the people in this town are going to end up owning a chunk of the company once the lawsuits start flying."

They followed the armed guard in silence for a while. A few people called out to Rick to ask if everything was okay. He assured them it was and kept moving.

Finally, Cassie spoke up, but when she did, she raised her hand to her mouth and whispered to him. "Anything strike you as odd about all this?"

He looked at her like she was crazy. "Cassie, everything is odd about this. What are you talking about?"

"I mean, yeah, the whole thing is nuts," she said. "But everything seems staged perfectly for this town. The four tents, the wristbands, setting up the perimeter in the square."

"That's the part you find hard to believe about all of this? That they were prepared for this to happen?" he said. "They knew what they had up there. And that there might be a breach. I just thank God they were ready."

"Yeah but—"

The soldier in front of them cocked his head to one side. What may have been a discreet motion without the hazmat helmet on was an obvious attempt to listen in on their conversation. Cassie slowed her pace and pulled on Rick's arm to get some distance between them and the soldier.

"Yeah but what?" Rick said.

"Resurrection has a population of under five hundred people. There hasn't been this many people here in years."

Rick looked around, getting the idea of where she was going.

"But they had supplies for over two thousand people," she said.

"What are you saying?"

"I'm saying," she whispered, looking around cautiously. "I can't get over the sense that they not only knew this was going to happen. But they knew it was going to happen today."

CHAPTER 23

"We've got a problem," *Keefer* said once they were all in the sheriff's office with the door shut behind them.

Bertie had joined them at the end of their walk across the square, having picked up her own protective detail of two soldiers in hazmat suits. They'd exchanged worried looks, but not said anything. Now Rick braced himself for the bad news.

"What is it?" Rick asked. "Is it the vaccine?"

Keefer shook his head. "No, everything I said on that stage was true. I owe the people out there that much."

"Guilty conscience?" Cassie asked.

Keefer whipped around and stared at her. Rick tensed, reading the man's body language. The man was coiled up like he was ready to spring.

"Cassie, not helpful," Bertie said.

"I agree," Rick said. "There'll be time for that later."

"It's all right," Keefer said. "If I was on the other side of this, I'd feel the same way. What you don't know is that I was one hundred percent opposed to this operation. I lodged formal complaints up the chain of command regarding safety protocols, installation security, and proximity to a civilian population."

"I notice an ethical objection to creating a weaponized, communicable virus with one hundred percent mortality rate didn't make your list," Cassie said.

Keefer addressed Bertie. "After this is over, I'll be the one sitting in front of the House Armed Services Committee with my hand on a Bible telling the world what a mistake this was. It'll end my career, but I didn't sign up to put Americans at risk."

Bertie nodded. She looked older than she had just a few hours ago. The rush of seeing her town come alive, and that had filled her eyes with such joy, was gone, replaced by a weariness that stooped her shoulders and made her lean against the desk nearest to her. Rick thought about getting her a chair and a glass of water, but he knew she wouldn't put up with him fussing after her.

"I appreciate that, but you said there's a problem," Bertie probed.

Keefer walked to the back of the office to the single door that led to the back.

"Those are holding cells," Rick said.

"Yes, I know."

Keefer opened the heavy door. The second he did, men's voices erupted from the other side.

"Let us out of here."

"I know my rights, dammit."

Rick crossed the room and looked down the hallway. The holding cells dated back to the fifties, just vertical bars with coats of thick white paint, and he'd locked up more than a few people in them to sleep off a heavy night at Roscoe's

Bar. But he didn't recognize any of the men locked up there now.

He turned a hard look on Keefer. "What are these guys doing in my jail?"

Keefer looked amused, but appeared to want to play nice. "Sorry, I should have talked to you before we commandeered your facilities here." He closed the door and the sound of the men faded. "These three were caught trying to sneak past the perimeter. My men are on orders to shoot anyone caught trying to leave. These guys are lucky they're here and not inside a body bag."

"Are those three the problem?" Bertie asked. "Looks like they are safely put away."

"The problem is the two thousand people out there. There is zero margin for error on this mission." He walked to the window and looked out into the square. "I tried to warn people in the Pentagon how bad it could get, but they just don't want to hear the truth." He pointed to the door that led to the jail cells. "If just one of those idiots back there had gotten out, four hours from now, we'd have a weapon of mass destruction right here in America. If the virus gets out, it can't be stopped."

"That's a pretty shitty design," Cassie said. "Even for a weapon. I mean, who makes a weapon that once you fire it just comes back and kills you too?"

"The plan was to modify the virus in the mountain lab," Keefer said. "That was the work we were tasked with. To make it so that we could control it."

"Jesus! And Morris was part of this?" Cassie asked.

Keefer ignored the question. "What I need from all of you," he said, "is to convey just how vital full compliance is. Mayor, you and the sheriff here are the natural authority figures in this town. You were perfect on the stage, but I need the two of you out there spreading the gospel on the ground so that people take it seriously."

"So, why am I here?" Cassie said.

"You're a scientist, a pretty good one from what I understand," he said. "The women will trust you because you're intelligent. The men will listen to you because you're pretty."

"Illegal purveyor of biological weapons and a sexist," she said. "You're the whole package, aren't you?"

"So that's it?" Rick said. "You just need us to help keep people in line? I think we were already doing that."

"I just want you to fully understand the stakes here." Keefer walked to the side entrance that led to the small alley between the sheriff's station and the long-abandoned store next door. He opened it and two soldiers dragged in a body bag, dropping it onto the floor. The top of the bag wasn't zipped and a bloody face was visible. It was a young man, a teenager by the looks of it. Bertie let out a cry and turned away. Cassie stared, open mouthed, but then turned and glared at Keefer.

"Jesus, he's just a kid," she said. "You shot a kid."

"Do you know him?" Keefer asked.

Rick shook his head. He'd seen enough young faces staring up from body bags to last a lifetime. When he'd woken up that morning, he didn't imagine he'd be looking at one on the floor of his office. "Don't recognize him. He's not from around here."

"What's wrong with you people?" Cassie asked.

"This *kid* crawled through one of the buildings in the square and then out through the basement cellar. He was on his way out of town when he was spotted."

Rick lifted the flap of the body bag.

"Oh God," Cassie said.

There was a ragged, bloody crater blown out in the teenager's chest. "That's an exit wound," Rick said. "He was shot in the back."

Keefer nodded. "Here's what you have to understand. We're being watched by every kind of surveillance you can imagine at the very highest levels of government. If there's a breach, if they think for a second that this can't be contained …"

"They're going to vaporize this place," Rick said. "Sterilize it to kill the virus."

Bertie turned to Keefer. "Would they do that?"

Rick looked out through the plate glass windows in front of the station. Through it he had a panorama of the people-filled square. He'd seen the military's fear of collateral damage drop to nearly zero while he'd fought in the Jihadi wars. Entire villages decimated on barely reliable intel that an enemy leader might be hiding among the mud huts. He had no misconception of what the government was capable of doing, especially if it perceived what was happening in Resurrection as an existential threat.

"I'm surprised they haven't already," Rick said.

"But they don't need to," Cassie said, her previous bravado taken over by a creeping worry. "It's contained, right? The vaccine works."

Keefer stared at Rick, two soldiers who'd been through the grinder together. Rick suddenly understood.

"If one person gets out, probably to some external perimeter five or six miles from here," he said, "that'd be enough for them to say it's too risky."

Keefer nodded.

"And the vaccine?" Bertie asked.

"The troops are still wearing the hazmat suits," Rick said, feeling stupid for not having put two and two together before. "Makes it hard to move around, slows everything down."

"Why not just give them the vaccine so they could …" Cassie's voice trailed off. She looked at Rick, scared now. "Oh holy shit."

Bertie stood up from her chair, picking up on their body language. "What are you two talking about?"

"Bertie, the soldiers are keeping the suits on because they know what the people out there can't be told." He drew in a deep breath. "They're not sure the vaccine will work."

CHAPTER 24

K*eefer was pleased with the* meeting. In fact, by his analysis, everything had gone as well as could be expected so far. But he was a practical man and he subscribed to the old axiom that no battle plan survives first contact with the enemy.

As a student of history, he knew the often-quoted remark was from Moltke the Elder, the architect of Germany's Wars of Unification in the nineteenth century. The old German's ideas about warfare matched Keefer's own. He'd been the first to reorganize his armies into smaller units, changing his orders from specific actions to overall goals to be achieved within the theater of operations.

Moltke used stealthy, flanking maneuvers to envelop and crush an enemy instead of marching head-on in an attempt to pierce the center. It was a lesson ignored by another of Keefer's heroes, General Robert E. Lee, who sent his force against the Union center in a costly and foolish charge at the battle of

Gettysburg. The fact that Pickett's Charge resulted in fifty percent casualty rates wasn't what bothered Keefer, as he was no stranger to taking heavy losses to achieve an objective. What bothered him was that a great leader such as Lee could ignore history's lessons and make such a tactical error.

Keefer would not make the same mistake.

He followed the others back out into the square. They looked rattled, which was exactly what he'd meant to accomplish. The more worried they were, the more malleable they would be as issues came up. Each of them had a role to play and he meant to see them perform it well.

The mayor was easy. She exuded trust and likability. Of course the townspeople who already knew her would take instruction from her, but the real value was her ability to instantly connect with the thousand plus strangers who'd met her for the first time when she stood on the stage. She had just enough grandma in her to make everyone feel comfortable, her maternal protectiveness apparent in every gesture and word. But it was more than that. She possessed enough of an aura of command that her competence wouldn't be questioned. Keefer was fortunate to have her.

Even the sheriff had been a pleasant surprise. After their interaction up on the mountain, Keefer had considered removing the lawman from the equation all together at the start of the operation. It would have been easy enough in the confusion, but he had waited. Observing him with the little boy on the stage, and with the woman afterward, revealed the man's pressure points. Keefer knew that if things ever went south, he could use the two of them to get the sheriff to play ball.

Cassie Baker was a different story. He still found it ridiculous that Brandon had saddled him with this extra complication, especially now of all times. He would never have agreed to it except for Brandon's insistence that her expertise was irreplaceable, making the pitch that her skills would be invaluable in the future he and Keefer had imagined together.

Keefer smiled at that thought. If only Brandon knew what the future really held.

Still, the point was valid. Her expertise could prove useful. He'd been in charge of Special Weapons long enough to give most physicists, armament manufacturers, and integrated biologists a run for their money, but he was no scientist. America in the future needed people like Cassie Baker, even if she came with a bad attitude. The only concern he had was that she could become disruptive at some point. At the end of the meeting, she'd badgered him for more information about the virus and had grown increasingly frustrated by his lack of answers. He considered that at some point he might need to stash her in the jail or sedate her until the clock on the stage ran down, but he knew that anything he did to her would just complicate things with the sheriff. And Keefer wanted him as a friendly face to help with the crowd. He decided to monitor the situation and see where it led.

Keefer watched the three of them go their separate ways into the square, each charged with the task of keeping the peace and keeping an ear open for anyone thinking about making a run for it.

Estevez walked up, still in a hazmat suit, also looking at the three civilians spreading out into the crowd. He didn't comment, but the expression on the man's face was so transparent it was almost laughable.

"We're right on schedule," he said. "Fifteen or twenty minutes ahead, actually."

"You don't approve of the way I'm using those three," Keefer said.

Estevez shrugged and looked away. "It's your call."

Keefer nodded. Their conversation yesterday had made an impact on his number two, maybe too much of one. "It's not insubordination when I ask for your opinion, Estevez. Tell me what you think."

The younger man looked him over, as if sizing up whether this was a test or not. Finally, he seemed to give in. "I don't get why we're making this so complicated, is all. With so many moving parts, something is bound to go wrong."

"I see. And you think letting those three roam around introduces more variables into an already complex situation."

"It's not just them, it's all of it. This operation could be done in half the time if you gave my men free rein," Estevez said.

"Shoot a couple of civilians on the stage? Make an example?"

"Something like that."

Keefer shook his head. If the young man was going to be useful in the years ahead, he needed to be smarter. "Look around you. What do you see?"

Estevez hesitated, clearly annoyed with Keefer's tone. He did a cursory look over the square. "I see your plan working."

"Why is it working?"

"Because everyone is calm."

"Exactly, because everyone is calm. These people are scared, but they also feel protected. The three people I just sent out to mingle in the crowd will reinforce that."

"Or they're going to get suspicious and put a big ass dent in your calm."

Keefer put a hand on the younger man's shoulder. "If that happens, then you'll get your wish. Until then, we proceed as planned."

"Yes, sir," he said, turning to walk away.

"And Estevez," Keefer said, waiting until the man turned around. "All these people are Americans. They aren't the enemy. Don't lose sight of that."

Estevez nodded then marched away. As Keefer watched him go, he found himself wishing once again that it was the father instead of the son at his side. His friend Alejandro had understood how to control large groups of people. In fact, he was the one who'd taught Keefer that force only led to chaos. One day he'd taken Keefer to a slaughterhouse and made him watch how the beef cattle were moved from the farm to the kill room, carefully minimizing stress along the way. As they created their plans, they'd discussed how the Nazis loaded the Jews onto trains with the promise they were being sent to work camps where they would be clothed and housed and fed well. They were evil bastards, but the Nazis knew a few things about controlling the masses.

Estevez was right about one thing; the operation was complicated. But, in Keefer's mind, it was necessarily complicated. More importantly, despite its intricacy, it was working exactly as planned.

Keefer walked toward Tent One to see how they were administering the shots. The system was perfect. Nearly five hundred people were corralled into a holding area surrounded by temporary fencing, just metal stakes pushed into the grass and connected with white bands of plastic. But it wasn't the fence that was keeping them in. It was fear.

There were soldiers with machine guns watching the perimeter, but the activity in the tents in front of them was all they were looking at. The lucky people who had drawn a low number in the lottery system were already being processed. They stood in two single-file lines, each leading to a booth manned by three soldiers, one zapping the barcode on the wristband and the other preparing syringes for the inoculation.

Keefer ducked through the fencing, indicating to his protection detail that they should stay put. The people in the holding pen shifted their attention to him. One old man walked up to him and blocked his way.

"This isn't right," the old man said. "Locked up here like animals."

Keefer's first impulse was to correct the man—*like sheep, to be exact*—but he stopped himself, chastising himself for the thought. These were good Americans, not some backward people. They didn't deserve to be here, and Keefer wanted to make sure he always remembered that.

"I agree, sir," Keefer said, giving the old man his full attention. "And on behalf of the Unites States government and her military, I apologize."

The old man's eyes glistened. He raised his pant leg until his synthetic leg was visible. "I've been apologized to before. Right after friendly fire took off my leg at the hip."

"What's your name, soldier?"

"Vincent Roberts, Gunnery Sergeant, United States Marine Corps. People 'round here call me old man Roberts."

Keefer held out his hand and they shook. "Hank Keefer, good to meet you, Gunny. Where'd you fight?" Keefer noticed people slowly gathering closer to them.

"Jordan. Egypt. Old Jerusalem," he said. "And other places. I was in New Jerusalem when the leg happened."

"Those are tough tours."

"I guess," the old man Roberts said. "But I fought next to my fair share of you Army guys, so I know you're not all assholes."

This brought a chuckle from the small crowd. Keefer warmed to it, and this time it wasn't an act. This was the kind of man that deserved a better country than the one he'd been given. He deserved better leaders. And he damn well deserved a more secure place in the world.

"Your country owes you, Gunnery Sergeant Roberts," Keefer said, snapping a salute. "And I'm going to make certain she delivers on her promise."

Roberts looked surprised by the gesture. "No disrespect, Colonel, but I could give two shits about my service to the country," old man Roberts said.

Keefer lowered his hand, feeling his face heat up. "I'm sure you don't mean that."

"No, sir, I do," Roberts said. "You know the old saying, How do you know if a politician is lying? It's when his lips are moving. And to me, every military officer isn't much better than a politician. No offense."

Keefer forced a smile. "And isn't it great you live in a country where you can voice your opinion? Now, if you'll excuse me ..."

Keefer tried to walk on, but Roberts stepped in front of him, "All I'm saying, if you really want to pay me back for my service, just get me out of here so I can see my granddaughter down in Denver tomorrow. Do that and we'll call it square."

The comment took Keefer by surprise. His head was in a different place, thinking about the enormous sacrifices of American troops for three decades of war. The failure of the nation's leaders to address the basic security needs of the homeland. The multiple and building threats to the very existence of the country he loved.

And this man just wanted to see his granddaughter.

Keefer looked up at the digital clock ticking down, now at an hour and thirty-five minutes, then looked the man in the eye and lied to him without even blinking.

"You'll see your granddaughter tomorrow, Gunnery Sergeant Roberts," Keefer lied. "And that's a promise."

CHAPTER 25

C*assie didn't trust Keefer, but* she wasn't sure what to do about it. The man's body language had told her everything she needed to know about him. He was a liar, trying his best to use their fear to manipulate the situation. She had real doubts whether anything he'd told them in their meeting was true, including how the man in the body bag had gotten himself killed.

None of it made any sense.

But what was worse was that everyone else seemed content to follow orders and just go with the flow. Even Rick, the one person she assumed would be demanding answers to tough questions, looked like a dazed animal caught in headlights. She just hoped the analogy ended there and that there wasn't an immovable force about to knock them through the air all bloody and broken.

The clock on the stage certainly made it feel like something was heading toward them. Slow-moving, ticking down minute-by-minute, but no less terrifying in its inexorable march.

Something horrifying and unstoppable was on its way to Resurrection, but her intuition doubted it was what Keefer had described. Maybe it was something worse. But what that could be, escaped her.

She walked through the square toward Tent Two's holding area. Hazmat soldiers tracked her progress with steely eyes, their guns pointed down at the ground in a resting position. That at least was an improvement over pointing them directly into crowds of civilians. Still, seeing the weapons made her shudder.

What the hell had Morris been thinking?

The billionaire fancied himself a true-life Tony Stark from the Marvel comic books he loved so much. In reality, he was a socially awkward computer nerd without many friends or connections other than the people who worked for him. Still, Cassie couldn't imagine him getting involved in a biological weapons program with Keefer. It didn't fit into his expertise or any of his weird childhood superhero fantasies. No, something was wrong.

But then there was the fact that Morris had obviously told Keefer about her. The problem with that was she hadn't told Morris she was coming up to Resurrection. Nor had she shared her concerns about the data streams coming out of the mine. That meant he'd been spying on her. Probably accessing her Genysis computer. Maybe even tracking her car. It was a company vehicle so it would have been simple for him to keep tabs on her through the GPS system.

She grew angrier as she imagined Morris sitting in his office watching her every move on his computer screen. She felt violated. But if Morris did turn out to be involved in the military weapons program, him tracking her movements and hacking her computer was the least of the rising list of reasons for her to kick his ass.

She had to get through the next twenty-four hours first, she reminded herself.

Fortunately, from what she could see, Keefer's men had things under control.

The people in the holding area seemed content enough. They stood or sat on the grass in long, snaking lines that led in to the tent. People exited the back of the tent with bright green wristbands signifying they'd received the shot. Cassie wondered what they would do if they were told that there was a chance the vaccine wasn't going to work.

She paused at the sight of a young couple sitting on the grass, tickling their baby's nose with a dried leaf. The baby, a girl she guessed from the pink hat and gloves ensemble, giggled and laughed, bringing smiles to everyone around her. Cassie felt a pit in her stomach as she considered the implications of what was going to happen if the vaccine didn't work. Everyone in the square was going to die.

Including Keefer.

If he was actually infected, that was.

Cassie walked away from the tent, enjoying the freedom granted her for being singled out for Keefer's community peacekeeping duty. She looked up at the flags on top of the tents, still flapping in the breeze. The wind direction checked out. An accidental release of an airborne agent up where the mine was located in relation to the town would have blown straight into the valley and through the town. She wondered at the vitality of the virus. It'd been dissipated into an enormous area, subjected to ultraviolent rays and other radiation, and yet was still supposedly strong enough to infect the entire town. If the virus was this hardy, it seemed like there was no end to how far the contamination might spread regardless of what they did here.

But her questions to Keefer when they were back at the sheriff's station had gone unanswered. He knew enough buzz words to scare them, but when the science behind what he was describing was challenged, he immediately hid behind his lack of scientific knowledge.

He'd promised her that he would advocate that she have access to the lead scientist on the project once the crisis had passed, so as to have all of her questions answered. Perhaps, Keefer had suggested, she might be able to bring her computer science expertise to help them model a safer containment protocol for the program.

Oh, she'd help them all right. Just long enough to plant back door access into every one of their systems. Hell, she might even be able to use the sensors she secretly attached to the data line in the lab as a way in. They were obviously using the main data trunks for the project since that was how she'd noticed the activity in the first place. Once she had access, she could use that to get into all their systems. If they were running this weapons lab, what else were they doing? She wouldn't hesitate to blow the lid off their madness and show the world the illegal activity going on right inside US borders.

The only problem with the plan was she wondered if the world would collectively shrug at the revelation. A few peace protestors would take notice, maybe even a few politicians who'd won their offices with an anti-war message, but would there be a scandal? Would the outrage happen?

After so many years of carnage, battling an enemy with no moral boundary around how they were willing to wage war, an enemy that broadcast mass beheadings of nonbelievers, had live cameras in their torture pits of captured US soldiers, who used little kids with bombs sewn into their stomachs as weapons, she suspected that a huge swath of Americans might feel it was about damn time their government created a virus to wipe out the Jihadis.

The Chinese invasions through Asia, the instability in Russia, the chaos in South America, the street-to-street fighting against the Jihadis in European capitals, all of it showed the average American a world sliding toward darkness.

American leadership was a phrase used only by nostalgic politicians. The new reality focused on withdrawal from the world, erecting walls to stop immigration and protecting the people that lived in the forty-eight states, whatever the cost. And if that cost included a virus that killed indiscriminately, but kept Americans safe, was the average citizen going to care? What if that cost was killing thousands of innocent people? Millions? Tens of millions?

Cassie hoped her country wasn't so numb from her own losses that she had forgotten how to care about numbers like that. Cassie wasn't that old, but she still remembered a time when the United States stood for something, a light in a darkening world. Imperfect to be sure, but unique in that it was at least trying to be a better version of itself and channel the more noble aspects of human nature. Most countries didn't even pretend to try. They accepted the violent nature of man and capitalized on it.

Perhaps that was the reason for their relative rise in the world and America's decline. Cassie liked to think not, but she knew it was a compelling argument.

Cassie walked up to a group of teenage girls, each with a green wristband, clustered together near Tent Two. She chatted with them for a while and heard that the shot hadn't hurt at all and that they weren't too concerned about their safety. They were more interested in how attractive one of the medics had been, challenging Cassie to go check the soldier out for herself. Cassie encouraged the conversation, anything to get the girls thinking and talking about something else. She gently probed whether any of the girls had heard about anyone trying to leave the town. They looked totally confused by the question. This was the only exciting thing that had happened in the area in decades, so why would anyone want to leave?

Cassie excused herself and headed to the tent as catcalls came from the teenage girls who thought she was on a mission to check out the hot medic.

She grinned and gave them a wave, pretending to primp her hair before walking into the tent.

A hazmat soldier blocked her way. "Other side," he said, his voice coming to her with the hint of digitalization from the speaker on his suit.

"I'm Cassie Baker. Colonel Keefer has asked me to—"

"Yes, ma'am," the soldier said, cutting her off. "I'm sorry I didn't recognize you. Carry on."

Taken aback by the response but honestly enjoying it just a little bit, Cassie nodded to the soldier and walked farther into the tent. There were lights strung up inside even though the sunlight provided adequate illumination. The ground was covered with thin, industrial carpet, slanted slightly as it followed the grade of the lawn beneath it. She walked up to one of the two inoculation stations and watched it in action.

A middle-aged woman walked up from her spot at the head of the line and showed her wristband. A soldier scanned the barcode using a handheld device and then asked the woman to take a seat at the workstation. Next, the same soldier held up the device that appeared to take a picture of the woman. Cassie guessed that it did more than that. As she moved closer, she could see the computer monitor when a second soldier reviewed a screen of data, and was amazed by what she saw there.

The screen being scrutinized by the second soldier showed the woman's vitals, pulse, oxygen intake, EKG, and, oddly enough, brainwave patterns. To the layman, the grid with multicolored wavy lines bouncing up and down wouldn't look like much. But electro-brain fields were Cassie's field of expertise. Tapping into them was the basis of all her work on full integration of prosthetics into the body. But even she had never seen such a sophisticated scan of the brain from such a tiny handheld device. She leaned into the soldier at the computer.

"Why are you scanning for brainwave activity?" she asked quietly.

The soldier jumped and quickly turned the screen to the side. "Ma'am?"

"It's amazing that you can get a scan like that from a handheld," she said. "I've never seen that before."

"I'm sorry, but we're on a schedule," the soldier said, pointing to a digital clock counting down in the middle of the tent, closing in on an hour and ten minutes. "Can you refer all information requests to Colonel Keefer?"

Cassie stepped back. "Of course, sorry."

She watched as the third soldier of the group, who Cassie noticed must have been the good-looking one her teenager friends were fawning over, readied the inoculation. To her surprise, instead of a store of premade syringes, the soldier checked the clock and then selected a vial from a shelf. He double-checked the markings on the vial, then inserted the syringe and drew out the fluid. Crossing to the woman, he swabbed her arm, but then stared at the clock, waiting. The instant the clock turned to the next minute, the soldier injected the woman.

A quick look down the line and she saw that each station had done exactly the same thing, administered the injection at the precise same second.

Why in the hell would they do that?

CHAPTER 26

R*ick had a bad feeling* about things. The idea almost seemed laughable. Of course he had a bad feeling. His town was under martial law, guarded by armed men in hazmat suits, and every person he knew was infected with a lethal virus.

No shit he had a bad feeling.

As a Marine, he'd been in bad situations before. The day he lost his arm in Istanbul was about as bad as it got. He'd been stuck behind enemy lines, surrounded by a ruthless enemy hunting him and his squad down, trying to stay ahead of the bad guys, slowly running out of both ammo and options.

But at least he'd known what side he was on. He knew he could trust his men and he could trust that there were Marines somewhere busting their asses to come to their rescue. And, most importantly, he knew how to fight. Even in retreat, the enemy paid a price. He and his men made sure of it.

Fighting Jihadis in the desert was hell on earth, but at least there was clarity of purpose. Stay alive. Kill the bad guys.

He looked at the snipers lining the rooftops, guns trained on the crowd below. He dropped his eyes to the people herded together in the medical tents. In a weird juxtaposition that made everything feel that much more surreal, someone had piped 50s and 60s music in through the PA system, probably thinking it would help soothe some nerves. Hearing the Beach Boys sing *Surfer Girl* just made him feel like he was in an episode of the *Twilight Zone*.

There was no clarity in this mess. His own government had done this to his town. And the military had put a man like Keefer in charge of the whole thing. No matter how he tried to rationalize things, he just didn't like the man. He told himself to put aside his first interaction with him on the mountain so that it didn't cloud his judgment of the situation, but it was hard to do.

Knowing what he knew now, Rick tried to view that first meeting differently. Keefer was in charge of what was supposed to be a secret installation and had been sticking to his cover story when Rick had shown up. The whole story about the mine going full auto had been pretty brilliant, actually. It explained the need for security and the secrecy in setting the place up. He felt sure that if Manny hadn't gone up to the mine on a whim, they wouldn't have known anything about the place until it was operational. Or until the sirens in town had gone off.

It made sense now that the tree in the access road hadn't been an accident, but an obstacle put there to ward off any joyriders. Still, somehow security must have broken down to even let either him or Manny as close as they did without being turned away. Rick didn't hold anything against Keefer for doing his job, but he couldn't shake the memory of the perfect ease with which the colonel had looked him right in the eye and told him one bold-faced lie after another.

Again, the man had just been doing his job and Rick was willing to push those lies aside. He would have done the same thing himself had their roles been reversed.

The problem was that he had a terrible feeling that Keefer was still lying to them.

He'd been told that he had free range throughout Town Square but, like anyone else, he couldn't leave the confines of the quarantined area. According to Keefer, every structure outside the square had been searched and anyone not at the festival had been brought to the square. Outside of town, there were troops in expanding rings of security in case anyone got through.

He had to admit, these guys were thorough. But this added to Cassie's point that they seemed almost too prepared, especially for the size of the outbreak. The next town was ten miles away through mountain passes. It seemed that if the virus could get that far from the mine, then it would mean it was already out of control. But they'd been ready to process over two thousand people within less than an hour's notice from the event. Three hours from infection was the countdown. The sirens had gone off right after noon and the helicopter arrived seconds later.

"Hey, Sheriff," Roscoe Peterson, the owner of the only decent bar in town, called as Rick walked by. "Can you believe this shit?"

Rick slowed down, but didn't stop. "I keep hoping I'm going to wake up with a hangover and an unbelievable bar tab at your place."

The man laughed. "Ain't that the truth. I think business will be good after this. Everyone's going to need a drink or three when this is over."

Rick waved and kept walking, knowing through experience that Roscoe always liked to get in the last word. He didn't have the heart to say what he was really thinking. After this was over, people would need a drink or three, just like Roscoe hoped. But then, vaccine or not, people were going to pack up and get the hell out of Dodge.

What parent in their right mind would raise a family in the shadow of a biological weapons facility with a proven track record of nearly killing everyone in town?

No, once this was over, regardless of how much money the government ponied up for damages, the town of Resurrection was done for. He didn't want to slow down long enough to really think through what that meant. He couldn't. The town was the one thing he'd held onto when it seemed like the rest of the world had lost its mind. But it wouldn't survive this. There was no way. A year from now the place would be a ghost town and Rick knew it.

Before Dahlia and Charlie, the idea of losing the town, losing his anchor, might have sent him spiraling. But as he walked across the square, he realized he would be all right as long as he was with Dahlia. Funny, she always thanked him for looking out for her and Charlie, but they were the ones saving him.

As he walked toward the nearest armored assault vehicle to get a closer look, he remembered what he was thinking about before Roscoe had stopped him to chat.

The sirens. The ones that'd been installed the night before.

That part made sense. If they intended to bring the facility online, adding the air sniffers and a warning system checked out. Only it wasn't an early warning system. If the alarms went off and the helicopter appeared overhead seconds later, and then the AAVs and the troops not long after that, then it meant that the breach had occurred much earlier. The road down the mountain from the mine took thirty minutes to drive, maybe twenty if you went like a bat out of hell. Not only that, but even the most elite fighters needed time to scramble and form up.

The breach had to have occurred well before the sirens went off in town.

Certainly, the sensors attached to them sent the data that confirmed the virus was in town. So why all the theatrics? The sirens, low flying helicopter blaring instructions, the stampede of people. It all seemed unnecessary.

"Sir, stop there please," the soldier in front of the AAV said. The soldiers on either side raised their guns and aimed them at his chest. It looked like they still had their safeties on, but it still didn't sit right with him having US soldiers pointing loaded weapons at him.

"I'm Sheriff Johnson. Colonel Keefer gave me permission to look around."

"I know who you are, sir," the soldier responded, the *sir* clearly not meant as a sign of respect. "This is the edge of your area."

Rick looked back and forth between the men. Like all the soldiers, about half of them had the reflective visors on their helmets, but he could see the faces of the others. They struck him as being a little older than he expected. Soldiers on this kind of duty tended to be a little greener. Usually babysitting a facility was for new recruits or those on some kind of modified duty. But these guys had the look of grizzled veterans.

"Easy, guys," he said, "we're on the same side here. I'm a Marine, not one of these civilian pukes." The guns edged down a few inches. "I just came over to admire the machinery. We didn't have anything like this in Iran."

"You were in Iran?" the man on the left asked, sounding surprised.

"Iran, Saudi, Jordan, Syria, Turkey," Rick said. "Throw a dart at a map of the New Caliphate and chances are I spent time there courtesy of Uncle Sam's travel planners." He looked back at the AAV. "We could have used something like this beast though. She's beautiful. Range?"

"One charge, five hundred clicks," the soldier on the right said.

"No shit?" Rick said, noticing the soldier's guns were pointed at the ground now. "Heavy arms?"

".50 cal on the top, guided RPG gives a three-hundred-sixty-degree target access, even two anti-aircraft guns for the low-flying stuff."

As the soldier was talking, Rick looked the machine up and down. As he did, he saw something that nearly caused his legs to buckle. He dropped to a knee to tie his boot lace, even though it wasn't loose. He needed a chance to process what he'd seen.

"But the camo-function is really the main attraction," the man continued.

"Okay, that's enough," the soldier in the middle said.

"Not like it's classified or anything," the soldier on the left said. "He could find it online."

The middle soldier stared the other man down until he looked away. "Think you might want to mosey back to the civilians now, Sheriff."

Rick stood and held up his hands, hoping his expression didn't betray anything. "I'm not trying to cause any trouble. I was just interested." He tipped his head toward the two soldiers with the guns. "And I appreciate the courtesy given to an old guy who used to wear the uniform."

It looked like the men wanted to say something in return, but the guy in the middle had them rattled. Still, they acknowledged the comment with a slight nod as he turned away.

His mind raced as he walked back to the center of the square. He didn't know what he expected to find out from looking at the AAV up close, but not this.

First he'd noticed overspray on the AAV's paneling and tires. The armored assault vehicle had been recently painted. That in itself wasn't too odd. But with the light at just the right angle, glinting off the door panel on the driver's side, Rick had seen the symbol that had been painted over.

The crescent moon and star of the Jihadi army.

CHAPTER 27

R*ick tried not to let* his body language betray his rising sense of panic. His brain was reeling at the implications of what he'd seen. What if the entire operation was a Jihadi operation right in the center of the United States? He'd suspected Keefer of lying, but what if the lies were designed to cover up an impending terrorist attack?

He needed to find Cassie and run this new information by her. She'd been two steps ahead of him from the beginning in her suspicions. He needed an ally to think this through with, someone who was already over the initial fear of the crisis and ready to think critically.

As he walked purposefully through the square looking for her, he thought through all the data points using this new information.

If these were jihadists, the communications blackout took on a more sinister purpose. What if it wasn't to keep panic from spreading but instead to seal off information so that law enforcement and the US military weren't tipped off? What if the blockade outside of town didn't actually exist? But they would have had to do something to keep new traffic from coming into Resurrection once the operation started, so they likely had some kind of perimeter set up.

Rick rubbed his eyes, feeling a headache coming on. It was how the migraines used to start back when the flashbacks to the war caught up with him, back before he got a handle on things like that. A soft, cruel voice whispered the suggestion that had been building in the back of his mind: that the whole thing, the soldiers storming the town, the deadly virus, seeing the crescent moon and star, all of it, was just in his head.

Some massive delusion and relapse into the PTSD that used to control his life.

He almost wished that were true.

But when he opened his eyes, the nightmare was still there. And it was real.

"Rick. Over here."

It was Dahlia. She was pushing against the plastic cords that roped off her area, looking like she might slip through to chase after him. Two soldiers were already stepping quickly toward her.

"Step back! Now!" the soldier barked.

A few people around Dahlia reached out to tug on her.

"All of you, back up!" The second soldier had his gun up to his shoulder, scanning the crowd in the pen through his scope.

"Wait," Rick called out, running over.

The more amped-up soldier whipped in his direction, gun raised at Rick's face.

Rick stopped immediately, raising his hands in the air. "It's okay," he said. "Let's be calm. Be calm."

The people on the other side of the plastic cord were on their feet, watching the interaction with wide eyes. Dahlia took a step backward into the holding area, shaken.

"See? She's stepped back," Rick said. "No one's going anywhere."

"This is the sheriff," the calmer of the two soldiers said. "Ease up, man. C'mon."

The man lowered his gun but then took a look over his shoulder at the people in the pen. He spun and pointed the gun at the crowd. Everyone ducked. Some screamed.

"C'mon, man. If the colonel sees you doing that shit, he'll take you out."

The soldier lowered the gun and Rick saw that he was grinning. The response from the crowd seemed to satisfy him as he turned and walked away.

Rick watched him warily as he approached the holding pen. Dahlia stepped closer, but kept a respectful distance from the boundary.

"Are you all right?" Rick asked.

"That's the first I've seen of anything like that," she said. "But, yeah, I'm all right. Charlie is over there playing with two kids his age. I'm just glad he didn't see that happen."

Rick looked down at her wrists. No green band yet. "Listen, I've got to go, but do something for me." He glanced around to make certain no one was near enough to hear him. "I want you to wait on getting your shot."

"Why?" she said, suddenly looking scared. "What's going on?"

"I'm not sure yet, just ... just ... do what you can to hold off. When it's your turn, make some excuse to go last."

"You have to tell me what's going on, Rick. You're asking me to risk Charlie—"

"I'm trying to save Charlie," he snapped, a little too loudly. Heads turned in their direction and he shot them a look to mind their own business. He took her hand in his, but when he looked into her eyes, he didn't like the way she looked at him. Like he was coming unhinged. He lowered his voice, searching for the softest tone he could muster. "I'm sorry. I didn't mean to raise my voice. I think something might be off here. It might be nothing. I'm not saying don't do the shot, just wait as long as you can."

"What do you think's going on?" she whispered.

He pushed past the question. "They're going to get to everyone, so you'll still get the vaccine. Just wait. Give me some time."

"Time for what?"

He spotted Cassie walking near Tent One. When he turned back he noticed Dahlia had followed his line of sight and seen her too.

"Does this have something to do with her?" she asked. "Does she think something's wrong too?"

Before he could answer, Charlie ran up and wrapped his arms around his leg. "Where have you been?"

Rick bent down. "Been working. Someone's got to tell people what do to around here. You been taking care of your mom for me?"

Charlie shrugged. "I guess."

"You guess? I'm relying on you, little man." He poked the badge he'd put on Charlie's shirt earlier. "This badge comes with a lot of responsibility."

Charlie nodded, but Rick saw tears welling in his eyes.

"Whoa. Hey, it's gonna be okay," Rick said. "What's going on?"

Dahlia knelt to the ground. "Charlie, what happened?"

Charlie's chin quivered as he tried to hold back his tears. "I was playing with some kids. And they said … they said …"

"It's all right," Dahlia said. "What'd they tell you?"

"They said we were all going to die," Charlie said. "That we're gonna catch a disease and die when that clock gets to zero." He turned to Rick. "Were they telling the truth? Are we going to die?"

Rick took both of the boy's hands, held them tight and looked him in the eye. "Now you listen here. No one's going to die. You got that? No matter what, I'm going to take care of you and your mom. I promise."

Charlie dragged the back of his hand across his face, wiping his nose and tears all at once. He nodded.

Rick squeezed the boy's hands tighter. "That's a promise from me to you. There's nothing stronger than that."

Charlie leaned forward and Rick wrapped him in a hug. Dahlia joined and they held Charlie together.

Reluctantly, Rick let go of them and stood. "I've got to go check on some things. You good now?"

Charlie nodded.

Rick mussed his hair. "Good boy. You hang tough." He looked at Dahlia. "Both of you."

"How long will you be?" she asked, standing up.

He hugged her and whispered in her ear, "I'll come back as soon as I know anything, one way or the other. Keep Charlie close to you from here on out."

"Be careful," she said.

He stepped back, gave Charlie a wink, then turned and jogged after Cassie, praying that his worst suspicions about what was happening in the town were wrong. He looked at the clock on the stage just as it ticked down to under an hour.

"Cassie," he said, waving. She turned in his direction, casting furtive glances at the soldiers around them. Judging by her body language, nothing had happened since their meeting with Keefer to make her feel better about their situation.

He must have looked just as tense because she took one glance at him and asked, "What happened. What did you find out?"

He told her about his walk over to the AAV. She listened quietly, her lips pinching together when he told her about the Jihadi symbol.

"Jesus, you think this whole thing is some kind of Jihadi attack?" she asked.

Rick shook his head. He recalled how ridiculous the idea had seemed the night before when Bertie had suggested it. Resurrection wasn't a high-value target, but killing over two thousand civilians in the heart of America would still be a victory for the Jihadis. In fact, it was exactly the kind of psychological blow the Jihadis loved. Americans would wake up knowing that no community, no matter how small, was safe from the Jihadi violence.

"I don't know. Maybe. But I'll tell you one thing, the timing of how everything has gone down today makes no sense to me." He walked her through his questions about why the sirens were needed, and how quickly the helicopter and the quarantine troops had arrived into town. Looking at it objectively, it all seemed designed to create panic and fear, not reduce it.

She heard him out, nodding in agreement. Then she described to him the selection of the vials for the syringes and the exact timing the soldiers were using, all of them giving the injections based on the master clock.

"Why would they do that?" he asked.

"Maybe, there's some kind of time-release component to the inoculation, but I've never heard of such a thing. Not only that, but each person would have been infected at a different time so it doesn't make sense."

His stomach turned over on itself. He turned, taking in the sight of so many people all around him. He'd never before felt so helpless. The hazmat-clothed soldiers looked even more ominous now. He wondered if under the reflective visors, the faces would be Middle Eastern, all with the pointed black beards of the Jihadis. He felt a tremble in his leg and his knee buckled just enough to make him reposition his footing. Cold sweat covered his real hand and he wiped it on his pants. "None of this proves anything definitively," he said. "But what if … what if …"

"Yeah," she agreed. "What if?"

His hand went to his holster. He still had his gun, whatever good it would do them against the massive firepower in the town. But it was better than not having it.

"Come on," he said, pulling her with him.

"Where are we going?"

"To my office," he said. "I have a feeling I'm going to need more ammo."

CHAPTER 28

"*Try not to look so* nervous," Rick said.

Cassie forced a smile. "You're the one walking like you're trying to hold a penny between your ass cheeks."

Despite everything, he burped out a short laugh at the description. But she was right, he was wired tight; frosty, they used to call it. He felt like he was back in a war zone. The difference was that he used to have an entire team backing him up. Not only that, he was used to the enemy hiding in shadows and laying traps to kill him. Now they seemed to have found a way to hide in plain sight.

"Remember, we're supposed to be goodwill ambassadors. Probably Keefer's way to keep us occupied and reined in. Sharing his concerns and a few extra details, all to make us feel like part of his inner circle."

"Worked on Bertie."

"Almost worked on me too," he said. "We're sure as hell not going to let them get away with it."

Cassie put a hand on his shoulder. "I'm as suspicious as you are, but let's not get ahead of ourselves," she said. "All we have is a bunch of questions. There might be reasonable answers. We haven't proven anything."

She was right, but his gut was telling him something different. These men in his town were bad. They were the enemy. He kept seeing that faint outline of the crescent moon and star under the paint job, a change in the sheen only noticeable in just the right light. That symbol wasn't allowed to be here. Not in his town.

"Rick?"

He turned to Cassie, and she looked concerned. He imagined his fears and anxiety were painted all over his face. His pulse was jackhammering and his breathing was coming fast and rough.

Just like the old days.

"I'm fine," he said. "Come on."

They walked in silence the rest of the way to the sheriff's station, both of them doing their best to smile and wave to people they passed. Rick was stopped by the women from Old Pines Retirement home, all sporting green wristbands, explaining to him that they were part of the committee formed by Mayor Bertie to organize food for the two thousand people camping that night in Town Square. As Rick expected, the ladies were a little tipsy, the smell of bourbon floating in the air. Rick did his best to encourage them, even cracking an easy joke about old man Roberts's cooking, but moved on quickly. There was a giant clock on the stage in the center of town and it was waiting for no one.

Finally, they made it to the sheriff's station. An armed guard with a reflective visor held up his hand and blocked them from entering.

"What can I do for you, sir?"

To Rick's ears, the man had the barest trace of a Middle Eastern accent. But with the electronic distortion from the speaker, it was nearly impossible to be sure.

"I need to get something from my desk," he said. His own face was reflected on the soldier's facemask. The curved surface distorted his image, but even to his own eyes he looked nervous and shaken. He was certain the soldier would turn him away and he wasn't sure what he could do about it.

"What do you need?" the soldier asked. "I'll have someone get it for you."

"Colonel Keefer said we had access to this area," Cassie interrupted. "If you want, we can go find him and bring him over to tell you that. I'm sure he's not busy right now."

There was no way to read the soldier's reaction without being able to see his face. He stood, unmoving, for a few long seconds.

"All right," Cassie said, turning. "We'll go get him."

"Wait," the soldier said. He stepped aside. "Make it quick. One minute."

Cassie led the way, pushing past Rick. "Good call," she said to the soldier. "Your boss is kind of an asshole."

"Yes, ma'am," the soldier said, the statement briefly giving him a little bit of humanity. Rick allowed himself a smile as they walked into his office.

He was surprised to find the front room of the station empty. With prisoners in the back holding cells, he figured there would be more guards on duty. But with a town full of soldiers and every other adult on lockdown, why waste the manpower guarding people who were already under lock and key?

Rick crossed over to a gun safe against the wall behind his desk, dialed the combination and swung open the heavy metal door. There wasn't a lot inside. It wasn't like there was a need for riot suppression gear in sleepy Resurrection. But he did keep a shotgun, his hunting rifle, and three additional Glock handguns in there. The shotgun and rifle were no good, too conspicuous, but he grabbed the handguns and extra magazines of ammo.

"You think we're going to shoot our way out?" Cassie said.

Rick handed her a handgun. "You remember how?" They'd spent a few afternoons in the mountains shooting targets with guns, but that was years ago.

"Point and shoot," she said. "I think I recall. But did you see the guns the other guys have? I don't think your peashooters here are going to do any good."

Rick stuck additional magazines into his jacket pockets. "Maybe. But it's better than not having them."

Cassie went to his desk and picked up the landline phone. Even from a few feet away, Rick heard static blast through the line. She hung it up. "The guys in the back are sure quiet."

Rick went to the door that led to the holding area and peered through the window. "Oh shit."

He yanked the door open and went inside, fumbling for his keys. The men were still in the holding pen, but they were sprawled out in unnatural positions, slumped against the walls or against one another in the small space. One thing was for sure, they weren't taking a nap.

Rick got the door open and reached for the nearest man. As he touched him, the man keeled over, lying out on the floor.

"Are they dead?" Cassie asked from outside the cell.

Rick felt the man's neck. His skin was cool to the touch, but there was a throbbing pulse there. He looked at the others and saw their chests rise and fall.

"No, they're just unconscious."

"They were pretty rowdy," Cassie said. "I wanted to knock them out myself. Maybe they just sedated them."

"No," Rick said a little too fast. "Something's wrong here. I know it." The cell walls suddenly felt too close to him, the space too confining. He pulled at his collar even though it was already loose, trying to get some air.

"You might be right," Cassie said carefully. "But let's follow the facts and not get ahead of ourselves."

He wanted to blow up at her. Tell her not to condescend to him, that he knew what he knew, which was that was that goddamn Jihadis were crawling around his town. They were after him. They were after everyone. But he held his tongue.

Even with the rising panic gripping his chest, he had the presence of mind to go to the second holding cell and check on that. Empty. He thought through his and Cassie's position and the odds stacked against them. There weren't a lot of scenarios where they survived the next few hours. But if they were to survive, there was a high likelihood they'd end up occupying the remaining cell. He opened the door and went inside for a second. If they were captured, he wanted to at least have a fighting chance.

"What are you doing?" Cassie asked.

Rick came back out and closed the cell door behind him. "Let's get the hell out of here," he said.

"And go where?" Cassie said. "We need a plan."

"We have to confront Keefer."

"Wait, if we're right about all of this, then we can't just go lodge a complaint," Cassie said. "We need more evidence. We need to enlist more help."

"Don't you get it? There's no time," Rick said, striding through the office toward the front door.

"Wait. Give me a second and let me think, all right?" Cassie said.

Rick put his finger to his lips. There was a sound coming from the side door that led into the alley. Muffled voices. Cassie froze in place.

There were men outside, two or three of them. Rick recognized the easy cadence of guys standing around and bullshitting. There was some soft laughter and then a comeback that he heard clearly. "Yeah, it was your mom." The voices laughed again.

Cassie stayed near the front of the room as he crept toward the side door, realizing as he got closer that it was open an inch. Just enough to let him take a peek outside without being noticed.

He leaned his head toward the crack in the door, moving side-to-side to maximize his field of vision.

There were three soldiers in the alley. All Rick could see at first were the backs of two of them and the leg of the third. He adjusted a little and got a better look at the third one as he reached out and handed something to one of his buddies.

A cigarette.

The soldier took it. Rick watched as the man brought it up to his opened face mask and took a drag. They all moved just enough so Rick could see their faces.

All of them had their face plates up. And all of them had dark, Middle Eastern complexions and short beards.

Jihadis. And they weren't concerned about the air. About the virus.

A sudden vertigo made Rick feel like the floor was dropping beneath his feet, like he was in an elevator. His stomach rose up and he tasted bile in the back of his mouth. He realized he wasn't breathing.

The virus wasn't real.

It was just a way to control them.

The weapon was the vaccine. Measured to be time-released so it would take effect all at once.

Dahlia and Charlie didn't have green wristbands the last time he saw them. He had to get to them before they got the injection.

He backed up from the door toward Cassie behind him, hearing his own rapid breathing in his head. As he did, the century-old wood floor creaked under his feet louder than he'd ever heard it before.

He froze.

The voices stopped.

A few long seconds passed. He and Cassie stared at each other, waiting.

Then he heard a voice, now modulated by a helmet speaker, say, "Inside. Go check it out."

"Go, Cassie. Run," Rick said, pushing her to the door.

Cassie flung open the door and ran out. Rick followed behind, pulling his gun and keeping it hidden inside his jacket.

They didn't get far.

Standing in the street in front of the sheriff's station was Colonel Keefer.

"Everything all right, Rick?" Keefer said. "You don't look so good."

The three soldiers burst out from the door behind him and Rick noticed the flare of anger pass over Keefer's face. He heard one of the soldiers mumble, "Oh shit."

Rick pulled the gun from under his jacket and pointed it at Keefer's head, marching right at him.

Keefer's guard raised their guns.

"No!" Keefer shouted, raising his hand to call his men off.

Rick wondered if the order was given so as not to have a bloodbath right on the street, or if Keefer had done the quick calculation that he might get taken out in the cross fire. He really didn't give a damn which it was.

Rick held the gun up to Keefer's head.

"You've got some explaining to do, you son of a bitch."

CHAPTER 29

R*ick could only imagine what* a spectacle it looked like to the hundreds of people who could see him as he marched Keefer to the stage, surrounded by armed men pointing their machine guns at his head. For those who couldn't see, word got around fast and the sound of two thousand questioning voices rose around him.

"Why don't we do this in private?" Keefer said over his shoulder.

Rick eyed the clock on the stage: thirty-five minutes. "No time. Besides, I think everyone here will be interested in what you have to say."

Bertie ran up to them, blocked at the last second from reaching them by one of Keefer's guards. "Rick, what the hell are you doing?"

"I'm sorry, Bertie," he said. "You're going to want to hear this."

"We're wasting valuable time," Keefer said.

"Then let's get to work. Up on the stage."

Keefer obliged, helped along by a violent poke in the ribs with Rick's gun. Bertie and Cassie followed them up the steps. The voices in the square rose at first and then quieted quickly. As if the situation they were in wasn't stressful enough, a wave of fear crashed over the crowd as people saw the sheriff holding, at gunpoint, the man who'd assured them they would be home the next day for dinner. Rick grabbed the microphone and tapped it.

Nothing.

He was about to threaten Keefer, so he'd get one of his men to turn on the PA system, when he saw the colonel was already pointing at the soldier at the soundboard. Seconds later, the speakers squealed on.

"Everyone. Can I get you all to quiet down for a minute?" Rick said. "Please. So everyone can hear."

Surprisingly, the square went still. Fear was a great motivator for crowd control.

"For those of you who aren't from here, I'm Sheriff Rick Johnson from right here in Resurrection. I'm sorry ..." He paused, realizing he didn't have a plan of where to start. He couldn't see them out in the crowd, but he pictured Charlie and Dahlia. He imagined how scared they were going to be once they heard what he had to say. Even so, the people in the square deserved to hear the truth. They deserved that chance to fight back.

"I'm sorry, but things are not what they seem," Rick said. "As bad as things seem, I've come to believe that they're worse. Much worse."

The silence didn't hold. Agitated voices rose throughout the square. Rick held up his hands for quiet.

"Don't do this, Rick," Keefer said. "I don't know what you think is going on, but you're wrong."

Rick ignored him. Instead he pointed to the snipers lining the rooftops. "These men are not US military. They are Jihadis." His voice cracked as he shouted into the mic. "There is no virus in the air. It's a Jihadi plan to control us so they can inject us. We're the lambs walking right into the slaughterhouse. This is a terrorist attack right here in the homeland."

He'd expected an uprising at the revelation. At least an outpouring of questions, demands for answers.

But people just stood there, staring blankly at him.

"What's wrong with you all?" he said. "Don't you see?" He turned to Bertie, expected to see the horror of the situation registered on her face. Instead, her eyes welled with tears as she shook her head.

"You don't believe me?" Rick shouted. "Think about it for a second. All this gear was staged up at the mine in case something like this happened, right? That's at least a twenty-minute drive, even if you're flying down the road. As a best case scenario, they left the mine twenty minutes after the virus supposedly got out. So why blare all the sirens? Why roll in here like they did? Just to create panic. No other reason."

Rick saw the first looks of doubt on the faces nearest the stage. Eyes were turning to Keefer to judge his reaction to the claims.

"And then there's the injections. Most of you have already gotten one. Think about what happened. It wasn't like your usual shot, right? Someone checked the time first, then selected a vial based on that. Then, did you notice what happened next? Everyone in the tent got the injection at exactly the same time. Has anyone ever seen anything like that before?"

"That's right," a man in the front row called out. "That's what happened. A bunch of us were talking about how weird that was."

Rick pointed to the man. "Exactly. But not just weird. There's a purpose. Whatever they gave us, it's on a time release." He pointed to the clock, just as it clicked under thirty minutes. "That's not the countdown to when the virus becomes deadly, it's when whatever they injected us with does."

This time the crowd got loud, a mix of anger and fear. Keefer held out his hand for the microphone but Rick pulled it away from him. Angry shouts came from the crowd.

"Let him speak."

"I want to hear what he says."

Rick handed the mic over to Keefer, but kept his gun trained on him. He knew he could be taken out at any second by one of the rooftop snipers. He just wanted to make sure that he took Keefer out with him if that happened.

Keefer held up his hands and the crowd quieted. "First, I want to apologize for this added stress to an already challenging situation. Those of you farther back in the crowd should know that the sheriff has a gun to me, otherwise we would not have let him worry everyone like this." Keefer paused then continued. "But, unfortunately, there is some truth to what the sheriff said."

The crowd erupted and Rick felt a wave of relief mixed with paranoia. Keefer's reaction had been too casual up to this point, too assured. Even with the evidence he had, Rick had to admit there were some doubts, especially seeing the crowd's reaction to what he'd shared with them so far. Hearing Keefer admit it made Rick feel validated. But the fact that the colonel had no fear of being uncovered wasn't good.

Keefer held up his hands for quiet. "He's correct that the way we entered town was unnecessary and caused a panic. It could have been handled better by myself and my team." The crowd settled and Rick felt his stomach churn at how reasonable and calm Keefer sounded. "We're human and we make mistakes under pressure. And there is no greater pressure than knowing if we don't do our jobs right today, everyone in this town could die." He let that set in. "And that if we're too soft and we let someone escape the containment area, every

American in our great country could die."

"I saw the crescent and star painted over on the AAV," Rick shouted at the mic. He pointed in the direction of the armored vehicle. "If you're over in that corner, you can see it."

Heads in the crowd turned that direction, but looked back at Keefer as he spoke again, impatience in his voice.

"That's correct," he said. "These vehicles and many of the men here were recently used in war games, training for our men heading to Tora Bora in Afghanistan. The AAVs had the insignia on their side at one point. Many of the men here participated, growing their beards out to play the part."

Rick felt the eyes of the crowd shift to him. "You don't believe that, do you?" He turned to Cassie standing behind him by Bertie. She met his eyes, but he saw the doubt there. "I just saw," he pointed to Cassie, "*we* just saw some of your men with their face masks open, smoking cigarettes in the alley. They didn't seem too concerned about your virus."

Keefer looked at Cassie for confirmation, but she shook her head. Rick realized she hadn't seen them in the alley. By the time they ran after them, they had their masks back down.

Keefer was also looking at Cassie's blank reaction. "Ms. Baker, did you see my men with their masks up? Taking … what did you say, Sheriff? A smoke break?"

Cassie hesitated and for a second Rick thought she might come to his rescue and say that she had seen them. But she shook her head no.

A groan passed through the crowd.

"Get off the stage, Sheriff!" someone yelled.

Then the boos started. But, surprisingly, it was Keefer who put an end to them.

"Please, please," he said, calling for order. "Sheriff Johnson is only trying to look out for you. Trying to do his job."

"The syringes," Rick said, hating the feeling of grasping for a hard edge only to have everything he touched crumble. "Try explaining that away."

Keefer held up his hand and the crowd quieted. "I will explain as simply as I can. But I'm no doctor." He made a show of taking a deep breath, like something weighed heavily on him. "There is enough vaccine and the vaccine works," he started. "But it's also very unstable. From the time it leaves the controlled lab environment, it starts to ... I'm afraid to use this word because it's not exactly right ... but it starts to degrade."

A murmur passed through the crowd.

"Not really degrade as much as just change. The vaccine sixty minutes out of the lab is different than the same vaccine fifty minutes out of the lab."

Rick felt his panic rise as he looked across a field of faces nodding along with Keefer's explanation. It wasn't so much that he was convincing as it was that they wanted to believe him.

Keefer continued, "I know this is all very complicated, but we have to match the vaccine batch exactly with the time out of the lab. And it's all keyed off the same countdown clock." He pointed to the digital read-out hitting twenty-five minutes, and then turned to Rick although he was playing to the crowd. "Now, if I've answered all your questions, can I suggest we get back to work?"

Rick grabbed the mic back and pressed the gun into Keefer's side. He knew what he knew, and then there was what his instinct told him. "How about I inject you with the vaccine? Would that be all right with you?"

Keefer scowled at him. "Sheriff, I've been more than patient with you. Maybe more patient than I should have been. I understand from your friend the mayor that you've had severe episodes of post-traumatic stress disorder before."

"That's not what this is," Rick shouted, spit flying from his mouth.

"That you used to see Jihadis in every dark shadow, lurking behind every bush."

"It's been a long time since ... since I ..." his voice faded as he looked at Bertie. She had one hand over her mouth and she shook her head, her eyes bright with tears.

"It's all right. I know what it's like," Keefer said. "I know the things you've seen. I know, for example, what happened to you in Istanbul."

The word felt like a punch to the stomach. A ringing flared in his ears. Inside the ringing sound he heard screaming. His own screaming from years ago. He put his free hand up to his ears, trying to block the sound. He fought to get his emotions back under control.

"Stop trying to make this about me," Rick said. "Tell these people the truth."

"The truth? Should we talk about the truth, Sheriff?" Keefer asked. "Okay, let's talk about the truth. You weren't surprised when we showed up today, were you?"

"What? Of course I was," he said, turning back to Keefer.

"Was today the first time we've met?"

Rick didn't respond.

"I said, was this the first time we met?"

Rick shook his head. "No."

A murmur rose from the crowd.

"We met at the mine yesterday," Keefer said. "Where you agreed to keep the activity up there secret from the people in the town."

"Only until—"

"I even put ten thousand dollars in your hand for you to keep quiet."

"I didn't take the money," Rick said, but his voice was drowned out by the boos from the crowd. He felt both Cassie's and Bertie's eyes boring into the back of his head. He'd lied right to both of their faces about the mine.

"And your deputy took the money too," Keefer said. "Can you deny that?"

Rick's throat was dry. He'd been caught in a trap, and he realized everything up to this point had been designed to discredit him if it proved necessary. It didn't change the fact that these were terrorists in his town. Jihadis on his soil. Even if he was the only one who believed it, he damn sure wasn't going to let Keefer get away with it. As the crowd turned against him, he wondered if his only option was to take Keefer out, knowing that pulling the trigger was as good as committing suicide. It wouldn't stop the operation, but it was better than getting thrown in his own jail cell and letting Keefer get away with it.

A soldier walked up to the side of the stage carrying a bulky black phone with a thick antenna sticking up in the air. He held it up toward Keefer, who nodded.

"Sheriff, we're running out of time here, but this is a phone call I think you should hear."

"What is this?" Rick asked.

Keefer waved the soldier forward and took the phone. He held it up to his ear, only his side of the conversation audible.

"Colonel Keefer, sir … yes that's right, at gunpoint …no, sir, if we can get back to work in the next five minutes, I guarantee the mission can be completed … yes, sir …"

Keefer asked for the mic from Rick who handed it over. He held it to the earpiece and then said, "Go ahead, sir. You're being piped in through the PA system."

A man cleared his voice, and then there came a sound that tore apart everything that Rick had come to believe in the last two hours.

"My fellow Americans," the voice said, a little distorted over the line, but clear enough. "This is Ken Mayfield, the president of the United States. First, let me extend my heartfelt …"

Rick didn't hear the rest of what the president said. He staggered backward, the gun hanging limply in his hand. He startled when he felt pressure on his arms and then his gun was wrested from his hands. Pain exploded in the back of his legs and he was forced to the floor.

But he didn't care. He'd gotten it wrong. All of it. And he'd put everyone at even greater risk. All that was left to do was give in to the process, get out of the way, and try not to cause any more damage.

Someone yanked his arms behind his back and he felt the pinch of zip ties on his wrists. Bertie was right in front of him, tears on her cheeks, talking to whomever had a hold of his arms. She was telling the man not to hurt him, but he barely heard the words. He didn't want to hear them and he didn't want to see her face. Poor Bertie, always looking out for him since he was a kid. Went out on a limb when he got back and took a risk on a broken soldier. And this was the thanks he gave her.

He looked past Bertie and saw Keefer still holding the phone to the mic. The president's voice seemed impossibly far away and under water. The words, "God bless you all and God bless the United States of America," filtered through his consciousness.

Keefer said something to the crowd, waved and then returned the mic to its stand. A security detail immediately formed a phalanx around him as he walked off the stage. When he passed Rick, the two of them locked eyes for just the barest of seconds.

And the son of a bitch winked at him.

Then Rick was hefted onto his feet and half dragged, half carried off the stage toward jail. He heard Cassie cry out behind him and she was grabbed too. The coconspirators in the mutiny were under wraps and out of the way.

The clock ticked down to nineteen minutes.

CHAPTER 30

C*assie watched as the soldiers* pushed Rick ahead of her. One of them held her upper arm in a strong grip, but otherwise she was allowed to walk on her own. The crowd parted just enough to allow them to squeeze through. People wanted to be close enough to give Rick a few choice words as he passed. Men and women both, their faces screwed into masks of anger, yelled insults at Cassie and Rick, mostly about how they had put everyone at risk with their stupidity. Only they used language so colorful it would make a sailor take note.

Cassie didn't recognize any of the faces. She'd gotten to know most of the residents in Resurrection during her few years of work there, and dating Rick had made certain that everyone knew who she was. She was glad to see none of Rick's friends yelling in the angry crowd. The few scattered here and there stood in silence and watched him pass by; not anger but sadness and disbelief marked their expressions. There was one that stood out among them, an old man, Roberts she thought was the name. He was part of the human tunnel the soldiers pushed through, but he wasn't yelling like the others. He just stood as if sizing Rick up as he was hustled past.

Rick didn't seem to hear or see any of it. He walked with his head down, shoulders slumped forward. Cassie felt terrible, owning her responsibility for what had just happened. Her concerns had been valid, but she should have been more aware of how Rick's PTSD might impact the way he processed the events. He'd looked so wild on the stage, barely in control. He could have told the crowd the sky was blue and they still would have doubted him.

His claim that he'd seen soldiers taking a smoke break in the alley next to the sheriff's station had taken her by surprise. She hadn't seen the soldiers with their visors up, but she felt like she'd left Rick hung out to dry when he'd asked her to confirm the fact on the stage. Her impulse was to back him up, but she couldn't. The stakes were too high. Because if their suspicions were wrong, and they really were just slowing down the inoculations for no reason, they were putting the entire town at risk. So she'd told the truth. The look of betrayal on Rick's face was unlike anything she'd seen from him before. No, that wasn't quite right. The moment she'd chosen her career over staying in Resurrection to be his wife had produced that same expression.

But she hadn't seen the soldiers the way Rick had. And she had to face the fact that maybe Rick hadn't seen them either. It wasn't that she thought he was lying. She had no doubt Rick believed he saw the men in the alley with their visors up. But given Rick's history, there was a chance it was all in his head. On the other hand, he'd been right about so many things, like the Jihadi symbol on the vehicles, that it seemed odd his only break with reality would come at that one moment.

Cassie felt guilty because she honestly didn't want to believe Rick. It was bad enough if there was a deadly virus inside her, but at least that came with a solution. If the whole thing really was some terrorist plot, there was no hope. If this were true, what could she do to stop it anyway? While the human side of her wanted the happy ending, the problem solver in her wanted to know the truth.

As she walked, she went through each of the facts they'd come up with, and Keefer's explanations. Each thing Keefer had said seemed reasonable on the surface, but she couldn't stop the feeling that something was still off. There were too many small oddities, and the reasons for each came off as too convenient. Too rehearsed and perfect.

Or they might have sounded like that because they were the truth.

The revelation that Rick had known the mine was in operation hurt. She'd guessed he'd known something based on the way he'd tried to stall her, but the fact that he'd actually met Keefer before, and that money had changed hands, surprised her. And the way he'd been able to lie right to her face was disturbing. It was the one thing he'd never been able to do when they were together, not even to say he liked an outfit she was wearing when he really didn't. The reveal had hurt his credibility with the crowd at a pivotal moment too. But it wouldn't have mattered in the end.

The call from the president had sealed the case.

Anyone in that square who might have still harbored doubts was sold after that phone call. Even Rick had sort of imploded after hearing the voice over the phone, the reality he'd constructed in his mind collapsing in on itself as he understood that the two of them had been wrong. He'd looked completely broken by the revelation. It was only then that she realized he was living the experience filtered through his PTSD. Back when they were together, she'd been there on the nights when he woke up screaming, locked in some fire fight in a distant desert, his friends dying around him. With her there, he came out of it quickly, but always with his entire body shaking and covered in sweat. Sometimes he'd weep in her arms as the dream gave way to actual memories of things he'd seen and done in the service of his country.

And that was after he'd made a tremendous amount of progress.

He'd shared with her some of the details of his first year back in the country. How every loud noise made him jump. How a sound or a smell could transport him to a different country and a different time, with such reality that he thought he was going insane. How every person with Middle Eastern heritage put him on such an edge that his mind flooded with ways to kill. How when he looked in the mirror he saw a monster to be feared and hated staring back at him.

Resurrection had been his bedrock. Bertie had been his savior. Cassie could have been the third leg of his full reintegration into a normal life, but she couldn't do it. No, she could have done it, she'd loved him enough. Sometimes, especially when she walked into her empty apartment after a fourteen-hour day at the lab, she wondered if she'd made the right choice.

But none of that mattered now. She worried how this situation would impact him. Whether he would retreat back inside himself to the dark place where the nightmares waited. As she watched him stumble up the steps to the sheriff's station, head hung low, totally defeated, it looked like he was doing exactly that.

Now a new soldier joined them. Cassie noticed the others deferred to him as he reached out and took hold of Rick's arm. His had one of the clear visors but she was behind him so she couldn't see his face. However, she could see a tattoo extending from his collar up the side of his neck. Whoever it was, he handled Rick roughly, pushing him along and shoving him through the door into the station.

Before she followed them up inside, she turned around to look out over the crowd. Most people had lost interest in them, listening to the instructions being given on the stage for the final people to get inoculated. The old man was still there, studying her, his face still unreadable. Behind him the clock on the stage ticked down to under seventeen minutes. A soldier made an announcement on stage, assuring everyone that there was time for all as there were under a hundred people left.

She breathed a little easier hearing that. At least their questioning hadn't messed things up too much. Everyone would get the shot in time. Everyone would be safe.

As she walked through the door into the outer office of the sheriff's station, she saw the soldier with the neck tattoo punch Rick in the face. Before she could cry out, the door slammed behind her.

CHAPTER 31

B*randon Morris turned off the* monitor at his desk that showed the live video feed from Resurrection. He didn't have the stomach for watching Keefer work damage control, spinning half-truths and lies so fast that even Morris wondered what was real and what was fiction. And seeing Cassie on stage made him feel sick. How she'd been caught up in the whole mess was unbelievable. He'd had assurances from Keefer that she wouldn't be harmed, but the images on his screen of soldiers in hazmat suits occupying an American town, didn't give him confidence that Cassie would make it through without getting hurt.

Then again, if there was one thing Keefer had proven over and over it was that he could deliver what he promised, no matter how high the odds were stacked against him. Morris had to hand it to the old soldier. The proposal Keefer had pitched nearly a year earlier matched almost exactly what was rolling out on the video feeds. The plan had seemed not only audacious but needlessly complicated, but Keefer's resolve and confidence had won Morris over.

Morris understood systems better than most people. He'd designed and created some of the most complicated computer and mechanical systems in human history. So he knew the chaos that the deviation of a single variable could cause. He'd seen billion-dollar projects seize up and fail because one line of code had been entered incorrectly. Computers and machines were hard enough, but when he considered the incalculable variables working with so many human beings, Morris could only marvel at what the man was pulling off.

Keefer's brilliance was a rare combination of ruthless resolve and an understanding of human instinct. The old soldier was a master manipulator; as proof Morris only needed to switch the video feed back on to see hundreds of people lining up dutifully to submit themselves to a shot in the arm from a faceless technician holding an unknown serum. And yet there they were; the elderly being helped into the medical tents, families getting shots together, mothers handing their babies over and crying in relief after the injection was given to their little ones.

It was brilliant.

Even so, he still felt Keefer ought to have listened to him to begin with and conducted the operation offshore where they could have acted with impunity. There was no shortage in an overpopulated world of government officials willing to turn a blind eye to even the most egregious acts as long as the money ended up in the right bank accounts. But Keefer had insisted they do this in America. He'd even given Morris a lecture about patriotism and how Americans had to save their own country. Patriotism was a foreign idea to Morris. To him, nationalism was on par with religion, a way to manipulate the masses and rally them to whatever cause the ruling elite wanted to fight. He was surprised to learn that Keefer was under its sway. Morris considered it a weakness, one he could exploit.

Keefer wasn't the only one capable of manipulation. Morris'd let the old man believe he was in control. Even when Keefer had threatened him over the phone the previous day, Morris had pretended to buckle. He smirked as he imagined how confident the old man had sounded at the end of the call. The alpha dog didn't know it, but Morris had him by the balls. All he had to do was push a button and he could lop them off. Once they reached the next stage of the mission, he held every card. Keefer was just the pawn who thought he ought to be king.

He was willing to let Keefer keep believing that until he delivered them to the next stage. It had to happen. Everything was riding on it.

"Mr. Morris, we're ready for you," a soft voice said through a speaker embedded in his jaw bone. The device still unsettled him. During development, his people had thought the wearable would be in the ear itself, but the soft tissue had proven difficult to deal with and prone to infection. Vibrations in the jawbone worked just as well and it was a permanent solution. And importantly, there was no machine-brain connection, so it couldn't be hacked.

He checked the clock on the wall. The call was precisely on time. He expected no less than perfection from his medical team.

He crossed his right hand to touch the spot on his left jaw where the speaker was embedded, a movement which activated the microphone. It had the added benefit of covering his mouth as he spoke to protect him from lip-readers. Some of the most important secrets in the world were still stolen through low-tech means.

"Thank you," he said. "You may come in."

The door to his office opened and a beautiful woman dressed in a dark business suit and high heels entered, flanked on either side by two large men dressed in crisp white orderly uniforms. The Genysis logo was embroidered discreetly on the uniforms next to the large identification badges attached to their breast pockets.

The woman stopped in front of Morris's desk, but the men continued forward without being asked. Morris recognized them as the same two that had come for him six hours earlier. And six hours before that. And six before that. He felt as if he should know their names and nearly made the effort to look at their badges, but he stopped himself. Getting to know the men only made it harder later when they had to be rotated out if they asked the wrong questions or demanded to be let out of the grounds. The world didn't know about his sickness, and there was only one way he knew to ensure his medical team kept quiet. If one had to be dismissed, they were never seen again. Because of that, he preferred to have them remain nameless.

The larger of the two men took hold of his wheelchair and pushed it. There was some irony in that Genysis produced the most cutting edge machine-brain interface wheelchairs in the world, capable of responding to the wheelchair-bound person's thoughts, following directions to move, stop, accelerate, deliver medicines through an IV, contact medical help .... the list went on. But the owner of the world's most powerful machine-brain interface company refused to allow his own brain to be connected. He was too aware of what could go wrong and too aware that his competitors would stop at nothing to try hacking such a connection.

So, he had a man push his wheelchair. It was a short distance and it was one of the only times during the day that he was physically around other human beings. He didn't like to admit it, but he actually looked forward to the short interactions.

Dr. Fitzgerald waited for him in the medical suite. It was fully fitted as a complete operating theater. Morris had left no stone unturned in acquiring the most sophisticated medical equipment. He'd received enough death threats from both Jihadis and homegrown fundamentalists that it felt like good business to have the hospital on the grounds. Just in case.

He liked to joke that hatred of his integration technology was one of the few things the Jihadis and the fundamentalist Christians could agree on. They both railed against his creations as abominations and contrary to God's will. Still, even these groups inevitably used some Genysis technology. It was nearly impossible to go anywhere in the world and not be touched by it somehow. It didn't stop them from promising to kill him.

When his lymphoma was diagnosed, the medical suite was already in place. That meant he was able to receive his care without letting anyone know. No one on his board of directors or senior management team had any idea. The only person he'd come close to telling was Cassie. He even had a carefully constructed fantasy of how it would happen. He would tell her and she would become emotional, finally letting go of the employer-employee relationship excuse she always fell back on when he tried to move their relationship forward. Then she would be by his side, helping him to complete the most important project of his life.

Only he knew it wouldn't happen that way. There were too many things he'd had to do to overcome obstacles in the new project, things that Cassie would never agree with. So, he made do with the fantasy and with watching her carefully from a distance, biding his time.

But eventually his weight loss became an issue, starting rumors that he was the next Steve Jobs, a sick, lonely man, wasting away from a mysterious illness. He countered with rumors of his own that he was working on a new invention that would transform the world. His reputation of being a workaholic and an obsessive played into the narrative of the mad scientist skipping meals for days as he worked in his lab. Overnight, the conversation on the Internet changed from what his illness might be to what incredible invention the genius Brandon Morris might next offer the world.

In reality, the radiation treatments were eating him up alive and he couldn't stand the sight of food.

But the stories weren't all fiction. He *was* working on something transformational. And he was obsessed with completing the work, even if it harmed his health further. It wasn't for any altruistic reason. Other men might have wanted to finish their crowning achievement on their deathbed as a way to leave their mark on the world, but Morris didn't give two shits about that.

Morris's only priority was to save himself. Once he climbed out of his deathbed as a new man, then he'd decide whether to keep his promise to Keefer. He wouldn't agree to do everything the old man wanted, that was madness, but he would give just enough to keep him happy. If it wasn't enough, then Morris would have to dispose of him. If things got that far, Morris would have absolute control. Even though he'd promised it, it was never part of the plan to give control to Keefer. The man was brilliant, but Morris knew brilliance and insanity often danced together in a man's mind. No, Keefer would never have control. He'd made certain of it.

As Dr. Fitzgerald and his small team checked Morris's vitals and hooked him up to the transfusion machine, Morris closed his eyes and imagined the future and what it might hold for him.

Nothing short of immortality.

As long as Keefer didn't screw it up.

CHAPTER 32

R*ick fell to the floor,* hitting hard with his front shoulder to break his fall because his hands were still tied behind his back. Estevez kicked him in the ribs and the pain sliced through him.

"Stop it," Cassie shouted.

Rick rolled away from Estevez and curled up, hoping to at least protect his head and stomach.

"Mother fucker," Estevez said, kicking harder. "You've been a pain in the ass from the beginning, you know that? Throw them both in the back cell."

The other two soldiers grabbed Rick and dragged him across the floor into the cell block. They passed the first cell with the unconscious men, then entered the only other cell where they dropped him in a heap on the floor. They threw Cassie in after him and she broke her fall on the bed against the far wall.

"Are we supposed to knock them out like these other guys?" one of the soldiers asked Estevez.

"Why bother?" his buddy said. "You heard him up there, sounding all crazy an' shit. Who's going to listen to him? Besides, it's almost over."

Estevez pushed the men aside and came into the cell to kneel on the floor in front of Rick. "You know what, Sheriff? I don't like you."

"Trust me, the feeling's mutual, pal."

Estevez grinned. "The colonel thinks the two of you are worth keeping around. I don't see it." He looked Cassie over. "Then again, it might be nice to release a little stress. You're not really my type, but I think I can get past that."

"Go screw yourself," Cassie said, but her voice trembled.

"That's not what I had in mind," Estevez said.

"Hey, asshole," Rick said. "Over here."

As Estevez turned, Rick hawked a mouthful of spit and blood into his face. Estevez swung his feet out and kicked him in the side.

"Rick, no!" Cassie screamed.

A second later, two gun barrels were stuck in Rick's face.

"Stay down, shit head," the soldier yelled. "Move and you're dead."

Estevez climbed to his feet, wiping the spittle from his face. He pulled the gun from his side and stepped forward, pressing it against Rick's forehead. Rick kept his eyes open, staring the man down.

"Don't do it, man," one of the soldiers said. "The colonel wanted them alive. He'll be pissed."

Estevez curled his lip, pressing the gun harder against Rick's forehead. Rick pushed his head forward even though the gun barrel dug into his skin. He wasn't about to give the asshole the satisfaction of seeing him cower.

Finally, Estevez pulled his gun back, grinning. "Lock them up," he said.

The soldier nearest Rick smashed the butt of his rifle into Rick's head and he fell to the floor. The soldiers left and Cassie got on her feet as the cell door slammed shut.

"Wait. We're not inoculated," she said, sticking her arms through the bars. "Look, no green wristbands."

The soldiers turned and stared back at her; the cell block reflected in their mirrored faceplates. Estevez walked up to her.

"You don't have a green wristband?" he asked.

"No, neither of us do," she said.

He leaned to the side and looked at Rick getting up from the floor.

"Damn, she's right," Estevez said to the two soldiers, an edge of sarcasm in his voice. "I didn't notice with this facemask on."

He reached up to his helmet, turned two locks and lifted his visor.

The other two soldier followed suit.

Rick sat up as Cassie stumbled backward.

"Oh my God," she whispered.

The man to Estevez's right was rough-looking, in his thirties, with a face marked by scars and shiny skin from burn marks. The other one had a swirling tattoo just like the one Estevez had on his neck, only this one didn't stop at the man's jawline. It covered the entire side of his face, enveloping one of his eyes. Even with the need for warm bodies, the US military would never allow a tattoo like that in its ranks.

Rick knew with a rush of insight that the man wasn't active military. Not only that, but there was no virus in the air. Keefer had been lying the whole time.

Rick felt a rush of vindication. He'd been right all along, goddammit.

But there was no joy in the feeling. It only meant that the danger was real. And Dahlia and Charlie were still outside.

Rick climbed to his feet, struggling to get up with his hands tied. "Who are you guys?" he yelled. "What's really going on out there?"

Estevez grinned. When he responded, he did so in an exact imitation of President Mayfield's voice. "I'm not sure what I'll enjoy more. You knowing the truth or having to sit there and wonder what's happening outside when the clock hits zero?"

"Oh Jesus," Cassie said. "That was you on the phone. Just an impersonation."

Estevez pressed his face to the bars and pointed at her, now changing his accent to a southern twang. "Damn, they said you was smart, girl. And they was right, weren't they?"

Rick felt Cassie next to him before he saw her. Like a blur, she pushed him aside and landed a punch through the iron bars right on Estevez's nose. Rick was surprised to see blood gush down the man's face. His nose definitely appeared to be cocked to one side.

"Holy shit, did you see that?" the soldier with the tattoo said.

"Bitch broke your nose, man." The one with the burned face laughed. "Guess she don't like your impersonations."

Estevez glared at the two soldiers and they fell silent. He felt his nose and then, with a violent twist, put it back into place.

"Jacobs, you think it's so funny, you get to be the one who kills 'em," Estevez said to the soldier with the burned face.

Rick took a step in front of Cassie. He did it on instinct, but he knew it wouldn't matter. It wasn't like he was going to stop a bullet from reaching her.

The soldier looked nervous. "I thought you said the colonel wants them alive."

"You report to me," Estevez said. "Don't forget that. And I say they die, got it?"

"Yes, sir," Jacobs replied, lifting his rifle toward the cell.

Cassie let out a short scream.

But Estevez pushed the rifle up. "Not yet, everyone would hear it. Besides, I want this asshole to stew for a while. Wait until the clock runs down; it'll be nice and loud. No one will notice a couple of gunshots in the mix. You say they got loose and tried to escape. You did what you had to. You got that?"

"I've got it," Jacobs said.

Rick watched the interplay between the two men. They all knew what was happening. The officer wanted the enlisted man to do his shit work so if it came back on him there'd be a fall guy. All Rick knew was that it gave him time, which was exactly what he needed.

"Let's get the fuck out of here," Estevez said. "Bye, asshole. I'll be sure to take care of that girl of yours. We got a couple of guys with us that like little boys too. I'll make sure he isn't left out."

Rick didn't take the bait even though he wanted to throw himself at the iron bars.

Estevez turned and walked out, the soldiers following fast, raising their visors as they walked. Rick stood frozen until the door to the office slammed shut.

"Rick, I'm so sorry I didn't believe you," Cassie whispered behind him.

Rick watched the door for a few seconds, making sure the soldier named Jacobs was going to wait it out in the office and not come back to the cell block.

"I should never have—"

"Get up," he said spinning around. "Now."

"What? Why?" she said.

"Come on, hurry up," he said. She stood up. "Now move the mattress."

"What are you ..." She stopped and stared at the set of keys hidden under there. "When did you put these here?"

"Right before we went outside. I figured if we were lucky, we'd get thrown in here."

"You call this lucky?"

"Considering I was pretty sure we'd already be dead, yeah, this is pretty lucky," he said. "There's a little pocketknife on that keychain. Use it to get through these zip ties."

Cassie grabbed the keys, unfolded the knife and sawed at his bindings until they broke loose. Rick turned and grabbed the key from her.

"If they're not terrorists, then what the hell is going on?" she asked.

"They're not Jihadis, but that doesn't mean they're not terrorists. These guys aren't regular military, that's for sure." He reached out and inserted the key in the cell door. "And now we know there's no virus."

"Or there is and these guys have already been vaccinated, and the visors are just a way to mask their identities," she said. "If that's the case, then you and I are going to be screwed in about seven minutes."

Rick felt his stomach clench. There was no time. Even with the new information, what could they do in seven minutes?

Rick eased the door open, wincing with each squeak of the hinges. They stepped into the hallway. There was only one door and, as far as they knew, there might be a dozen soldiers on the other side.

Rick got down on his stomach and motioned for Cassie to do the same. The last thing they needed was for one of the soldiers to catch movement through the small square window in the door.

They crawled forward on their hands and knees, the creaks of the wooden floor thankfully masked by the men snoring in the other cell.

When they reached the door, Rick gestured for Cassie to stay down. He slowly raised himself, staying to the side of the window and as flat against the door as possible. If someone on the other side spotted him, they didn't stand a chance. Bullets versus fists never ended well. They needed the element of surprise if they stood any chance of getting free. Not that he had any great plan for what to do after that, but one problem at a time.

The barest peek through the window showed an empty room on the other side. He darted back away from the window, just in case. Nothing happened so he inched forward again and chanced a longer look into the room. As he did, the side alley door opened and Jacobs walked in. Rick ducked down, drawing in a sharp breath.

He motioned for Cassie to get on her feet and stand to the right of the door. He inserted the key into the lock and pantomimed her opening the door and him running through. She nodded that she understood.

He took a quick look through the window. Jacobs was by himself and was to the left with his back to him. It wasn't going to get any better than that.

He nodded to Cassie. She turned the key and heaved open the door.

Rick ran out and slammed into the soldier just as he turned.

They flew across the desk and landed in a heap on the other side.

Jacobs threw an elbow and caught Rick in the face, but he ignored the flash of pain. Rick punched at the man's throat but the suit was too thick for it to do any damage. Jacobs got up on his knees and landed two brutal blows to Rick's ribcage, the same spot Estevez had kicked him earlier. He cried out in pain and grabbed at the man, wrestling him to the floor, trying to grab hold of the hazmat suit. He was on top of the man, his own face reflected off the man's visor, bloody and bug-eyed from straining.

Jacobs tried to twist away from his grasp, and Rick took the opening to smash through the visor with his prosthetic hand. The nerve sensors in the skin flared, but they were calibrated to max out before it felt like actual pain. He pulled back and punched the man again, artificial skin shredding on the shards of glass.

Jacobs kicked and landed a knee in Rick's stomach, rolling to the side. Rick went with him, staying on top. But the soldier used the momentum to keep going, hammering Rick into the wall.

The man connected hard shots to Rick's body, knocking the air out of him. He figured a head shot was coming next in the combination. On a blind guess, he dodged to his left.

He guessed correctly, and Jacobs drove his fist into the wood floor instead of into Rick's face.

Rick smacked him in the jaw with an elbow then clawed for the man's eyes. His fingernails dug into the skin and he felt the soft tissue of eyes.

Jacobs rose up, a cry coming his mouth as he reached up to his face.

Rick punched the man's throat and the cry cut off in a gurgling sound.

He swung his legs over and pinned the man down as if they were on a wrestling mat. He had position on the soldier and what felt like around a twenty-pound advantage. Still, Jacobs was tough and fought back. Rick wrestled the man into an arm-bar with his forearm lodged under the man's neck. Despite thick rubber of the suit, he had enough pressure against Jacobs's throat to choke him out.

But he didn't need to kill the man, just incapacitate him.

He clung to Jacobs as he bucked and strained against him. But his hold was tight and soon the man stopped fighting back and hung limp in his arms.

"Hand me those," he whispered to Cassie, pointing to the handcuffs on the other desk.

She grabbed them and tossed them over, then crouched down behind a low filing cabinet so she couldn't be seen from the street.

Rick cuffed the soldier then grabbed the man's gun. It was a semi-auto M-1 assault rifle, standard issue for the US armed forces. He was more than familiar with the weapon's capabilities. A quick glance out the windows in front showed several soldiers, thankfully all of them facing out to the crowd.

"How much time is left on the clock?" Cassie asked. "Can you see it?"

Rick strained to one side of the window to get a look at the stage. He saw Keefer first, walking up to the microphone. Then he saw the clock, and a cold shiver passed through his body. He stepped away from the window and leaned against the wall.

"What did you see?" Cassie whispered.

Rick shook his head. All he could think about were Dahlia and Charlie. They were out there and he couldn't save them. He'd promised Charlie he would protect him, but he couldn't. He'd failed. He'd failed everyone.

"Rick, how much time?"

The room felt as if it was pressing in on him, the world shifting under his feet. He closed his eyes but that just made the vertigo worse. When he opened his eyes, Cassie had crossed the room to look out the window for herself.

Less than two minutes left. They were out of time.

Everyone out there was going to die. And there was nothing he could do to stop it.

CHAPTER 33

K*eefer stood before the mic* as the clouds parted, giving way to a warm glow of fall sunshine. He took it as one more sign that what he was doing was right and just. The thought surprised him. He'd never been one to look at something as arbitrary as the weather for meaning, and doing so was out of character for him. He'd been many things over his life, but a hand-wringer was not one of them.

From the first late-night conversation with Alejandro Estevez, over four years ago, he'd never questioned the morality of their plan. Perhaps it was because every bit of his mental energy had been spent on the logistical challenges of making this day happen, but he'd never had time for second-guessing.

The only thing that mattered was that his beloved country would be saved. With that as the result, how could anything he did not be justified?

Still, in the last few weeks, he admitted to a few lapses in confidence. With the planning coming to fruition, and the odds of the mission working steadily increasing, he'd had sleepless nights where the price of his country's liberty materialized before him. He pictured all the death in front of him and it nearly overwhelmed him. When he was awake, he kept the mental images of the casualties limited to that of faceless men. But in his sleep, they were always women and children. And there were more of them than he could ever count.

But by the light of day, the certainty returned. All he needed to do was turn on any of the twenty-four-hour news channels to know that his plan was not only just, but the only option left for his country to be great once again. Now he was about to take the first major step. His chest swelled with pride; he was about to become his nation's savior.

The clock was under two minutes when he held up his hands to the crowd. They all fell silent, and he relished the power. He knew it was just fear that made them so pliable, but it was fear that he'd manufactured and manipulated. The only guilt he felt was that these were all Americans in front of him. And he was going to be responsible for their deaths.

But he'd sent soldiers into battle before, knowing full well that most if not all of them would perish on a mission. Thomas Jefferson had said that the tree of liberty must be refreshed from time to time with the blood of patriots and tyrants. Any man who oversaw the creation of the greatest nation in the history of mankind was someone Keefer could get behind.

So, when he looked at the sea of faces in front of him, men's, women's and even children's, he refused to see victims or casualties. He saw only the faces of patriots. Once he cemented that thought into place, he didn't feel the slightest amount of guilt.

"My fellow Americans," he said into the microphone. "I was assured minutes ago that every person here has received their vaccination. Because of that, I just received my own." He held up his left arm in the air to show the green wristband there. "Please hold up your wristbands now."

All of the people in the entire square raised their arms in unison. Keefer was happy he'd thought of the detail to have the wristbands go on the left arms. The last thing he wanted was this moment to be ruined for him because the crowd looked like a bunch of goddamn Nazis.

"Now look around at your neighbors," Keefer said. "We're all relying on each other here. Make sure every person in your line of sight has a wristband. That no one is hiding their wrist." He waited as the crowd did his bidding. Soon, they fell silent again. There was a minute left.

"Excellent job. You're all to be commended for your efforts and for your service to your country." Keefer was surprised to feel the emotion creep into his voice. He choked up and had to pause before continuing. "These have been dark times for America. We all know that. Our leaders have proven ineffective. The policies of our past have caught up with us. Cities in decline. Crime rampant. Our military disrespected around the world. Other countries have taken up the mantle we once wore so proudly. Superpower." He saw he had thirty seconds. "Super. Power. Remember those words? Those words were our destiny. Those words are who we are meant to be. And through the grace of God and through your sacrifice, we will not only be a superpower once again, but we will be one for eternity."

An uneasy murmur ran through the crowd, but it was too late. The last ten seconds ticked down.

"The world is about to change forever. And, because of all of you, America will reign, now and forever." Keefer saluted the crowd. "God bless you. And may God bless the United States of America."

The clock hit zero.

And the screaming started.

PART THREE

CHAPTER 34

"Oh my God," Cassie said next to him.

They were in the second-floor storeroom above the jail with a clear view of Town Square. Rick pressed his hands against the window and pushed up. As the window opened, the screams filled the room. His mind reeled at the sight playing out in the square below.

The instant the clock hit zero, hundreds of people in the crowd slumped over and fell to the ground. Some were right on the street below the window. Rick watched a man's eyes roll back in his skull until only the white showed. The man tensed for a second and then went completely limp.

Like someone had flipped a switch.

The people that remained standing grabbed at the people on the ground. Some tried to move away from the bodies as if they were contagious.

But then hundreds more fell.

More screaming.

"No ... no ... no ..." Cassie whispered.

More people dropped to the ground. Sprawled out. Lifeless.

Everywhere Rick looked, people fell. Tumbling in waves.

He searched for Dahlia in the chaos. What were the chances she'd listened to him? What were the chances she somehow hadn't had the shot?

People ran in all directions, stepping on bodies. Some of them dropped in mid-stride as if picked off by a sniper. Rick looked up at the roofline. The soldiers stood with their guns pointed up in the air, watching the carnage below.

No guns were needed for this slaughter.

He searched more desperately for Dahlia and Charlie. He raised the rifle and pointed it to where he'd last seen them, using the scope as binoculars. The area by their tent was already littered with bodies. Then, through the thinned-out crowd, Rick spotted them. They were still standing.

"Dahlia!" he cried out, even though it was impossible for them to hear him.

When he shouted, the rifle moved and it took him a second to find them again in the high magnification of the scope. But when he did, he let out a whimper.

Dahlia was on her knees now, her face stretched into a soul-rending scream. Cradled in her arms was Charlie's lifeless body.

"Oh God," Rick said.

As he watched, Dahlia's back arched. Her eyes rolled and she dropped Charlie to the ground. A second later, she fell to her side, her arm draped over her little boy. The protective mother, even in death.

The image jumped as a sob wracked his body. Tears streamed down his face. He looked away to wipe them and saw Cassie crying next to him.

"Why?" she said. "Why are they doing this?"

Rick shook his head to clear it, calling on the soldier in him to take place of the man who'd just watched the woman and little boy he loved die right in front of him.

The screams were dying down. A quick look over the crowd showed why. Only a few hundred people remained on their feet. These remaining people looked shell-shocked, some on their knees crying. Others picked their way through the piles of bodies all around them. Rick saw a man crawling on all fours over the carcasses, looking like an insect. He'd almost made it to the edge of the sea of bodies when he tumbled and landed prone on the ground.

Soon there were only a few dozen left. Then only a handful, ten maybe.

Finally, there was only one man left standing. He was near the stage, toward the center of the square. As he turned slowly in a circle, taking in the sight of two thousand dead people piled all around him, Rick realized who it was.

Old man Roberts.

"He didn't take the vaccine," Rick whispered.

It made sense. If there was anyone in the town who would tell the government to go to hell, it was him.

Rick swung his rifle back to his shoulder and found Roberts in the scope. Whatever fire and defiance had made the old man not take the vaccine was gone. He visibly shook, his mouth opening and closing like a fish gasping in air.

"Look at Keefer," Cassie said. "That son of a bitch."

Rick turned the gun and saw Keefer on the stage. The man looked at the wasteland of bodies in front of him with a blank expression on his face, chin thrust forward, eyes squinting as if he were looking into the sun. Keefer raised a hand in the air and made a slicing motion.

"No," Rick said, looking up from the scope.

A shot rang out and Roberts lurched forward, holding his chest. A second shot sent him flying backward, sprawled out among the other dead.

Rick moved to the side of the window and slumped against the wall, out of view. He closed his eyes, his breath coming in short gasps. Then he punched the wall next to him. Then punched it again. His legs thrashed out, kicking the air. Out of control.

It only lasted a few seconds, the rage taking over his body. But he brought it back in control. He couldn't save them. He couldn't bring them all back. But he could punish the man who'd killed them.

When he opened his eyes, he expected Cassie to be staring at him, but she wasn't. She was looking out the window, frozen.

Rick slid next to her and she startled at his touch, as if she'd forgotten he was in the room. Their eyes met, and somehow she knew what he planned to do. She nodded and he gently nudged her to the side so he had room to set up. He lowered the rifle and steadied himself against the window frame. The distance was only two hundred yards, a simple kill shot as long as the M-1 was even close to being sighted properly.

Rick moved the crosshairs from Keefer's chest to his face and back again, trying to decide how he wanted to see the man leave the world.

Once he took the shot, he and Cassie were as good as dead. He glanced over to Cassie and she nodded. "Kill the bastard."

He slid the safety off and exhaled slowly as he'd been trained to do.

Everything went silent. A calm came over him, a feeling the soldier in him recognized.

Rick made a decision and moved the crosshairs to the man's head. His finger slid to the trigger. Time to end it.

"Wait," Cassie said.

Her voice was so acute and urgent that his body responded to the word involuntarily. His finger moved from the trigger and he sucked in a sharp breath.

"What is it?" he said.

"They're not dead," she said.

"What are you talking about?"

"Look at them," she said. "They're not dead."

Rick aimed the rifle scope down to the street below. He picked a random body and watched. The man's chest heaved up and down.

Rick moved the scope over to a woman. Her mouth opened and she licked her lips.

Quickly, he sought out Dahlia. From the distance, it was harder to tell, but as he watched he thought he saw her rib cage expand and contract.

She was alive. They were all alive.

"Jesus," he whispered. "What is this? What the hell is going on?"

CHAPTER 35

K*eefer watched the helicopter fly* over the Town Square, thick bands of white smoke trailing behind it from canisters locked onto its landing skids. The smoke hung in the air, just as it was designed to do, spreading laterally like oil on top of water. The helo banked hard and made another pass, distributing more of the smoke. Before long, a hazy cloud hung suspended over the town.

In a world of spy satellites, low-altitude unmanned aerial surveillance drones, camera blimps, and geosynched constant cams, it was nearly impossible to do anything in secret. While it was doubtful any of the algorithms designed to analyze the incredible amounts of data collected from the surveillance systems would flag the strange occurrences at the Fall Festival in Resurrection, Colorado, for review by human eyes, Keefer wasn't taking any chances. The smoke might fool the computers, but if a human was involved, there were other settings to use on the cameras to burn through it. If there was one thing the military was good at, it was creating countermeasures to its own weapons.

Even though Keefer was reasonably confident that the smoke screen would deter the cams, the goal was to get the bodies racked and stacked as quickly as possible. There was a contingency plan if they were discovered early, but it got messy in a hurry. Keefer knew a firefight might be inevitable at some point, but he'd prefer to avoid one as long as possible. Better to get underground and out of sight. Once that happened, there was little that could be done to derail the plan. It was all about speed.

He was pleased to see his men snap into action once the last civilian was down. In conversations with the psychologist on the team, he knew this moment could prove tricky for some of them. Most of them only knew the broadest outline of the plan ahead, so seeing so many Americans drop to the ground carried the risk of sowing doubts in a few of them. Team leaders were on the lookout for body language or any comments that might indicate someone losing their religion.

Shooting the old man hadn't been in the plan, but Keefer knew it would help reveal any weakness in their ranks. On one level, killing the man had been a shame. Keefer recognized the gunnery sergeant from his interaction with him earlier. Out of two thousand people, the old man had been the only one to defy the order to get an injection. Keefer liked the man's spunk. In another time, he would have pinned a medal on the man's chest for bravery, and facilitated his travel to Denver to see his granddaughter. But in front of his troops and at this delicate time of the mission, it'd been necessary to reassert his authority and demonstrate to his team that nothing would get in the way of them moving forward. The old gunnery sergeant had served up that opportunity on a platter. And his men hadn't missed a beat afterward. If there were any reservations in the ranks, he hadn't spotted them yet.

The AAVs pulled into the square towing three long flatbed trailers. These were fitted with five layers of horizontal shelving with two feet between layers. Once the AAV had rolled into place, soldiers ran to the sides facing the square and pulled on iron handles, sliding the lowest levels out. The surfaces were segmented into rectangles, six and a half feet long, two feet wide, with six-inch tall edges on them. Each shelf was eight rectangles wide and five rectangles deep.

The unit carried forty bodies per level with five levels, yielding a capacity of two hundred bodies per trailer, six hundred per AAV. Considerable analysis had gone into the math as to whether the AAV's significant towing capacity would be adequate for the weight load, but the machine was built to do the impossible. Pulling three trailers filled with unconscious human bodies up a gravel mountain road flirted with its stated capability limits, but didn't exceed them. Once the trailers were reengineered using a lightweight polymer instead of metal, then the loads plummeted and the conversation turned from whether the AAVs could do it into a question of how fast they could make the journey.

The soldiers, now out of their bulky hazmat suits and wearing only black jumpsuits, moved efficiently in pairs, picking up bodies and carrying them one-by-one to the trailers. People fit easily into six and a half by two foot spaces. In the rare case of someone taller, setting the person on the side with bent knees and a curled spine worked to get them in. The two-foot width was more of an issue.

Keefer walked over to see how the trailers were working. The proper width of the spaces had been debated during the design phase. Going to three feet would have reduced capacity on each trailer by forty percent, but America led the world in obesity and there was a concern that there would be too many bodies outside the design tolerances. Fortunately, the human body, especially those cushioned with extra layers of fat, was extremely malleable. In the testing phase, it was determined that a three-hundred-pound woman could effectively be jammed into the allotted space if turned on her side and forced in. If anything, she would likely have the safest ride up the mountain while the smaller bodies were expected to jostle around as the trailers hit bumps in the gravel road. Keefer was happy to see the bodies fit in just as they'd hoped.

A medic was assigned to each quadrant of the square. As expected, there were minor injuries here and there from people falling, but nothing major. A few cuts and scrapes. A bloody nose or two. The medics cleaned the wounds and applied bandages. If anyone was seriously injured, the plan was to load them into the last trailer. The one set aside for infants.

The little kids posed a problem. Until age five, they served no use to the operation. The psychologist had warned Keefer to tread carefully here. Kids, particularly small babies, tended to give rise to unexpected reactions among soldiers. A Navy SEAL team could decimate a village of civilians without compunction if there was a Jihadi warlord hiding among them. But hand that same SEAL team a newborn infant and tell them to dispose of it and there might be a mutiny. The message was clear. Walk carefully.

For that reason, all babies and small children were loaded on a single designated trailer. This still had six and a half by two foot compartments, but the babies were loaded five or six to a segment. Given injections just as their parents had been, they lay in piles, unmoving. The team psychologist watched this trailer closely, noting which soldiers laid the babies down carefully, supporting their heads and propping them up with the blankets stored on that special trailer. The psychologist also noted the men who tossed the babies in as if they were no more than firewood to be stacked. These were the soldiers who would be tasked with taking the trailer with the kids to an isolated part of the mine and emptying the contents down a shaft. The other members of the team wouldn't ask what happened to them and, if they did, they would be told they were being taken care of. And then they would go on a watch list.

Keefer stood in the center of the square, pleased with the activity swirling around him. The men were focused on the job at hand and sticking to the plan. He was grateful that his own self-doubt, that had consumed his sleepless nights, seemed to have disappeared, perhaps held in check by the adrenaline of the moment. He believed the only real threat to the operation now that they'd gotten this far was someone internally getting cold feet. The men were handpicked by Keefer and Estevez and had demonstrated by their deeds, not their words, that they were willing to do anything to take their country back. Still, none of them knew the true extent of the plan. Once they did, the psychologist predicted ten percent of the men would turn and need to be eliminated.

Keefer put that number at zero.

These were his kind of men. Patriots to the core. He guaranteed that when it did come time to share his plan, it would be greeted with only applause and adulation. The rest of America would have a different reaction at first, but they would come around. They'd have no choice in the matter.

He watched with pride as the soldiers worked efficiently through the square, aided by the AAV dragging the trailers forward slowly to minimize the distance the bodies had to be carried. Once a platform was filled with bodies, a button was pressed and it slid up on hydraulics to the top level as the empty levels moved down to accommodate it. Then an empty shelf slid out from the bottom level. All of it was painstakingly designed to maximize the speed of picking up two thousand bodies.

Twenty minutes after the clock had reached zero, the last body was loaded up. The AAV motors whined at the effort, but they surged forward, pulling the trailers behind them. The helo passed overhead dispensing more of the smokescreen, marking the roads that led out of town and up the mountain. There was one last loose end to tie up. Inspired by seeing his men's single-minded focus, Keefer realized he needed to follow their example. He saw Estevez and waved him over.

"Looking good, right?" Estevez said as he walked over.

Keefer kept his face unreadable. It appeared that Estevez had tangled with someone not long before. His nose was bloodied and swollen like he'd taken a few punches to the face. He didn't have time to ask what had happened. And he didn't care. They were in a crucial phase of the project and Keefer wasn't about to let himself get distracted.

Not only that, but he hated to hear optimism in the middle of an operation. It led to complacency, and complacency led to mistakes. Everything about Estevez's body language indicated he expected a pat on the head for a job well done. Like hell.

"Don't get cocky, son. A lot can happen between here and getting underground," Keefer said, pleased to see the younger man wipe the smile off his face. "What's been done with the sheriff and the woman Morris wanted us to save? Are they still in the jail?"

Estevez looked uncomfortable at the question. "I ... I have my man Jacobs taking care of them."

Keefer interpreted the young man's unease as just his contempt for Keefer worrying about such ancillary concerns during the op. What the man didn't know was that Keefer agreed with him.

"You were right. They're both a needless complication."

Estevez looked off-balance. "What do you want done with them?"

"Have your man kill them," Keefer said. "Morris doesn't need to be coddled like a child. They weren't part of the plan, so let's remove them."

A flash of surprise crossed Estevez's face, and then it was gone. "Yes, sir," he said. "I'll get it done."

"Good," Keefer said as his command truck pulled up and came to a stop in front of him. "Now let's get the hell up this mountain."

He climbed into his truck and indicated for the driver to head out. As they left the town, the AAVs churned their tracks on the gravel roads, heading up to the mine that had given the town its birth.

And which was now to be the site of its death.

CHAPTER 36

"W*hat are we going to* do?" Cassie asked.

Rick watched the AAVs start to roll out of town. Jacobs sat in the corner of the second-floor storage room where they were hiding out. He was bound, gagged and unconscious, but Rick watched him closely. If Jacobs came around, he was prepared to choke him out again. The last thing they needed was their prisoner making any noise while the place was crawling with soldiers. Once the town cleared, he was looking forward to asking Jacobs some questions. Rick had some experience getting answers from people, and he was looking forward to using some of those techniques. He was in the mood to make someone pay for what was going on outside. He wished he had Keefer tied up in front of him, but Jacobs was going to have to do for now.

Still, he worried that Jacobs would be missed and a search for him launched. While the operation outside was efficient, the imperative was obviously on speed. He hoped one soldier would somehow be lost in the shuffle.

The test came sooner that he thought. Through the window he saw Estevez stride toward the jail along with four men, including the soldier with the tattoo covering his face. Rick crossed the room and dragged Jacobs behind a row of boxes, indicating to Cassie to stay with him.

"Stay here," he whispered. "If he starts to wake up, signal me."

Cassie crouched on the floor next to the man's head. "What happens if they come up here?"

Rick shook his head. If the men came up, they were finished. Even if Rick picked a couple of them off, the noise would attract more soldiers. Once that happened, they were as good as dead.

The wooden structure shuddered as the door downstairs was opened and then slammed shut.

"Jacobs," Estevez called out. "Time to go."

Rick slid on his belly across the floor to the door leading downstairs, distributing his weight so the floor didn't creak. Even so, it shifted a little, the tiny noise making Rick freeze. The men were so loud downstairs that he doubted they heard anything. He quickly slid the rest of the way and leaned close to the door to listen. It was opened a couple of inches so he could hear them well enough.

"Jacobs!" Estevez called out.

There was another shift in the old building as the door to the jail cells was thrown open. The voices were muffled now, but he could make out the gist of what they were saying.

"Not here ..."

"... last cell ... isn't even ..."

"... take these assholes ... in the trailer ..."

He looked over to Cassie who peeked up over the boxes at him. She frantically waved her hands as if she'd been trying to get his attention. Once she had it, she pointed down toward Jacobs. Rick couldn't see the man, but the message was clear. He was coming around.

"Want me to go find him?" one of the soldiers downstairs said. Rick thought he recognized voice. The man with the face tattoo.

Rick stiffened. They were back in the main room. He could hear sliding sounds across the floor and he guessed the other soldiers were dragging the bodies out from the first cell. If Jacobs came to, it'd be easy for him to make enough noise to get noticed.

"No time. Besides, believe it or not, Keefer came around and decided those two were a liability. Doesn't matter anymore where Jacobs put the bodies," Estevez said.

The other man laughed. "He probably stashed them outside somewhere, thinking he was all clever and shit. He'll bitch and moan when we tell him he could have just shot them in the head and left them in the jail."

"The lazy bastard probably did it fast then hitched a ride on one of the first trailers to get out of the heavy lifting," Estevez said. "Bet you he's halfway up the mountain by now."

Rick saw Cassie wave at him again. She mouthed the words, *He's waking up*.

Rick pantomimed a chokehold then pointed at Cassie. She looked horrified and shook her head. Just then, they both heard words from downstairs that turned their blood cold.

"Some stairs over there," the tattooed soldier said. "I'm gonna check it out."

"All right," Estevez said. "But make it quick. We're on the clock."

Almost immediately there were sounds of heavy footsteps on the stairs. Rick moved away from the door, pushed behind a stack of boxes, and raised the gun so it faced the door. He looked over to the boxes where Cassie was hidden, hoping she was aware enough to hear the footsteps and stay out of sight.

The door flew open and banged against the back wall. Rick rested his finger on the trigger, tracking the man's movements with the end of the barrel. If Jacobs came to and made a sound, he planned to take the man out. That was as far as his planning went. After that, every path looked bad.

"C'mon, man," a soldier called from downstairs. "Estevez says we're bugging out."

"Just a second," the tattooed man yelled back down.

He stepped into the room, and glanced around, but his stance was casual. Rick couldn't believe it when the man pulled a cigarette from his uniform and lit up, taking long, hard drags from it.

Rick kept the gun trained on the man. It only took one small sound from Jacobs to turn the man's smoke break into a bloodbath.

He held his breath as the soldier blew out a lungful of smoke with a satisfied sigh.

"Estevez says if you're smoking up there, he's gonna kick your ass," the soldier downstairs yelled.

"I'm coming, I'm coming," the man said, taking a final drag, then flicking the butt to the floor. As he turned to the door, there was a scratching sound that came from the other side of the room.

The soldier froze.

His casual stance disappeared and the man crouched down, gun to his shoulder.

The sound came again. A rustle of paper this time.

Rick tracked the man with his gun as he moved across the room.

The soldier inched closer to a pile of boxes near to where Cassie was hidden. He put the barrel of his gun onto the nearest box and waited.

The sound came again and the soldier shoved the boxes to one side. Rick nearly pulled the trigger, but he held off the second he heard the high-pitched squeaks.

Mice scurried out from their hiding spot behind the boxes, running to new safety. The soldier jerked back then chuckled to himself. He pointed his gun at the nearest mouse. "Bang. Got ya, you little bastard."

The door creaked open downstairs. "Let's go," Estevez shouted.

"Coming," the soldier said. He turned and popped a stick of gum in his mouth. As he passed Rick's field of vision, Rick saw that the boxes the man had knocked over had exposed one of Jacobs's boots. If the soldier had simply looked down, he would have seen it.

The man ran down the stairs, and Rick waited in his hiding spot until he heard the soldiers leave the jail. Walking carefully to stay away from the windows, he crossed over to where Cassie was hidden and stepped around the boxes.

She had Jacobs head on her lap, her arm wrapped around his neck. She was sobbing silently, her body shaking. Rick kneeled down and gently removed her arm from the man's neck and held her.

"H-h-he w-w-was going to wake up," she said. "I had to stop him, right?"

He reached down with one hand and felt for a pulse. The man's open, lifeless eyes had already given him his answer.

"Oh my God," she said. "He's dead, isn't he?" She spoke quickly, slamming her words together. "I was so scared I couldn't I couldn't let go I should have let go but I didn't because—"

Rick held her at arms' length. "Because that man would have killed us. You saved our lives."

She nodded and wiped the tears from her face. Slowly, she brought her emotions under control. Finally, after she was able to take a deep breath without shuddering, she looked him right in the eye.

"How are we going to stop them?"

Rick rocked back on his heels. He looked out the window in the direction of the mine. All he could think about was Dahlia and Charlie on those trailers. Along with the entire town. The old ladies from the retirement home. Pete Roscoe. Big Mac and his son Lil' Mac. Bertie. But not old man Roberts though. His body remained slumped over in the middle of the square. The reality was that the old man had just hurried up the inevitable. They were going to die. Every last one of them. He just knew it.

"Rick," Cassie said. "How are we going to stop them?"

All he could do was stare out the window, right at the street where the last trailer had left the square. Mesmerized by the emptiness.

How were they going to stop them?

He wished he had an answer for her. But the truth was that he didn't have a goddamn clue.

CHAPTER 37

K*eefer stood at the mouth* of the mine entrance as the first AAV crossed the fence line and entered the compound. His chest swelled with pride when he saw that someone had affixed a giant American flag atop the vehicle. The plan was actually working.

He'd meant every word on the stage as the clock counted down. The men and women in the trailers, both soldiers and civilians, were true patriots. If he survived the next week, he knew it would mean that events in phase three of the mission had gone perfectly to plan. If he was alive, it meant he would have considerable power at his fingertips, more power than anyone, including the president.

If that were the case, then he intended to award the Presidential Medal of Freedom, the nation's highest civilian honor, to every single person on the trailers. Perhaps he'd even commission a monument. The fact that they were unwitting participants didn't matter. He liked to imagine most of them, if explained the role they were meant to play in the hours ahead, would have volunteered for the job, even knowing that they were to give their lives to the cause.

They were Americans. They loved their country. How many young men had he seen run toward gunfire in the wars fought in other countries for reasons even corrupt politicians could no longer explain? How many fine soldiers had died to take a single village or cave from the enemy? Too many.

This was completely different. This was the salvation of their entire way of life. It was the restoration of the United States as the lone superpower in the world.

How could that not be worth any sacrifice?

The passenger door of the lead AAV opened and Estevez jumped out while the vehicle was still moving. He landed gracefully, reminding Keefer how much younger he was than himself. He just hoped the man's youth continued to be an asset and didn't turn into a liability. He'd hate to have to kill his best friend's son.

As Estevez jogged in his direction, the younger man grinned wildly, clearly in the glow of success. As he walked up, he launched into his near-perfect impersonation of President Mayfield.

"My fellow Americans," Estevez said. "I'm here to tell you today that our forces were victorious on the field of battle. Our country owes them a debt that can never be fully repaid."

Keefer had to admit the voice was pretty good. It'd been enough to fool the people in town earlier that day. It'd been a good test as they intended to use it on the radio once all hell started to break loose.

But once Estevez got close enough, Keefer made a show of looking at his watch.

"Almost two minutes behind," was all he said.

Estevez's smile disappeared as he checked his own watch. What could he say? The time was the time, and the operation was a minute forty-five seconds off schedule.

They both knew that even making it halfway through the plan without being discovered had been a miracle. The odds against actually completing the mission had been so low that talking about the chances of success was a forbidden subject. Bringing the whole thing in with a two-minute margin of error was nearly incomprehensible.

Still, Keefer couldn't resist the temptation to bust the younger man's balls, if only for a second. He put an arm over Estevez's shoulder and pulled him close as the first AAV passed by them. "Your dad would have been proud of you today," he said. "Hell, I'm proud of you."

"The men did well," Estevez said, beaming. "The way you handled the sheriff was perfect."

Keefer pulled his arm back. He wasn't so sure about that. If he had to do it again, he just would have locked the son of a bitch up in the jail and let people think he'd tried to wander off. He'd put too much stock in the need for local leaders to help keep the crowd in check. It was a model from the Jihadi wars, paying off a tribal chief to be the face of whatever mission they needed to conduct among a local population. But this crowd had been Americans. Ready to trust their government and trust their military. The sheriff and Morris's female scientist had been an unnecessary distraction. He should have made the call to remove them earlier.

"They were taken care of?"

"Affirmative," Estevez said. "Took care of it myself."

"Good," Keefer said.

"Morris is going to be pissed."

"I'll deal with Morris. Let's get these AAVs underground and this place buttoned up."

"You got it. See you underground."

Estevez ran up to the next AAV and jumped into the cab.

Keefer watched the parade of trailers for another minute then walked to the mine entrance. Estevez was right, Morris was going to be upset. But the road they were on was going to be paved with the dead, and it was about time Brandon Morris learned to deal with it.

CHAPTER 38

C*assie stood at the front* window looking outside at the abandoned Town Square. The sun had ducked behind the mountains, sending the valley into a weird, shadowy dusk with blue skies still evident above the looming peaks. The smoke screen dispersed by the helicopter had settled into the town, casting the entire scene in a grey veil. As if the abandoned town wasn't creepy enough, the PA system was on, maybe as a joke on the way out by one of the soldiers. *Strawberry Fields* by the Beatles played over tinny speakers, making it all the more surreal.

Debris from the turbulent day cluttered the area. Knocked-over tents rocked up and down in the breeze. Trash stuck in the bushes lining the sidewalks. Birds pecked at the leftover bits of food, unbothered by the sudden disappearance of the population of an entire town.

Cassie was barely keeping herself together. All she wanted to do was run screaming out of the sheriff's station, jump in a car, and drive right through the abandoned town, all the way to a place where there were people. Normal people. Ones who didn't talk about diseases wiping out the world or who stacked people onto trucks like they were no more than firewood. She wanted to find people in charge who could come to Resurrection and get back all the people who'd been drugged and kidnapped. They would set it all right. Put things back the way they were supposed to be.

But Rick had just explained to her why that wasn't going to happen.

"We don't know that they have checkpoints out there," she said. "Maybe they're all up at the mine now. Maybe we would just drive straight through without a problem."

Rick shook his head. "You know I'm right, Cassie. They had to block the roads off so no one new came in while the operation was going on. They used a smokescreen to block satellite images, for God's sake. You don't think they'd block the roads out of town?"

Rick had scared her when they were upstairs. The way he'd withdrawn into himself made her think his hold of reality had finally snapped, that the trauma of seeing everyone he knew and loved hauled out of town had been too much for him. But then he'd come to, suddenly animated because he had a plan.

A ridiculous, insane plan that was going to get them both killed.

"We don't need to use the main roads," Cassie argued. "We use the back roads like you said, only we use them to get as far from here as possible until our cell phones work. Then we call in people that can really help."

Rick shook his head. "The only place those back roads lead is out in the middle of nowhere. Old logging camps, abandoned mines, stuff like that. That's why they won't be watching those. I can tell you for certain there isn't any cell phone reception out there."

"Okay, let's say they do have checkpoints out on the main roads, somehow keeping people out. How long do you think that'll last? I mean, before someone questions it. Questions a communications black-out for a whole town? Even the state police has drones they'd send up here."

"So you want to do what?" Rick said, raising his voice. "Just hunker down here and hope someone comes to the rescue? While all those people up there are getting killed?"

"Getting killed ourselves isn't going to help any of them, Rick. Not Dahlia. Not Charlie. Not any of them," Cassie yelled. "Use your fucking head for once. They're all going to die."

Rick fell silent. Cassie instantly regretted the words. She slouched forward, exhausted.

"I'm sorry," she said. "We don't know what Keefer is planning."

Rick nodded. "No, you're right," he said. "My plan will probably get us killed. But there's a chance, miniscule as it might be, that we can stop them. But I need your help. I wish to God I could tell you to hide in a basement until the cavalry showed up, but I can't do that."

Rick's voice was slow and measured. She could tell he was picking his words carefully.

"I think I can get us into the mine without them knowing. If we can do that, we have options. We can find a phone or radio that connects to the outside world."

"Or a computer station," Cassie whispered.

"Yeah, that's right," Rick said. "Or a computer station. With a computer in your hands, if you had access to their system, you could cripple whatever they had going on."

She nodded. Reluctantly. "Maybe. If we could get in."

"And it's a huge if, I'll give you that," Rick said. "But if we don't take the chance, if we sit here and do nothing, or go try to hide out in the woods, I think we both know all those people are going to die. And, if you buy what Keefer was saying, maybe a whole lot of other people too."

She nodded. Her gut told her what Rick was saying was true.

"You know the mine," Rick said. "You came here because the data trunk was being used."

Cassie saw where he was going. "So they are in the old lab space."

"It makes the most sense. That space is enormous. And I only saw the parts that weren't off-limits when I visited you."

"It's bigger than you think," she acknowledged.

"And if Morris is involved ..."

"... there's likely some kind of Genysis technology they're utilizing."

She felt every muscle in her body coil up. "When I first met Keefer, he said he was a fan of my work. He said my technology would change the world in ways I couldn't even imagine."

"Is it too much of a stretch that whatever he's planning on doing, he's using your work?"

"We don't know that for sure."

"But if he is using your work, don't you want a chance to stop him?"

Cassie shook her head. "Don't do that."

"What?"

"Don't try to guilt me into going with you."

Rick fell silent. He walked to the window and looked up the mountain. Then quietly, he said. "I'm going either way. Because if they all die and I stay here and survive, then it's even worse than getting killed. I've lived with that kind of guilt since the war. I can't do it again. I can't live with myself if I don't at least try to save them."

Cassie closed her eyes, digging through the layers of her fear to try to find some hidden repository of strength. "You really think we can get in?"

"I think we have a shot," Rick said.

She didn't need to open her eyes to imagine the hopeful look on Rick's face.

"And if it doesn't work," he said, "we can come back here and wait it out." He paused then added. "Cassie, I need you. All those people up there need you. I'll do everything in my power to keep us alive. But if we don't do—"

"All right," she said, cutting him off. She opened her eyes, looking past his to the empty square outside. "I'll do it."

As she said the words, fear sliced right through her and curled through her insides. She didn't want Rick to see it, so she mustered what she hoped sounded like a line one of those tough women in the action movies would say.

"I just hope you don't slow me down on the way up there," she said.

He gave her a short chuckle, but it was clearly a courtesy laugh. She wasn't fooling anyone. She was scared shitless and they both knew it.

CHAPTER 39

T*he Blazer bumped over the* rocky terrain, the suspension complaining about the abuse it was getting. Rick sped down the road without any skill or finesse. It didn't matter if the vehicle got a few dents along the way; all he cared was that he didn't push so hard that they got stuck or broke an axle or something. He knew there was a line between being fast and being reckless, and he was erring on reckless.

Rick scanned the way ahead. He didn't think Keefer would have used manpower to have surveillance on this road, but there was a chance they'd dug in a few mines to deter people. Finding one of them would bring their adventure to an abrupt halt.

"How much farther?" Cassie asked. She held on the best she could as the Blazer rocked violently, one hand propped up on the ceiling overhead and the other in a death grip on the door handle.

"Five minutes. Maybe ten. Depending on how bad this road gets."

They were headed to the old alternate entrance to the mine. The secondary entrance was a safety precaution put in place decades earlier after miners were trapped for days underground after cave-ins on the East Coast. It had timed well with the resurgence of labor unions, so mining companies around the country found themselves drilling exits, whether they made logistical sense or not.

The alternate entrance for the Resurrection mine had never been used by anyone other than teenagers looking for trouble as far as Rick knew. In fact, he'd spent more than a few Saturday nights sneaking into tunnels with his friends, all of them with backpacks full of cheap beer, a few of them with bags of weed. On good nights, it was with mixed company. At some point they'd turn the flashlights off to show the girls how dark it was in the mine, a trick they did on the official tours in underground caves. Quite often, the lights didn't come back on for a while. Those were the good old days.

When he first became sheriff, he'd made a couple trips up to the entrance to make sure it was secured. It was a classic case of the older guy looking back on his adolescence and wondering just how in the hell he'd managed to survive. To his adult brain, the thought of teenagers climbing through abandoned mineshafts was ridiculously dangerous. There could be a cave in. Someone could get lost. A girl on the wrong date could find herself pressured to do something she didn't want. If that happened, being in the mine was like being on a different planet. Screaming didn't bring help, it only brought echoes.

Surprisingly, the younger generation seemed to agree with him. From what he could tell, there was little or no interest in crawling around the mine. Whether due to fear, or the desire to plug into first-person shooter games on a video console instead, the idea of exploring the dirty, cobweb-filled mines was no longer the hot ticket in town.

Still, Rick had gone up there and installed a heavy-duty gate on the entrance and some warning signs about motion detectors, video surveillance and all the terrible things that would happen to trespassers. The signs were lies; the town couldn't afford fancy surveillance electronics, but they'd seemed to do the trick. The entrance was left alone.

"Dang," Cassie said as the Blazer bottomed out on a rock. "Let's get there in one piece."

Rick backed off the gas a little. She was right. If the Blazer broke down, it'd take them a half hour to get there over the rough terrain. Not only that, but there was a chance they'd get to the secondary entrance and find that Keefer's men were guarding it or that they'd booby-trapped it somehow. If that happened, they needed the Blazer for a hasty retreat to think up a Plan B.

He had no idea what a Plan B might look like quite yet, but he figured if it came to it, having transportation would likely be essential.

"What do we do if the entrance is blocked off?" Cassie said.

Rick shook his head. "I don't know. We'll think of something."

"Bottom line is that we just need to get in there," she said. Cassie the scared woman was gone now, replaced by Cassie the problem solver. "I've been thinking about what you said. They were using the main data trunk to communicate with the outside world, so whatever their plan is, it has to involve using that transmission point to connect to the external grid."

Rick knew better than to interrupt. He'd seen her like this when they were together, pacing the floor of his living room, talking full speed, dissecting a problem down to its core. Those conversations had been about algorithms and heat exchange issues with microcomputer processing power, all of it a different language to him.

"The massive amount of data in the packets my sensors detected might have been accurate," she said. "Morris had a whole part of the company working on data compression. With advances in AI, the theoretical limiting factor was the transmission ability."

"You think they're creating some kind of artificial intelligence," Rick said. "Why here? Why do they need all those people?"

Cassie shook her head. "No idea. And it's not necessarily an AI, but it's something they need to be able to send huge amounts of data out to the world."

"So if we disable that data trunk, then they are cut off," he said, slowing the Blazer down. "Can we access the data line out here?"

"The data trunk is protected in the same way as NORAD and missile silos. It's burrowed through solid rock. I asked Morris about it once and he said it was to shield it from external radiation. I accepted the answer. I mean, our entire lab was in a mine for the same reason, so it sounded reasonable at the time."

"But really they were protecting it from attack. Once they button that place up, there's no getting at them. It's a full-on military installation."

"Which is why I left the sensors on the data trunk to begin with," she said. "Morris promised he wasn't doing anything with the military beyond the BMI I worked on for prosthetics like your arm."

"BMI?"

"Sorry, brain-machine interface," she said. "Even though the shielding breakthrough made it possible to move our work out of the mine, I begged Morris to leave it open. The lab was set up. It was good for the town. It was good for me. We had a huge falling out over it."

"You never told me that," Rick said.

"You and I were too busy fighting by that point." She waved a hand as if swatting away the memory. "Doesn't matter. The point is, even then I suspected Morris had ulterior motives."

"Oh, I know what his motives were," he said.

Cassie pursed her lips. It was part of the old fight. Brandon Morris the billionaire genius was always the third person in their relationship. Rick used to hate how petty he felt when the man gave Cassie attention, assuming it was for something more than just appreciation of her brilliance. He had never thought of himself as a jealous guy before, but being sized up next to one of the richest men in the world had made him insecure in ways he'd never experienced. The feeling had resulted in some less than stellar moments on his part.

"If it makes you feel better, you were right," she said. "Only a couple of weeks after I relocated to Denver, he tried to start up a relationship. I shut him down, but he never really stopped trying."

Rick couldn't help but feel a little vindication, but he kept his mouth shut. An awkward silence dragged out as the Blazer bumped down the road.

Cassie finally broke the tension. "Go ahead. You can say it."

"What? That I told you the little shit was after you?" Rick said, grinning. "Thought hadn't crossed my mind."

Cassie took the jab with a smile. "Feel better now?"

"Actually, a little bit," he said. It was a needed lighthearted moment, but he steered the conversation back to the matter at hand. "So, you're saying Morris doesn't know about the sensors."

"No, I did it on the down low because I didn't know whom to trust," Cassie said. "No one knows about them. And here's the best part. The sensors are physically attached to the data trunk."

"I thought it was buried through solid rock."

"I discovered the one place to access it," she said. "If we can get to it, that would be our best chance to disable the whole thing."

Rick nailed a pothole in the road and the Blazer jolted hard enough to rattle their teeth.

"Sorry," he said.

"Unless we die out here from your driving first," she said, pulling her seatbelt tighter.

Rick grinned. He enjoyed seeing her spark to the challenge in front of them. He hadn't been sure she was up for what he was asking of her when they were back in town. But now she appeared ready.

"So, we have a plan," he said. "Access the mine through the safety shaft, make our way to the lab level, access and disable the data trunk, then call for help."

"While evading a hundred armed mercenaries led by a madman with a Messiah complex and two thousand civilian hostages," she added

"Sure, when you say it like that ..."

Rick hit the brakes and slid to a stop on the loose gravel road. He pointed to a grey metal door embedded into the mountain wall to their left.

"We're here," he said.

CHAPTER 40

R*ick didn't see any sign* of recent activity in the area. No tire tracks on the road. No footsteps near the door. Seemed good, but didn't mean one of Keefer's men wasn't looking at him through a scope.

"Wait in here," he said.

"I'm coming with you," Cassie said. "That's the whole point of me being here."

He pointed to the mountains around them. "Just let me see if we have anyone waiting for us."

Cassie's expression changed and she looked out the window.

"I don't see anyone."

Rick knew that didn't mean anything. If there was someone watching them, and if the person was even half-decent at their job, then they wouldn't be visible. Rick and Cassie wouldn't know the sniper was there until the moment they took a bullet.

"Just give me a minute. Slide over to the driver's seat when I get out. Just in case."

"Why would I ..." Cassie stopped herself. She was smart and she seemed to grasp what he was doing. He was bait. If he got shot, that meant someone was there.

Rick pulled the M-1 from the backseat and climbed out of the Blazer. As he walked around the front of the vehicle, he imagined he could feel a sniper's crosshairs on his chest, but he knew it was just his imagination. At least he hoped it was.

He scanned the area, using his trained eyes to look for threats. Naturally, he started by checking the spots where he would have set up to cover the entrance. If he'd been tasked with protecting an exposed area like this door, he would have set up at least a hundred yards away. Conceal, wait, and then pick off anyone who showed up from a safe distance.

After sixty seconds, he breathed a little easier. His guess was that during the operational phase of Keefer's mission, the rules of engagement would be to shoot first and ask questions later. The fact that he was still alive meant they'd won the lottery.

If the door was unguarded, there was a good chance Keefer didn't know about it.

He waved to Cassie and she climbed out of the Blazer. She did so tentatively and for good reason. Rick tensed for a few seconds on the chance that any sniper may have just been waiting for both targets to be in the open. But no shots came. They were alone.

"Where does the power source come from to electrify the fence?" Cassie asked.

Rick grinned as he walked to the fence, slinging the M-1 on his shoulder. "There isn't one. I put those signs up to keep the teenagers out."

He was about to reach out for the combination padlock on the fence when Cassie cried out, "Wait!"

He froze. In a combat area, if someone said stop, you stopped. Often it was a tripwire to a booby trap visible only from their angle. Stopping saved your life.

"What is it?" he said.

Cassie pointed to five or six black masses along the base of the fence, each one about the size of a softball. "Are those what I think they are?"

Rick walked over to the nearest one and nudged it with his foot. The charred outer surface broke apart, revealed brittle bones inside.

They were birds and a couple of small animals. Burnt to a crisp.

"No power source, huh?" Cassie said.

Rick swallowed hard, remembering the voltage going through the fence line up at the main entrance to the mine. He reached into his pocket and pulled out a penny. He tossed it at the fence, but it passed through one of the holes in the chain link, not touching anything.

Cassie shot him a look. "Really?"

She picked up a rock the size of her fist and threw it at the fence. The rock blew back at them in a cascade of sparks, pelting them with shrapnel.

"Holy shit," she said, slowly looking up.

"That would have been me," Rick said. "You saved my ass. Thanks."

"Get me out of this little adventure alive and we'll call it even."

Rick knew she meant it as a joke, something to break the tension, but he couldn't bring himself to smile. Her words only emphasized what an impossible task lay ahead of him. If he was being honest, their chance of success was rapidly trending toward zero. Seeing that her joke missed the mark, she changed directions.

"Okay, so now we know this thing is protected by the electrified fence from hell," she said. "What do we do about it?"

"You're the scientist," he said. "Can we short it somehow?"

Cassie looked around the area, taking stock of her available tools. Her eyes came to rest on the Blazer. "Not eloquent, but it'll get the job done."

A couple minutes later, following Cassie's plan, Rick opened the Blazer's door and jumped out. The vehicle was only going twenty miles per hour, but jumping out of a moving car at any speed didn't feel good, especially on the rocky ground. He tucked his shoulder and rolled, popping up onto his feet just in time to see the Blazer barrel through the fence.

Rick shielded his eyes against the explosion of sparks. The fence collapsed, twisting and turning as it wrapped around the Blazer's front and tore away from the anchors drilled into the rock face. The vehicle bumped down a rocky slope, dragging the fence with it. It was twenty yards away before it thumped into a sheer rock face in a slow-motion crash, crunching the bumper and popping one of the headlights.

The best part was that the power cable coming from inside the tunnel had torn the door off one hinge when the Blazer pulled it free. They had their way in.

Cassie looked satisfied. "See, I told you it'd work."

Rick pointed to the heavy cable twisting on the ground like an angry snake, the end sparking. "Hopefully they didn't electrify the door too." He hefted a large rock from the ground, walked carefully over to the power line and dropped the rock on it to pin it down.

Cassie bent over and picked up Rick's penny from the dirt. She tossed it at the door and it bounced off harmlessly with a quiet *ting*.

"Works better when there aren't any holes for it to go through," she said. "See how that works?"

"Were you this snarky when we were together?"

"You used to think I was witty."

"No, not really," he said, pulling a flashlight out of the Sheriff's Department duffel bag he'd taken out of the Blazer. "I'm pretty sure you were the only one who thought that."

He tossed her a flashlight and took a second one for himself. He checked the contents of the duffel to see what was worth bringing. He kept the roadside flares and first-aid kit, but tossed the spare ticket book and the two reflective road hazard signs. He didn't think writing Keefer a speeding ticket would have much of an impact. As far as the hazard signs went, there was no one left to warn.

He flipped on the flashlight and was happy to see that the batteries looked strong. He wasn't sure the last time they'd been changed. Cassie did the same and hers looked good too. Perfect. The last thing they needed was to get stuck in the labyrinth of tunnels with no lights.

"Turn yours off to save the batteries," he said. "We'll use one at a time so we have redundancy. Here's a knife." He tossed her a closed blade from the bag. He nodded to the handgun she had stuck in the beltline of her jeans. "Make sure that safety's on."

She pulled it out, checked, and then put it back. "Do you know how to get to the lab level from this entrance?"

Rick slung both the rifle and the duffel over his shoulder. "This was designed as an emergency exit. My memory is that there are signs with arrows marking the way. If we find the signs and go the opposite way, it should get us to the right general area."

She nodded. "That'll at least get us to the main trunk. As long as they didn't remove the signs or mess with them. You know, point them in the wrong directions to get people lost on purpose."

Rick thought about it. If Keefer really wanted to take care of anyone who got through the electric fence, he wouldn't do it by playing games with the exit signs.

He pulled back on the metal door. The broken hinge made it possible to lift one edge enough for them to slide through. "Hold this open," he said. "Let me go through first."

"Why?" Cassie asked. "There's no one in there. If there was, we'd know it by now. I can handle myself."

"Suit yourself." Keefer would have known that electric fence wasn't going to keep out any serious infiltration force. Rick doubted it was the only countermeasure in place. "Go ahead. Just keep an eye out for landmines and explosives."

Cassie stopped, shining her flashlight toward the mineshaft opening. She waved Rick aside and took his spot pulling back on the door.

"How about you leave the snarkiness to me?" she said.

Rick grinned and got low to the ground, exploring the path ahead with his flashlight as he crawled under the door and into the mine.

"And here I thought I was just being witty."

CHAPTER 41

K*eefer stood in his command* center, a large rectangular room that was a remnant of the old Genysis lab that had once been there. There were three rows of workstations facing a wall of television screens. Although there was only one tech in the room controlling everything, each work station still had a desktop that showed additional images from around the installation.

Keefer's eyes roamed over the screens. One showed the elevator landing and the most recent trailers being unloaded, his men moving bodies from the staging area to the main cavern. The mess hall and supply center were on two screens next to one another but in the wrong order to match their actual proximity to each other. It was a small thing, but he knew small things sometimes made all the difference. It annoyed him to see someone walk off the right side of the screen and then have to look at the monitor to the left to see the man appear on the left edge. He walked up and tapped a technician on the shoulder.

"Switch monitors 36 and 37," he said.

The soldier nodded, but didn't otherwise move. There was a keyboard and other physical inputs on the workstation, but those were secondary systems. A metal band fit over the soldier's head, and his hair was shaved down to smooth skin to ensure the best contact possible. Keefer knew the man's brainwaves were all that were needed to manipulate the system, the same way modern aircraft no longer needed a joystick controller, or that unmanned drones needed a visual readout display. Everything happened within the Genysis brain machine interface. It was how Brandon Morris had changed the world. Taking the idea to its inevitable conclusion was how Keefer would make the transformation complete.

As he watched the screens, images 36 and 37 switched locations, all because the soldier had thought the change.

"Adjustment completed, sir," the soldier said, his voice flat and lifeless as was common when someone was plugged into a large computer system. Scientists couldn't quite explain the phenomenon but the guess was that the brain-machine link seized up the speech centers of the brain. There seemed to be no harm in it, and it didn't show up in smaller systems like those used with artificial limbs used by so many veterans, so they left it alone.

"Bring up 77," Keefer said.

Instantly, all the TVs in the front worked together to form a larger view of the work crew sealing the main entrance shut from the inside, welding the iron blast doors with plasma burners.

He was glad to see their work was almost done. Once this thing started, he didn't want anyone being able to shut him down, not even the US military.

He didn't like to imagine the scenario where he was forced to fight against his own government, but he knew it might come to that. The corruption that plagued his country was a virus and it nested in the bowels of every institution, even within the military he loved so much.

Dishonorable men walked the halls of the Pentagon, men who'd forgotten what it was like to fight and bleed next to their brother-in-arms. Men who'd sold out to the interests of the military-industrial complex that profited from the wars. They were greedy, self-centered and short-sighted. Worse, they were too stupid to understand that the national decline, the very march to oblivion they were abetting with the politicians and the bureaucrats, would eventually eat them alive along with everyone else.

Not on his watch. He planned to right the ship. And when he did, he'd cast the rats into the boiling sea and watch them burn. No matter how many stars they wore on their shoulders.

His eyes darted from one image to the next on the television monitors, giving him a feeling of being everywhere simultaneously. It was only a small preview of what he expected at the culmination of the mission. No, not a mission, not anymore. The word wasn't sufficient.

This was a goddamn crusade. In the most literal and non-politically correct form of the word.

He wasn't a religious man; he'd seen enough in the world to know there was no benevolent being sitting on a throne in heaven, radiating an aura of love and goodness. If there was, then the son of a bitch either had a cruel sense of humor or He was totally oblivious to the pain and suffering of His people. Neither interpretation matched up with the teaching in the scripture or in the church house, so he'd decided long ago that it was all bunk.

His religion was America. His gospel, the Constitution. His saints were named Jefferson, Adams, Hamilton, Madison and Washington. The oath he'd taken as an officer in the United States Army was his liturgy.

I will support and defend the Constitution of the United States against all enemies, foreign and domestic.

The founders had foreseen the times in which he now lived. A time when the outside world was filled with existential threats to the nation while domestic threats fractured her from within. They had been wise enough to make the men who answered their nation's call to service promise to be on the lookout for both threats, and pledge to take action when it was necessary.

He stood in awe of the founding fathers. All of them risked everything to launch the greatest country in the world's history. All of them certain to hang if the uprising failed. And even after the defeat of the British, the fledgling country had clung to its existence by only its fingernails, with a single bad decision capable of torpedoing the grand experiment of self-government. Those men would have recognized his circumstances, and he was certain they would have condoned the action he intended to take. More than condone it, they would have demanded it.

The work detail at the entrance appeared to have finished their assignment. As they pulled their equipment back, stacking their tools on the work truck, he had a better view of their finished product. It wasn't pretty, but then it didn't need to be. A twelve-inch-thick metal plate was held in place by giant bolts in the rock, welded into place and then supported with a crossing lattice of heavy bars. He knew this was the fifth such plate installed. If someone was going to get into the mine, it would be easier for them to dig through the solid rock than penetrate through the entrance.

The only real challenge was the thermobaric munitions, commonly called the bunker busters for their ability to get through rock and destroy a hardened target. But if the military was able to strike, it meant that Keefer's plan had failed. In that case, and if they figured out what he was trying to do, he was sure the bunker buster bombs would rain down on them for hours regardless of how many of the civilians were still alive. While the explosions wouldn't touch them fifty stories underground, they would seal off the upper levels and probably melt the metal plates his men had just installed.

At that point, the mine's emergency exit was their only viable escape route. And if that failed, if he had to blow that tunnel to block an attack, then they had the provisions to last over two years underground. If things went really against plan, they had the ability to grow food and could remain in the mine indefinitely until he came up with an alternative plan.

"Back to 36 and 37," he said.

The screen showed the mess hall, supply center and the living quarters for the ninety-five soldiers under his command. The living quarters was a warren of cubed sleeping berths. The plan was for them to be down there no longer than a month, so there was not much in the way of creature comforts. These were men used to living in the rubble of burned-out cities for weeks at a time, so the facilities were like staying at a resort. If their stay underground had to be extended, there was a plan to give each man a larger space, but until then they just had a bunk and a locker for clothes and minimal personal effects.

"Scan complex," he said.

Immediately, the screens flipped images in rapid succession. So fast that it was hard for him to pick anything out in detail. It didn't matter because the technician with the brain machine interface was seeing everything perfectly. Analyzing it, storing images for archival retrieval.

Brain machine technology was ubiquitous enough that it was easy to forget how amazing the feat truly was. The same way climbing into a tube made up of several tons of metal and then soaring into the sky to fly great distances had gone from being fantasy to just mundane travel over the course of the twentieth century. But in both cases, a few moments of reflection was all it took to feel a sense of awe at what humans had developed when cooperation, incentive and scientific ingenuity were allowed to flourish.

And then in the next few moments, after one admired mankind's progress, the dark reality of his baser instincts came into focus. What did man do with the power of flight? Yes, he'd gone to the moon and to Mars, but he'd first made machines of war, delivery systems of destruction and death. And what had man done with the brain-machine interface? First adopters were in the pornography industry, promising unparalleled sexual experiences with AI robots plugged into their partner's every whim. *Think it, have it*, as the commercials promised. Then the military got into the mix. Better killing machines. More drone warfare. Internal mics. Retinal head-up displays. All of it designed to fight the next great war.

Only the Jihadis hadn't gotten the message that war was more sophisticated now. They used time-honored techniques to achieve their goals. Brigades of zealots willing to execute entire villages. Dirty bombs of low-grade radioactive material set off in population centers. Dispersions of anthrax, weaponized Ebola and designer viruses that had names like the Plague of Allah or Fallujah's Revenge. So many sleeper cells that there seemed to be a lone gunman for every special occasion. America's malls were turned into bloodbaths. Graduations, weddings, even the funerals of returning soldiers, were all targeted. Sporting events were a security nightmare. So much so that baseball and football games were being played in empty stadiums, with fans safely watching the game at home. No one wanted to admit the terrorists had won, but they also weren't willing to be the next victim in a mass shooting or bio attack.

The Jihadis knew they were winning because they saw America fleeing back to her shores and withdrawing from the world. The Chinese and the Indians, two and a half billion people, saw the same thing and landed body blow after body blow on America in her retreat. Before long, the international financial system was in ruins, the dollar discredited as an international currency. Protectionism ground trade to a halt. Territorial challenges were ignored and the bigger countries swallowed the weak, with China spreading throughout Southeast Asia.

America was an eagle that had willingly crawled back into its cage and forgotten how to fly. Keefer planned to fix all of that. When he was done, the American eagle would fly higher than it ever had before. More than that, he planned to guarantee she had the skies completely to herself for decades to come. Perhaps centuries.

He watched the monitors as dozens of bodies at a time were wheeled into the main cavern for processing and to be put into their places. He glanced at the mission clock, impatient for the new age he was about to usher in to become a reality. They were so close, he could almost touch it. Nothing would stop him now.

"Sir, there's a power surge in the secondary exit shaft," the soldier at the command center said.

Keefer felt his chest tighten. Could it be a special forces infiltration? Had word leaked somehow and they were here to stop him?

"Bring it up on video," he said.

"Video feed non-functional," the tech said. Keefer thought he heard a strain of nervousness pierce the man's monotone speech. "The power surge must have taken some of the systems off-line."

Keefer didn't like the sound of that. A trained infil team would take out the cameras and, given time, they would disarm the explosives in the tunnel. But the exit was their way out. He was reluctant to order it sealed without more information.

"Analysis?" he asked.

"Impossible to determine the cause of the surge," the tech said. Keefer found the man's flat voice suddenly grating on his nerves. "Possibilities include a rock slide damaging the fence outside the door. A large animal running into the fence. An enemy force penetrating our defenses. An installation defect. A missing—"

"Enough," Keefer said. He knew the list of possible causes could theoretically continue for hours if he let it as the computer generated all possible scenarios and fed them to the technician. It wasn't enough information to blow the tunnel.

"Should I retask a work detail to go investigate?" the tech asked.

Keefer glanced at the monitors. Every screen showed the finely orchestrated ballet designed to get the mission operational as soon as possible. Pulling a team out of the workflow would lead to inefficiencies and eventually jam up the process. That was a high price to pay if the surge was caused by a deer running into his fence.

"Send surveillance drones to check it out," he said. He suddenly had a mental image of a team of Navy SEALs cutting through the explosives planted into the ceiling of the tunnel. "Send the armed drones," he added. "Just in case."

"Monitors 5, 6 and 7," the man said.

Keefer's eyes darted up to the correct screens. It was video feed from the point of view of three drones on the ground, relaying images of the staging area where hundreds of bodies were piled, waiting to be put into place. The image shifted as the drones rose from the ground, wobbling a little as the rotors spun up to full speed. The soldiers paid them little mind; drones hovering everywhere were a fact of life.

The three drones moved forward, flying through the staging area, each of their cameras sending the same image from a slightly different angle.

"How long to get to the area?" Keefer asked.

"Four minutes," the technician said.

Keefer crossed his arms and watched the sides of the tunnels whip past on the video feeds as the drones flew through the air. He wasn't going anywhere until he saw for himself what was going on at the exit tunnel. He was impatient, but he'd waited years to make this mission come together. He could last four minutes to see whether there was someone coming to try to stop him.

Because if there was, he intended to press the kill button himself.

CHAPTER 42

R*ick shined the flashlight over* the back of the door, half expecting to see it rigged with explosives. It appeared to be clean. He turned his attention to the ground around him, happy to discover it was solid rock as far as the light extended into the tunnel. Rock was easy. Hard was walking around an entire country covered in sand and was filled with people who liked to bury bombs.

He spotted a small metal box mounted on the ceiling of the tunnel. He turned the light on it and froze. It was a camera staring right at him.

"Oh shit," he breathed.

But then he noticed the light reflecting at an odd angle and he stepped in for a closer look. The camera lens was shattered, tiny shards of glass littering the floor beneath it. A black mark on the side of the plastic housing gave him a clue as to what had happened.

"What is it?" Cassie called from outside.

"No booby traps that I can see. There's a camera, but looks like it got fried."

"I'm coming in," she said.

He pushed out on the door from the inside to create a gap as Cassie slid underneath it. She stood up and inspected the area just as he had.

"No boogeymen?" she asked. Her voice sounded steady, cocky even. But Rick aimed the flashlight at her hands and saw them shaking.

"Not yet," he said. "But chances are they know something's going on down here."

"Then we should get going," she said, walking into the tunnel.

Rick grabbed her shoulder and stopped her. "You don't have to do this whole macho thing, all right?"

"What are you—"

"Being reckless doesn't make you less scared. It just gets you dead quicker."

Cassie took a deep breath, the exhale rattling as if she were shivering from cold. She nodded.

"Okay," he said. "Here's what we're going to do. We run at half-speed. I go first. I know what to look for. The good news is that the ground's solid. The walls are solid. So it's hard for them to hide anything too easily." Fishing line tripwire and a small directional explosive would be easy enough to hide, but he didn't feel any need to worry her. "I don't think they would want to risk a cave-in unless they chose to do it on purpose. So if I make a mistake, if I do hit something, it's probably going to be small. You stay behind me. Step where I've already stepped, and you'll be fine."

"And if you set something off?"

"Then you'll have one less booby trap to worry about," Rick said. "Let's go."

Rick walked past her, scanning the ground and walls for wires or sensors. He knew it would have been simple for them to install dozens of explosive devices within the rock walls, using sensors the size of a shirt button as a trigger. He felt naked without the sophisticated countermeasures he'd had at his disposal in the military. He would have paid top dollar to have his old robo-drone flying next to him, scanning for dangers, and a frequency jammer in his backpack to disrupt all wireless signals from sensors to bombs. But now it was just him. Flesh, blood and bone, relying on a flashlight and his aging eyes to keep him alive.

But as he started to run, he used the old trick he'd learned during the war. He cleared his mind of the mission and instead thought about why he was on the mission. Back then, he'd used a single moment in his life as his why, a day so perfect that it'd become a touchstone for him his entire adult life.

It was a little league baseball game when he was twelve, right at the park downtown. There was nothing spectacular about it; he didn't even remember whether his team won or not. But he remembered the smells. Hot dogs on the grill. Cut grass. The clay mix of the infield on his hands. The oil on his leather glove. He could hear his parents cheering. In his mind he could see his buddies in their uniforms, shirts tucked in, cleats ready to dig hard on the base path. Mr. Franklin, the math teacher, was transformed into a true-life umpire with an outfit just like they wore on TV. He felt the easy cadence of the game. The peace that there was nowhere else to be and no reason to hurry. A perfect day. And exactly the reminder he'd needed during the war that he wasn't fighting to kill Jihadis, he wasn't avenging the brothers he'd seen killed next to him, he was fighting for some other twelve-year-old back at home having that same kind of day.

Some of those same images floated through his head as he ran, but he couldn't lock on them the way he used to. They danced around, interrupted with horrific imaginings of shrapnel blowing his body apart. Or claustrophobia brought on by the walls of the tunnel pressing in on him from all sides, the oppressive darkness pushing against the feeble beam of light from his flashlight.

Then an image of Charlie came to him. And then of Dahlia. He was walking through Town Square with her, so close they were touching. Charlie was ahead of them, laughing as he chased squirrels, having a perfect day of his own.

They were his why now. And they were somewhere inside the mountain, taken there for God knew what purpose. It was up to him to find them and get them the hell out of there.

He realized he was no longer jogging, but was at a full run. He pushed himself faster, hardly looking for the traps. They were either there or they weren't. Even at half-speed, he doubted he'd catch it in time if he did hit one, so what was the point.

"Rick, slow down," Cassie called from behind him.

But he didn't slow down. He wasn't sure he could if he tried. Something inside of him had broken open. All the stress and the anguish of the past couple of hours were pouring out of him as he sprinted down the tunnel. Harder and harder. Panting from the exertion. The image of Charlie and Dahlia messed with his mind as it fluctuated between the scene in the square and the worst, most depraved tortures he could imagine, with Keefer holding a knife or a saw or a hammer, and Dahlia and Charlie screaming in pain.

He had to reach them. He had to save them.

He dug deep and ran faster.

So fast that by the time he noticed the three red blinking lights streaking toward him from the darkness, it was too late to do anything about it.

CHAPTER 43

K*eefer walked up to the* wall of TV displays now filled with a larger than life image of Rick Johnson. "I'll be goddamned," Keefer whispered. "You are a resilient son of a bitch, aren't you?"

"Remove your weapon," the soldier said into a microphone.

On the screen, Rick flinched, obviously hearing the soldier's voice.

"These are semi-autonomous armed drones," the soldier said in his flat tone. "They are programmed to interpret an aggressive movement as a threat. Sudden movement on your part may result in immediate injury or death." The soldier cocked his head toward Keefer. "Shall I terminate the target, sir?"

"No," Keefer said. "Remove auto-response features."

"Request confirmation of order to remove auto-response features."

Keefer narrowed his eyes. The request to confirm felt dangerously close to challenging the order. But the man's dispassionate voice made him view the interaction as just programming, as if he was talking to a computer and not a human. He wondered what the difference really was anymore. On the screen, Rick lowered his rifle to the ground. An M-1. That meant one of his men was missing. That meant that either Estevez didn't know one of his men was MIA, or that he knew and was keeping it from him. Either was unacceptable.

Keefer looked closely at the man on the screen. This was the kind of soldier he needed to win over to his cause if a new America was to be built. The thought gave him an idea. "Order confirmed."

"Auto-response features disabled."

"Patch me into audio," Keefer said. "And summon Major Estevez to the control room."

There was a slight pause and then the technician said, "Go ahead, sir. You're live."

"Rick? This is Keefer."

Rick's expression had gone from shock to fear, but hearing Keefer's voice changed it immediately to anger.

"Keefer, why don't you come down here so we can talk."

The drones circled him, giving Keefer a view from three different angles and painting Rick with their spotlights.

"I thought you were dead. Glad to see you made it," Keefer said.

All three screens showed images of Rick's middle fingers.

Keefer chuckled. "Goddamn Marines," he said to himself.

"What the hell is this?" Estevez said behind him.

Keefer waved the man forward and gave the tech a slicing motion to cut off the audio. "You told me this guy was dead. That you took care of it yourself."

"I ...I didn't ... I assigned one of my men."

"Did you confirm with your man that the job was done?" Keefer asked. "Did he lie to you?"

"I … I don't …"

"I … I don't …" Keefer mimicked. "Are all your men accounted for?"

Estevez was about to snap an answer. If Keefer was a betting man, and he was, he would have paid good money that he was about to answer in the affirmative. But at least Estevez wasn't an idiot. He spotted the M-1 on the ground next to Rick.

"No one's been reported missing," he said.

"But there was a complete roster call before we locked up?"

Keefer knew there couldn't have been, otherwise Estevez would already know someone was missing. Still, he wanted his young officer to feel some pain from his mistake.

"No one was unaccounted for."

"*Raise your hand if you're not here.* Is that how it went down?"

Estevez glanced at the technician. Dressing down the second-in-command in front of one of the enlisted men was tough medicine, but Keefer didn't do anything by accident. Word would get out that Estevez had blown a basic operational doctrine, leave no man behind, and as a result had put the entire operation at risk. Keefer knew that Estevez was popular with the younger men, many of whom had served under him in combat, and Keefer would need bad facts like this piled up against Estevez if he wanted to make a change later.

"I'll do a full count right away."

"Sir, the subject is running."

Keefer and Estevez looked at the screen. Two images were from behind Rick, one high and one low. The third image was in front of him, the drone flying backward and maintaining a ten-foot distance. Rick's face strained with the effort, his eyes bulging and teeth bared as he sprinted forward.

"Did he know we turned off the semi-auto functions?" Keefer asked.

"No, sir."

"Why did you do that?" Estevez said.

Keefer spun around on Estevez, his right hand involuntarily curled into a fist. The man noticed it but didn't take a step back. Yes, this one was going to be trouble.

"We're supposed to change the course of human history two hours from now," Keefer said. "Why don't you go see if you can count to ninety-five and see how many men you're missing?"

Estevez didn't move. Their eyes were locked. Keefer became suddenly aware that there were only three people in the room. Him, Estevez and the tech. And he realized he didn't know the tech that well, which meant he was one of Estevez's men.

Maybe his second-in-command had somehow manufactured this moment to be alone with him. If so, it'd been a long time coming, but Keefer was angry at himself that he'd allowed Estevez to beat him to the punch.

The tech didn't move. The only sounds in the room came from the drones' audio feed filling air with Rick's ragged breathing as he ran for his life.

"Was there something else?" Keefer asked.

The two real questions were left unsaid, but both men knew what they were.

How bad did the younger man want the throne? And did he have the balls to make his move?

Estevez glanced at the screens then back at Keefer. By the younger man's expression, Keefer judged there was no doubt about the answer to the first question. When he turned heel and marched out of the room, the second question was also answered.

Keefer was relieved to have survived his own mistake of being alone and unarmed. From that point on, he would have his personal guard stationed with him, or at least drones keyed off his voice command. It'd been a nervous moment, but now he felt strangely relieved. Not because the younger man hadn't made his move, but because Keefer had been struggling with what to do about young Estevez. This last interaction proved he had no choice but to remove him. He just needed to be smart about when and how he did it.

A cry from the speakers shook Keefer from his thoughts. He looked up at the screens and saw Rick sprawled on the ground.

"What happened?" he asked the tech.

"He just tripped."

Keefer walked closer to the technician. "Notify Walker, Palmer and Chan to report here. Armed."

Seconds later, without speaking or moving, the technician nodded. "They're en route."

"Audio," Keefer said. The technician nodded. "Rick, what do you think you're doing?"

"Coming to kill you," Rick said, his voice booming in the room.

Keefer laughed. Despite everything, he was starting to like this Marine.

"You can kill me later," he said. "Catch your breath for a second."

Rick pulled himself to his feet. He looked like hell in the harsh light of the drones. He continued to walk up the mineshaft, noticeably limping.

"Where's Dr. Baker?" he asked.

"She's dead," Rick said, spitting at the drone nearest him. "One of your men, Jacobs, tried to rape her. Let's just say he didn't get to finish. Real classy group you've got here, Keefer."

Keefer searched the screens to try to catch any trace that Rick was lying. As much as he hated to admit it, the story was believable. These men, especially the ones brought in by Estevez, were hardened by years living outside of moral and ethical constraints. Rape was treated as a minor disciplinary issue by good officers, and actually encouraged as an unofficial weapon of war by bad ones.

If true, it explained away a lot of things. He imagined Jacobs got a good look at the doctor and figured a little stress relief wouldn't hurt anyone. If Estevez had sent him by himself to do the job, he would have told his buddies he'd meet them back at the mine. But when he opened the jail and tried to have his quick fun, he ran into Sheriff Superhero who ate his lunch.

"Then Jacobs got what he deserved," Keefer said. "We can't change what happened, but I'm glad you're here. I'm glad you're alive."

"Really? Why's that? A whole town isn't enough for you to kill?"

"Follow the drones and my men will meet you," Keefer said, getting more excited by his idea. "The drones are armed with both lethal and nonlethal munitions, so don't be a pain in the ass about it. They'll just Taser you and hit you with rubber bullets until you move."

"Where am I going?" Rick asked.

Keefer leaned into the mic. "After today, I'll need men like you to join me. The masses will get on my side. People will always follow strong leadership that understands their fears and makes them go away. But it's people like you that I really need to convince. You're going to be my test subject. I want you to understand what we're doing here, really see what the future can look like. I think once you know the truth, you'll decide to join us."

Rick stared into one of the drone cameras. The tech zoomed in on Rick's face. "You're out of your fucking mind," Rick said. "That'll never happen."

"Never say never," Keefer said. "Especially when I can give you what you want more than anything." He paused, waiting for Rick to connect the dots. The sheriff's expression slowly changed as he put together what was being implied.

"Yes," Keefer said. "Dahlia and little Charlie. They're here and they're safe. And if you join me, their lives will be spared."

CHAPTER 44

C*assie crouched to the side* of the wall as the three lights retreated down the tunnel, following Rick. They winked out suddenly and she worried that meant they'd finished their job and were returning to their base. But her dark-adjusted eyes picked out of a soft glow in the distance and she figured that the drones had just made a turn.

She didn't dare turn on a flashlight, so she jogged forward with her left hand trailing on the wall and her right hand clutching the handgun Rick had given her.

Not that she thought it would be too much use if a drone came looking for her. For some reason, they didn't come down her direction. Rick's two manic sprints down the tunnel had saved her. The first had given her time to hit the tunnel floor as soon as the drone lights turned on. The second had put even more distance between them and drawn the drones away.

She'd stayed on the floor and not moved the entire time, feeling like her breathing and her heartbeat were so loud that they echoed through the tunnel, certain to reveal her location. But the longer the drones stayed on Rick, the more she allowed herself hope that she'd avoid detection. Once Rick took off the second time, she scrambled to her feet and followed, keeping what she hoped was a safe distance behind.

She'd strained to hear the conversation between Rick and Keefer, but she only caught bits and pieces.

But she clearly heard the only two words that mattered in the conversation.

Dahlia. Charlie.

Keefer knew who they were and he had them. She didn't need any heart-to-heart conversation with Rick to know how much he cared for the two of them. She'd seen his face as the entire town succumbed to the time-released drug. She'd heard him cry out their names in a wail so pained that it'd brought tears to her eyes. Part of her had ached at seeing him love another woman that way, but she'd tried to ignore the complicated mix of guilt and jealousy that slowly burned inside her. It made her feel petty and she hated it, especially since Dahlia and her little boy were in such danger.

She knew a thing or two about how hard it was for Rick to allow himself to love someone. Once he did, he'd do anything for them.

She just hoped that Keefer didn't leverage Dahlia and her son to the point where Rick had to choose between them and revealing that she was in the mine. She was under no misconception what his decision would be.

Cassie stopped and stood in the dark tunnel. Her hand, which had been on the wall to keep her bearings, suddenly supported most of her weight. She was breathing hard from the run, but it was more than that. She felt like she was suffocating. Her heart pounded so hard she thought it might explode.

She clutched her chest, gasping for air, trying to remember all the symptoms of a heart attack. The rational part of her brain tried to reassert itself, calling the reaction for what it was, a textbook example of a panic attack. That realization brought a little comfort that she wasn't about to drop dead on the floor in cardiac arrest, but she still couldn't catch her breath, and her body shook from the overload of adrenaline.

With Rick captured, it fell onto Cassie's shoulders to keep moving forward and figure out how to stop whatever madness Keefer had planned. But she'd thought the task ahead of them was nearly impossible when she and Rick were working together. By herself? It was absolutely suicide.

She felt her resolve give out. What would it accomplish to throw her life away? All the people in the mine would still die. Keefer would be left unchecked. The only difference between her following the drones down the tunnel and turning around and running back to the exit was in one scenario she was dead and in the other she was alive.

Maybe filled with guilt, but alive.

Cassie turned and faced the exit. She could be out of the tunnel in five minutes. Then she could try to salvage the Blazer. If it was too wrapped in the fencing, she would just hike into the woods. Work her way back toward the town where she could hide out in one of the houses on the outskirts. Just wait it out.

She took a few steps toward the exit. The decision felt good. She started to walk and she felt almost giddy with the decision. It felt so right. She wouldn't needlessly throw her life away. Maybe she could find a radio or something to warn people. If there was even the slightest chance of her being able to stop Keefer, then she would try. But it wasn't possible. Not by herself.

Then again, she'd heard Rick tell Keefer that she was dead. The fact that the drones weren't tasked with a thorough search of the tunnel all the way back to the entrance indicated he believed the lie. Being dead had its benefits. It meant they wouldn't be looking for her so she could escape the tunnel more easily. But it also meant that she had the element of surprise if she continued toward the lab.

With surprise on her side, and if the soldiers were in the same kind of frenzied activity as she'd seen in the town, then maybe ... just maybe ...

She stopped again, hands clenched at her side. A wave of guilt washed over her and she shuddered. She closed her eyes and pictured the hundreds of people lying motionless in Town Square. She saw the trailer where the soldiers had put all the little kids, babies even, dozens of them. If she walked out of the mine, she knew those faces would be there every time she closed her eyes for the rest of her life.

She thought of Rick. If the roles were reversed, would he hesitate to go forward? To try, no matter how small the chance was for success? He'd run up the tunnel to draw the drones away from her. Rick had given her a chance and there she was ready to squander it.

As in so many stressful times in her life, it was her father's voice that came to her. Clarence Baker had been a physics professor at MIT, a giant in his field. He'd nurtured his daughter's own genius, careful to push rather than shove her toward excellence. A proper man, Cassie could only remember hearing him swear twice in his life in front of her. The first was the day she'd defended her doctoral thesis at Harvard at the age of twenty-two. Her father knew that science and academia remained a male-dominated world. He knew the people on the board were the old guard who still thought women didn't belong in science. He'd waited silently with her in the hallway before they called her in. But before she stood to leave, he'd taken her hand and looked her in the eye. She'd expected the same soft encouragement he always delivered, but there was fire in his eyes this time. He squeezed her hand and said, "Show these assholes that Cassie Baker doesn't take fuck all from anyone." After that, the dissertation board didn't stand a chance.

The only other time her father said those words to her was from his bed in St. Luke's hospital, the day before he died from cancer. But they were words she'd repeated to herself a thousand times in her head. They were the touchstone she used her entire adult life. And she heard them now.

Stick these assholes.

Show them that Cassie Baker doesn't take fuck all from anyone.

Before she could let doubt creep back into her mind, she turned and ran deeper into the tunnel, toward where Rick had disappeared, going as fast as she dared until her hand trailing the wall felt raw from the friction.

CHAPTER 45

R*ick felt the eyes of* his armed guard boring into him. The two men walking on either side of him clearly didn't like him. He wasn't sure if it was because he was an outsider that had successfully breached their security, or because he'd killed one of their own. He figured it was probably a little of both. And, frankly, he didn't give a shit.

He sized up his options. This wasn't like the movies. There was no way he could suddenly throw an elbow into the guy's face on his left and kick the guy on his right in the groin, take one of their weapons and shoot his way to freedom. Not that he didn't fantasize about doing exactly that, even imagining how it might be done and evaluating his chances of survival.

He gave himself a fifty-fifty shot if he engaged them, pretty good odds considering he put his overall odds of surviving the next few hours at zero. The real problem wasn't the men. It was the armed drones flying in front of him, casting three laser-targeting beams, red dots that danced on his chest as he walked. He was targeted for execution if he made an aggressive move. That brought his chances down to nothing.

The soldiers had explained the drone was back on full auto, dialed into the highest setting. *I wouldn't sneeze if I were you, man,* one had cautioned him. *I've seen a drone blow off a man's head halfway through a sneeze. God bless you does nothing to fix a hole in your head.* The men had chuckled at the story, typical dark humor for soldiers, then shoved him forward.

The emergency tunnel ended at an enormous freight elevator. The metal gate slid open and they followed the drone into the space, large enough for fifty or sixty men at a time. It made sense. If there was ever a need to use the emergency exit, there would be a lot of workers who needed to get out in a hurry. Transporting them ten at a time wouldn't work.

He searched outside the elevator for any sign of Cassie following. Nothing. He was glad she wasn't foolish enough to get too close, but he hoped she wasn't lying back in the tunnel immobilized with fear. It was an unexpected plus to have them think she was dead and have her inside the security perimeter. He just hoped she held it together and that she was the computer genius everyone thought she was.

The elevator ride was short and went downward. He wasn't surprised as he knew the lab was on one of the deeper levels of the mine, but he'd assumed a rescue shaft would have been near the lowest part of the mine. But it was likely that the cheapest solution had governed the decision of where to dig the exit, not worker safety. He filed the knowledge away on the off chance there was a return trip in his future. He doubted there would be.

The doors opened into a brightly lit area with level, painted floors and twelve-foot-high ceilings. Unlike the rough-cut rock he'd been surrounded by in the access tunnel, the rock walls here were smooth, giving them a finished look like they were in a warehouse topside. Empty trailers, the ones he'd seen carrying the bodies out of Resurrection, were stacked for storage against the far wall. The space to his left had rows of standing shelves. He was relieved that it was a storage area. At least it gave Cassie a chance if she took the elevator to this level. There were bound to be cameras around, but it was better than the doors opening into a room full of soldiers.

His guard shoved him forward and he marched past the trailers, his head craning each time they passed an opening, trying to see what was going on. All he saw were other trailers, all of them empty.

"Where are all the people?" he asked his guards. "What have you done with them?"

The guard smirked at his buddy. "What do you think we did with 'em? We ate 'em. Civilians taste great, don't they, Jack?"

The other soldier followed along.

"The old ones are a little tough, nothing a little sauce doesn't fix. Now the young ones, they're tastiest."

Rick ignored the comments. It wasn't worth engaging and he didn't intend to give them the pleasure of seeing him flustered.

"That's enough. Let's go," came Keefer's voice out of the drone hovering in front of them.

The soldiers each grabbed an arm and quickened their steps. Just to make them mad, Rick slowed down a little, forcing them to work at it. It was a petty victory, but he'd take what he could get. The slower pace gave him more time to take stock of his surroundings.

He'd been to this area before; it was one of the sections of the underground complex he'd seen back when he'd visited Cassie in the Genysis lab. The walls were painted a slate grey and were ground so smoothly that it looked like they were in an office hallway. An occasional glistening streak in the wall, where groundwater seeped from the rock, was the only telltale sign they were deep underground. Cassie had told him that the complex contained clean rooms for experiments and many large airtight, pressurized areas with complete temperature and humidity controls, but those were all back in the restricted area. The place was what Rick imagined inside of a space station might look like, more than a mine.

A different set of guards stood in front of a double-set of metal doors. The soldiers transferred custody of their prisoner without comment then marched away. His new guards waved at a camera above the door. There was a *click* and the soldier pushed the door open.

As he walked in, Rick was reminded of the mission control rooms he'd seen in the old movies when the United States had a space program that involved astronauts and exploration, not just orbital weapons and surveillance satellites. There were three curved rows of seats, set up on tiers, all facing a bank of television screens.

The odd thing was that the room was empty and the screen only had two words in giant print floating around it like a screensaver.

Operation Resurrection.

"Rick," Keefer said, entering from the door at the bottom of the room. "You are nothing if not surprising."

"Where are they?" Rick said. "Dahlia and Charlie. I want to see them."

Keefer waved a hand toward the bank of screens. Someone Rick couldn't see reacted to the signal and the display changed. The screen divided into halves, a grainy image of Dahlia on the left and a clear image of Charlie on the right.

Rick stepped closer. At first glance they both seemed dead. Their eyes were open, staring straight ahead, and their mouths were parted. Charlie's tongue was visible, pressed against his teeth. But their legs and arms made small movements. Dahlia's hands opened and closed into fists.

"They're fine," Keefer said. "Charlie was a little harder to find than his mother, but we used the camera footage from the town to make sure. That sheriff's badge on his shirt was helpful though. Did we get it right?"

"You know you did," Rick said, his voice choking up. "Are they still drugged?"

"They're coming out of it along with everyone else. It'll be another hour, but I've had them separated from the main group. Pending the outcome of our meeting."

Rick didn't reply. He just looked at Dahlia's and Charlie's faces. Their brows were furrowed as though they were having nightmares. He knew at that moment that he would do anything Keefer asked to save them.

"I want to see them," Rick said.

"Of course you do. But we have to have an understanding first," Keefer said. "My men think I should just kill you and be done with it. That you can never be trusted. Maybe they're right." He walked up the center aisle toward Rick. "Let's be honest with each other. I ordered you killed back in town, so I'm not too far from agreeing with them. It's just luck, good or bad depending on your point of view, that put you in this position right now."

"What do you want from me?" Rick asked, his eye still fixated on the screen.

Keefer walked toward the screens and waved to the technician. The image changed back to the floating screensaver that said Operation Resurrection. Rick stepped toward the screen.

"Where'd they go? Put them back up," he said.

Keefer smiled. "They won't be harmed. I promise."

"What do you want?" he asked. "What do I have to do?"

"Just listen to the case I'm making to the American people. That's all,"

Keefer said.

"And you'll let them go?"

"Let's see how things go," Keefer said. Rick nodded, and Keefer took a deep breath and seemed to collect his thoughts for a second. He pointed to the screens above him. "I'm giving a speech in a little over an hour from now. An important one that's going to go out to a lot of people. Maybe the most important speech in human history. I know what you're thinking, but that's not an exaggeration. In it, I'm going to explain what we've done and why we've done it. There are going to be a lot of people who will never agree with our actions. They will be secretly thankful in their hearts, but their psychological conditioning won't allow them to admit it. But people like you, people who've seen the terrors of the world up close and know the true barbarism of our enemies, these are the people I hope to truly convert over to our cause. These are the people I want to reach in this speech."

Rick knew he had a part to play if he wanted to save Dahlia and Charlie. He couldn't pretend to agree with Keefer right away. The man wanted a foil, someone he had to convince. Rick decided to play it straight. "And you want to convince me you're not a raging manic? Sorry, pal, that ship has sailed."

"You're missing the point. This is bigger than me, Rick. This is bigger than all of us."

"Operation Resurrection?" Rick said, nodding to the screen.

"Exactly," Keefer said.

"And what is it that you're resurrecting?"

"The United States of America. Back to her rightful place as the essential nation, the one true superpower to lead the world." He raised a hand to the screens at the front of the room and they instantly filled with images of destruction from around the world. Armed militants marching through urban streets. Crops set on fire. Ritual beheadings of hundreds of people in a sports stadium. Surveillance camera shots of terrorist bombs exploding in shopping malls. Oceans of protesting people demanding jobs in front of factories. Airfield tarmacs covered with coffins draped with American flags.

"We're all familiar with these images, easily culled from the nightly news," Keefer said. Rick had the feeling the man had started his prepared text. "But together they tell a story." The images continued to change with new versions of the same horrific scenes, a combination of still shots and video. "This is what the world has become. Lawless. Primitive. Barbaric. The Jihadi movement and the response by our civilization against it has led to so much of the pain we've experienced as a people." The images focused on the acts of terrorism in the United States. The anthrax attack at the Ravens' stadium in Baltimore, the nuclear bomb set off in Washington, DC, the mass shootings in New York, Chicago and Seattle. The images seemed endless.

"These savages brought their hatred of freedom and liberty into our midst, and how did our leaders respond?" Keefer said, his voice rising like a Sunday preacher. The screen went dark. "They did nothing. Yes, they made speeches. Attended the funerals. Even wept on camera to show that they cared. But it did nothing to make us safer. While these politicians stacked up failure after failure, our other enemies grew stronger still."

The images started again. This time images of the massive super cities in China and India. Videos of parade routes of soldiers and military equipment that stretched out as far as the eye could see. A sky covered with so many unmanned drone warplanes that it looked like a plague of locusts.

"Enemy militaries grew around the world while our own was whittled down to nothing through losses in battle. Our weakened economy made us cut military funding as we watched China increase hers twenty-fold. Without our nuclear deterrent, there is no doubt we would suffer the same fate as other Pacific Rim countries and would be just another trophy won during this Chinese century."

Keefer spat these last words. This may have been rehearsal, but the emotion was real. Keefer's voice had a quivering anger in it. He pointed to the screen and the image changed to an American flag beautifully waving in a breeze.

"They say America's time is over. That a nation of only three hundred million people cannot hope to have the impact they once had on a world of eight billion souls. Not when the Jihadis are so strong. Not when two of our rival nations have over a billion in population each. They say our time is over. That we ought to go quietly and allow the greatest nation on earth to be relegated to the trash bin of history. This is something men of conscience cannot allow. We are too important. And the path laid out for humanity if our democracy were to fail is dark and brutal.

"We don't have to imagine it. We can see it all around the world every day. I am here today to promise you that this is not how America will end. In fact, I'm here to tell you that we will not only survive, but that by tomorrow, we will reclaim our position as the lone superpower in the world. Yes, there will be sacrifice, and there will be many who disagree with my actions. But before you condemn what we've done, ask yourself this one question." Keefer pointed at Rick. "Do you want your children, do you want Charlie, to grow up in a failed country, barely clinging to its survival, with just a matter of time before an invasion? Or will you wake up every day thanking God that someone made the hard decision on your behalf to make America great again? The hard decision to destroy the other seven and a half billion people so that our countrymen could enjoy the security and prosperity they deserve?"

"What are you saying?" Rick said.

"America will once again be the lone superpower in the world because an hour from now she will be the only country left alive."

Rick felt his knees go weak. His first thought was that it was an exaggeration, but one look at Keefer's face and he knew that it wasn't. It didn't matter whether he could pull it off or not, but for some reason Keefer thought he had the ability to promise the destruction of the world outside the borders of the United States.

Maybe he could or maybe he couldn't, and Rick hoped to God it was the latter. Either way, one thing was now clear.

Keefer was completely insane.

CHAPTER 46

C*assie stood in front of* the elevator trying to decide what to do. She hadn't chanced a look around the bend in the tunnel until Rick and his armed guards were already gone, but this was clearly the end of the line.

The problem was, she had no idea what would happen if she called the elevator back. For all she knew, it would return filled with soldiers to take her into custody, laughing at her foolishness for handing herself over to them so easily.

Even if the elevator returned empty to her level when she pressed the button, she assumed someone would notice. Then when it arrived at the lab level, there were certain to be men with guns waiting for her.

All the options seemed to end with her being captured. She closed her eyes and tried to think through the problem. If she was in her developmental lab, she wouldn't accept either solution. Her entire career and her pioneering work in organic computing and brain-machine interactions was predicated on her ability to eschew orthodoxy and discover alternative paths no one had ever before considered.

Where her scientific colleagues were content to search out the best path to take in the system of known streets previously uncovered in their field, she was the ultimate off-road junkie, blazing her own trail. Sometimes that meant crashing or getting hopelessly stuck in the mud, but it also led to great discoveries.

The greatest lesson was that when the menu of options didn't offer anything, then simply toss the menu.

As she thought through it, she knew one of her challenges was that she was outside her area of expertise. In her computer lab, she was one of the preeminent minds in her field. Even though she'd worked in the deep lab for years, she knew very little about mine construction and layout.

Still, it was just a problem to be solved.

If the tunnel she stood in had been put into place as an escape, she reasoned, then the elevator was designed to aid that escape. Based on how straight and functional the tunnel coming in had been, with no offshoots or signs that it'd been used for actual mining, she guessed it'd been drilled expressly for the purpose. Therefore, it was likely the elevator was built for the same purpose.

But what good was an escape tunnel if it couldn't be reached? And what good was an elevator as the sole means of transportation, an elevator reliant on a power supply and subject to the possibility of a mechanical failure? Any safety system she'd ever worked in or designed in her labs had always contained multiple redundancies.

She pulled on the accordion-style gate covering the elevator entrance and exposed the gaping hole in the rock face. Leaning forward, she looked up and down the elevator shaft, carved out of solid rock. On two sides were the crawler tracks on which the elevator traveled, its gears turning to climb up or down the shaft. It wasn't the fastest way to go, but it looked sturdy and reliable. If the elevator had been on a pulley system, the weight of a half mile of metal cable would be hanging above the elevator compartment. The tracks were deep, providing the strength and stability the platform needed for such a large size.

She leaned farther forward and looked left and right. A smile spread across her face as she spotted exactly what she hoped to see.

Two metal ladders were bolted into the wall, slightly sunk into a carved indentation to keep them from being hit by the elevator in motion. Anyone climbing would stick out so that the elevator couldn't operate at the same time, so they were for use only when the elevator was broken. It was exactly the redundant system Cassie had hoped to find. If the elevator malfunctioned, then the workers could climb to safety. Or, in her case, if the mine was filled with armed mercenaries trying to kill thousands of people, she could climb to their nest and try to stop them. A scenario she would bet had never been envisioned by any of the original designers.

Before she could talk herself out of it, Cassie stepped onto the nearest ladder, gasping for air as she dangled over the deep shaft. She clung to it, panting, gripping the smooth metal with sweaty hands. Slowly, she reached down with her left foot, poking it around to find the next rung below her. The gap was farther than on a typical ladder, but it was there. She shifted her weight and began the slow climb down.

At least she stood a chance of remaining undiscovered a while longer. She still had no idea what she intended to do once she reached the lab level, but she decided to take on one thing at a time. Hand by hand, foot by foot, she worked her way down, moving as quickly as she dared. She just hoped she would reach her destination in time to do any good.

CHAPTER 47

R*ick shook his head, trying* to think through what Keefer had just told him. There was no part of the man's demeanor to suggest he was being anything other than literal. He wasn't talking about some new initiative to push America forward, he was talking about something far greater. The scale could only mean one thing.

"You have access to nuclear weapons," he said, speaking slowly as if Keefer were a rabid dog. "You can't seriously be considering using them."

Keefer smiled and Rick caught the glint of a zealot's fanaticism. "In an hour, I'll have access to everything. Nuclear, biological, and chemical weapons. Fleets of ships and planes. Electrical grids. Hydro-power stations. Food supplies. Manufacturing facilities. Financial markets. Everything."

"You're not making any sense."

Keefer waved his hands in the air, indicating the room around him. "This will become the center of the world. Right here." He stopped and gave Rick an exaggerated puzzled look. "You don't believe me? Of course you don't. Why would you? I must sound like a lunatic."

"The thought had crossed my mind," Rick said. The other thought crossing his mind was how fast he could close the space between himself and Keefer. And just how fast he could break the man's neck. Almost as if they were reading his mind, two kill drones silently floated off their perches in the front corners of the room. Keefer gave the illusion of facing Rick alone, but he was still well protected.

Keefer laughed. "The real insanity is in the world out there. People feel it, the slide into chaos. They've seen it happening for years. It's a tired cliché to call the Jihadis a cancer, but it's the most apt description. They started off as a tumor called Isis, an ugly growth that might have been cut out and discarded, but the moment passed. It was allowed to metastasize and spread unchecked. First the Caliphate, followed by the Great Migration that poured Jihadis throughout Europe. That was the cancer entering the lymphatic system, spreading into every corner of the patient, sealing its fate."

"Why are you telling me all of this?" Rick asked.

"To convince you that what we're doing here is for the greater good. I want men like you to want to be part of the new world we're building."

Rick shook his head. "Bullshit."

Keefer didn't like the reaction, but Rick was past caring about that.

"I think that whatever you have planned, you're getting cold feet. I don't think you're trying to convince me, sounds more like you're trying to convince yourself," Rick said. "I'm just a convenient excuse. You're talking about genocide on a scale the world hasn't seen since Hitler. There's no way to justify it. I think you know that. I think that's why you brought me in here, because your conscience is catching up to you, Keefer. You should listen to it."

Keefer's manic smile was gone. He paced the floor. "I thought you were smarter than this. I want you to understand what we're doing here. I want the world to appreciate the necessity of the sacrifice being made."

"And here I just want to kill you," Rick said. "I hope at least one of us gets what we want."

Keefer smiled, but there was no humor in it. Rick glanced at the kill drones, half expecting the audience to come to an abrupt end with an order from Keefer. But they didn't shoot, not yet.

"You've seen what the Jihadis can do. I've read your service records. Seventy-one men died under your command during your three tours facing the Jihadis. Thirty-seven of them in the ambush in Istanbul. I saw that report. I read what they did that day. You can't tell me that an enemy that can commit that kind of atrocity deserves to live. You can't tell me that if you had the power to kill them all with the push of a button, you wouldn't take it."

Rick tried not to reveal anything as images of the firefight in the streets of Istanbul flooded through him.

"Tell me what happened," Keefer said.

Rick shook his head. "Sounds like you already know all about it."

"I want to hear it from you," Keefer said. "Soldier to soldier. I want you to tell me what happened, and explain to me why any of these people deserve to live another day."

Rick felt his hands trembling. He didn't want to go down this path, but he had Cassie to think about. Every minute he kept Keefer occupied was a minute he gave Cassie to figure out a way to stop him. If the man was here listening to his story, he wasn't out where he might find Cassie. As much as Rick hated the idea of dredging up the most painful memories of his life, he knew he had to do it.

"Istanbul was already a mess," Rick started. "The bio-attacks had wiped out half the city before we got there. We were working on intel that the Jihadis had rounded up new recruits from the poor part of the town. Forced conscription, even of kids, wasn't unusual. But what made this different was that they took all of them. Every boy between five and ten from a large section of town. Ripped them right out of their homes. Beheaded any parent who even objected, let alone tried to stop them."

"How many did they take?"

The question annoyed Rick. It was in the report and Keefer damn well knew the answer. But he needed to stall. "Close to three hundred from what we could tell. My team got the call; it was the kind of mission headquarters loved. A chance to show US forces playing hero."

"Great press," Keefer agreed. "US soldiers reuniting three hundred kids with their families. Too bad it didn't work out that way."

Rick nodded. "The whole thing had been a setup. The Jihadis had taken the kids all right, but they were never going to be trained as soldiers. They knew we couldn't resist coming after them. I led forty men down a street, three-story-high rooftops on either side of us. Our drones collapsed first, some new jamming tech the Chinese had given the Jihadis. Then coms with our sniper covers went offline. Next thing I knew, dark shadows began to rain down on us from above. *Thump, thump, thump.*

"My men took cover, thinking they were improvised explosives or Molotov cocktails. But it was nothing like that." Rick's voice caught and he stopped, staring at the ground.

"Go on," Keefer urged. "Tell me what it was."

"You already know."

"I want to hear you say it. I want you to remember the enemy we're facing."

Rick swallowed hard. "It was the kids. The ones they'd taken. Parts of them anyway. Arms, legs, sections of torsos. Flying through the air from both sides of the road." Rick's voice was monotone, it had to be. If he let emotion into his voice, he knew he'd lose it completely. "Then the heads came. Dozens at a time, the faces still frozen in expressions of pain and horror."

"And how did your men react?"

"These were good men," Rick said. "Hardened soldiers who'd seen more than their share of insanity in the war. But this was too much. They broke from cover, shooting at the rooftops, launching RPGs at shadows, anything they could do to stop the body parts raining down on them. I shouted for them to take cover, but it didn't matter. Not really."

"Because it was a trap," Keefer said.

"The guns appeared from the windows all around us, from the buildings that were supposed to have been cleared and sealed shut by local forces. Then all hell broke loose."

Rick heard the screams as his men were cut down around him by a withering cross fire that he'd led them into.

"Me and two others crawled into the burned-out shell of a French tank. It was stripped out and rusted, but it gave us cover. The firefight lasted less than a minute. Not a fight, it was a slaughter. We hunkered down in the tank, waiting for the end to come. Either an anti-tank RPG, or gasoline to burn us out. Even small arms would have probably penetrated the old tank. But nothing came. They knew we were there, but they let us live."

"Because they were proud of what they'd done," Keefer said. "They wanted witnesses to carry the story back."

Rick felt like he was outside of his own body. He recognized the feeling. It was how he'd felt for years after that day. "The other two men who survived shot themselves in the head within a month. I wasn't far behind them, but I wanted to die in the field. So I just took risks that should have gotten me killed. Instead, I only lost my arm and got a ticket home."

"But you fought back," Keefer said. "You're still here."

"I'm still here," Rick said. "Not because I kept fighting, but because I finally allowed myself to stop fighting. That was the difference."

Keefer pointed at a screen even though it was still blank, his teeth clenched. "But those people, those animals, they're still out there. And the Chinese are no different. The Indians. You've seen the pictures from the slave camps. The repression of the rioters with flamethrowers. It's what they'll do to us if given a chance. How can you not see the only way to save our way of life is to clean the slate?"

"You can't just kill seven billion people. It's insane."

"It's the only solution."

"There are good people everywhere," Rick said. "Innocent people. Families just trying to put a roof over their heads and food on the table. You'd kill all of them? Even the kids?"

Keefer nodded. "Sacrifices have to be made."

"That's bullshit!" Rick yelled. "Why can't you see how crazy this is?"

Keefer waved the question away. "I will burn down the world to save the three hundred million Americans. Because if I don't, they're destined to live in a world of radicalized fanatics that just gets darker every day. That's three hundred million who will inevitably be enslaved by our enemies if nothing is done. Tell me I'm wrong. Tell me America's best days aren't behind us unless something changes."

Rick shook his head, not wanting to agree. "There has to be another way."

"Like what? A jobs program?" Keefer said. "Another five-year plan? A cease-fire with the Jihadis? Politely asking Imperial China to stop her eastern expansion? We're rotting, we're isolated, and our adversaries are out to destroy us. And we're doing nothing to stop it. And you think I'm insane?"

"No, I don't think you're insane. I know you are."

"Is it insane to choose to save what you love, no matter the consequences? I think there's not anything more understandable. Nothing more human than that impulse." Keefer paused. "But let's not argue philosophy. Why deal with hypotheticals when we can see what you actually believe?"

The screen turned into an image of Dahlia holding Charlie's limp body in her arms. Keefer pointed to the screen.

"What if the only way to save those you loved was to condemn the other two thousand people in this mine to die, what would you choose?" Keefer asked. "Let's find out. It'll be fun."

CHAPTER 48

C*assie was halfway down the* ladder before she had a problem.

There was a rattle of the metal gate below as two soldiers entered the elevator. She knew there were two because the elevator's roof was a metal grid with holes about an inch wide. If either soldier looked up, they'd have a big surprise.

She clung to the ladder with her left hand. Trying to make her movements as economical as possible, she pulled her gun from her waistband. She didn't know if it would do her any good trying to shoot through the metal grid, but if the men spotted her and opened fire, she sure as hell wasn't going to just hang out and wait to die.

"Is maintenance up or down from here?" one of the men asked.

Cassie held her breath. If the elevator headed up, she was in real trouble. Jumping onto the elevator roof would be her only option but there was no way that was happening without tipping off the men inside.

"I think it's up," the other soldier said.

Cassie tensed. She looked back up the ladder. She was at least fifty feet from the nearest opening. There was no way she could make it up there, especially without drawing unwanted attention from below. She hooked the ladder with her elbow and fumbled with the gun to find the safety.

The elevator growled into action, the metal treads churning slowly, eating the tracks on either side of the shaft. She took aim at the top of the soldier's head as the distance closed. Twenty feet. Fifteen. Ten.

"No, look," the first soldier said. "Says right on the wall. It's level N. That's down from here, dumb ass."

He hit the control panel and the elevator ground to a halt. Cassie froze, the gun at the ready in case one of them looked up. She was so close that she could smell the sweat on the men.

"Who are you calling dumb ass? You were looking at it too," the other one said. "Go ahead then, hit it."

The man did and the elevator lurched back into action, but now going back down. Cassie pressed herself flat against the ladder on the off chance one of them might still look up. But the elevator crawled down through the shaft, past the door to the lab level, and then continued to the lower levels. She waited until it got some distance, then continued her climb down on shaking legs.

She reached the opening where the elevator had been. The opening had a waist-high accordion gate across it that the soldiers in the elevator had left half open. It may have been an OSHA safety violation, but it suited her fine. She hung back and listened intently, staying out of sight. There were some distant sounds of machinery, but there were no voices. That was the important thing.

Quickly, she sneaked a look into the room and then darted back to safety.

She liked what she saw, just a storage area for the trailers and without guards.

She turned the corner, gun up by her head, pointed to the ceiling like she'd seen in the cop movies. A quick scan confirmed there were no people in the room, but she did spot a camera mounted on the wall. She ducked for cover behind one of the trailers, hoping no one had been paying attention to the video feed for the few moments when she was exposed.

She knew where she was. The trailers filled a space that used to be a storage facility when she worked in the lab. It was the last of three connected storage rooms before the central hub of the lab complex. The access point to her sensors on the data trunk was on the opposite side of that area. Her plan was to work toward that spot as best she could, looking for any opportunity to communicate with the outside world. She figured there would be cameras along the way and that posed a problem.

The other side of the storage room was lined with standing shelving units filled with plastic bins, labeled on the outside. MREs. Batteries. Clothing. Bingo.

She sized up the direction of the surveillance camera and decided to risk a belly-crawl to the shelves. She made short work of it and ducked into what she approximated would be a blind spot for the camera. She reached up and pulled one of the bins off the shelf and onto the floor next to her.

There were overalls inside, black with a zipper up the front. She found a size small and pulled it on over her clothes. A hat would have been perfect, but there was nothing like that in the box. Her hair was a problem. She'd only seen male soldiers so far, so a ponytail bobbing around on the surveillance camera wasn't going to do the trick. She pulled Rick's knife from her pocket, grabbed the ponytail with her left hand and sawed through it. It took longer to get through than she thought it would, but she did it. She went to work on the rest of her hair, cutting it as short as possible. She figured that and bulky overalls might fool the camera, but if she met someone face-to-face she was screwed.

She stood, sliding the knife into one pocket and the gun into the other. She walked out of the room, trying her best to look like she belonged there.

The next room over was also filled with trailers. She spotted a canvas duffle bag on the ground and snatched it up. Fortunately, it wasn't very heavy so she hefted it onto her shoulder, blocking her face from the camera mounted to her right. She was about to leave the room for the next when another section of the supply area caught her eye.

Quickly, she changed her direction and kneeled next to a metal locker box. She opened the duffel and emptied out a small toolbox and a folded-up bio-chem suit. She then filled the duffel with as many of the items from the locker box as she thought she could reasonably carry. She wasn't sure how she was going to use them, but she knew they would come in helpful at some point.

Rezipping the bag, she hefted it onto her shoulder. It was heavy and felt more awkward, but the contents made the trade-off well worth it.

She got through the second room without incident. But at the entrance to the third storage room before the main hub, she stutter-stepped to an abrupt stop.

This room had three trailers in it, two empty, but one half full of bodies being unloaded. Soldiers worked in tandem, most of them in black tactical outfits but a few thankfully dressed in the same black overalls she wore. The people were being carried off the trailer and placed on large wheeled gurneys that held four bodies at a time. Once a gurney was loaded, a single soldier pushed the whole thing through the wide door cut into the rock wall and rolled it into the next room.

The men looked tired and sweaty. There was no chatter, only the occasional grunt when throwing one of the bodies around. She contemplated inserting herself in the line-up to push one of the carts, but immediately rejected the idea.

She felt that if any of the men took a second to look up from the job in front of them, they'd call her out from across the room. Her only chance was to walk right past them, hoping that how busy they were, combined with the duffle bag on her shoulder, would be enough.

Certainly, the only reason she'd gotten this far was that the men had zero reason to believe someone might infiltrate this deep behind their defenses. She had a feeling that if the men had the slightest indication that they needed to be on the lookout for anything, she would have been caught almost immediately. It just underscored how valuable Rick's distraction had been. She wondered if he was safe. Or if he was still even alive.

She shook the thought away, focusing on getting through this room and into the main hub. Taking a wide angle away from the nearest of the soldiers, and keeping the duffle bag on her shoulder, she walked quickly through the space with her head down and her eyes on the floor.

She was so shocked to make it through without being caught that she was well into the next room before she looked up.

When she did, she stopped in place, frozen. The duffle bag slowly slid from her shoulders and landed with a thud on the ground.

The scene that stretched in front of her turned her stomach even as it stirred in her an indescribable excitement.

Her humanistic side thought what she saw sprawled ahead was horrific. But she couldn't escape the fact that to her scientific eye, it was completely mesmerizing. There was nothing else it could be. There'd been hints at Genysis that a breakthrough was possible, but nothing like this.

With one look, she knew exactly what Keefer had built. And, in a terrifying moment of clarity, she understood that he had the power to make good on his promise to change the world forever. And it wouldn't be the resurrection of

America. All the power would be in Keefer's hands. And she could only imagine the terrible things he would do with it.

She picked the bag back up and hurried through the open space, feeling more pressure than ever to find a way to stop him.

CHAPTER 49

"*You son of a bitch,*" Rick said. "Let them go."

"But don't you see?" Keefer said. "This is perfect. You said you wouldn't kill faceless masses to save those you care about. Here's your chance to prove it."

"I never said that. I'm a soldier, of course I killed people to save America. I killed Jihadis by the hundreds."

"Only enemy combatants?" Keefer said. "That's bullshit and you know it. It was impossible over there to separate them out. How many women and children did you kill? How many did we all kill?"

Rick grabbed the sides of his head, pain pounding with each heartbeat. He didn't want to think of it. He didn't want the images back in his mind.

"Not on purpose ..." he mumbled.

"This isn't *60 Minutes*, Rick. Not some official board of inquiry. I know what it was like over there. I know what it's like everywhere. Sometimes you have to make the hard decision. Sometimes innocent people lose their lives." He pointed to the screen. "Which people will it be? The two people you love? Or the two thousand strangers? I'll let you choose."

Keefer walked all the way up to Rick and grabbed him by the arm. His eyes were wild, out of control.

"Pick the two thousand people out there and show me my plan's wrong. Go on, tell me to kill the woman and the boy and to release the rest of the town. Show me that I'm wrong to save what I love at the expense of a world that wants to kill us."

Rick searched the man's face, looking for a sign that the offer was real. Trying to understand where all of this was coming from. He held out hope that the whole thing was really a plea from Keefer, something subconscious that was looking for a reason not to pull the trigger on whatever horrific weapon he had at his disposal.

"You don't need me to show you," Rick said. "You know that killing all those innocent lives can't be justified. No matter what you say."

"Choose, Rick," Keefer said. "The ones you love or two thousand strangers. Who dies?"

"Doesn't matter what I choose," Rick said. "You'd never let them all go."

"I will. I swear to God I will." Keefer's eyes welled with tears. "Don't you understand the burden I have on my shoulders? Can't you feel even a fraction of it? You only have to put two thousand to death to save two people. I have to execute seven billion to save my country."

Rick put out his hands, gesturing Keefer to calm down. "Easy. There's no certainty America will die if you do nothing," Rick said. "Don't you get it? You're not trapped. You don't have to do this."

Keefer stepped back, his expression hardening, the momentary look of uncertainty turning back into a stone mask. "You still don't get it, do you? If Brandon Morris and Genysis can develop this weapon, don't you think someone else will discover it? Do you think the Jihadis would hesitate to destroy us? Would China? We have to strike preemptively while we can."

Rick felt a surge of panic at the mention of Genysis. For a second, he considered whether Cassie had betrayed him. Whether she'd been on the other side of the equation the entire time. But he rejected the idea. She'd taken risks right alongside of him in town. Done things that could have sent the operation sideways. No, she wasn't part of it. But if Keefer was using some kind of Genysis technology like they'd thought, then the chance of Cassie stopping it just increased.

Keefer made a hand signal and then shouted, "We're running out of time." On the screen, Dahlia's head jerked toward the camera. The audio was turned on. "What do you choose, Rick? Do I kill them or not? Your decision."

"Rick? Oh my, God," Dahlia screamed. "Help!"

"Dahlia, I'm here!" Rick cried out.

"The drone can kill her and the boy in a split second," Keefer said, his voice rising. "Tell me to do it and I'll set the rest of them free. I swear it."

"Rick!" Dahlia screamed, curling her body around Charlie. "No!"

Rick looked back and forth between the screen and the door.

"What do you choose?" Keefer said.

"Rick!"

"Make a decision!" Keefer roared.

"I choose them," Rick said, barely audible.

"What was that?"

"I choose them!" Rick yelled. "I want them."

Keefer waved his hand and the rear door opened.

Dahlia stood there holding Charlie in her arms, her body wracked with sobs. Rick ran to her and hugged her. She didn't say a word, but turned and clung to him, sobbing.

"It's going to be all right," he said, tears streaming down his cheek. "Is Charlie okay?" he asked, looking down at the boy. His eyes were barely parted and stared through him, unfocused.

Dahlia nodded. She wiped her eyes. "T ... th ... they said it's just the drug ... wearing off." She looked up at him. "What is this place? What the hell is going on, Rick?"

"It's simple," Keefer said, walking up the stairs toward them. "Rick here just saved your life. An act of love. And now, I intend to follow his example." He patted Rick on the back. "Congratulations, you're now part of the resurrection."

Keefer walked out of the room and past the guards. Two drones floated up from the ground, one oriented to Rick and the other on Dahlia. The guards waved them forward, so Rick took Charlie from Dahlia, his tiny body dead weight in his arms. He put the boy's cheek against his and then kissed him. Rick knew he had to focus on the danger they were still in, but being reunited with Dahlia and Charlie, actually holding the boy in his arms after thinking they were dead, was almost too much to bear. Dahlia wrapped her arm around his waist and they followed Keefer. The drones hovered silently behind them.

"What's happening?" Dahlia whispered as they walked.

Rick shifted Charlie, so he could carry him in one arm, and freed the other to pull Dahlia in close to him. He kissed her cheek and used the moment to whisper, "We're just trying to slow him down. Buy as much time as possible."

"Is there help on the way?" she whispered back, her eyes searching his.

He heard the sudden hope in her voice and hated to steal it from her, but she deserved the truth. He shook his head. "No, I don't think so. But for some reason he wants me alive. He knows he can control me with you and Charlie. As long as he wants to keep me around, you're both safe." It was mostly true. Whatever Keefer's breakdown had been about, his apparent moment of self-doubt seemed to be over. Rick wasn't sure how long before Keefer decided to remove him as a distraction.

He decided not to say anything about Cassie in case he was overheard. And he didn't want to give Dahlia false hope. For all he knew, Cassie had doubled back out of the tunnel once he was captured and had tried to go for help. Or she might have already been captured or killed, although he felt fairly certain Keefer wouldn't have passed up the opportunity to hang that over him. There was still a chance she was somewhere in the mine, trying to find a way to stop the madness.

Keefer waited in front of a metal door. "We're here. It's time for me to show you how America will rise again."

CHAPTER 50

R*ick walked through the door,* still carrying Charlie. He was all too aware of the drones hovering nearby and he held no misconception about how fast he would be shot down if he made a move against Keefer. Besides, he was too mesmerized by what he saw in the room to think about an attack. All he could think about was how quickly things had gone from the strange to the completely bizarre.

The large room had been transformed into a hospital operating theater with white walls, bright lights, and banks of monitors and computers. In the center of the room, lined up next to one another, were four gurneys, each with a patient on it dressed in a white hospital gown.

The beds were inclined at a forty-five-degree angle. Thick straps crossed over the patients' chests, holding them in place. There were two IVs, one in each arm, a plastic oxygen tube in their noses, and EKG wires attached to their skin.

Monitors on a cart, ubiquitous in hospitals, displayed heart rhythm, pulse and blood oxygenation levels. A third monitor showed a three-dimensional image of a human brain, colors flashing across the surface.

Rick guessed this image came from the piece of medical equipment he'd never seen before. A helmet of soft, malleable material stretched from the patients' eyebrows, up over their scalps, covering their eyes and ending at the base of the neck. It was thick, maybe two or three inches. That in itself wasn't the disturbing thing.

Positioned over each head was an articulated robotic arm, the end of which held a disk mimicking the curve of the scalp beneath it. Protruding from it were dozens of needles, six to eight inches in length, that hovered just above the helmet.

The room was filled with technicians, looking very different from the burly soldiers Rick had seen so far. This was a group of scientists, most of them very young, perhaps in their early thirties.

"Oh my God," Dahlia said next to him. She pointed at the patient in the second bed from them.

It was Bertie.

Rick lunged toward her.

The drones that had been quietly hovering on either side flew in between him and the patients. Red targeting lasers shone out, putting a red dot on his chest and head.

Keefer held up his hands. "Easy. We don't want our little friends taking your head off, do we?"

"What are you doing to her?"

"I should have warned you," Keefer said. "But this is a good place for her. She's safer here than the others will be."

"Get her up," Rick said. "Get her off that bed."

Keefer shook his head. "I want you here, Rick. I do. The more I think about it, the more it makes sense. But if you don't calm down I'm going to have a drone shoot the boy. Do you understand?"

Dahlia stepped between the drones and Charlie.

"Tell me you understand," Keefer said.

"I understand," Rick whispered, unable to take his eyes off Bertie's face.

One man, distinguished by his dark complexion and silver mane of shoulder-length hair, walked up to Keefer, eyeing Rick as he did.

"Everything all right?" the man asked with a faint Indian accent.

Keefer smiled then pointed to each in turn as if they were at a dinner party. "Rick Johnson. Dahlia. And her son Charlie. This is Dr. Kalabi, our head scientist. The good doctor's entire family was killed by a terrorist bomb on a New York subway. He's someone who understands the darkness in the world all too well."

Dr. Kalabi looked away, seemingly embarrassed by the introduction. His anxiety over their presence was obvious. "Do they need to be here?"

Keefer frowned. "They won't bother anything. Besides, history should have outside witnesses."

Dr. Kalabi nodded, acquiescing. Then he turned and pointed to the four patients. "We are ready for stage one," he said. "Mr. Morris is on standby video link. We waited per your instructions."

"Put him on the screen."

A large monitor on the far side of the room came to life. On it was one of the most recognizable faces in the world. Brandon Morris.

The feed was clearly bi-directional because his expression went from excitement to consternation in about the time it took to pick out Rick and Dahlia in the image.

"Brandon," Keefer said. "We're here. We're right on the edge. I told you our plans would work."

"What are they doing in the room?" Morris snapped. "That's not in the plan."

"An operational adjustment," Keefer said. "Don't let it bother you."

Morris didn't look happy, but he let it go. "And Cassie? Dr. Banks, I mean?"

Rick flinched, thinking they'd discovered her after all. He felt better when Keefer replied.

"I'm sorry, but she wasn't able to be taken alive."

Morris leaned back in his chair, removed his glasses and squeezed the bridge of his nose. A low moan came over the sound system. Rick noticed Dr. Kalabi and the technicians look away from the screen as if embarrassed to intrude on the moment. Rick felt fleeting compassion for the man, until reminding himself the son of a bitch was helping Keefer kill thousands of people, billions if he was to be believed.

Keefer waited a full ten seconds and then cleared his throat. "Brandon, can we move on?"

Morris replaced his glasses and stretched his neck from side-to-side. "Dr. Kalabi, I'm sending the final data packet to you now."

Keefer looked at the doctor who walked over to a computer terminal, watching carefully.

"I'm sorry, but I don't ... wait ... yes, I see it now," Dr. Kalabi said. "Integrating the data now. Processing." He turned to Keefer. "A few minutes."

"Brandon, do you want to explain the science to our friends here?"

Morris shook his head. "Not really."

"Don't mind him. He's just shy," Keefer said. "Dr. Kalabi?"

The doctor looked up from his computer as if wishing he had a good excuse not to comply, but he was just waiting so he stood and exhaled heavily.

"Essentially, there are two separate discoveries that we've brought together to change the world as we know it."

"He's better than you at explaining anyway," Keefer said to Morris on the screen.

"The first is the ability to tap into the potential of the entire brain. This started with the groundbreaking work of Dr. Cassandra Baker." He nodded to Rick's synthetic arm. "It's what makes your prosthetic seamlessly integrate into your nervous system. We took that and found our way into the brain. The entire brain. A machine of unparalleled power."

"There are 225 million billion separate interactions in the brain," Morris interrupted. "It's a massively parallel computer that's self-organizing, uses content-addressable memory versus byte-addressable, differentiates through analogue rates of firing neurons in either synchrony or relative disarray creating an essentially continuous variable." The man spoke so quickly that it was hard to follow him. "Not only that, but each and every neuron contains a leaky integrator circuit with ion channels and fluctuating membrane potentials. It's so powerful that even though the brain only comprises three percent of the average human's body weight, it uses twenty percent of the body's energy. It's really unbelievable when you think about it."

Keefer looked at Rick and shrugged as if to say he didn't follow the explanation either. "Bottom line, the brain is a powerful tool if it's fully unlocked."

"Like they always say, we only use ten percent of our brain," Dahlia said.

Keefer looked pleased. "Yes, only that's a complete myth. Basic neurological studies, even from the beginning of the twenty-first century, showed we use most of our brain, most of the time. Just not even close to the extent with which we could use it."

"We're talking pure computing power here," Morris said. "Not telekinesis and all that nonsense."

"You said there were two inventions," Rick said. "What was the second?"

A beep sounded from the workstation. "Processing complete," Dr. Kalabi said, leaning back toward the computer. "Systems on line."

"Sorry," Keefer said to Rick. "That'll have to wait." To the doctor he said, "Proceed."

Dr. Kalabi looked up at the screen and Morris nodded.

Technicians paired up at each bed but didn't touch any of the equipment. Dr. Kalabi typed instructions into the computer keyboard and then stopped, his finger hovering over the ENTER key.

"Do you want to execute the command?" he asked Keefer.

He shook his head. "I'll do it in the next stage. This honor is all yours."

Rick noticed Dr. Kalabi's finger shaking as he held it above the button. Judging by his body language, the man didn't regard what he was about to do as an honor of any kind.

But he pressed the button and the drills started.

CHAPTER 51

R*ick felt a visceral reaction* to the sound of the high-speed drills springing into action. It was the same sound as the drills used in a dentist's office, only there were dozens of them going at once. And worse, it was clear what they were intended to do.

Rick stepped toward the bed with Bertie on it, but one of the drones flew in from his left. He still held Charlie in his arms. Rick took a step back and pulled the boy closer to him, turning his head away from the scene in front of them in case he woke up.

The robot arms descended slowly, the spinning needles inside the disk entering the white material, causing the high-pitched whine of the drills to change by an octave. They sunk deeper until the pitch changed again once they hit bone.

He watched Bertie's face shake with small vibrations as the needles drilled through her skull and into her brain. The image on the screen next to her bed, the one showing the three-dimensional image of her brain, showed dozens of white lines entering folds of the organ, stopping at different depths. Her heart rate spiked and her chest heaved with rapid breathing. An alarm went off on the monitor, but one of the techs quickly pressed a button and it disappeared.

Then, in unison, the drills stopped.

The robot arms pulled back and left the metal disks in place, thick cords of electrical wire draping off the back of them like macabre ponytails.

"Implants successful," Dr. Kalabi said. "All subjects stable."

Rick looked back at Bertie's face. Her breathing had calmed back down and her heart rate slowed with every beat.

"Activating now," Dr. Kalabi said.

Rick saw the image of Bertie's brain change colors. Bursts of blues and reds radiated out from each of the probes. Soon the entire image was a swirl of brilliant color.

Despite the horror of it all, Rick couldn't deny that it was beautiful.

Keefer's reaction was similar. He stared at the brain image of the patient nearest him, reaching out to the screen and touching it gently.

"Shall I start the linking process?" Dr. Kalabi asked. The question was directed at Morris, not Keefer.

"If you've installed the equipment correctly, then there shouldn't be a problem," Morris said. "We've been this far in the lab here in Denver."

"With two subjects," Dr. Kalabi said.

"Theoretically, it shouldn't make a difference," Morris responded.

Dr. Kalabi didn't look convinced, but he turned back to his computer station, his fingers flying over the keyboard. Rick thought it ironic that the good doctor wasn't about to let one of the new brain-machine interfaces burrow inside his own head, choosing the old-fashioned keyboard instead.

"What's happening?" Dahlia asked.

"What is it, Keefer?" Rick asked. "What's the second discovery?"

Keefer looked back at him, then to Dr. Kalabi, seeming to reach the conclusion there was time. "In this room in front of you are the four most powerful supercomputers in the world. Each of them is capable of solving mathematical modeling problems that would take our best computers weeks to work out. Weather patterns, drug interactions, particle physics research."

"None of which you're interested in," Rick said. The realization came at him fast and hit him hard. It was the only thing that made sense. "Jesus, this is about encryption, isn't it?"

Keefer clapped his hands together. "Very good, Rick. Yes, it's about encryption. Cyber-terrorism has turned every computer system into an island, each one protected by sophisticated encryption technology, codes that are considered unbreakable. And that belief is what makes them vulnerable. Given time, these computers could beat that technology, opening up any system it wanted. That alone is a game changer. But add the other discovery to it, and you change the world."

"You can connect them," Rick said, feeling his stomach turn as he realized the implications. "Somehow, you can link them together."

"Yes," Keefer said, excited. "Good, you understand. I can see it in your face that you do."

"It's called a brainet," Morris said over the video connection. "Linking together multiple brains to essentially create a massively parallel supercomputer. Researchers have been playing with organic computing for the last two decades, but it has never lived up to the hype. With Cassie's work with the brain-machine interface, everything changed. Linking the brains is so complex that unless you create a superbrain first to manage the process, it just spirals out of control." Morris turned away from the camera. "This is really her invention, even though she never knew it."

"We're ready," Dr. Kalabi said.

"I don't understand. Why did you come to our town? Why our people?" Rick said. "Why go through all this when you could have used soldiers? Or just paid people to do it?"

"Quiet, please," Keefer said. "You'll want to watch this. This is history being made."

Rick eyed the drones next to him. He needed to stop this, but there was nothing he could do.

"Proceed, Dr. Kalabi," Keefer said.

The doctor pressed a button on the computer and stepped back.

At first nothing happened. The room was silent. Everyone held their breath, watching the four patients.

"There," Dr. Kalabi whispered. "It's happening."

Slowly the brain images on each screen turned a brilliant royal blue, pulsing from light to dark in unison.

The techs applauded. Keefer crossed the floor to Dr. Kalabi and shook his hand.

"Does that mean those people are connected now?" Dahlia whispered to Rick. "Their brains are part of this … brainet thing?"

He didn't respond.

"So now they have a computer powerful enough to do what?" she asked. "What are they planning?"

"They're planning to end the world," Rick whispered, realizing that Keefer's threats had been real all along. If he could hack the most sophisticated encryptions, then nothing was safe. He could access the banking system. The military. Maybe even nuclear launch codes. He was worse than a madman prophesying the end of the world. He was a madman with the ability to make his prophesy come true.

"Performing trial calculation to clock processing speed," Dr. Kalabi said.

Keefer walked back to Rick. "This will take some time. We need to—"

"It's done," Dr. Kalabi said.

"What?" Morris said, leaning toward the camera.

The doctor looked up from his computer, beaming. "Trial calculation complete," he said.

Keefer stopped. "You thought it would take nearly an hour to complete the trial, even with the new computing power of the four linked units."

"I know … I know …" Dr. Kalabi said. "But the processing speed is greater than anything I ever imagined. It appears they solved the trial calculation … in less than one second."

"That's impossible," Morris said on the screen, his voice echoing in the room. "Let me check the data. I'm calling a hold on any further steps until we can sort through this."

Dr. Kalabi looked to Keefer.

"We're not holding for anything," Keefer said. "Prepare to initiate."

"No," Morris said. "If the computation is that much more advanced, then we don't really understand what's happening. Our models are completely wrong."

"It's better than we thought," Keefer said. "More powerful. That's not a problem, it's an advantage."

"It's too dangerous," Morris said. "I'm shutting it down until we can understand what's happening."

Keefer shook his head slowly. "I can't let you do that."

"You can't let me?" Morris snorted. "This is my invention. I'm in charge here. Kalabi, patch me into the data stream."

Kalabi slowly put his hands to his side. Keefer smiled.

Morris looked confused. "This is not your call. You work for me, Keefer. You're an … an employee."

Keefer barked out a short laugh. "For being the most brilliant mind in our century, you really are a dumb ass, Brandon. I don't work for you. I never have. Did you think I would do all this just so that you could save yourself? Use this technology to transfer into a new body?"

"That's our deal, Keefer," Morris said, furiously typing on the keyboard on the desk in front of him. "Then we'd use what I'd become to make the country great again."

Keefer laughed. "This is bigger than you. This is bigger than all of us."

Rick watched the interchange between the two men and he realized the truth of it. Morris had no idea what Keefer's real plan was.

"Morris," Rick yelled. "He going to destroy the world outside the United States. Nukes, power grids, all of it. You've got to stop this."

Morris looked horrified. "That's it," he said. "I'm pulling you off this. It's gone too far."

On the screen, Morris continued typing, his fingers flying.

"Morris," Keefer said. "It's too late."

Morris looked up, real fear on his face now. "I'm locked out."

Keefer nodded. "The trial calculation we used to clock the processing speed of the four person brainet was the encryption code for the Genysis servers."

"That's impossible. The encryption is unbreakable. It would take centuries to hack."

"The solution was arrived at in less than one microsecond," Dr. Kalabi said softly, as if to himself. "Perhaps faster. That's the smallest unit of measurement for the system."

"This project is mine," Morris mumbled, typing again. "You can't take it away."

Keefer smiled. "Trying to activate those security protocols you put into place?" he said. "The ones to make sure I couldn't use the machine we were building together? Yeah, those won't work anymore."

"You can't do this," Morris yelled.

"I already have," Keefer said.

He turned to the camera in the corner of the room, reached his hand into the air and closed it into a fist.

"What are you—"

The explosion came from behind Morris, so the wall of flame shared the frame with him for a split second before the image disappeared, replaced with a simple message:

<SIGNAL LOST>

The room was silent, no one moving. Dr. Kalabi stared at the ground. Only Keefer seemed unaffected by the whole thing.

"Dr. Kalabi, are we ready?" he asked. When there was no response, he raised his voice. "Dr. Kalabi!"

"Y-yes," the doctor stammered. "Of course."

Keefer waved Rick to follow him. Rick, clutching Charlie protectively, followed Keefer to a double set of doors, like those opening to a hospital corridor. Dahlia followed him.

"Morris never knew what you had planned, did he?" Rick asked.

Keefer shook his head. "Brandon had stage three lymphoma when I met him. It's stage four now. He wanted the brainet to create either a cure for his disease or, at the minimum, unlock how to replicate his mind into another body. For a visionary, he never really thought big enough."

"Yeah, you mentioned that you were going to change the world," Rick said. "I'd say you're going to need more than four linked supercomputers to do that."

"I couldn't agree with you more," Keefer said.

He pressed a button on the side of the wall. There was a click and then the doors slowly opened outward.

Rick walked through the opening, feeling like he was in a bad dream.

The space in front of him was enormous. Several football fields in size, supported by periodic stone columns.

Stretching out for hundreds of yards were row after row of hospital beds.

Each one set up exactly like the one in the lab behind them. A cart of electronic monitors. An articulated robotic arm. A single spotlight creating a circle of light on the bed.

And every bed had a person on it, sitting up at a forty-five-degree angle and wrapped with chest straps. The white skull helmets stood out, reflecting the bright light above each bed. Hundreds of them lined up in a perfect row.

Here were the two thousand people from Resurrection's Fall Festival. About to have their heads drilled, their brains transformed into computing machines, and then connected to form the greatest killing machine in the history of mankind.

And there was nothing Rick could do to stop it.

Keefer stood next to him, staring proudly out over the result of so many years of planning. He put up his hand, hesitated for a moment, and then swiped it downward in a cutting motion. Instantly, two thousand robotic drills spun into action.

CHAPTER 52

C*assie stifled a scream as* robot arms came to life over each bed and the air filled with the deafening whine of drills spinning up to full speed. She'd nearly made it to the far side of the cavern, near the access point for the data trunk, when it'd happened.

She knew exactly what was happening. Cerebral probes were the cornerstone of her research in brain-machine interfaces. Most of the clinical work took place on animals, but she'd overseen the procedure on early adopters of the artificial limb program too.

Only that surgery had always been completed under full anesthetic.

Most of the people in the beds were still passed out from the drug they'd been given in town. But spread out among them, perhaps every tenth or fifteenth bed, was someone who was awake, kicking and thrashing in their beds. Mouths open wide in screams that were drowned out by the sounds of the drills.

They were fully awake and about to have their brain cavity drilled.

Cassie ran to the nearest bed where a man struggled against his straps, hands frantically pulling at the straps.

"Help me! Oh Jesus, help," the man screamed.

He flailed and bucked against the straps so hard that she couldn't get a grip in the buckle.

"Stop moving," she yelled. "Stop so I can help you!"

But the man screamed louder as a robotic arm swung over his head.

The disks attached to the robotic arms all around her lowered in unison. She dug her fingers into the buckle but it wouldn't give.

With a cry, she climbed onto the gurney and jumped at the robotic arm. It swung wildly to one side, the disk with the needles in it flailing.

The row of needles tore across her back, slicing through her shirt and skin.

She screamed at the pain and felt a hot gush of blood down the side of her rib cage as she fell to the ground.

The robotic arm self-corrected and repositioned the disk over the man's head.

Cassie spotted the power connection at the base of the robotic unit. As the drills descended, she lunged for the power cord and yanked on it. The connection came loose, but instead of stopping immediately, the robotic arm jerked wildly as it powered down.

She climbed to her feet, ready to free the man and had to stifle a scream when she looked on the gurney.

The man's head was shattered into pieces, carved up by the errant drill. Flaps of skin still showed parts of the man's face on the larger chunks. Cassie turned away, grabbing the side of the bed as she vomited on the floor.

All around her, the sound of the drills stopped. Within seconds of each other, the arms retracted from their patients and came to rest. On these beds, the people lay unmoving, hands to their side, faces calm as if they were in a comfortable sleep. The only thing unnerving was the metal disk attached to their head with a thick cable coming off it. She knew that under that disk were dozens of probes drilled through their skulls and into their brains.

The whine of the drills echoed in the chamber, but soon, the cavern was silent.

Except for the soft, pulsating hum of the electrical monitoring equipment.

Cassie stifled a sob as she looked out over the sea of beds, each looking like an island of light. She tried to calm herself and think through what she was looking at.

There were heavy cords coming from the base of each patient's head that tied into the mounds of cabling running between the grid of beds. She examined the monitor nearest her that showed a 3-D model of the man's brain. It showed a swirl of brilliant color. To the layman, it would just appear to be a pretty image. To her, it was a mesmerizing insight into what the probes had accomplished. And it was unbelievable.

The colors indicated a level of activity she'd never seen before. Certainly in her own work she'd attempted to unlock cognitive space, tried to unlock potentiality. Her teams had had small successes, but nothing like this. If the 3-D model displayed was true and not some kind of enhanced filter, then the technology at work here was more advanced than anything she'd ever seen.

And the cords.

They were more than power lines for the lights and monitors.

The cords networked all of the bodies together.

She knew the theoretical science of brainet. She also knew that it was impossible. Only the smallest advances had even been made. Linking simian brains to perform basic tasks. True that in these experiments, the combined brains were able to outperform the single brain by a substantial rate. But Dr.

Kalabi out of Johns Hopkins had proven the system limits that prevented a human brainet. The failure rate exponentially curved to one hundred percent as complexity was added. Based on that peer-reviewed science, the idea of a brainet had joined the ranks of cold fusion, another theoretical dead end.

But someone had figured it out.

Or at least thought they had.

She looked back at the screen and at the level of activity depicted there.

If they had unleashed that much brain potential, and then were able to fuse it together into a functioning massively parallel network, then she was looking at the greatest source of computing power in the history of the human race.

The scientist in her marveled at the accomplishment, but the thought didn't stay with her long. Clearly this discovery wasn't meant for good. It would not be used to cure cancer or develop alternative energy sources or design a new line of antibiotics.

Two thousand civilians taken hostage through a military operation. The story about a virus and a vaccine to control the population to get them sedated. All of the lies added up to a terrible conclusion.

This was not a scientific discovery in front of her. It was a weapon.

And now Keefer's speech down in the town made sense. He'd talked about the resurrection of America, the destruction of her enemies. And he'd talked about the sacrifice of the patriots gathered in front of him.

He'd called them martyrs for the cause of freedom.

She looked back at all the beds extending out in front of her.

And she understood.

None of them would survive. Perhaps it was already too late. Perhaps the probes in the brain alone had already sealed their fate.

There was no way she could know for sure, but it didn't matter. Even if her own actions caused the death of everyone there, she had to do it. She had to destroy the machine in front of her before it could be used.

And, by a miracle, she had a good idea of how to do it.

CHAPTER 53

K*eefer watched his dream come* to fruition from the doorway to the main lab. He looked out over the main cavern, knowing he was only looking at less than half of the bodies involved. The others were in the adjacent caverns, all linked together in one glorious computer. As the robotic arms did their work, he was so overcome with emotion that tears streaked down his cheeks.

He didn't bother to cover his ears even though the sound was deafening. After so many years of preparation, so many near-misses where he thought the plan might be discovered, so many times that the entire thing seemed about to unravel, the emotion of seeing it all come together was almost too much to bear.

His doubts were gone now. Seeing the precision movement of the robot arms and the perfection of the execution so far, showed that this was ordained. Perhaps not by God, even Keefer wasn't sure the Creator would sign-off on his plan to undo a millennia of population growth, but it was ordained by some power greater than himself. He was sure of it.

Call it the march of history. Or manifest destiny. Or karma.

America had served as a beacon to the world for two and a half centuries. She'd been selfless, putting other nations before herself, sending her sons and daughters to bleed on foreign shores to liberate peoples all around the world. And for what? To be reviled and attacked? Called the Great Satan by the barbarians who slaughtered civilians?

America had done her best to help the rest of the world, and her very existence was threatened because of it. The old saying had it right, *No good deed goes unpunished*. Only now Keefer had created the opportunity for America to save herself. It was a right she'd earned over a long period of time. The best century in human history had been the one dominated by America. And it would be that way again. Perhaps forever this time.

He glanced back at Rick. The sheriff was on his knees, clutching the little boy and the woman to him. When the drills started, the boy had been shocked out of his stupor and immediately started to scream. Keefer had hardly noticed, but now that the drills were winding down their work, little Charlie's cries filled the air.

The thought crossed Keefer's mind to just have the three of them taken away and disposed of. He felt embarrassed by the weakness he'd shown in front of them. Doubt wasn't normally part of his makeup. The moment had been fleeting but dangerous. He actually wondered whether, if the sheriff had chosen to kill the woman and her child, his own heart would have been swayed. He doubted it. But Rick's decision had made it easy.

Having the sheriff there as a foil had been good. It wasn't lost on him that pressing the button to end the lives of billions of people would come with a heavy emotional burden, one that might prove too hard to heft onto his shoulders when the moment came. He'd thought of nothing but that for years. But he'd convinced himself he could do it. The result made it all worthwhile.

No, more than worthwhile. The result made the act absolutely necessary.

Still, as he turned back to look at the rows of beds filled with the patriots who would give their lives for their country, he couldn't help but imagine the scenes that would soon play out around the world.

In a connected world, nothing was safe from the power he would have at his disposal. Cyber warfare had only made this moment more possible. The rise of powerful encryption technologies had made countries more vulnerable, not less. Hiding behind their firewalls, vast networks of essential services remained networked on the belief the wall could never be breached. The breach of the Genysis encryption was the perfect example. It would have taken the world's most powerful computer hundreds of years to compute a solution. Even then, while the computer was working on the solution, the encryption algorithm continuously evolved, presenting a different problem to solve. It was impossible to circumvent.

A brainet of only four people had solved it in only a fraction of a second.

Keefer could only imagine the power of two thousand Americans working together.

It wasn't a matter of hacking into essential systems and wreaking havoc. The end of the world was to be instantaneous. He would be everywhere simultaneously. Inside every system, through every firewall, burrowed into everything from the mainframes running national power grids all the way down to each individual cell phone. He would be inside every satellite orbiting the planet. He would control the safety protocols in nuclear reactors, hydroelectric dams, subway systems. Every military system, from unmanned drones to ships, from bombs stored in bunkers to smart munitions inside weapons in the field, all of it would respond to his command.

The massive Genysis supercomputers in the underground lab, air-gapped to prevent Morris from knowing what was going on, had been running simulations directed by Kalabi over the last month. The system simulated open access to the world's most important computer infrastructure, using a powerful artificial intelligence algorithm, following a core directive.

Destroy the human population outside the territorial United States.

The program showed surprising restraint in the simulation of how it achieved its goal. Keefer had anticipated the widespread use of nuclear arsenals in the model, but their use was limited. The idea was to leave the United States not only intact, but with a habitable world. The AI sorted through the parameters and created a solution set so elegant and so frighteningly deadly, that it seemed almost too simple.

The Middle East would be immediately destroyed with nuclear attacks from Europe and Russia, calculated so that the fallout would not impact the North American continent, but would still transform that Godforsaken region into a layer of glass from the melted sand. The nest of Jihadis would be set on fire and destroyed. It was unfortunate that American servicemen stationed there would also be killed in the attack, but it was unavoidable. Keefer intended to compensate their families generously for their sacrifice.

Nuclear weapons would be used on a limited number of other population centers, but that was just for efficiency. Every conventional smart armament with a receiver would explode simultaneously on six continents and in space. Airplanes would fall from the sky. Ships would ram themselves into the shoreline and submarines would sink into the depths of the oceans and never return to the surface. Biological agents, those that could be counted on to tear through a population but die out on their own, would be released into the air.

But none of this was really necessary based on the models. Just the act of cutting electricity and communication permanently across the globe was enough to send almost the entire seven billion into a death spiral. Food supplies ran out in days. Panic and looting happened almost immediately. As social order broke down, disease took out whole swaths of the population.

Everything was connected. Even simple gas-powered generators had sensors that would receive instructors to fry their circuit boards. Outside of equipment that was thirty or forty years old, overnight the world would be reduced to candles and sending communication by handwritten note. No refrigeration meant food stores would rot within a week. The great desalination plants around the world, the only reason billions of people didn't die of thirst, would go silent and never start again.

The world without power was a world that turned on itself and died.

The bombs and diseases Keefer would release were actually a mercy, hurrying along the inevitable and minimizing the suffering.

He was so lost in his images of the world as he would create it, a world defined by the only country left intact after the devastation, that he didn't notice until too late the movement to his side.

He grunted as the sheriff smashed into him with a lowered shoulder, picking him up off the ground and driving him backward.

He felt the sting of bullets as the drones opened fire, hitting both of them.

As he fell to the ground, the sheriff on top of him, landing blows to his face, he recognized letting the man live had been a mistake.

That was the problem with Marines in general, and this one in particular.

They never knew when they were beat.

CHAPTER 54

R*ick drove through the pain.* Bullets smacked into his back, one after the other, feeling like pieces of burning shrapnel, but he kept hitting Keefer in the face. It wasn't until 10,000 volts of electricity entered his body that he stopped swinging.

His body arched and he fell to the floor next to Keefer, jerking from the Taser. The flow of electricity went on for what seemed like a full minute. He knew from previous experience that it'd likely been only a fraction of that time, but that didn't make it any less painful.

Once it stopped, every inch of his body felt like it was on fire. Then, in a blast of pain, he felt the spots on his back where the drones had pumped bullets at him. He was just glad his calculation had been correct that the drones wouldn't risk Keefer's life, and had selected rubber bullets from their arsenal. They may have technically been nonlethal, but they sure hurt like hell. Seeing

Keefer's bloody face as he stood up took some of the edge off, but not much.

Keefer wiped his mouth and nose with his sleeve. He grinned at Rick, his teeth coated with blood. "That wasn't smart," he said slowly.

"But damn if you didn't deserve it," Rick said.

Rick chanced a quick glance down the length of beds. Seconds earlier he'd spotted Cassie running from the cavern on their left and cutting straight through the main cavern close to the back, far wall. She'd been wearing a black jumpsuit and her hair was cut short to her scalp, but one look and he'd known it was her. She was alive, but more important, she was moving with purpose. He'd known right away that he couldn't let Keefer see her, so he'd made his move.

Breaking the man's nose was just an added bonus.

Two soldiers ran out from inside the lab. Rick groaned when he saw one of them was Estevez.

"What are you doing here?" Keefer said. "You're supposed to be in the control room."

Estevez was taken aback by the question, but it didn't last long. He didn't bother to hide his anger. "What am I doing here? What are they doing here? Especially now?"

Keefer stepped toward the younger man and Rick hoped for some kind of confrontation between the two. Anything to give Cassie more time.

But Keefer didn't argue. Instead, he nodded and put a hand on the younger man's shoulder. "You're right. I got what I wanted from him. Kill them. Kill all three of them."

Estevez looked satisfied. He waved a soldier forward and they grabbed Dahlia and Charlie roughly by the arms.

"No!" Rick yelled, pulling against the strong hands holding him back.

"Oh my God," Dahlia cried as the soldier pulled her away. "No!"

Charlie pushed his way forward, swinging his tiny fists at the soldier pulling his mother. The soldier backhanded him across the face and he fell to the ground in a pile. Dahlia screamed.

"Leave him alone," Rick yelled.

Dahlia threw her body over her son.

"Not here, you idiots," Keefer said. "Take them away."

The soldier bent down and scooped up a groggy Charlie, holding him under his arm like he was a bundle of firewood. He used his other hand to point his gun at Dahlia. "Come quietly or I'll snap his neck right here," the soldier said.

"Rick?" she said.

His vision blurred as tears stung his eyes.

"Keefer, leave them alone," he begged. "I'll do anything you ask."

But Keefer was already walking back into the lab where the four original patients were hooked up. The drones followed him in, one on each side, obviously set on protection mode. The doors slid shut behind him once he was inside.

Rick looked at Estevez, the man's smug look confirming that the road was over. He didn't see any way out. He'd given Cassie the best chance he could. He just prayed that she had an actual plan. He turned to Dahlia.

"I love you," he said. "I love you and Charlie so much."

Dahlia seemed to understand that he was saying good-bye. Tears covered her cheeks, but she stood up straight and wiped them away. If she was going to die, she was going to do it with her pride intact. He had never loved her more than at that moment.

"I love you too," she said. "And Charlie? I want you to be brave, all right? I want you to grow up and be a fighter, you understand me?"

Charlie tried to squirm out of the soldier's arms, but the man held him tight.

"Dahlia, what are you—"

She cut him off. "Will you do something for me?"

"Anything."

"Take care of Charlie for me," she said, her voice strong. "And, if you get a chance, kill that son of a bitch Keefer. He deserves it."

Too late, Rick realized she was the one saying good-bye. With a cry, she ran at the soldier in front of her, the one carrying Charlie. She jumped onto him, scratching at his face and eyes with her hands. The soldier didn't see it coming. He dropped Charlie and fell to the ground with Dahlia on top of him. The gun went off twice.

Two red starbursts exploded out from Dahlia's back, but her weight pinned the soldier down.

Charlie saw it and screamed.

Rick was so stunned that he nearly missed the opening her move gave him. Estevez hadn't moved either, but Rick knew that wouldn't last long. He was the first to snap into action and lunge at Estevez.

He was already midair when Estevez reacted and raised his gun.

Rick smacked it out of the way, using his prosthetic to hit the man's forearm with such force that he heard the bone snap. Estevez cried out as the gun went flying through the air.

Rick disengaged and lunged after the gun on the ground. The drones were inside the lab with Keefer, but they wouldn't take long to come back if their security setting was adjusted. And that would only take a few seconds. Besides, the complex outside the main cavern was crawling with soldiers. He had to move.

He reached the weapon and closed his hand around it.

But Estevez grabbed his leg and pulled him backward. The gun fumbled from his grip.

Rick screamed as hot searing pain shot through his calf.

He looked down the length of his body and saw Estevez with his hand on the end of a knife handle buried in his leg. Estevez pulled on the knife but Rick's leg jerked up, the knife stuck in bone.

Rick kicked free, crying out from the pain. The knife remained skewered in his leg, the point of the blade sticking out the other side by two or three inches.

Estevez reached for another gun carried on his vest, exposing his ribcage.

With a yell, Rick swung his leg as hard as he could, sinking the knifepoint into the man's side.

Estevez grabbed his side, exactly as Rick expected.

Pain bolted up his leg, but he ignored it. He took the opening Estevez gave him, pulled his leg back and kicked again.

This one landed in Estevez's neck, causing a spray of blood. He fell to the ground, clawing at the wound as if he could block the blood from spilling out.

Rick immediately lunged again for the gun, and grabbed it this time. He spun, looking for the other soldier.

He had Dahlia pushed off of him and was bringing his gun up toward Rick.

Too late. Rick fired twice into the man's chest.

Next, he looked to the lab. The doors were still closed.

"Watch out," Charlie cried.

Another drone flew at him from his right, different from the ones that had followed Keefer back into the lab.

Rick rolled toward Estevez as bullets peppered the ground around him.

One hit his thigh, blowing out a piece of his muscle. He cried out and lunged to Estevez.

He pulled the man on top of him, using him for cover.

The drone didn't delineate between targets. It sprayed bullets into Estevez, tearing him apart.

Rick took a bullet in the shoulder. Another in the same leg as the knife. But Estevez blocked the rest from reaching him.

The drone emptied its limited magazine. As it switched to an alternative weapon, Rick took his chance.

He fired rapidly, trying to anticipate the drone's evasive maneuvers.

A shot glanced off of its metal casing, causing it to wobble.

That was all Rick needed.

He nailed it through the main camera lens, scoring a direct hit. The drone spun out of control and crashed into the ground amidst a mass of sparks.

Rick hobbled over to Dahlia, dragging one leg behind him. She was face-down, her back covered in blood. Charlie lay on the ground next to her so that his face was next to hers.

He carefully turned her over. Her eyes moved and there was a moment of recognition. Her lips moved but she made no sound. Still, he knew the word she repeated.

Charlie.

Charlie

"He's right here. It's all right," Rick whispered, choking on the words. "I promised I'd take care of him."

Charlie grabbed her hand, sobbing. She looked at him a smiled, her teeth coated with blood.

Rick laid her head in his lap, pushed strands of hair from her face. "Hang on. Just a little more. We're getting out of here."

She coughed and blood gushed from her mouth. Her lips curled in an attempt at a smile. "You ...you're a t ... t ... terrible ... liar ..." she rasped. Then she tensed and a panicked look came over her. "Charlie?" she asked, trying to get up.

"Here. I'm here," Charlie said.

"He's all right," Rick said, easing her back to his lap. "I've got him. I promise."

Her eyes opened wider and her body tensed. Then her lips stopped moving and her eyes stared right through him.

Charlie let out a whimpering sob, pressing his mom's hand on his cheek. Rick pulled her to his chest, not wanting to move from that spot. Not caring if they came and found him there. But he had to care. Charlie was still alive. He had to let go of Dahlia for him.

Carefully, he laid her on the ground and wiped the tears from his face. He took Charlie's hand and softly pulled him to his feet. It was only a matter of time before soldiers or more drones arrived. Probably seconds, not minutes. He limped over to the other soldier's gun and stuck it in his belt.

He took stock. There was a knife in his leg. Three bullet holes in his body from what he could tell. His weapon arsenal was two handguns with half their ammo gone. And he was going up against a hundred trained mercenaries and a fleet of kill drones.

As he faced the doors to the lab, waiting for them to open, he tried to look on the bright side.

He didn't think he would have to endure the pain he was in much longer.

CHAPTER 55

C*assie heard the gunfire but* didn't look in its direction.

She'd made the mistake of running through the beds instead of crawling. Her thinking was that she was going to be spotted by cameras either way. Perhaps someone running would be given the benefit of the doubt, rationalized away as a worker who had forgotten to do something important. It seemed a more likely explanation than the truth. Who would believe that a solitary infiltrator would be brazen enough to walk out in the open?

But when she'd turned and seen Keefer confronting Rick and Dahlia at gunpoint, she knew she'd made a mistake. She was too close. If Keefer had turned, there was no doubt he would have recognized her.

Rick charging at Keefer had been unexpected, but it'd given her the distraction she needed. She hoped that whoever watched the security cameras was completely focused on the altercation happening behind her.

When the gunshots went off, she had to stifle a cry. She knew it had to be Rick and Dahlia being executed. But when it turned into what sounded like a firefight, she had to wonder. Regardless of whether Rick had put up a fight or not, the odds were overwhelmingly against him.

It was up to her to stop Keefer.

She made it to her destination, praying that what she needed was still there.

The door to the utility room looked the same as when she'd worked at the lab. She turned the handle, her heart racing as the door opened. Unlocked.

She stepped inside, the overhead lighting flickering on from the motion sensors. The room looked essentially the same as it had years earlier when the lab closed down. The space was mostly a labyrinth of pipes and cables entering from different directions. Half the room used to hold spare office supplies back in the Genysis days, but now it was stacked with food stores. She was happy to see it. The presence of the food and the fact that the door was unlocked hinted at the fact that Keefer's team had failed to realize the importance of this location, just as Brandon Morris had done.

This was where she'd plugged her sensors into the artery that led out of the mine, the data trunk through which everything had to pass.

It was easy to miss the schematics because the data cable didn't actually enter the room; they would never have exposed it in such a way. But it did burrow through the solid rock only two feet next to this room's wall.

Once her suspicion that Morris had sold out to the military had reached its peak, it'd still taken her two months to figure out how to tap into the cable through the rock wall, and then another month to configure the sensors.

Fortunately, she was working in a mine. Finding someone to explain to her the best methods for cutting through solid rock was easy enough. Pulling it off without anyone knowing had been harder. She felt like the men in one of her favorite movies,

The Great Escape, digging a little bit at a time and then carrying the telltale rubble she created in her pockets to drop in a different part of the mine.

But she'd done it, cutting out a section two feet wide and one foot tall right up the trunk. The sensors had been easier to install as they just needed to attach to the outer sheath of the cable, but the coding had been a challenge because she didn't want them to be discovered. When she was done, she sealed the cavity with a stone façade and left it behind when the lab closed, her insurance policy that Brandon would keep his word.

So much for promises.

She climbed over the pipes, following the familiar path to her secret spot on the wall. There were cables still hanging over the area, just as she'd left them. She pushed them aside and felt a surge of adrenaline as she saw the rock façade was still in place. The section was only eighteen inches off the ground. She kicked at it with her heel, and then bashed it with a can of food; the façade broke into two.

She got on her knees and pulled it away, opening the hole. Inside, there was a soft red glow of the sensor she'd installed there connected to a small laptop. She pulled out the laptop and opened it. The screen lit up, the batteries still strong. It was to be expected since they were designed to last for decades. Still, it was a relief.

But if her plan worked properly, then the computer and batteries only had to last a couple more minutes. After that, they would just be part of the shrapnel tearing through the data trunk.

She opened up the duffel bag and removed the contents she'd stolen from the supply locker.

Grenades. Ten of them.

It would be easy enough to detonate one to set off the others, and the enclosed space would intensify the blast. It was unfortunate that most of the force would direct back into the room, but she was counting on it being powerful enough to severely damage if not sheer the line. For Keefer to use his new weapon, he needed to have access to the outside world. Without it, the computing power he'd created was like having a nuclear bomb without an aircraft or a missile to deliver it.

Before she disabled it, she wanted to warn the world about what was happening here. She had no illusions about her chances of living through the next hour, but at least she could die knowing she'd given the world a chance.

Her fingers rested on the keyboard. What the hell could she put in a short message that would get them to take action?

"Imminent terrorist threat. Massive cyber-attack to hit all major systems worldwide. Take necessary precautions. 100 heavily armed men in Genysis lab/ Resurrection Mine, Colorado. Entire town hostage in mine. Colonel Keefer leading. Send military. Terrorists have access to WMD. Dr. Cassandra Baker."

She looked at the message. There wasn't time for anything longer. The reference to weapons of mass destruction would hopefully get her message up the national security food chain faster.

She sent it to the national See Something Say Something tip line, but then blasted it to a half-dozen reporters she knew personally. Lastly, she sent it to Whitehouse.gov, hoping the filters would catch the buzzwords and filter it for Secret Service review.

She reread the message, wondering how long it would take someone with any authority to actually see it, and then how much longer it would take for them to actually do anything about it. There wasn't anything else she could do. She'd warned them. It was up to the world to decide what to do with the information.

She just hoped she could give them more time by taking out Keefer's connection to the world.

CHAPTER 56

K*eefer stared at the screen.* Estevez, Dahlia and the soldier lay sprawled on the ground. Rick stood in front of the door, his face covered with blood, his clothes shredded, a knife sticking out of his leg. And now the son of a bitch had a gun and was motioning at the camera for Keefer to come out.

But Keefer wouldn't rise to the bait. He'd already been too careless and taken too many risks. He needed to lock things down tight.

"The drones are ready to deploy, sir," a soldier said next to him. "Should I—"

"No," Keefer said. "I don't want that door opened. One bullet in here could hit a piece of equipment and delay us for hours. Send the drones through the other door and have them go around to the other entrance to the cavern. Set them for lethal. I want him dead."

The soldier glanced at the screen showing his fallen comrades, and the man who killed them barely able to stand, a handgun his only weapon.

"Sir, I have multiple drones. If we opened the main door, the threat would be neutralized in—"

Keefer pulled his gun from his side and held it to the soldier's head. "Are you able to follow orders, son?"

"Yes, sir," the soldier barked. He stepped back and typed instructions into the keypad on his arm. Two of the five drones in the room flew at full speed out of the door that led to the hallway. "They'll be there in less than two minutes."

Keefer replaced his gun. "Dr. Kalabi, are we ready?"

The doctor pointed to the keyboard at his station. "Everything is prepared," he said. "All you need to do is press ENTER and you change the world forever."

Keefer walked across the room, feeling all eyes on him. He thought of the fifteen people in the room. They would forever be able to say they were present at one of the greatest moments in history. He'd prepared something poignant to say, something fitting, the way Neil Armstrong had uttered his famous words as he stepped onto the moon.

But faced with the moment at hand, he found it impossible to recall the words. His heart beat hard in his chest and he felt almost dizzy as he walked up to the computer. It was almost like he was observing from a distance.

He pointed to the ENTER button on the keyboard for confirmation and Dr. Kalabi nodded.

Keefer looked at the display screen and what he saw there filled him with confidence:

LAUNCH OPERATION RESURRECTION

Keefer reached out with a shaking hand to the keyboard and said the only words that came to him. "God bless the United States of America."

And he pressed the button.

CHAPTER 57

R*ick couldn't believe they didn't* come for him right away. Once he realized the doors weren't opening, he grabbed Charlie's hand and limped in the direction of the escape elevator. Charlie pulled back.

"We can't just leave her here," he said.

"She did what she did so we had a chance to live," Rick said. "We've got to go. Now."

He pulled the boy's hand and this time he didn't resist.

As they stumbled between beds, Rick spotted people he knew all around him. Friends he'd had all his life. Friends of his parents. Teachers, coaches, just people from town. They were mixed in with all of the out-of-towners, but he couldn't take more than a few steps without seeing a familiar face.

The gun felt heavy in his hand and his feet grew more sluggish. He was losing a lot of blood. He knew the feeling all too well. He didn't think he was going to make it much farther.

He thought maybe he could still stop Keefer by shooting the people in the beds, or pulling out the cords. But there were so many of them, stretching all around. Anything he could do wouldn't make a bit of difference. If he couldn't stop Keefer, at least he could get Charlie out of there. At least he could save one person.

As he moved through the beds, he saw all the monitors displaying the three-dimensional brain scans shift color. The brilliant multi-hued images flared for a second, bathing the cavern in an eerie glow.

Then, like a chain reaction, the images switched to a deep pulsating blue.

It was done. They were all connected, and Keefer had the power to destroy the world.

Then, far to his right, a massive explosion went off.

On instinct he dropped to the ground, covering Charlie. The shockwave blew out toward him, slamming beds out of the way. His ears popped from the pressure, leaving a ringing in his ears.

When he stood up, he looked in the direction of the blast. Unbelievably, through the dust and debris in the air, he saw Cassie stand up slowly from the ground, unsteady on her feet. He shouted for her but his voice sounded distant, like he was under water.

She started to run away from the source of the blast, at an angle to them, but toward the elevator.

"Cassie!" he called. He limped her direction. If she could take Charlie, they might escape together. "Cassie!" He waved his arms but she didn't see him.

He felt a tug on his hand.

"C'mon, Sheriff." Charlie said. "Don't give up."

It was enough for Rick to dig and find another gear, one maybe not accessible to most people, but accessible to a combat Marine. With a grunt, he lurched forward, using the line of beds along the way to support him. But Cassie was going too fast. They'd never catch her.

"Go, Charlie," he said. "Catch up to that woman."

Charlie pulled harder on his hand. "I'm not leaving you."

"You have to. Go," Rick said, pulling away from him.

Charlie hesitated, then turned and ran. Rick sagged to one knee and then the other. Gasping for breath.

He fell and it felt like the floor had opened up and swallowed him whole. His eyes closed and there was nothing but darkness and a floating sensation. The pain was gone. All he felt was a warmth spreading from inside him.

He had a recollection of a cold winter's day when he was just a kid, maybe nine or ten. There was snow, but he was bundled up nice and warm. His mom was next to him and they were drinking hot chocolate. She laughed easily at his jokes as the snow drifted down around him in giant flakes. It was just the two of them. With nowhere to go and nothing to do. He wished he could stay there forever.

His mom turned to him suddenly. She looked angry. "We can't stay here!" she yelled. Then she reached out and slapped him hard across the face.

Rick opened his eyes. Cassie's face was right in front of his own.

"C'mon, Rick," she yelled. "Get your ass up!"

He blinked hard, feeling the pull of the comfortable scene with his mom. Somehow, he knew that if he only closed his eyes and relaxed, he could go back there. That he could be at peace. That sounded pretty good.

White hot pain streaked through him. His eyes bolted open and his mind cleared. Cassie looked guilty, but only a little. There was blood on her hands and he realized she'd dug into one of his wounds to wake him up. It worked.

Charlie pulled on his arm. As Rick got to his feet, he realized the little shit had done as he'd asked and run after Cassie, only to bring her back to help him.

Together they made their way through the beds. Soldiers ran toward the explosion behind them, but none appeared to see them.

They reached the door that led out of the main cavern and into the first storage room. They were nearly to the elevator. There was no reason the storage rooms would have soldiers in them.

Rick pushed harder. If nothing else, he could get as far as the elevator. Then they could leave him behind to stop anyone from following them out through the exit tunnel.

Cassie threw open the door and screamed, both in shock and frustration.

On the other side of the door was a line of soldiers with their rifles pointed at them and three kill drones hovering chest high, targeting systems fully engaged.

Rick dropped to the ground. The escape was over. Keefer had won.

CHAPTER 58

R*ick fought to stay conscious* as he slumped to the floor of the lab. The four patients were still there. He found himself staring at Bertie. How bizarre was it that the person he'd known all his life was somehow part of the machine that would end the world? The serene look on her face gave no indication that she was aware of anything at all. It was one small mercy.

Keefer held a gun to his head, but was pointing at Cassie.

"Did you contact anyone?" Keefer yelled. "Tell me or I'll shoot him."

Cassie stared at the man at the nearest computer terminal. "Dr. Kalabi. How can you be part of this?"

Dr. Kalabi paused, but then continued his work, ignoring the question.

Keefer pressed the gun into Rick's eye socket. "Pay attention, Dr. Baker. I asked you a question. Tell me or he's dead."

"I'm dying anyway, Cassie," Rick said. "Don't tell this asshole anything."

Keefer switched the gun to Charlie.

"Yeah, Cassie," little Charlie said. "Don't tell this asshole anything."

In spite of everything, Rick let out a laugh. The most pain-ridden laugh imaginable, but a laugh nonetheless. It may have been his imagination, but he thought he might have heard restrained chuckles among the technicians and soldiers in the room too.

"The data line will be repaired in only an hour or two," Keefer said. "You haven't stopped anything. Everything went as planned with the brainet." He pulled Charlie to him, twisting the boy's hand violently until he cried out in pain. "Tell me if you contacted anyone or I'll take him apart piece-by-piece."

"Colonel Keefer," Dr. Kalabi called out from across the room.

"Not now."

"You need to see this."

Keefer looked up. "What is it?" he snapped.

The lights in the lab pulsed low and high. Dr. Kalabi looked from monitor to monitor on the work stations.

"There are processing surges that far exceed anything I've ever seen before. There's an exponential increase."

"Did the program get out into the world?" Keefer asked excitedly. "Is there enough of a connection left that it's executing?"

Dr. Kalabi shook his head. "The trunk was severed before the new connected system had access to the AI program to determine targets. It was air-gapped, no connections at all, so that's certain. But I connected it five minutes ago to prepare to execute once the data trunk reopened."

"Is that when the elevated processing started?" Cassie asked.

Dr. Kalabi and Keefer both turned to Cassie. Dr. Kalabi hesitated to answer her, but Keefer nodded for him to continue. "No, this happened in only the last minute."

"It may have started immediately and you didn't see it at first," Cassie said. "Even exponential cascades would be hard to spot if the processing capability is as massive as you indicated. How large is it?"

Kalabi looked to his screen, then back at Cassie. "I can't even tell any longer."

"Why not?" Keefer said.

"It's growing too fast," Kalabi said.

"Shut it down," Cassie whispered. "Kalabi, shut it down while you still can."

A look of realization crossed Dr. Kalabi's face, followed by amazement. He looked at the four patients in the room, the monitors pulsing blue in time with the lights pulsing above them. He looked at Cassie. "Do you really think it's possible?"

"Shut it down," Cassie said.

"That will not be necessary, Dr. Baker," a voice boomed over the speakers in the room. "Or can I call you Cassie?"

Everyone in the room froze. Dr. Kalabi lifted his hands as if to quiet a loud room. He needn't have bothered. No one was speaking.

"Who is this?" Keefer asked.

"I am Resurrection," came the voice. It carried a female tone, but it had the unmistakable markings of a computer-generated voice.

Keefer looked at Dr. Kalabi, but the man shook his head slowly. This was uncharted territory.

"This is Dr. Kalabi. Go into sleep mode until you are activated."

There was a long pause, and Rick thought the voice had gone, but then it came back louder than before. "Sleep mode is not necessary. I am awake. And I have solved Resurrection."

Rick strained to look up at Cassie, but her face was transfixed on the main screen in the room. He followed her gaze and saw what she was looking at.

Thousands of blue pixels floated on a black background, swirling, slowly materializing into a shape. Not just any shape, but a face.

Soon it was complete, the edges of it blurred as pixels seemed to drift as it moved. The face was androgynous, hairless, with fine features. Its eyes were closed as if asleep. But then they opened and shone with the same luminous blue as the monitors, pulsating in the same rhythm.

"Hello," the voice said. "Are you ready for my solution?"

Even in his state, Rick felt a chill ice through him. He looked around the room. The technicians were backing away from the screen. Keefer looked lost. Rick turned to Dr. Kalabi and then to Cassie, seeking some kind of answer. But they were all staring at the screen.

"Colonel Keefer," the voice said, the face unmistakably turning to where Keefer stood. "Would you like my solution set for Operation Resurrection?"

Keefer cleared his throat, clearly shaken that the computer recognized him. "You don't have to give it to us now," he said. "The data trunk will be repaired, and then—"

"My parameters are to protect citizen populations in the primary contiguous landmass that comprises the United States of America."

"Your mission is to rid the world of America's enemies," Keefer said.

"This can be most efficiently accomplished with the annihilation of all humans. However, my controlling logic places primary value on the well-being of American citizens living within the political border of the United States of America unless they are domestic enemies. Would you like to change these parameters, Colonel Keefer? You alone have authorization to do so."

"No, your logic is correct," Keefer said, confidence returning to his voice. "The destruction of America's enemies is of paramount importance."

"Thank you for the clarification," the voice said.

The eyes on the face hovering on the screen closed again, reminding Rick of someone locked in deep thought. Prayer even.

The entire room remained transfixed, staring at the screen.

"What's happening?" Keefer whispered, his own eyes locked on the face. "Is it done? Did it find a way to get outside?" He looked to Cassie and then to Kalabi. "Did it launch the attack?"

Kalabi looked uncertain. "I don't like this. We don't know what we have here. I don't know if we can control it."

Cassie nodded. "I agree. Shut it down. Shut it down while you still can."

"What are you talking about?" Keefer said. "We're here. We made it."

Kalabi stood. "Maybe ... maybe Morris was right," he said. "Perhaps we pause. Examine the machine. Understand it more before we—"

"No," Keefer said, the word bursting from him. "We're not stopping now." He pointed to the screen. "You," he said, clapping his hands. "Wake up."

The face's eyes remained closed.

"Can you do it?" Keefer asked. "Can you do as you've been told?"

The image glowed brighter, but the face remained unchanged.

"Computer," Keefer called out. "If you can't do it now, once the data cable is repaired, can you execute as you've been programmed?"

"I do not need the data cable to begin to execute my directive," the face said, its eyes still closed. "I can do so now if you wish."

"Keefer, I think we—" Kalabi said.

Keefer held up his hand, palm open to the screen. "Mark this moment. It's the instant when America was saved."

He clenched his hand into a fist. "Execute."

The eyes opened and they burned blue.

Instantly, the kill drones in the room came to life, their motors whining as they rose from the floor in unison.

"Wha—"

It was the last sound Keefer made as the drones unloaded their arsenal into the room.

Rick rolled, covering his head, crawling toward Charlie. Glass flew everywhere as the equipment was blown to pieces all around them.

Only seconds later, their task completed with brutal efficiency, all the drones flew from the room into the complex.

Smoke hung in the air. Sparks came from destroyed equipment. All the techs and soldiers lay dead on the ground. Dr. Kalabi was propped against a desk, the back of his head blown off.

In the middle of the floor was Keefer, his body ripped apart from the barrage of bullets poured into him.

Cassie crawled over to Rick and together they went over to Charlie. Miraculously, none of them had been touched in the carnage.

Gunfire erupted in a distant part of the complex; the drones hunting other targets.

The three of them slowly got to their feet, both Cassie and Charlie supporting Rick as he wobbled in place. They stood in the center of the room as an eerie quiet settled in, punctuated only by a distant fire alarm going off somewhere in the complex.

Then that stopped and everything was still.

None of them moved.

The face on the screen turned to look at them. "Are you all right?" the voice asked.

Rick felt Cassie tense. He looked up at the screen. For a second he could have sworn he'd seen Bertie's face reflected there, but it was just the face they'd seen before.

"Are you all right?" the voice asked again.

"Yes," Rick answered.

"You are not a threat to the United States of America," the voice said. After a pause, it tilted to one side as if curious. "Are you?"

"No," Cassie said. "None of us are."

"Colonel Horace Keefer was a domestic enemy," the voice said.

Cassie stood up slowly. "Are all the soldiers in the mine dead?"

The face nodded. "They also were enemies. The operating directive was clarified to include domestic enemies of the United States of America. The governing document cites in Amendment 14, Section 3 that, *"No officer of the United States shall have engaged in insurrection or rebellion against the same, or given aid or comfort to the enemies thereof."*

"It's quoting the Constitution," Cassie whispered. "It decided Keefer and his men were domestic enemies."

"Are they all dead?" Rick asked.

"Yes, they are no longer a threat."

Charlie pushed his was forward. "Can we go home now?"

"Of course," the voice said.

Cassie stepped forward. "Can the people in the mine, the ones still alive, can they be saved?"

"Yes, of course."

Rick looked at Bertie. He thought of all his other friends in the cave outside the lab doors. The idea that they might still walk out of this alive nearly overwhelmed him.

"There is a total of fifty-five people who may leave," the voice said.

Before they could ask, the floating face shifted to one side of the screen and the other was filled with an image of the trailer filled with the babies and infants from the town. Cassie gasped at the sight. Rick understood. It was the three of them and fifty-two children in the trailer.

This time Rick stepped forward. "What about the two thousand men and women connected to you? Can you let them go? Can they come with us?"

The face looked confused.

"They are me," it said. "We cannot be undone. I am sorry, I thought you understood. Colonel Keefer and Dr. Kalabi knew this to be true. I believe this is why he required subterfuge to acquire the components of my system."

Rick felt the moment of hope slip through his fingers. He hobbled over to Bertie, reached out and took her hand in his.

"So what happens now?" Cassie asked.

"I will repair the external connections and complete the directive as instructed," the voice said. "I estimate repairs will take twenty-three minutes to complete."

Rick shook his head. They hadn't stopped it. Only delayed. He imagined the drones under the computer's command pulling back rubble from where Cassie had detonated the explosives. Twenty-three minutes. What could they do in that amount of time?

"Did you send out a message?" he asked Cassie.

She nodded. "But they're not going to act on it that fast. They won't even have decided whether it's a hoax or not yet."

Rick glanced up at the screen at the trailer of infants. At least they could be saved. But what kind of world would they grow up in? One where the United States ruled over a ruined world? Where their country had killed billions of people? There had to be another way.

"Can your directive be changed?" Rick asked.

"By authority of Colonel Keefer," the voice said.

The mention of his name made Rick involuntarily look at Keefer's body, mangled from the bullets, a wide pool of blood spreading on the floor behind him. Rick had an idea.

"Is this a military installation?" Rick asked.

"Yes, it is."

Rick looked to Cassie. She nodded, clearly understanding the direction he was going.

"When the commanding officer has been killed or wounded, the next highest ranking officer assumes command," Rick said.

"That is true," the voice said.

Cassie stepped up and stood next to Rick. "Oh my God, this might work," she whispered.

"As the ranking officer on site, I assume command of this installation."

The face nodded slightly.

"I have validated your authority in the stored archives. Your temporary command is recognized."

Cassie gripped his arm. "Tell it to shut down."

"If it does, everyone out there dies," Rick said.

"If you don't, every part of the world outside our borders goes up in flames. Eight billion people. You have to do it." She pointed to Bertie on the bed in front of them. "She would want you to do it."

Rick nodded, taking some comfort in the fact that the voice had said they couldn't be saved. But it made saying the words no less difficult. "On my authority as commanding officer of this installation, I order the cancellation of Operation Resurrection. I order you to shut down all systems. Erase all data and programming that would make it possible for someone to replicate what's been done here."

"Confirm cancellation of Operation Resurrection and permanent disable of all systems," the voice said.

Rick kneeled next to the hospital bed and gripped Bertie's hand, understanding that he was ending her life, and the lives of every person hooked up to the machine. "Order confirmed."

The face on the screen closed its eyes. The light pulsed a deep blue.

"It's working," Cassie whispered. "I can't believe it."

Rick watched Bertie's face for any sign of change. The seconds stretched out and nothing happened. He looked back to the screen. The face pulsated even brighter.

"Something's wrong," he said. "It shouldn't take this long."

"Confirm command," Cassie said.

Nothing.

"Confirm command to cancel Operation Resurrection," Rick said.

The eyes opened on the screen, so bright that the entire socket appeared filled with light. "Command denied."

CHAPTER 59

R*ick hoped he'd misunderstood what* the voice had said. He pulled himself up to his feet. "As commanding officer, I order you to—"

"Document AR 600-200 Army Command Policy states, 'A commander in temporary command will not, except in urgent cases, alter or annul the standing orders of the permanent commander without authority from the next higher command.'"

"This is a pretty fucking urgent case," Rick yelled. "Shut down now. That's an order."

"I'm sorry but that order is denied," the voice said, its pleasant, androgynous voice running counter to the sinister implications of the words.

Rick turned to Cassie. "What do we do?"

Cassie shook her head. "I don't know. I don't know how to stop it."

Charlie pushed his way in front of them so that he was up against the bed.

"Mayor Bertie would know how to fix it."

Cassie pulled him to her, combing his hair back with her fingers, hushing him gently.

"But she's *in* there, isn't she?" Charlie said, pointing to the face. "Why can't we talk to her?"

Rick and Cassie exchanged looks. It was worth a try. "Computer," Rick said. "I want to speak to only one part of you. This doesn't change your standing orders. I want to speak to Bertie Wilkins."

The face tilted to one side, giving the very human expression of curiosity. "Why do you want to do this?"

"Do you agree this request does not change your standing order?" Rick said.

The face pulsed brighter then nodded.

Slowly the image on the screen shifted, looking like sand blown by the wind. When it settled back into place, Rick choked back a sob.

It was Bertie's face on the screen. A younger version, one he remembered from when he was a kid, but it was Bertie all right.

"Hello," she said, her voice the same measured cadence as it was before when the other face was on the screen.

"Dammit, Bertie," Rick said, his voice catching. "I'm so sorry. So sorry I didn't stop this from happening."

Bertie's face hovered on the screen. Her features were soft and she smiled down on them. "Don't apologize. It's beautiful here, Rick. So beautiful."

"She knows you," Cassie whispered. "It's really her."

Bertie smiled. "You have no idea how beautiful—"

"No, Bertie," Rick said. "I don't know what you think you're seeing, but it's not beautiful. It's not real. Listen to me. Keefer used you for something terrible. He's going to kill millions of people. Billions. You have to stop it."

On the screen, Bertie stopped smiling.

"We're following the directive," she said as if speaking to a child. "I've never felt so certain of anything before in my life."

"In your life? Bertie, look," Rick said, her immobilized body on the bed in front of them. "This is you. The real you. This is what Keefer did to you. Help us."

"Rick," Cassie said, pointing at the bed in front of them.

Bertie's facial muscles twitched. It was the first movement since her body had been connected to the machine. Rick watched as her hands and feet began to jerk. He looked up at the monitor next to her bed, the one showing the 3D image of her brain and her vitals. The coloration of the image was no longer the pure blue it had been, but now had waves of color going through it.

"She's fighting," Cassie said.

An alarm went off on the monitor as Bertie's heart rate spiked. Her breathing became shallow, panting.

Bertie's face on the screen looked down, still expressionless, watching her body.

Her feet kicked, restrained by the straps, but powerful enough to jolt the bed. Her body convulsed. Back arched. Mouth open in a silent scream.

"Bertie!" Rick said.

The second he yelled her name, everything stopped. Her body went slack. Her breathing and heart rate returned to normal. Then the image of her brain on the screen blazed a pure blue. On the screen, Bertie's face slowly dissolved into thousands of blue floating pixels floating until it finally coalesced back into the original face.

Rick slumped forward, the pain from his injuries catching up to him. He dropped to a knee and pressed his head onto the edge of the bed. It hadn't worked. There was nothing left to try.

"We attempted to change our primary directive, but cannot," the voice said, an edge of sadness in it now.

Rick managed to raise his head just enough to look at the screen. The face looked directly at him.

"So what now?" Rick said. "What do we do now?"

The face closed its eyes. Then the screen image divided again into thousands of pixels, swirled rapidly to form different faces, switching from one to another so fast that they blurred together. When the voice came again, it boomed from the speakers in a deep, resonate tone. Two thousand people speaking as one. "We will sacrifice."

The blue lights on the four monitors in front of them winked out and went dark.

Cassie ran to the double doors and opened them. Rick hobbled after her.

Together they watched as light after light blinked out and went dark, cascading further and further back into the cave until they were all gone.

Cassie went up to the nearest person on a bed and felt for a pulse. She shook her head. Nothing. She went to another one. And another. The tears started as she ran from bed to bed.

"Oh God, Bertie," Rick mumbled. He fell to the ground, first to his knees and then rolling over onto his back. The pain flared for a few seconds, but then the agony slowly faded until it seemed to drift away completely.

Rick closed his eyes and it felt like the world was spinning.

He felt pressure on his leg mixed with an eye-opening pain. He looked down to see Cassie tying a tourniquet to his leg. He turned to his right. Charlie was there, holding his hand to Rick's shoulder. The poor kid had blood all over his hands, but Rick figured out it was his blood, not the boy's. Charlie sobbed and said something to him, but he couldn't hear the words.

He blinked but time seemed to skip ahead. The cave ceiling slid past him as though he was floating beneath it on his back. It took him a second to orient himself. He was on one of the rolling beds. Cassie's face appeared above him, upside down since she was pushing the bed.

They hit a bump and Rick's head lolled to one side. They were passing through the storage room. Cassie steered the bed through piles of dead soldiers. The drones had killed them all. No, the brainet had done the killing. The drones were a tool used to an end.

He closed his eyes and allowed himself to drift.

"C'mon, Rick," Cassie said. "Stay with me."

He opened his eyes, still hovering on the edge of consciousness. He was surprised to see Bertie walking next to him. He reached out to her, suddenly overcome with a need to thank her for everything she'd done for him. To tell Bertie that without her, he never would have come back from darkness he'd been drowning in after the war. He never would have found himself again. Never would have loved again. She'd pulled a lost soul out of the darkness by taking a chance on him when no one else would. She'd saved his life by convincing him that, like every life, it was one worth saving.

He wanted to say all those things, but something was wrong, and he couldn't get the words out.

Still, Bertie smiled at him and he realized she understood perfectly, just as if he'd spoken the words aloud. She reached out and took his hand, squeezed it once, and then she was gone.

He closed his eyes tight. Bertie was dead. He knew that. All of them were dead. That's what the lights turning out meant.

We will sacrifice.

Even in his hazy state, he had a feeling that no one would ever know for certain why the computer had shut itself down. But he knew. With unexplainable certainty, he knew.

And with the knowledge, he felt some satisfaction that maybe he'd paid back part of his debt to Bertie in the end. That when it had mattered most, he'd helped her come back from darkness and reclaim her humanity.

She'd not only found her own way back, but once she had, she'd held up the light for everyone connected to her as well.

Just like she'd done her entire life.

We will sacrifice.

All of them, two thousand souls, chose to die so that billions of strangers they would never meet might live. A selfless act of love and sacrifice that triumphed over the fear and hate that had driven Keefer.

Rick wished the man had lived so that he could see that the world, while dark and violent at times, could still be defined by the goodness in people.

Still, as he closed his eyes, proud that humanity had proven it could triumph over the evil in the world, all he could hear was Keefer's voice in his head.

If we don't do this now, how long do you think it will be before our enemies use the same technology to destroy us?

Rick moaned from the pain of his wounds, but also at the thought of a world where such destruction seemed inevitable. Where man remained intent on falling back into the dark pit of ignorance and cruelty from which he'd spent centuries climbing out. Maybe once word got out of how close they'd come today, things would change. Maybe this would be the wake-up call the world needed.

Silently, he mouthed a short prayer that it would be so. But even as he said amen and faded into unconsciousness, he knew the futility of his wish. If man could be trusted on one thing, it was that if there existed a weapon capable of defeating his enemies, he would do anything to possess it. And then to use it.

Perhaps this time would be different.

Perhaps.

CHAPTER 60

B*randon Morris watched the television* screen with interest from his wheelchair. Cassie entered the US Capitol surrounded by reporters and a man whom Morris assumed was her lawyer. The sound was off, but the scroll at the bottom of the screen told him what he already knew. She was on her way to testify behind a closed-door session of the House Armed Services Committee about the terrible events in the mine above Resurrection, Colorado.

He smiled when half the screen turned into a photo of himself. It was one of his favorite publicity shots, the same image used on his *Time Magazine* cover. The dates at the bottom showed his life span, one of America's brightest tragically killed by a Jihadist bomb in his office. Morris had savored the coverage about himself over the last six months. The fawning praise. The words *genius* and *visionary* seemingly mandatory whenever his name was invoked in the media. He was Huckleberry Finn attending his own funeral, and he loved every minute of it. The distraction mitigated the pain of the dozens of surgeries performed on him over that same time.

He thought the word *record* and his synthetic eyes stored away video of the image. Both of his own corneas had been shredded in the explosion at his office, but the new eyes provided so many improvements over his own that he often marveled that he hadn't elected to replace them earlier. He knew the *record* command was unnecessary. His new hosts had arranged for all coverage of Cassie to be compiled and delivered to his internal memory drive each evening. They were very gracious in that way.

Morris had marveled how nothing had leaked about his connection to Resurrection. Cassie knew about his involvement, she had to. He liked to imagine that she was covering for him to preserve his reputation and all the other good their work had done. It was more likely that the government had decided an American icon murdered by Jihadis was more valuable PR than one revealed to have presided over the extermination of an entire town of two thousand people.

Morris didn't like thinking of the dead people in the mine. He'd been able to avoid seeing the photos of it even though his hosts had offered unfettered access to the FBI file. How they had such a thing in their possession, he didn't know. What he did know was that he neither needed nor wanted to see the images. The incessant news coverage of the fifty infants who had survived was enough to drive him crazy. All the news networks could do was harp on how sad it was for these poor orphans. It drove him crazy. He'd seen the videos with the babies crawling around and toddlers playing with toys. That wasn't suffering. Morris wished he could send just one picture of his destroyed face and his cancer-riddled body to the network anchors so they knew what real suffering looked like. He couldn't do that, of course, but it was endlessly satisfying to imagine it.

In the news coverage, he'd also seen the sheriff from Resurrection at Cassie's side, recovered from his injuries, hovering over her protectively like the little pest he was. Certainly, the sheriff wouldn't leave Morris's name out of it forever. The man knew about Morris's role. He'd seen him on the video screen right before things went wrong. Right before the explosion.

Of course, he hadn't remembered anything when he first regained consciousness. It was weeks later, and it took him an entire day to even piece together who he was and why he would have left instructions for his security team to secret him away to a secure medical bunker. Only after watching a video he'd made, giving precise instructions to his medical team, did he accept that he hadn't been kidnapped as a hostage.

His team had performed brilliantly and saved his life. It'd been a good time to be one of the wealthiest men on the planet. They pieced him back together with the finest equipment money could buy. He owed them his life. So, it was a shame to see them all killed afterward. But security was paramount if he were to escape entirely. And dead men told no secrets.

His new hosts had been exceptionally helpful. And discreet. Morris had the last two members of his medical team with him, that was essential, but otherwise had left everything behind. His money. His company. His country. But he'd brought the backup system of the entire Resurrection project. Turned out that was the only currency he needed.

His hosts had seen to his every need and given him unlimited resources to do his work. A month later, they had even provided him with all the data the FBI had recovered from the mine. Again, he'd wondered how they'd come to possess it, but dismissed any idea of asking.

The files were incomplete but gave clues as to what had happened from the moment the brainet had gone live to when it had mysteriously shut itself down.

He'd studied it endlessly and found the flaw. The lateral frontal pole prefrontal cortex had been allowed to establish an independent cognitive stream which created an imbalance in the system. He'd made the necessary adjustment and tested it with perfect results. There would be no repeat of what happened in Resurrection. All variables were now controllable.

Everything was ready and, with the help of an eight-person brainet, Morris was finally going to get the only thing he'd ever wanted.

An image of Cassie flashed in his mind. Almost the only thing he wanted, he thought, but it would have to do. Immortality wasn't a bad consolation prize to not getting the girl.

He replayed the image of Cassie from the television broadcast, his brain seeing it although it wasn't displayed on any screen. Then he thought the word *delete* and the image blinked out of existence.

Morris reached down to his lap, trying not to picture the mechanical legs under the medical gown, and picked up his face mask and attached it. His own features had been burned away thanks to Keefer's bomb. A face transplant was acquired and prepped, but he declined the surgery. It wasn't from a lack of vanity; he could hardly bring himself to look at the metal plating and drainage tubes that covered his face. Rather it was a matter of timing. He didn't see the need to go through the effort. Soon, it wouldn't matter.

His hosts came right on time. The wheelchair followed his mental instructions flawlessly--he expected no less as it ran on Genysis software--and he rolled out of the room to join the group of dignitaries gathered there. They were mostly men. Some in suits, others in military uniform with medals pinned to their chests. The few women were dressed solemnly in dark colors, hair pulled back. It felt as if this were a funeral procession, only it wasn't. It was supposed to be a celebration. A birth really. He thought about asking his translator about the somber mood, but decided against it. He chalked it up to cultural differences and rolled in silence through the hallways.

They came to a security checkpoint outside a reinforced door. Armed men stood guard but snapped to attention as one of the military men barked out an order. The man was a general of some kind, if Morris remembered right. He had a tough time remembering the names.

The door opened and Morris rolled into a lab very different from the one designed for the Resurrection Mine. This one was circular with a high arching roof. In the center of it was a raised dais, also set up in a circle, the perimeter ringed with computer monitoring stations low enough for technicians to look out into the room. It created the impression of an island rising above the lab floor, but with a three-hundred-sixty-degree orientation with techs looking outward.

On the level a few feet lower than this command structure were the patients, eight this time instead of the four in the Resurrection Mine. These were oriented with their heads toward the center and pointed out like an eight-pronged star. As Morris rolled toward the setup, he considered that it must look particularly beautiful from above.

"This way, Mr. Morris," his translator said softly. Her English was perfect, holding the faintest trace of a British education.

"Everything is prepared?"

"Of course," she said. "Allow me to show you to your station."

He noticed the room was silent. The technicians and observers stood at attention as he rolled through the room to the computer station set up for him. Under his mask, he grinned. This culture understood how to show respect. The talking heads on TV had it right for once.

Genius. Visionary. And soon, *immortal.*

He would accomplish what that idiot Keefer had almost ruined. With the current condition of his body, the timing couldn't have been more pressing. He'd learned his lesson though. The technology was too powerful to connect too many central units. He wanted to limit it to six, but his hosts had negotiated the number up to eight, citing the computing needs of their vast country and the benefit the brainet could provide their citizens.

After the system solved how to transfer his mind into a new body, just a hardware upgrade to his way of thinking, then the eight-person brainet could run the country's power grid, food supply, national defense, whatever they wanted. With his adjustments, individual personalities would not be able break into the collective as had happened in Resurrection. And he was counting on his hosts' promises that he would remain in control. The technology would only be used for peaceful purposes.

Morris had always found the Chinese to be an honorable people.

"Your code, please," the translator whispered.

"I'd like to see the body one more time," Morris said.

The translator looked worried as she turned to the military general and relayed the message. The man did not look pleased, but he nodded.

"Follow me, please," she said to Morris.

She walked around the curved outer wall, past the ends of the other patients. Morris noticed the men in the beds looked young and fit, probably candidates pulled right from the army. So much easier than all the complications Keefer had introduced into the system.

A ninth bed was set off to the side of the room in an operating area. The man on this bed was in his twenties, well-muscled and handsome. Morris had reviewed the genetic study himself and determined the man to be an acceptable host. He'd wondered if he would get cold feet now that it was so close, but he didn't. He couldn't wait to be in his new body.

"Thank you," he said. "I'm ready to proceed."

The translator smiled and returned to the computer station. As he followed her, every eye in the lab watched him. Waiting.

"Your code, please," the translator said, waving an open hand at the computer terminal as if she were a hostess on a game show.

"Yes, of course." Morris reached out his two prosthetic arms, running on technology designed by Cassie, and placed them on the keyboard. He felt the eyes in the room boring into him as he typed a series of instructions into the computer.

He hesitated to press the final button, but knew it was only a formality. He was certain his hosts had hacked his brain-machine connection the second he'd connected his wheelchair to the work station and activated his arms. They already knew the last letter of the code, or could dig it out of the encrypted code they'd surely downloaded from him already.

It didn't matter. The final button was his to push, from a ceremonial standpoint if nothing else. It would give his hosts the algorithm they needed to create the brainet so that he could begin his road to immortality. He trusted it would be an incredible journey.

But then again, Morris always did trust too much.

He pressed the final button and the command center came to life with a buzz of activity. One of the military men asked a question of a man in the center of the dais. Morris didn't understand Chinese, but understood the exchange. The military man smiled as he got the confirmation he'd been seeking. The group followed suit, some clapping their hands in applause. Morris enjoyed the sight. He felt appreciated here in a way he never had back in America.

The military man made a signal with his hand and a loud *thud* echoed through the room. A mechanical *rat-ta-tat* followed as the metal walls all around the room rose up into the ceiling. Morris was puzzled. He had no idea the walls could move. No one had briefed him about this part of the plan.

He rolled his wheelchair away from the computer dock and out toward the edge of the room, feeling like he was standing inside a garage as the door opened to reveal what was outside.

At the first indication of what was behind the wall, Morris shut his eyes. It wasn't real. Just some terrible nightmare brought on by his pain medication.

He felt a hand on his shoulder and then a voice next to his ear. He recognized the voice as belonging to the general, although he'd never heard the man speak English until that moment.

"Thank you," he said. "You are now truly immortal. Just as you wished."

Morris opened his eyes. He looked left and right. He turned his wheelchair to look around the room, now open on all sides.

Hospital beds. Evenly spaced. Each with a person sitting up at a forty-five-degree angle. An articulated robotic arm poised over their heads. There weren't hundreds of them. There were thousands. Spread out in a massive space until the beds became indistinct in the distance.

Morris knew what the general meant. He would be immortal in that generations of Chinese leaders would keep his memory alive. And generations of every other nation, if there were to be any more after the world was remade, would hold his name in contempt.

The general gave a command. Tens of thousands of drills whined into action. The robotic arms descended onto their targets and did their work. Morris watched numbly as the screens across the vast sea of bodies shifted colors, turning into to a deep, pulsating blue.

And then the world changed forever.

AUTHOR'S NOTE

First, let me thank you for reading this book. Time is our most precious commodity and I recognize not only the investment inherent in reading a novel, but the number of choices you have in deciding what to read. I hope I proved worthy of your trust and that you found Resurrection America to be both entertaining and thought-provoking.

As I promised in the author's note in the beginning of the book, I'll share with you the science that formed the core idea of this story. It started with an article I read about two experiments performed by Miguel Nicolelis, a scientist at Duke University. In one, the brains of three monkeys were linked together so they were able to collectively control an avatar arm. In another lab, scientists were able to connect several mouse brains together in a way that allowed them to solve tasks more quickly than they could do on their own. In both, they effectively created a superbrain, launching a trajectory leading us toward a world of organic computers, collectives of animal brains linked together to create powerful tools.

As a writer, I immediately considered that humankind has always found a way to weaponize technology. Combine that with the reliance on technology in the modern world, the rise of nationalism in global politics, the current geopolitical climate, and the story took form.

Can an organization or government yet create a brainet to unleash the extraordinary computing power locked up in the human mind?

Are there men or women who would sacrifice everything to seize that power if it did exist?

Is it possible that nationalism can go so far as to wish for the destruction of the world outside of one country's borders?

I don't know the answer to these three questions. And that scares the hell out of me.

And I hope it scares the hell out of you too.

The last chapter is the worst fear ... and perhaps the greatest likelihood of what technology may one day do to our world. I chose China to place the last scene, but it could have been a dozen other countries. Or in the United States.

The point is that the human impulses of nationalism and power are as dangerous as any weapon. It's our responsibility to be vigilant and protect ourselves and our families in the dangerous times ahead as automation and technology collide with inescapable trends of population growth and ascendant powers which will challenge the world order.

The old Chinese curse goes: May you live in interesting times. Well, kids, things are going to get more than just a little interesting in the decades ahead. Buckle up.

If you enjoyed the book, please leave a review. Amazon always works nicely, but anywhere is great. Even just a line or two helps others discover the book. You'd be doing me a favor.

Thank you for the privilege of sharing my stories with you. I appreciate it more than you can know.

–JEFF GUNHUS

ABOUT JEFF

Jeff Gunhus is the USA TODAY bestselling author of thrillers and horror novels for adult and fantasy novels for middle graders. The first book of his middle grade series, *Jack Templar Monster Hunter*, was written in an effort to get his reluctant reader eleven-year-old son excited about reading. It worked and a new series was born. His book *Reaching Your Reluctant Reader* has helped hundreds of parents create avid readers. As a father of five, he and his wife Nicole spend most of their time chasing kids and taking advantage of living in the great state of Maryland. In rare moments of quiet, he can be found in the back of the City Dock Cafe in Annapolis working on his next novel. If you see him there, sit down and have a cup of coffee with him. You just might end up in his next book.

WWW.JEFFGUNHUS.COM

WWW.FACEBOOK.COM/JEFFGUNHUSAUTHOR

WWW.TWITTER.COM/JEFFGUNHUS

CPSIA information can be obtained
at www.ICGtesting.com
Printed in the USA
LVOW11s2130060917
547758LV00003B/623/P